Feel . . .

■ . . . the fear of trying to free a trapped motorist as a mountain of floodwater hurtles toward you.

■ . . . the desperation of trying to save a man who's literally been scalped by a giant grizzly bear.

■ . . . the heartbreak of holding a dead child in your arms.

■ . . . the horror of seeing a car accident victim impaled by a metal fence.

■ . . . the humor of performing mouth-to-snout resuscitation on an unconscious springer spaniel.

■ . . . the joy of giving an elderly heart attack victim another Christmas with her grandchildren.

Angels of Emergency

These are their remarkable stories.

By Donna Theisen
"What to Do Until the Ambulance Arrives"

Books by Dary Matera
Are You Lonesome Tonight?
(with Lucy De Barbin)

Get Me Ellis Rubin
(with Ellis Rubin)

Quitting the Mob
(with Michael Franzese)

What's in It for Me?
(with Joseph Stedino)

Strike Midnight

ANGELS OF EMERGENCY

Rescue Stories from America's Paramedics and EMTs

DONNA THEISEN AND **DARY MATERA**

HarperPaperbacks
A Division of HarperCollinsPublishers

Stories by Bonnie Allen and Ralph Hendricks reprinted and edited with permission from *Emergency* magazine.

HarperPaperbacks *A Division of* HarperCollins*Publishers*
10 East 53rd Street, New York, N.Y. 10022

Cover photographs by FPG Int./T. Tracy and
FPG Int./Terry Qing

First printing: July 1996

Printed in the United States of America

HarperPaperbacks and colophon are trademarks of
HarperCollins*Publishers*

❖ 10 9 8 7 6 5 4 3 2 1

Acknowledgments

On April 24, 1995, one of the most famous paramedics in the world died in a manner that sends chills through all of us in the emergency medical service profession—he shot himself. Eight years earlier, Robert O'Donnell, then thirty years old, courageously slid down a dark shaft drilled twenty-two feet into the earth and rescued "Baby Jessica," the Midland, Texas, toddler who toppled into a narrow well. O'Donnell's heroics came at the end of a fifty-eight-hour rescue operation that captured the attention of the nation.

A top-rated television movie dramatizing the event quickly followed. O'Donnell was tapped to play a reporter. It was the best of times.

Despite the heroism and heady fame, friends and relatives say O'Donnell's life fell apart after he saved the child. Five years later, in 1992, he divorced his wife and quit the Midland Fire Department.

Three years after that, he quit everything.

"There's a deal that happens when people are in these real stressful situations," his brother, Ricky O'Donnell, told reporters. "It's so hard to deal with this afterward."

Many people, including a number of television commentators and radio talk show hosts, were stunned and confused by O'Donnell's suicide. How, they wondered, could a dramatic, successful rescue with such a wonderfully happy ending result in life-threatening stress?

"You'd think that it would be a life-affirming experience," one radio announcer commented.

You'd think so—unless you were a paramedic or an EMT.

What the reporters and broadcasters failed to consider was how many Baby Jessicas Robert O'Donnell lost during his eleven-year career. How many times did he arrive too late to do anything but suffer the emotional agony of witnessing a tiny life cut short? How many children died in his arms? How many mangled teenagers did he pull from crushed cars? How many families did he see ripped apart by sudden, tragic accidents?

When the television crews shut off their bright lights and the movie producers packed their equipment and left town, Robert O'Donnell had to go back out on the streets. He returned to a world where nine times out of ten, Baby Jessica doesn't make it.

This book is written for Robert O'Donnell—and for all the medics around the world who know exactly why he put a shotgun to his head in a Texas pasture.

It's written for those who are carrying on despite having to live with the horrors that haunted Robert O'Donnell—without even experiencing that one brief moment of fame and exhilaration.

Kudos to Patrick and Carol Walsh and the Lee County, Florida, paramedics, who collected two thousand toys for fifteen hundred displaced children after Hurricane Andrew.

To all the paramedics, EMTs, and dispatchers for their input and enthusiasm, and for the way they bared their hearts and souls. To Dary Matera, for his patience in working with a novice writer and sharing my dream. To Vicki, for typing and being my "favorite" daughter. To Dr. Harvey Tritel, for keeping me going and for caring.

To our agent, Connie Clausen, and editor, Eamon Dolan. Finally, to Joe, for patience, confidence, nagging, and money to get this done. I love you all.

Donna

Special thanks to Fran Matera, Ph.D., of the Walter Cronkite School of Journalism and Telecommunication, Arizona State University, for providing editorial assistance.

Any paramedics, EMTs, first-responders, dispatchers, or ER personnel with a story to tell for *Angels of Emergency—Part II,* please contact Dary Matera, 1628 S. Villas Lane, Chandler, AZ 85248, or Donna Theisen, 89 Glenmont Drive West, North Fort Meyers, FL 33917.

Dary

Contents

Introduction ■ — xiii

CHAPTER 1 — Nutshell ■ — 1

CHAPTER 2 — Getting the Shiny Badge ■ — 8

CHAPTER 3 — Dialing 911 ■ — 27

CHAPTER 4 — Win Some . . . ■ — 65

CHAPTER 5 — . . . Lose Some ■ — 95

CHAPTER 6 — Coping ■ — 110

CHAPTER 7 — Fear ■ — 127

CHAPTER 8 — Laugh Till You Cry ■ — 150

CHAPTER 9 — The Weird and Bizarre ■ — 177

CHAPTER 10 — The Horror, the Horror ■ — 203

CHAPTER 11 — The Weird and Bizarre, ■ — 221
Part II—Pathos, Bathos,
and Poignancy

CHAPTER 12 — Win Some More ■ — 246

CHAPTER 13 — Oklahoma City ■ — 271

CHAPTER 14 — Gripes and Suggestions ■ — 293

Epilogue ■ — 309

Contents

INTRODUCTION

CHAPTER 1

CHAPTER 2

CHAPTER 3

CHAPTER 4

CHAPTER 5

CHAPTER 6

CHAPTER 7

CHAPTER 8 — The Body and Mind

CHAPTER 9

CHAPTER 10 — The Word and Name

CHAPTER 11

CHAPTER 12

Introduction

When the last of my four children prepared to leave the nest in 1980, I decided, like many women today, to return to the work force. Actually, in my case, *return* isn't the appropriate word. I had pretty much spent the first forty-three years of my life as either a dependent child or a codependent housewife. Eschewing an easier profession, I halfheartedly responded to an intriguing ad in the local Ohio newspaper: *"Wanted: emergency medical technicians. Will train."*

To my surprise, I was accepted. (I don't know how many others even applied.) Off to EMT school I went, scared to death.

"I'm not coming back tomorrow," I vowed after the first class. "This is crazy. I'm too old, too inept, too out of it, too everything to do this."

"I'm definitely not returning," I swore after days two, three, and four, again to no avail. Despite all my fears and misgivings, something kept drawing me back to the classroom.

I learned how to take vital signs during the second week of training and was allowed to ride with real EMTs as an observer. That was a thrill. I remember sitting in the squad building, alternately praying for a run and feeling ashamed about my eagerness. Someone would have to be sick or injured in order for me to experience a real-life rescue.

Fate intervened, ending my internal debate. A student

fell through the ice covering a frozen pond and had to be fished out by his friends. He needed to be transported to the hospital for a thorough examination. Fortunately, he turned out to be okay.

I was more than okay. The fear and excitement combined to give me an adrenaline rush like I'd never experienced before. I didn't know it at the time, but I'd caught a bad case of emergency medical service fever.

That put an end to any doubts I had about sticking it out and finishing the course. I was determined to earn that red badge EMTs wear on the left arm, and I absolutely craved the supercool Star of Life patch with the international EMS symbol—a staff with a snake wrapped around it set against a blue cross—that medics wear on their uniforms.

Newly inspired, I passed the course, survived the state certification exam, and earned my precious badges. *Hot damn,* I thought, *now I'm going to ride ambulances and save lives!*

Looking back, I'm not really sure why I picked such a stressful, harrowing career. My naïveté played a part, as did some desire to help people in need. After being a mother for so long, I guess I figured I had experience playing nurse.

Another factor was that EMTs were in short supply in the rural community outside Dayton, Ohio, where I lived. That made a job available immediately upon finishing the three-month course. Initially I found the rescue work to be so fascinating and gratifying that I continued my training and completed the year-long paramedic course in 1984.

A personal shake-up—an empty-nest-syndrome divorce—resulted in a psychological slump and a move to Florida. I never recovered from the one-two punch enough to sit for the required paramedic certification exam in my new state. However, now that I needed a job instead of merely something to occupy my time, I continued to ride under the flashing red lights as an advanced-level EMT.

Time passed. The calls piled up, more than five thousand in all. Memories blurred into each other. I experienced great rushes of exhilaration—along with every form of human heartache and misery imaginable. Like virtually all EMTs, paramedics, and dispatchers, I started feeling worn down and burned out. I began questioning myself again: "What am I doing here?" I quizzed my partners: "What are you doing here?" I pestered everyone in the lifesaving business: "What are we doing here?" I wondered why I was getting up in the middle of the night to drive a fishtailing ambulance through a pounding thunderstorm to respond to a drunk who smashed his car into a tree. My boots constantly filled with mud. Mosquitoes feasted on my flesh. I was assaulted, spit on, and cursed. The elderly died in my arms. Children perished in ways I never imagined, and babies . . . they were the worst.

Hey, what's going on here? my mind screamed. This wasn't like television. This wasn't *Emergency* or *Rescue 911,* where all the patients are heroically saved after the commercial break and every story has a happy ending. Instead, it was overwhelmingly tragic and frighteningly dangerous out there.

Desperately seeking relief, I went to the library to see if there was anything that would give me a boost. I was looking for a book that would let me know that I wasn't alone, that other paramedics, EMTs, and dispatchers had suffered through the same rip-your-guts-out emotional upheaval that I was experiencing. I wanted to know how they handled it and what they did to get through the day when they hit rock bottom and felt like quitting.

Unfortunately, I found nothing remotely close to that in the library or on the bookstore shelves. I knew there was a real need for a compilation like this, so I decided to do it myself. In 1985 I began a comprehensive, ten-year study of the emergency medical service profession—apparently the first of its kind. The purpose of my research was to analyze the psychological impact that the stressful EMS career has on its practitioners and help develop coping mechanisms and techniques.

The result, suffice it to say, has been illuminating.

So has the response. Virtually everyone I surveyed was anxious to relate his or her experiences. They eagerly shared their funniest, nastiest, saddest, messiest, most frightening, most horrifying, and most satisfying "war stories." For many, just talking about it was an emotional release. It seemed as if the stress had been bottled up inside them for years.

From coast to coast, I kept hearing the same comment after introducing myself: "It's about time somebody did something like this."

Donna

ANGELS OF EMERGENCY

Rescue Stories from
America's Paramedics
and EMTs

1 Nutshell

It's just after midnight. The call comes in: "Code twenty-seven, eleven twenty-four Carver Street." You cringe, because the code number means the problem is unknown and the address is in a dangerous part of town. You and your crew sigh, then roll out the unit, sirens blaring and red lights flashing.

Your heart pounds as you pin your long blond hair into a bun and double-check the supplies. The driver radios the dispatcher to try to get more information about what to expect. Are the police there already? Will they arrive in time to provide backup in case things get ugly? You remember that not everyone sees you as an angel of mercy coming to help. Many people, especially those living in poverty-racked neighborhoods, view paramedics as another form of cop.

"No further information on the call."

The dispatcher's words tighten your chest. You give your partner a shrug and whisper a silent prayer.

"We're going in blind."

The driver skillfully moves the Chevy unit down the street, easing through intersections and darting in and out of the traffic. Cars are pulling over to the side of the road—most of them, anyway. A thousand feet ahead, a pickup truck is still in your lane, ignoring the lights and sirens.

"Move it, you stupid son of a bitch," the driver screams.

The annoying truck fails to yield. The driver is forced

to bounce the unit over the median, jarring your teeth and scattering equipment. As you squat down to gather everything up, your partner says, "I have the trauma bag. You grab the O₂."

Five minutes out, the driver turns into the projects. He stops in front of a decaying apartment building. "This is it," he yells. "Everybody out."

You and your partner hit the side door. The first thing you see is a crowd of people. Few are smiling. Some look absolutely menacing. They don't want you there. Fear grips you. Then, off to the side, a single person is screaming and waving to you. She's a heavy, powerfully built woman. "Hurry! Hurry!" she cries. "My boy's been shot! He's spittin' blood!"

The woman ushers you inside the dark, frightening building, into a maze of littered hallways that smell of urine. The walls are covered with gang graffiti. The floors are dotted with old and new body fluids. A trail of fresh blood leads up a set of rickety stairs blackened with grime. A terrifying thought strikes you—is this a real rescue, or a rape and robbery setup?

The woman leads you into a small, neatly kept apartment, a pocket of order in an ocean of disorder. As you enter you notice family pictures hanging on the wall: photographs of sons, daughters, parents, grandparents, and grandchildren. One shows a young, happy couple in the wedding garb of another era. You recognize the woman who led you into the building. She was much thinner then. The man in the picture, you figure, is long gone.

You make your way into a small bathroom and find a teenager lying on the floor in a pool of blood so large that steam is rising from it. He's been shot twice in the stomach and is moaning in agony. From the size and position of the gaping wounds, you know he has little chance of survival. Still, you have to try. You kneel down over his once strong body and check his pulse. It's weak.

"Is he going to be all right?" the sobbing mother asks. "He's all I got."

You look up but can't find the words to say anything. In the doorway, you see more faces—the same angry, sullen faces from downstairs. They've followed you into the apartment and are now watching the show. Apparently no one but the mother cares if this boy lives or dies. Anger boils away your fear.

"Everyone clear the door!" you shout in a firm, authoritative voice. "Clear the apartment! *Now!*"

Remarkably, the crowd obeys. As they spread apart, you see your partner and driver appear with a gurney. It won't fit into the bathroom, so you have to lift the gut-shot youth out into the foyer.

"Is he dead?" someone asks.

"If he ain't now, he soon will be," a cynical voice answers.

You ignore the harsh diagnosis and prop the youth on the stretcher. The return trip down the dark stairways and through the dank halls goes faster now that you know your way.

"He's a good boy," the mother says, following along. "He was going to enroll at the community college next fall. He's not into drugs or anything like that. He's a good boy."

Outside, you maneuver through a crowd that has now swelled to more than a hundred. You finally reach the back of the ambulance, only to discover that two crack addicts are inside, looting the expensive medical equipment.

"Get out of here!" you scream. "Can't you see we're trying to save this boy's life?"

The two men stroll leisurely out the door, clutching anything they can make off with.

"Ain't no skin off my ass if he croaks," one says as he passes.

Inside the unit, you attempt to administer an IV of lifesaving fluids and find that they've been stolen.

"Dammit!" you scream to the crowd peering through the still-open doors. "Doesn't anybody here give a shit about anything?"

"We give a shit about your tight ass, lady," a coarse voice says. Many in the crowd laugh.

"Let's go!" you shout to the driver, eager to leave.

On the way to the hospital, you locate a backup IV kit and start the youth on D5W TKO solution to keep him from dehydrating. The first stick blows as his veins collapse. As you prepare another cath, he gasps and goes into cardiac arrest.

"We're in code!" you shout. "We're in code!"

You pound on his bloody torso and start CPR.

"One one thousand. Two one thousand. Three one thousand."

With the first few compressions, you hear the sickening sound of the cartilage breaking away from his shattered sternum. The youth fails to respond.

"We're in code," the driver radios the hospital. "Seventeen-year-old male. GSW. ETA eight minutes."

You continue on.

"Five one thousand. Six one thousand . . . "

The teen gasps and takes a painful, gurgling breath.

"Hold on, kid! Hold on!"

You feel his fingers tighten around your hand.

"That's it. Hold on. Only a few more minutes now."

At the hospital, the driver pops open the double back doors. You leap to the pavement and pull out the gurney, then push the rolling bed into the building and aim it toward the trauma room. Inside, the ER team takes over. Your job is done.

You lean against the wall, happy to be relieved of the

burden. Your heart pounds. Your mouth tastes like a bushel of cotton. Your clothes are soaked with blood and sweat. As you head for a scrub sink, you catch a glimpse of the mother being led into the ER. She is clutching her son's pajamas. "In case they keep him for a while," she says. You avoid eye contact.

After washing up, you go to the nurse to make your report. Then you gather your crew to return to headquarters. You forget a small detail and wander back to the nurse. Before you reach her, you see a doctor pull a sheet over the teenager's face. Your heart sinks. Gathering strength, you clean the gurney, replace the supplies—both the ones that were used and the ones that were stolen—pick up your oxygen tank, and head for the station.

You don't tell your partners the patient died.

Two blocks down the road, the radio jumps to life, giving you a start. "Unit twenty-seven, unit twenty-seven. Code four. Carver and Washington." You pause, stunned. Your head drops, and the fear returns, stronger than before. It's another call at the same frightening location.

"Oh, shit!" the driver exclaims as he hits the reds and switches on the siren. "Here we go again." Although he's trying to be brave, you sense the fear in his voice. A disturbing thought crosses your mind: *Is this a real call or a setup to get us back? To get* me *back?* A second, even more disturbing thought follows: *What the hell am I doing here?*

Paramedics, emergency medical technicians, and dispatchers—there are 600,000 of us in the United States, and probably a few million more working around the world. We come from all walks of life, in all ages, shapes, sizes, and colors. We're male and female, and rarely does anybody notice or care about the difference.

People just demand that we get there fast and perform miracles.

We're a special breed. We must possess a deep compassion for humanity. We must have the skills and knowledge to do our job. We must never, ever crack under pressure, because every call is pressure.

Our pay is low, starting in the mid-teens and rarely going over $40,000, regardless of education or experience. It's usually less than the pay of a garbage collector or a bus driver. There is no path for career advancement, because there is nothing above or below us. We work long hours, usually twenty-four on, forty-eight off. We miss family dinners, birthdays, anniversaries, and holidays. Many of us need to work second jobs to support our families.

Our training encompasses hundreds of hours in a classroom and equally as many in a hospital. We must endure even more hours of continuing education to retain our certification. We are subjected to written tests, usually every two years, mandated by state law. We are put through unannounced spot field checks three or four times a year.

Every day we face death and anguish, sorrow and pain. We're bombarded with verbal and physical abuse. We've been beaten up, robbed, cursed, maligned, spit upon, and killed. Even in good times, we're frequently overcome with despair. We feel unappreciated and overlooked.

Off duty, there's still no escape. The images of horror and human suffering reel through our minds well into the night. We're torn with grief, guilt, and depression. We must constantly battle such job-related physical problems as extreme fatigue, nausea, an inability to concentrate, emotional outbursts, loss of appetite, and insomnia.

Ask us why we stay, however, and our faces brighten. Once emergency medical service gets into your blood, you're hooked. Maybe we can make a difference, save a life. That's the biggest rush of all.

Despite the pitfalls, we have great pride in what we do. We have a deep sense of purpose and personal satisfaction.

We're angels of emergency. These are our stories.

Donna

2 Getting the Shiny Badge

A neat thing about our job is that once in a while, we get the opportunity to bring life into this world—as opposed to a lot of times seeing life leave the world.

DOUG CARRELL, PARAMEDIC, NEBRASKA

If any of you are considering becoming an EMT or a paramedic—and if what you just read in the previous chapter hasn't scared you away—then a brief explanation of the training and career aspects of the emergency rescue vocation is in order.

As with so much about the still-adolescent EMS profession, the training, both in class and on the job, can be confusing. Education and licensing requirements differ widely throughout the fifty states, not to mention foreign countries. To further complicate things, some cities and counties insist that their EMS crews also be firefighters, which involves an entirely different type of training. And try as they might, the best EMS academies can only teach emergency medical science. They can't begin to touch upon the almost infinite array of physical and emotional calamities you'll face out on the streets. Make no mistake, EMS is a career that deeply affects the physical and mental state of its dedicated practitioners. All too often, it threatens their lives as well. And the stress? That can be unbearable. On the up side, it's a career that pays off in great rushes of adrenaline and immense personal satisfaction, especially when you save a life.

Good or bad, exhilarating or depressing, it's definitely a job that not enough people want to do. The need for talented, compassionate EMS workers will always be strong.

The EMT classes are moderately difficult but not too hard. Anyone with a high-school degree or equivalent is welcome, regardless of sex, age, race, or religion. As I mentioned in the introduction, I started my career at age forty-three, when the last of my four children prepared to leave home. My work experience up until then? Two decades as a housewife. Believe me, if I can make it, so can you.

The basic training itself usually consists of a three-month, four-hundred-hour EMT-ambulance course given at a local vocational school, at a community college, in the basement of a grammar school or church, or in a converted storefront. The instructor generally opens the first class with films of actual emergencies. That's to see if the students have the stomach for it. If you can sit through the videos without running for the door, you've passed the first test.

Next you'll learn the inside-outs of ambulances—where everything is and what everything does. If you think paramedics carry little more than a few bandages and a bare-bones first-aid kit, think again. Those vans are loaded. The daily checklist is three pages long and covers hundreds of items, including a defibrillator unit, cardiac paddles (for electric shocks), an EKG display, an EKG recorder, external pacemakers, assorted oxygen tanks, seventeen sets of keys for locked drug boxes, nineteen types of bandages and splints, eleven extrication devices (backboards, pry axes, window punches, etc.), five different stretchers, a mobile trauma box containing twenty-five basic rescue necessities (alcohol preps, bandages, IVs, syringes, etc.), twenty-two drugs, thirty-six advanced life support supplies (lactated ringers, IV butterflies, six different catheters, four types of syringes, etc.), nineteen drug-box items (scalpel, scissors, thermometer, etc.), thirty-eight kinds of airway supplies (oxygen masks, tubing, Magill forceps, nasal cannulas, etc.), thirteen lifepack and telemetry items (defibrillator pads, electrodes, EKG paper rolls, batteries, etc.), twelve unit-cleaning supplies, eight maps of the area, and thirty-eight miscellaneous items such as cold packs, surgical masks, restraints, stethoscopes, bedpans, penlights, bite sticks, ammonia capsules, blood pressure cuffs (three types), EMS command vests, and teddy bears.

After you've mastered this, the fun stuff starts. You'll plunge headfirst into anatomy and physiology. When you finish, you'll know, or should know, all the proper names and functions of the human body parts. Remember that annoying "the kneebone's connected to the shinbone" song? You'll be singing it in the shower.

Basic first aid and emergency medical treatment follows, focusing on the calls ambulance crews encounter most frequently—falls, burns, broken bones, auto accidents, cuts, bumps and bruises, strokes, heart attacks, breathing difficulties, and knife and gunshot wounds. Depending upon the state and course, the instructor will then attempt to cover as many combinations and variations of the above as possible. For example, say a woman is shot and stabbed during an attempted carjacking. She gets away, has a stroke and heart attack from the stress, crashes the car, bangs her head, burns her arms, then falls out and breaks her leg. You'll know what to do. If she's pregnant, you'll also know how to deliver her baby, which is always a treat.

Some EMT courses toss in a trip to the auto wrecking yard. There you'll learn how to use "slim jims" and other neat tools designed to help you break into cars quickly.

This includes the granddaddy of them all, the "jaws of life," a scary-looking device that can cut open a car as if it were a sardine can. You'll be taught the critical technique of how to use the jaws without inadvertently beheading the victim trapped inside.

The junkyard training also comes in handy if you ever lock your keys in your own car. Plus, should you fail the EMT course, you're qualified for a career as a locksmith, welder, or car thief.

The second field trip is decidedly more harrowing. You'll be bused to the local county hospital emergency room—a real swinging place. Depending upon how hands-on your particular course is, you may end up having to do some chores while you're there, such as mopping up who-knows-what from the ER floor, emptying those fragrant bedpans, holding puke pans for drunks, and other similarly delightful tasks.

Once you survive the ER visit and EMT course, you're ready to take the state boards. The tests, as previously mentioned, vary widely from state to state. In general, they consist of about 150 true-false and multiple-choice questions. In the multiple-choice section, they usually give you four possible answers to choose from. Two will be like that recent hit movie, *Dumb and Dumber*. The other two will be very similar to each other, meaning one's correct and the other's trying to be sneaky. The trick is to eliminate the dumb answers and then guess correctly between the remaining two.

The test results arrive in the mail about a month later. It's an anxious wait, but most people who pass the course nail the qualification exam. Remember, there's a great need for warm bodies on the ambulances, so they want you to succeed. They're not trying to weed you out.

Once you're certified by your home state, you're ready to ride shotgun on a speeding ambulance. Good luck. You'll need it.

After six months to a year on the job, you may want to consider whether you'd like to go further. If you're enjoying what you're doing, and you still have your wits about you (to an EMS worker, that can sound like a contradiction), you can take a stab at moving up to become a full-fledged paramedic. That'll send you back to the classroom, this time for up to a year. (Most states require 1,400 hours of classroom and hospital study.) On this level, the training is obviously more intense. It resembles that of a first-year medical student, without being quite as exhausting and stressful.

Again, if you have any doubts about your abilities, consider that this over-the-hill housewife successfully made it through the paramedic academy as well.

In paramedic school, you'll finally learn what's in those little plastic bags that are always hanging near patients. The course will also teach you how to make sense out of those squiggly lines on the little monitors in the ambulance and emergency room. You'll be taught how to dispense drugs, draw blood, and worm a nasty-looking intubation tube down a victim's throat to help oxygenate them. Sometimes that tube is all that's oxygenating them.

You know those fancy terms you hear mentioned on *E.R.* or *Rescue 911* all the time—*sinus tachycardia, PVCs, tubing?* You'll suddenly know what they mean. Your friends will be impressed!

In fact, as the year progresses, you'll find that you're speaking a new language—paramedicese. This consists of all the ten-dollar medical terms and quick abbreviations that are scattered throughout this book, plus hundreds more. Your spouse won't understand a word you're saying anymore—but that's not always a bad thing.

Be prepared for weekly exams, biweekly exams, and every-third-Tuesday exams. Plus you'll spend hundreds of hours in hospitals. And this time you won't be limited to the ER. You'll get to know the entire building and its personnel up close and personal—pediatrics section, recovery room, intensive care unit, maternity unit, operating room, IV team, respiratory therapy team, and whatever else the hospital lists in its promotional brochure.

Yet even with all that wandering around, it's the wild and woolly ER that'll draw you back like the mob sucking in Michael Corleone. There you'll discover that the harried ER doctors are the most friendly. That's because they know that one day you'll be a critical part of their support team. (They can also use all the help they can get!) If they think you're halfway on the ball, they might even let you sew some stitches, clamp a bleeding artery, or hook up a number twelve EKG (you'll know what that means).

Best of all, during the intensive hospital training, you'll get to wear those nifty little paper masks, shoes, and hats that make doctors and nurses look like walking toilet paper rolls.

By the end of the course, you'll be able to make a complete assessment of a sick or injured person in about ninety seconds. This includes tilting, squeezing, pinching, feeling, listening to, looking at, and sometimes smelling the patient in order to give the proper on-site treatment while radioing a rapid-fire diagnosis to the waiting ER doctors.

Sail though the class, pass the finals, and it's back to the state boards. As before, the rule of pollex (a *pollex* is a thumb, as you'll learn) is that if you've passed the course, the boards will be a breeze. But don't lollygag. Grab your number two pencil and sit for the exam as quickly as possible. As with high-school Spanish, you'll start forgetting the stuff the moment the last bell rings unless you immediately put it to use.

The nerve-racking wait for the postman to deliver the pass/fail news is just as long for potential paramedics as it is for EMTs, four to six weeks—only with the paramedic exam, you'll probably know if you aced it or not as soon as you walk out of the testing room.

The letter finally arrives. You've passed! Now you're a big-time paramedic. You can pull rank and attitude on all those wet-behind-the-ears rookie EMTs and first-responders. You'll be able to furrow your brow and bark words such as *cannulation* and *defibrillation* with authority and meaning.

But invariably the first thing you'll say after ripping open the letter is what we all say at that point: "Hey, when do I get that shiny badge?"

STORIES AND COMMENTS

■ When I was young, I used to come home from school and run to the television to watch *Emergency*. Of course, I was only a kid and didn't realize it was Hollywood.

My dad passed away, and I took a job in a carpet store. The place was pretty dead. I was looking through the paper, saw an ad for dispatchers for a volunteer rescue squad, and decided to apply. They required that we obtain a first-responder EMT certification.

While I was going through the class, I was driving down the street and saw this girl on a bicycle hit a pothole and fly off. I immediately made a U-turn and went back to help. I didn't know what to do because I'd barely started the classes, so I just held her hand and told her to squeeze my fingers. I figured if she could squeeze my finger, her arm probably wasn't broken. After a few minutes she started smiling and laughing, and eventually she climbed back on her bicycle and rode off.

I figured that if I could make someone who'd just flipped off her bicycle feel better and smile, then maybe this was the profession for me.

My instructor advised me that if I really wanted to

become a paramedic, I should train in Florida. He said there was no future for paramedics in Canada. I took his advice and went to the United States. I've since worked EMS in both Canada and Florida.

I don't think I'd trade EMS for anything. I could never do a nine-to-five job. I'm an EMS person. I love my job. I've delivered five children in the field. I wear a Star of Life [the EMS symbol] around my neck. People say that if I was ever cut and bled, my Star of Life would bleed, because I eat, sleep, walk, drink, and talk EMS. Maybe that's good, maybe that's bad, but I think it's good. That's part of being good at the job—wanting to do it and liking it. I'm up at the crack of dawn, ready to come to work. No one has to push me out of bed.

And it all started with that little girl.

HOWARD LEVINSON, PARAMEDIC, MONTREAL

■ In EMT and paramedic school, it's really been one of my pet peeves that they don't teach us the *S* part of the job, the services part. We don't teach enough customer relations, customer service, what is excellence, and what does all this mean. We teach EMS workers medicine, and they come out a "medicine machine." They know medicine, but they don't know how to look somebody in the eye and say, "Hello, my name is so-and-so, and I'm going to take care of your mother today."

When I first took the administration job four or five months ago, we were averaging a complaint or two a week, all dealing with customer service—things like a medic putting his feet on somebody's brand-new sofa while filling out the paperwork. If the Sears delivery man did that, you'd call Sears and raise a stink. That's what I'm talking about, how to treat people. You don't treat them like they're captives, not like "You called us, therefore we're here and we're going to do it our way." Instead, it should be "You called us because you need help, and this is what we're going to do to facilitate your transport to the hospital." I'm not saying the medics have to give lectures, just a sense of "We care. We understand what you're going through, having seen it so often, and we're sympathetic toward what you're going through." When people need help, they're expecting an element of compassion to come with that. When you go to your physician, you don't want to be treated like "Next!"

MARTY WILKERSON, EMS ADMINISTRATOR, FLORIDA

■ I think that pretty much like all rangers, I became a medic in order to provide assistance to the visitor population in our national park [Denali National Park]. The other thing is, I think a lot of park employees feel that having EMS training is necessary to compete for jobs in the National Park Service. So many of the parks are in remote areas and don't have readily accessible medical care. It's pretty much imperative that the rangers have some sort of advanced medical training to provide support for the back-country-related injuries as well as the front-country injuries. You're not always going to have an ambulance there, or a helicopter to help stabilize the patient, so you've got to be able to take care of them to the best of your ability.

**NORM SIMONS, PARK RANGER AND
EMS COORDINATOR, ALASKA**

■ I like the fact that firefighters evolved into paramedics. Frankly, firefighters were getting stagnant. Because of modern construction techniques, there aren't nearly as many fires today as there were twenty years ago. In turn, there are a lot more medical emergencies.

Thus it was a natural process of evolution that turned

firefighters into paramedics. Studies have shown that the first few minutes after a serious injury, an auto accident, or a heart attack are the most important. Who else was prepared to respond as fast as firefighters? There was a tremendous void out there that wasn't being filled before, and we filled it.

Then when the television show *Emergency* came on the air, that sealed it. Everyone just assumed that all firefighters were paramedics, which still isn't the case today. But after *Emergency,* whenever somebody needed help, they dialed the fire department.

Today EMS calls are 75 percent of what we do. And that number increases every year.

It's my personal belief that the firefighting-paramedic profession is set to undergo yet another dramatic transformation in the next few decades. Something out there, some advancement in lifestyle or technology, will present another void that needs to be filled. Whether it's the use of dangerous chemicals, fusion, biotechnology, whatever, paramedics will be called upon to take care of the resulting problems.

ROD MORTENSEN, PARAMEDIC, ARIZONA

■ I think another reason why people enter the profession is that they've either been close to a relative who died, or found themselves in an emergency situation with a family member and weren't able to help them. It could have been years before. That was true with me. I saw my grandfather have a couple of heart attacks, and I didn't know what to do. So that might have something to do with it.

NAME WITHHELD, PARAMEDIC, CALIFORNIA

■ After my second year on the job of riding rescue with nothing more than a CPR and first-aid card, I realized that we weren't really providing a whole lot of help to people. At that time, I approached my chief and told him I needed more training. That wasn't an easy thing to do. He was the type that didn't believe in "doctors" in fire service. He figured that if you wanted to wear a stethoscope, you could go to one of the other fire departments that had all these little rookie fire-rescue guys.

Still, I was bound and determined to go to EMT school, and after nagging him for a few days, he let me go. I was able to learn a multitude of lifesaving medical techniques that helped me out on the street. I subsequently persuaded a number of my colleagues to take the course. Because of that, we turned what had once been considered a very backward rescue squad into a first-rate operation that was respected throughout our county.

With the proper EMT training, instead of just standing around with our fingers up our asses waiting for the ambulance service to arrive, we were actually able to help save lives.

TERRY PYE, PARAMEDIC, ONTARIO

■ I think there's a point you get to where the rewards aren't that great moneywise and so forth. These guys who have families and who have been here ten to fifteen years have to work their butts off on other jobs and stuff, and that's just not for me. I hope I'll get married to somebody rich and won't have to work. I'll stay home and have kids.

NAME WITHHELD, PARAMEDIC, WASHINGTON

■ I thought at one time I would be a veterinarian or a doctor, but they had you do those dexterity tests in grade school. They said, "No, you can never be a doctor. You don't have the dexterity for it." Well, that could have been learned. But they discouraged me so much that I thought,

I can't do it. so why should I bother? I went to Catholic school and I blame them for a lot of it because I think I would have excelled more if they had said, "Yeah, with a little practice and doing certain exercises, you can develop your dexterity." Girls were supposed to be mothers. . . .

We lived pretty close to a volunteer fire department, and I used to hear the whistle blow at night. It would just get my blood churning. I'd want to be out there with them. So I decided to start with advanced first aid and went through that. I'll never forget my first call. I thought the guys who responded were gods. This guy was in cardiac arrest, and just watching the medics perform the way they did, it was unbelievable to me. *I want to do this!* I said to myself.

This time, nothing was going to discourage me. I continued going to school and eventually became the first woman firefighter in my area. From there, I became the captain of our rescue squad. After that, I went to nursing school, then took the EMS courses.

EMT school doesn't teach you all the craziness that can happen. Every call is different. It's not textbook. You have to be aware of your surroundings. They never mention the violent patients that are literally going to pick you up and throw you off the back of the unit. They don't tell you how to react to these people, what you should do, how you should handle them. There's just so many things. They can teach you and teach you the books, but to actually go out and deal with the public is another story.

Sometimes the people are just too big. There's no way I can lift them. I once had to go to a neighbor and get help. Some people weigh over 300 pounds. I can lift about 270, but over that I have problems. I had to train and lift weights to be able to lift these people.

DIANE CRAWFORD, PARAMEDIC, OHIO

■ We had a SIDS [sudden infant death syndrome] case. The father was very upset, distraught. He wanted to thank us because we tried so hard, and all I could do was hug him. I felt terrible. My associates just dropped their heads.

"You know, sometimes this job really sucks," one of my partners observed.

"Yeah, no question. Sometimes it really does," I agreed.

On the other hand, there are an awful lot of positives. The people who call us, they want us. They need us. They're sick. They're hurt. They want help. We've had twenty, thirty in full cardiac arrest and we've been able to revive them. When that happens, you feel sensational.

TOM HARRISON, PARAMEDIC, WISCONSIN

■ I became a medic as a freak occurrence. I was working for a Kash-N-Karry grocery store stocking dog food. Three friends of mine decided to take the EMT course. One was a nurse, and the others were just interested in the medical field. They asked me to go with them, and I agreed. I guess I was looking for a job that was more rewarding that stocking dog food.

The school doesn't teach you about life. They don't teach you that people are going to spit on you and try to beat you up and are going to hate you even when you do the right thing. They can tell you what cyanosis [blue skin from lack of oxygen] is, but until you see it, you don't really know. They can let you intubate all the mannequins in the world, but until you're upside down in a vehicle in a ditch, in the dark, with a patient who has blood in their airway and who's biting down on the tube or fighting you with all their might, you'll never know what it's like. You'll never know until you experience it. And no matter how good your paramedic course is, it's impossible to teach those things. It's impossible to teach common sense in paramedic school. It's interesting to me that they call it "common sense," and yet it's so uncommon.

My advice to a new medic? Don't expect to save the world. Patients are going to die. Children are going to die. Teenagers are going to die. Mothers, fathers, and grandparents are going to die. There are times when God allows us to intervene, but there are also times when God's punched someone's ticket and there's nothing that I, as a paramedic, as a person with finite abilities, am going to be able to change.

The other advice is, don't expect to be appreciated. Even when you do save the world, a lot of people aren't going to notice; a lot of people aren't going to understand.

JEFF COLE, AEROMEDICAL PARAMEDIC, FLORIDA

■ EMS is tough on relationships. If your partner's not involved in the profession, be prepared for some rough times. They won't understand what you're going through after you've seen a dead baby or after you've transported someone burned beyond recognition. They just won't be able to understand the thought patterns that are going through your head at that time.

DOUG CARRELL, PARAMEDIC, NEBRASKA

■ One of the big beefs I have with the paramedic program is that they teach you how to succeed. They teach you the perfect call, the perfect solution to everything you do. They teach you how to do everything the way the books say it's to be done. But they don't teach you that you may fail, that you may not be able to intervene, and that sets you up for a big disappointment. Psychologically, I think that's one of the biggest problems I had in the beginning, because you're not going to get that IV on everybody. You're not going to get that perfect tube on everybody. You're not going to have that perfect call. And you're not going to save everybody.

They need to teach paramedics that they will fail every now and then. Not that they really want to teach that, but it's human nature and they need to address it.

Other than that, I think my education was strong.

As for my personal life, EMS has not really caused any problems there. My wife was a medic for ten years. I've been a medic for eleven. She's since become a nurse. It's worked out to our benefit. We've been able to raise our three children with one of us always being home. She worked one shift, I worked another. Our days off were arranged so she had a day to herself, I had a day to myself, and we had a day together. I don't know about anybody else, but it worked great for our marriage. We haven't had to have anybody else raise our children, and that's a big plus, because I love my kids and *I* got to raise them, not the television or day care.

Another reason I stay in EMS is because no two days are the same. I don't punch a time clock, and if you do your job, nobody screws with you, which I like a lot. There aren't too many jobs that I know of where you can do that. In most places, even if you do your job, they still mess with you, but not here.

SCOTT JOHNSON, PARAMEDIC, ILLINOIS

■ Becoming a paramedic was the turning point of my life. I'd have to say that. When I was twenty-three, I became a paramedic, and it changed my whole life.

MIKE SCHULZE, PARAMEDIC, NEW YORK

■ My son, seven, was playing with a friend on the monkey bars at school when the other boy slipped, got his arm caught, broke it, and nearly tore it off. It was one of those freak accidents that injures the child far more than you'd imagine. I responded and took the boy to the hospital. The interesting part is how this affected my son. He suffered through an extreme amount of guilt because he felt that since his father's a paramedic, he was therefore responsible for the well-being of his friends. The reality, of course, was that when the accident happened, he didn't know what to do. He couldn't stop the bleeding or take his friend's pain away, and that really crushed him. It took several weeks before he was able to deal with it.

It's kind of sad, and scary, that our children look up to us that way. They like what we do so much they automatically conclude that they should be able to do it. When they can't, it frustrates them. This is something we should all be aware of and deal with in advance.

RANDY MEININGER, PARAMEDIC, NEBRASKA

■ I originally wanted to become a doctor or a photographer, but being a photographer didn't pay real well and being a doctor meant eight more years of school. Being a paramedic, I basically do everything a doctor does except write prescriptions and earn a lot of money.

I love the job and would never give it up. Every day is a new learning experience. Well, yeah, I'd give it up if I won the lottery, but other than that, I'm going to continue to do it.

Paramedics are the best actors and actresses in the world because we have to convince people that they're going to be okay. Fifty to eighty percent of this job is psychology. If somebody is having chest pains, sure, the oxygen and nitro will help, maybe morphine will help, but at the same time you have to convince the patient that what you're giving them, what you're doing for them, will help. A lot of times it does, but the patient has to want to get better.

Being a paramedic has given me a different perspective on life and death. I live life to the fullest and I appreciate every day that I'm alive. I've seen too many people die who shouldn't have died and people live who shouldn't have lived.

VICKI IEZZY, PARAMEDIC, FLORIDA

■ Initially, when you first start this job, it's real hard dealing with some of the terrible things. As the years go by, you'll pretty much see everything there is to see. As time passes, it becomes easier to handle.

JOHN OBJARTEL, PARAMEDIC, IOWA

■ I've been through three marriages. That tells you something about EMS. Most of my career has been twenty-four hours on, forty-eight off. That doesn't promote a successful relationship. Plus, people who aren't in this business have a difficult time understanding some of the problems that you go through.

A mistake can cost a life. People in authority can end your career because of the mistake. We all know that there are a load of ambulance chasers [lawyers] out there who are ready to do whatever they can to make a buck. If it destroys someone's life or career, so be it.

PAT CRAWFORD, PARAMEDIC, FLORIDA

■ My grandfather had an ambulance and funeral service. My father took it over when he died. I guess I always wanted to be on the ambulance for the excitement. I'd see them running up and down the road with the lights flashing and sirens blaring, and it was a thrill. Being able to make a difference, lessen someone's pain or prolong their life—that appealed to me.

The only disappointment is that I'd expected that we could change the lives of everybody we touched. That's not the case. We do help, that's for sure. But on all these rescue shows, they only show the positive end to it. Everybody makes it on television. In real life, that isn't true. However, when someone does survive, it's a great feeling knowing you made a difference.

PATRICK WALSH, PARAMEDIC, ILLINOIS

■ I'm really sorry that I didn't get into EMS when I was younger. Aside from raising my children, EMS has been an experience like none other in my life. You walk in a door and see the terrified look on people's faces. They're in pain, or a loved one's in pain, and they're confused and frightened. They have no idea what to do. They look at you and say, "Oh, thank God you're here! Everything's going to be okay now."

It makes you feel sort of important.

This profession, hectic and heartbreaking as it can be, has given me great personal satisfaction. I remember this little old lady we were taking to the hospital. She had the whitest hair and clearest blue eyes that I've ever seen. I had an overpowering premonition that this would be her last ride. I must have had a despondent look on my face, because she touched my hand and said, "Honey, don't look so sad and worried. I know I'm dying, and it's okay. If you just sit here with me and stay with me so I'm not alone, that will be fine."

We said the Lord's Prayer together. After we finished, she had such a peaceful look on her face.

"Thank you," she whispered, squeezing my hand with her last ounce of strength. "Thank you for being here with me."

I'll always remember how important my presence was to this stranger. It was the kind of magical moment that I could never quite explain to my family. They couldn't understand my dedication to the job. Sometimes we'd be having a family gathering and my beeper would go off, and they'd just groan and try to talk me out of responding. They'd get mad at me for spoiling the fun.

"How can I just sit here and keep eating while someone's bleeding or can't breathe?" I'd ask.

"But we need you, too, Mom," they'd counter. "You're always running off."

"At least I come back. What's more important, that we finish dinner together tonight or that someone out there might never get to eat dinner with their family again?"

That argument usually got through, but they still weren't happy.

I guess I was so caught up in EMS that it consumed me. After the children were older, it became the most important thing in my life.

I often lie in bed at night and think of the thousands of calls I've been on. I recall the faces of the people I helped and comforted, and it gives me a sense of inner peace. If I saved one life, just one, then all the other stuff, all the death and suffering, has been worth it.

Almost without exception, the medics I've talked to and worked with feel the same way. They express it differently, in their own words, but deep down they feel the same.

It's no small irony that the symbol for EMS is the Star of Life. That adequately describes all the people working in EMS. We're all Stars of Life.

DONNA

3 Dialing 911

> *It never ceases to amaze me, the things that people will jam into their butts. I've had calls about lightbulbs, vibrators, dildos, pepper mills, you name it. There sure are a bunch of fun people out there! No gerbils, though—not yet.*

CES HERRERAS, DISPATCHER, CALIFORNIA

Today's best 911 systems are true technological marvels. The instant someone calls, their name and address pop up on a computer screen. Actually, it's the name and address that particular telephone is registered under, but it's usually enough to get an ambulance to the scene.

Which is not to say that a 911 caller should blow off answering the dispatcher's questions. The name and address must be verified, directions on how best to get to the location can help medics save precious minutes, and the dispatcher needs to know what the problem is in order to prepare the EMS crew and the hospital.

The automatic identification system is considered a backup in case someone passes out in the middle of the call, is attacked by a spouse or intruder, or is too overcome by emotion to communicate adequately. As veteran dispatch supervisor Melanie Carr explains, these emotions can be varied and powerful: "How many times does a person have a medical emergency in their lifetime?

People rarely face something like this. The range of reactions is extreme. You get people who are calm, like they've programmed exactly what they're going to say. Some people even read from a card that they've prepared in advance. Regardless of what questions you need to ask them, all they do is continue reading their speech. That can be frustrating. Other people are cool and collected. They'll answer questions fine, like normal conversation. Some are just on the edge. You can tell by their voice that they're struggling to hold themselves together. If you ask the wrong question or say the wrong thing, you're going to lose them. They go right over the emotional cliff.

"Then there are the people who are totally panicked from the start and all you get is little bits and pieces," Carr continues. "You have to pull the information out of them in a verbal tug-of-war before you can even begin the rescue process. That wastes valuable time. The public should know that we don't take our computer screen data for granted. If a person's down, having a heart attack or something, and the family member panics, they might not know who to call, so they call a friend on the other side of the county. Then that friend calls us, so we can be showing one address when the actual emergency is across town. Or they're calling about a car wreck that they saw down the street on the way home. Knowing this, the only time we exclusively rely on the on-screen information is in a case where somebody calls and then they gasp and drop the phone, and there's no other way of finding them. We then trace it back to that particular telephone.

"The computer identification does work to cut our prank calls down to almost nothing. That's because we have a way of finding them. They're not anonymous. They can't hide from us anymore. And they can be prosecuted. They can be charged for the cost of the response. The judges here in this county have done that. It'll cost someone four or five hundred dollars for each individual piece of equipment that responded."

Overall, the 911 system is the first link in the critical EMS chain. As hectic and difficult as things are for the paramedics and EMTs in the field, dispatchers may have the most stressful job of all. They field dozens of calls a shift—dozens of hysterical calls. Dispatchers have to calm the person, get the required information, then make instant decisions on whether or not to send an ambulance. Sometimes they even save lives by talking people through CPR, childbirth, poison treatments, and any number of other medical procedures.

All too often, they "witness" through their ears the same horrible tragedies that paramedics and EMTs experience in person.

It's debatable which is worse.

THE STORIES

■ "There's a UFO flying over my house! It's trying to get me!"

The lady sounded serious. I knew better than to brush it off as just another late-night crazy. There are a lot of strange things that go on in this world.

Years before, when I was in high school, my sister told me that she'd been abducted by space aliens. She said they had transported her through solid walls and beamed her aboard their ship. She never saw them and couldn't describe what they looked like, but insisted that they'd tattooed an invisible mark somewhere on her body that only they can see. The aliens, she explained, had similarly abducted and branded many other people.

My sister has stuck to her story for more than twenty years.

"Keep on laughing," she says. "One day you'll find out."

That experience came to mind as I considered how to deal with the terrified caller.

"Just lie still and let them take a look at you," I instructed.

"I'm scared! They're trying to get me!"

"They don't want to hurt you. They just want to study how we live. Lie still, let them have their look, and they'll go away."

"Are you sure?"

"Yeah. Just lie still. Stay calm. Don't be frightened."

"Okay." There was a long pause. "It's leaving! It's leaving!"

"Good. Do you need an ambulance?"

"No. They've left. I'll be okay now, I think."

"All right. If it comes back, call again."

"I will."

I can't confirm that a spaceship was actually hovering over that woman's house. However, if one was, I guessed correctly that it wasn't going to hurt her.

SHIRLEYVON, DISPATCHER, WISCONSIN

■ "There are space aliens living in my attic! They're cooking their food and going to the bathroom up there. They won't keep the place clean! I need you to get them out of here!"

"Okay. We'll send an officer."

We used to try to blow this woman off, but she kept calling and insisting her house had been invaded by creatures from outer space. Sometimes she'd say they were inside her head stapling her brain. On other occasions she'd report that they had taken up residence inside her refrigerator.

"They won't let me open it," she'd wail. "I can't get any food!"

The police officers and paramedics would go to her

home, make a show of shining flashlights in the attic or refrigerator, and order the aliens to leave.

One day an officer went running down the street, pretending to chase the aliens to the next block.

"They're gone forever now, ma'am," he announced.

Not quite.

"They're back!" she proclaimed a few nights later. "And don't send that cop who came here last time, the one who ran down the street. He thinks I'm stupid! He wasn't chasing anything!"

Graveyard shifts . . . we do the best we can.

TAMMY YENNIE, DISPATCHER, CONNECTICUT

■ "Oh, God, hurry! My baby isn't breathing. I don't know what to do. . . . Please, please—she ain't breathing. Please hurry!"

"Do you have the baby there with you?"

"Yeah, yes."

"How old is it?"

"She'll be two weeks old tomorrow." The caller is sobbing, nearly hysterical.

"Okay, cover the baby's nose and mouth with your mouth and blow in. Very gently. Not too hard. Blow in four times."

"Okay. Okay."

"Go ahead. Do it right now." After a pause: "Is the baby breathing at all?"

"No!" More sobs from the mother.

"You are going to have to calm down. Relax. We have help on the way."

"I can't. I can't."

"All right. Take two fingers now and find the spot in the baby's chest where it dips down. . . . Got it? Place them above that spot. Now gently press in. Not very hard, but gentle enough to compress the chest a little bit."

"Okay."

"Press in five times, then breathe into the baby's mouth and nose. Gently now, okay? . . . Count them out loud. Let me hear you."

"One, two, three, four, five . . . "

"Keep doing it."

"One, two, three, four, five . . . She's jumping!"

"What? Keep on doing it. Breathe in the baby's nose and mouth. Press, breathe. Press, breathe."

"One, two, three, four, five . . . "

Everyone in the dispatch center leaps to their feet. "Is that the baby crying? Is she crying? Come on, baby, cry! Cry! Cry!"

"Oh, yes, Laurie. Cry. Cry, baby, cry."

Once in a while you get a call like this one—the baby I helped save by talking her mother through CPR. We were all pumped up over that call. My partner and I left here at the end of the day and got a six-pack. We were all excited over this baby. It was such a unique situation. You knew that it had turned blue and was dying, and then you could hear the baby cry. It's not a common occurrence, but that kind of satisfaction feels pretty good. That may sound sort of corny, but I get satisfaction from knowing that what we do is important. Everybody likes to feel that their job is important.

This call received a lot of attention. I ended up getting the Employee of the Month award. I had to go down to the courthouse and get the award from the chief. All the attention made me feel good, although we felt better the day it happened.

When they went through the award ceremonies at the courthouse, they played the 911 tape. It was the first time I heard it. It brought tears to my eyes. I got all choked up and I couldn't say anything. It was kind of embarrassing, you know, because you're not supposed to do that.

I have the original tape at home. Every once in a while

someone brings it up and we play it. When the baby cries, it's just like, well, wow!

I have to admit, after I called back and got hold of the mother, I was thinking, *Man, I don't want to do this.* We have no obligation to make a call back and try to do anything. None of us are paramedics or EMTs. All we had was a CPR course. But I was thinking that it was so many miles out there in the country and the roads are bad. This was just a little baby, thirteen days old. It's one of those things you hate when it first comes up. But I had to do something. I couldn't just sit there.

There's a little bit of fear that you are not going to do something right or you won't be able to take control of the conversation. At the end, I was relieved that it was over.

I never met the baby or the mother. I was going to go up there and just see the baby, but I decided not to. First of all, there was a lot of attention brought on by the call, and I was kind of embarrassed by all of it, anyway. I thought it was best to let it go. I never heard personally from the mother. They interviewed her for the newspaper and she said some very nice things, but I never heard from her. I can't recall if they sent us a letter or not. But it was a good call. I felt good about it.

PAUL FULLON, DISPATCHER, FLORIDA

■ "There's blood all over my house! I don't know what it's from!"

So began a major mystery. The police and crime lab were dispatched and quickly became as puzzled as the homeowner. All members of the man's family were accounted for. No one was injured. Yet the home was splashed with fresh blood from one end to the other.

The crime technicians took samples while police officers and paramedics scratched their heads. It was obvious some horrible tragedy had taken place there. But what? Had strangers broken in, tortured and murdered someone, then disappeared with the body? Was there a missing girlfriend or child the man was not telling anyone about? Was the home haunted by violent ghosts?

The answer came in a sheepish call later that night.

"My cat just came home. Somehow its tail got cut off!"

The frisky feline, no doubt in great pain from the loss of its tail, had apparently run around the place in a frenzy shortly after losing its rear appendage. It had sprayed its blood far and wide, creating a ghoulish portrait of horror.

By the time the animal came back home, however, the wound had clotted and the newly bobbed cat seemed little worse for wear.

SHAWN MABEE-HILL, DISPATCHER, ARIZONA

■ "I'm locked in and I can't get out! I'm afraid if there's a fire, I won't be able to escape!"

The frantic caller's location didn't come up immediately on our 911 screen, so my partner kept talking to him.

"Where are you, sir?" he asked.

"I'm in a mental health center," he stated.

My partner and I looked at each other. Then, breaking tradition, my partner let all the stress of getting hundreds of bad calls and false alarms pour out.

"You dumb son of a bitch, you're *supposed* to be locked in!"

CHUCK VOGELSONG, DISPATCHER, VIRGINIA

■ I was working the night shift on a slow evening. A man called who was having a great deal of trouble communicating. He spoke in grunts and strange guttural sounds. It sounded like he'd had a stroke or a heart attack, or was severely beaten.

To complicate matters, his address wouldn't pop up on my screen. I called the police and the phone company, and they couldn't get a make on him, either.

I quickly developed a system of yes and no grunts, then painstakingly led him through the numbers and alphabet to try to determine his address. It took twenty nerve-racking minutes, going number by number, letter by letter, to finally work it out. Using this ad-libbed code, I was able to decipher his house number, street name, and even his apartment number.

I dispatched the paramedics and stayed on the phone until they got there. A medic came on and explained that they'd found an elderly man on the floor. He had a tracheotomy, and that was why he was having so much difficulty speaking.

Because of his operation, the medics had a hard time determining what was wrong with him. (Maybe a fan of *Wheel of Fortune* could have used my system and figured it out a lot sooner.) His problem happened to be the biggest catch phrase in the country at the time: "I've fallen, and I can't get up!"

NATALIE MARTINEZ, DISPATCHER, ARIZONA

■ A woman called, screaming hysterically.

"They've chopped him to pieces. Oh, my God! Oh, my God! I don't know what to do. It's a massacre!"

My adrenaline rushed. The lady kept screaming so much I had a hard time getting the necessary information out of her.

"Where are you? Where is this happening?"

Despite her refusal to provide those critical details, I was convinced that there was a big-time mass murder in progress. Finally the 911 computer screen flashed her number. I traced it. It was a pay phone at a mental hospital.

I called the main office and got in touch with a nurse.

"Is there someone on the hall pay phone?" I asked.

After a moment the nurse said, "As a matter of fact, there is! Ellen, get off the phone right now!"

I would have sworn that was a real call.

MELANIE CARR, DISPATCH SUPERVISOR, FLORIDA

■ We get tongue-tied once in a while, and it can be terribly embarrassing. And worse, once you get something twisted, it sticks in your brain and you can't stop.

I had this problem with the routine instruction "Did you copy the cancellation?" Much to my chagrin, it kept coming out as "Did you cancel the copulation?"

"No, never!" the paramedics would invariably respond. "We're still on for tonight, baby!"

CES HERRERAS, DISPATCHER, CALIFORNIA

■ We had a lady on our shift who kept stumbling over the term "head-on collision." She kept saying "hard-on collision." That always got the paramedics' attention.

SHIRLEYVON, DISPATCHER, WISCONSIN

■ "The Christmas tree's on fire!"

"What Christmas tree?"

"The tumbleweed tree!"

The caught my attention. The world-famous, one-of-a-kind tumbleweed Christmas tree is one of our city's major attractions. The forty-foot beauty is constructed entirely from Old West–style tumbleweeds. The tree is so large and bright we can see it from our dispatch center. I ran to the window. Sure enough, there was an enormous glow in the sky. The cherished tree was engulfed in flame. It looked like a giant torch!

For the next few minutes, the communications center

was inundated with frantic calls about the burning Christmas tree. We must have received fifty in a row.

Despite the public's quick reaction, there was nothing the firefighters could do. The dry desert brush burned like paper. The whole tree—lock, stock, and decorations—was totally consumed within minutes.

The fire investigators determined that someone had ignited it with a Molotov cocktail. By coincidence, two teenagers were rushed to a nearby emergency room complaining of nasty gasoline burns. The pair never confessed, and the police left it at that. If they were the guilty parties, they'd already punished themselves far worse than a judge could have.

Since it was two days before Christmas, there wasn't time to rebuild the famous tree. A citizens' group used wires, tinsel, and garland to jury-rig a replacement. It was pretty, but it wasn't our tumbleweed tree.

Some teenage Scrooges had definitely spoiled Christmas.

AMY AZCEK, DISPATCHER, ARIZONA

■ This woman called from a phone booth outside a store. We didn't have the address. She was really upset because she and her boyfriend split, and she stated that she was going to kill herself. She had a gun.

"You don't want to do that," I said. "Not over a boyfriend. It's absurd. What about your family, the people who love you?"

Suddenly the caller heard the beeps on the phone and realized that she was being taped.

"I'm being recorded, aren't I?" she demanded.

"Affirmative," I said.

"Well, I'm not going to talk to you anymore!"

"Give me your phone number and I'll call you right back on an unrecorded line," I promised.

She agreed. I dialed while my partner used the number to check her address. Bingo. We called for an ambulance and the police.

Meanwhile I kept talking to her, trying to convince her not to kill herself. In the background, I heard sirens.

Apparently so did she.

"You called the law!" the woman screamed.

The next thing I heard was two loud bangs. I stayed on the phone. Incredibly, she came back on and told me she shot herself twice in the stomach.

"It hurts!" she screams. "It hurts. Get somebody here. Quick!"

I flicked the switch to mute my initial response: "What did you think it was gonna do, tickle? Smart move, lady."

I switched back on. "Hang in there," I said. "You're going to be all right. The medics will be there any minute."

Fortunately, the woman hadn't hit any vital organs, and she survived. She was in a lot of pain—more than her boyfriend had ever caused her—but she made it.

MELANIE CARR, DISPATCH SUPERVISOR, FLORIDA

■ "There are birds in my tree!"

"Yes. So what's the problem, ma'am?"

"There are birds in my tree! I want you to send someone to get them out."

"We don't do that. We don't get birds out of trees."

The woman went ballistic, refusing to take no for an answer. She insisted that as a taxpaying citizen, she had the right to have birds removed from her tree. She eventually wore me down, and I dispatched an officer.

The woman greeted him on her stoop with her hands above her head, ducking madly. The officer kept turning around, expecting to find himself in the middle of a scene from the classic Hitchcock movie *The Birds*.

Nothing happened.

The trees on the property were more than a hundred feet tall. If there were any birds, they were way up there.

"They keep swooping down on me and my dog!" she ranted, bobbing and weaving. "Do something! Do something! They're driving me crazy!"

"There's nothing I can do, ma'am," the officer said, retreating to his unit. "That's where birds live, in trees!"

PATTI WALTON, DISPATCH SUPERVISOR, OHIO

■ This young guy, Peter, used to call us two or three times a week on the late shift and just talk for hours. We'd put him on hold, take a lunch break, handle ten calls, come back, and he'd still be yapping. He said he was going to college to become a paralegal, but I figured that was just his imagination. He'd ramble on about the law, chat about the car he had back in high school, then fast-forward to some guy peeing on his fence. It was hours and hours of stream-of-semiconsciousness nonsense.

One day he stopped calling and never called again. As happens with these types, he just faded away.

Eight years later, I was reading the newspaper and came across an item about a local court case. The attorney for the plaintiff was my old nightcrawler pal Peter! I couldn't believe it! The guy was a certified lunatic, and now he's a practicing trial attorney!

ED KARSTEN, DISPATCHER, ARIZONA

■ "I need an ambulance for Dora in four-A!"

That was all the woman on the phone would say. I couldn't get anything else out of her. When her address came on the screen, I realized why.

She was calling from a retirement community. That explained it. Everybody she knew lived in that complex. Everything they do centers around the complex. Naturally, the person needing the ambulance is in this complex. The caller thinks we should know that. It doesn't even occur to her that we wouldn't. She thinks that we're in the complex! She has no idea that when she calls 911, she could be in Angola, for all we know.

PAUL FULLON, DISPATCHER, FLORIDA

■ We had a regular named Ed who used to go to nice restaurants and order big, fancy meals. After wolfing down dessert, he'd fall on the floor and dramatically clutch his chest. We ran him a half-dozen times before we caught on to his scam. He was faking a heart attack to get out of paying the bill!

It got so that every time we received a call about someone having a heart attack in a restaurant, we'd ask the manager to describe him. More times than not, it would be our pal, check-dodging Ed.

GARY STILTS, DISPATCH SUPERVISOR, ARIZONA

■ We received a call from a man estranged from his wife. He'd taken the children out for the day and brought them back home. Then he snapped. In front of the children, ages six months to six, he proceeded to beat his wife, then stab her to death. Halfway through, he called 911. We could hear the baby screaming and the two other children crying and screaming.

"Don't hurt my mommy. Don't hurt my mommy!" a child pleaded in the background.

The guy told us that he killed his wife. He then dropped the phone and went back to stabbing her body some more. The line was open, so we heard it all.

We were on the phone trying to get the address, and we could actually hear this guy stabbing and stabbing her. The little boy was still crying "Don't hurt my mommy" over and over again. He was probably trying to pull his father off her.

We stayed on the phone and heard the medics and police break in. We heard the police arrest the guy. The police officers were angry and were calling him names.

The woman had been stabbed more than thirty times, right in front of her children. It was horrible. A horrible call. We were all sort of conferenced together on this call, all the dispatchers. It was one of those calls where we could have hung up, but you can't. It's like, *This is happening and I'm getting my units there as fast as I can, and I can't hang up.* You have to stay on the line. But you feel so helpless.

There is something in you that just won't let you hang up that phone. You just can't disconnect from that kind of tragedy. Maybe it's human nature or whatever.

It was the most awful call that I've heard in my career. It made our skin crawl. It was so vivid that the dispatchers who were working that night had to go through the CISD [critical incident stress debriefing] program. The police officers and medics also went.

MELANIE CARR, DISPATCH SUPERVISOR, FLORIDA

■ An extremely distraught young man called and said he was going to kill himself. He told me that he'd confessed to his father that he was gay, and the conversation hadn't gone well. His father was an influential doctor, and the young man was afraid that he was going to shame the family.

He'd come out of the closet, he said, because he was in danger of being exposed.

We talked for the next hour. He told me about his life, his loves, his family, anything and everything. He'd leave the phone for a while to kneel and pray, then come back and continue our conversation.

"This is not worth killing yourself over," I pleaded. "Your folks will eventually learn to deal with it. Give it a chance."

One of the police lieutenants grew weary of the stand-off outside the man's house and grabbed the phone.

"Enough's enough!" the lieutenant barked. "I want you to end this and come out right now!"

Bang! Bang! That was it. The guy killed himself.

I was so stunned and numb, it didn't affect me right away. As the days passed, though, I found that I couldn't forget it. I felt like I was reaching him, making some progress, then *bam,* it was over. I ended up having to go to stress debriefing. That helped, but it still hurts.

TAMMY YENNIE, DISPATCHER, CONNECTICUT

■ My wife had been a dispatcher for nine years when she received a call that pushed her over the edge. An elderly couple returned home from an evening out and found their VCR on the front lawn. Instead of going to a neighbor's house and calling the police, they foolishly marched inside. The burglar was still there. He whipped out a knife and slashed them both.

The injured woman crawled to a phone. My wife fielded the call and tried to determine the extent of the couple's injuries. The woman wasn't very forthcoming, so my wife was forced to concentrate on telling her how to treat herself.

The man was far worse off. He died at the scene.

My wife kicked herself for not insisting that the woman explain his condition. Although it's doubtful that a dispatcher could have done anything to save him, that didn't stop my wife from being haunted by feelings of failure and neglect of duty. She immediately took two weeks off to get herself together. When she came back, she couldn't handle the job anymore. She quit within the month.

We met and fell in love in that communications center. We'd worked together for nearly a decade. Yet ironically, our experiences led us in opposite directions. Although I understand the stress that made her leave, I don't feel the same way. I love what I'm doing. I can't imagine doing anything else. I've been fielding 911 calls for fourteen years now, and I plan to stay another twelve. I'd stay even if I won the lottery.

ED KARSTEN, DISPATCHER, ARIZONA

911 TAPES

■ **SOFT FEMALE VOICE AT 4:00 A.M.:** I have a rather strange situation. We have a pet cow. . . .

DISPATCHER: Let me see if I got this right. You have a pet cow?

CALLER: You got it right.

DISPATCHER: Okay.

CALLER: And she's stuck in the backyard and we can't get her out. . . .

DISPATCHER: Oh, wait, ma'am, your pet cow is stuck in the backyard?

CALLER: We've been back there shoveling, and we're trying everything we can. I finally got permission to call you.

DISPATCHER: My goodness. You've got a cow high-centered in your backyard?

CALLER: That's a new one, isn't it?

DISPATCHER: Goodness gracious. I just don't know what kind of truck to send out on that.

CALLER: Do you have some kind of winch?

DISPATCHER: [Breaks down laughing]

CALLER: [To someone with her] She's laughing so hard she can't talk.

DISPATCHER: As a matter of fact, we have a big truck with a crane on it. My supervisor's here, and I'm going to apprise her. I tell you what—let's do this like we do every other emergency and let's get your address first.

CALLER: [Gives address]

DISPATCHER: Okay.

CALLER: We're actually right here in the city, you know.

DISPATCHER: Yeah, I know that area [a small rural pocket]. Is the cow conscious, ma'am?

CALLER: Is she conscious? Yeah, she's conscious.

DISPATCHER: Conscious? Breathing? Okay that way?

CALLER: Yeah, she's breathing. But we thought we almost had her, that she could maybe try [to get out] again, but it seems like her back end just sinks down farther.

DISPATCHER: [Cracks up again] Haven't you had days when your back end will do that?

CALLER: [Laughs]

DISPATCHER: I tell you what. We'll get out there, or we'll get the proper animal control or somebody out there to help you. Okay?

CALLER: You got it. [Repeats address]

DISPATCHER: Sounds good. This is a pet cow?

CALLER: Well, by now she's retired, you know? She wandered out last night and got into something like . . . well, it used to be a cesspool.

DISPATCHER: [Fighting back laughter] Okay, we'll get somebody out there to help you. And calling was the right thing to do!

CALLER: Well, yeah, I had a hard time convincing the rest of them to call. I know you get cats out of trees, but this is different.

DISPATCHER: Oh, I know. It's just as important. I know we're laughing—

CALLER: That's all right.

DISPATCHER: —but I know you're scared and you've got

to get her out. So we'll figure out who to send and we'll be right out for you.

[The paramedics were dispatched. Using a ladder truck and crane, they successfully rescued the cow from the sinkhole.]

CANDI BRUNACINA, DISPATCHER, ARIZONA;
TAPE PROVIDED BY FIRE CAPTAIN JIM ARBAGEY

■ **DISPATCHER:** Fire department.
MALE CALLER: I need a paramedic.
DISPATCHER: To what address?
CALLER: Uh, let's see. I don't live here. [To other person in room] What's the address? [Consults with someone, then gives address and phone number]
DISPATCHER: What's the problem?
CALLER: The guy that lives in the apartment has inserted something into his rectum, and it won't come out.
DISPATCHER: Okay, does anyone have an idea what it is?
CALLER: [To other person in room] What is it, Morris? [To dispatcher] It's a dildo.
DISPATCHER: Okay. How old is the gentleman?
CALLER: He's forty.
DISPATCHER: They're on the way, sir.
CALLER: Thanks.
[The dispatcher calls back. A different man answers. He speaks in a hushed, pained voice.]
DISPATCHER: This is the fire department. We have a unit trying to locate the apartment and building number.
CALLER: [Gives directions]
DISPATCHER: You're the patient?
CALLER: Yes. My friends are out in front trying to find the ambulance.
DISPATCHER: How are you doing?
CALLER: I just feel real stupid. How else would I feel?

DISPATCHER: I really wouldn't know.

CALLER: Yeah, how appropriate. I don't know . . . loneliness does strange things to strange people.

DISPATCHER: Sometimes it does.

CALLER: May I hang up now?

DISPATCHER: I want to make sure they find the apartment. If you can just let me know if you hear the truck outside . . . do you hear anything at all, sir?

CALLER: No.

DISPATCHER: Are your friends outside looking for them?

CALLER: Yeah.

DISPATCHER: I'll let you go ahead and hang up. They'll be there in just a minute.

CALLER: Thanks.

NAME WITHHELD, DISPATCHER, NEW MEXICO

■ **DISPATCHER:** Fire department.

MALE CALLER: I have a friend of mind here and she's complaining of sharp pains inside her stomach and she's crying and screaming.

DISPATCHER: Okay. All right. What address is she at?

CALLER: [Gives address] She's eighteen years old. She was at the doctor two nights ago, at the emergency room.

DISPATCHER: What'd they say?

CALLER: Something happened to her at a party or something, like glass broke inside of her. She's complaining and crying. . . .

DISPATCHER: How did glass get inside of her?

CALLER: I'm not sure. She was with some friends. Some weird guys. They took her to the doctor and now she's over here and she's crying. I live right here. She came here because it's the closest thing.

DISPATCHER: Can you ask her if she can calm down and talk to me on the phone?

CALLER: She says she can barely breathe. She's on the ground [floor] crying.

DISPATCHER: Ask her if she can calm down enough to talk to me on the phone.

CALLER: [To patient] Hey, Vanessa, can you talk to the lady on the phone? [To dispatcher, with patient's screams in background] She can't.

DISPATCHER: Is there any chance she could be pregnant?

CALLER: [To patient] Is there any chance you could be pregnant or anything? [To dispatcher] She says no.

DISPATCHER: Can you ask her how glass got inside of her?

CALLER: Well, I—

[Call disconnects, and dispatcher calls back]

CALLER: Hello?

DISPATCHER: This is the fire department. What happened?

CALLER: She's on the ground. I don't know what happened.

DISPATCHER: First of all, I want to tell you help is on the way for her.

CALLER: Thank you.

DISPATCHER: She's having trouble breathing?

CALLER: She's breathing and she's, like, in a lot of pain.

DISPATCHER: In her stomach area?

CALLER: In her stomach and . . .

DISPATCHER: Does she have a medical history of any kind?

CALLER: She's had a baby in the past, I know that. But she's not pregnant. There's something, like, something piercing her inside, I guess.

DISPATCHER: And you're saying the other night she went to the hospital because glass broke in her stomach?

CALLER: She was there two nights ago in the emergency room. She was partying with some guys and they, like, put something in her when she was passed out. They took her to the doctor and the doctor said everything was okay, but she's, like, over here crying because there's something in her stomach.

DISPATCHER: So they didn't put glass inside of her?

CALLER: It was, like, a lightbulb or something. I'm not sure. Something freaky, you know?

DISPATCHER: Where did they put the lightbulb?

CALLER: Inside her private area.

DISPATCHER: Okay, so they didn't put it in her stomach?

CALLER: Well, it's, like, yeah, in that area.

DISPATCHER: Sir, your stomach and your vagina are very different. They don't even touch.

CALLER: I know. She's complaining about her stomach. Something in her stomach is hurting. The lower part of her stomach.

DISPATCHER: Okay, so there's nothing in her vagina right now?

CALLER: Um, not that I know of. See, I'm just a friend! I'm trying to help.

DISPATCHER: Okay, okay. We'll be there in just a few minutes.

NAME WITHHELD, DISPATCHER, ILLINOIS

■ **DISPATCHER:** Fire and ambulance. Do you have an emergency?

ELDERLY FEMALE CALLER: I've been trying to get Mr. Vincent's Beauty Shop and they [directory assistance] say it so fast that I can't understand it.

DISPATCHER: This is fire and ambulance. I have no idea where Mr. Vincent's Beauty Shop is.

CALLER: Well, it's in the mall.

DISPATCHER: I'm fire and ambulance dispatch. This is not directory assistance!

NAME WITHHELD, DISPATCHER, OKLAHOMA

CALLER: This is Sylvia. There are penises in my milk!

DISPATCHER: What?

CALLER: There are penises in my milk! Please come out and get rid of them.

DISPATCHER: We can't do that, Sylvia. I think if you drink your milk, they'll go away.

CALLER: Okay. Thanks.

NAME WITHHELD, DISPATCHER, KANSAS

■ DISPATCHER: Fire and ambulance.

FEMALE CALLER: I need an ambulance at 1012 Wilson now!

DISPATCHER: 1012 Wilson Street?

CALLER: Yes.

DISPATCHER: Can you give me an idea what the problem is?

CALLER: He's been . . .

DISPATCHER: Okay, is it a home or an apartment?

CALLER: It's an apartment.

DISPATCHER: What apartment number?

CALLER: He's been drinking and mixing medication.

DISPATCHER: What apartment number?

CALLER: 1012 Wilson Street.

DISPATCHER: All right, can you give me a cross street that goes with Wilson?

CALLER: Huh?

DISPATCHER: I need a cross street that goes with Wilson.

CALLER: You come down Westchester to Wilson Street.

DISPATCHER: I need—

CALLER: You assholes! It's off Westchester on Wilson.

DISPATCHER: Okay. What's the phone number you're calling from?

CALLER: [Screaming] Okay, you bitch! It's 555–0812.

DISPATCHER: Thank you very much.

NAME WITHHELD, DISPATCHER, MONTANA

DISPATCHER: Emergency.

CHILD'S VOICE: [Crying] My hand is being cut off!

DISPATCHER: Your hand is being cut off?

CALLER: My fingers.

DISPATCHER: Your fingers?

CALLER: Yes.

DISPATCHER: How did you do that, honey?

CALLER: My mom's [egg] beater is going, and I—my finger's stuck!

DISPATCHER: Have you got a towel or anything you can wrap around it and hold on to it?

CALLER: I can't get there!

DISPATCHER: Have you got anything to put around your finger?

CALLER: [Crying harder] The, ohhhhhhh, the, ohhhhhhh, the blood isn't going to get from my finger.

DISPATCHER: I know, honey. Just stay on the phone with me, okay?

CALLER: [Whimpers] Okay.

DISPATCHER: Just stay on the phone with me. There's nothing there that you can wrap around your hand?

CALLER: No.

DISPATCHER: Okay, well, we'll hurry. [Dispatches paramedics] Okay, honey, they're on the way.

CALLER: Okay.

DISPATCHER: Now you stay right on the phone with me.

CALLER: They're going to have to cut the beaters off.

DISPATCHER: Your hand's still stuck in there?

CALLER: Yes.

DISPATCHER: Is it bleeding real bad?

CALLER: Just a little bit.

DISPATCHER: Hold your hand real still.

CALLER: Okay.

DISPATCHER: What kind of beater is it?

CALLER: Um, an electric one.

DISPATCHER: Electric beater to what?

CALLER: We're making Jell-O.

DISPATCHER: Okay. Can you raise your hand up?

CALLER: No, 'cause the beater's still stuck on it.

DISPATCHER: Just be real still. Okay?

CALLER: Okay.

DISPATCHER: [Radios update to paramedics]

CALLER: Owoooooooooooo.

DISPATCHER: Don't cry. Everything going to be all right. Everything's going to be just fine. Just be real still and they'll be there in just a second, okay?

CALLER: [Whimpering] Okay.

DISPATCHER: Is the front door unlocked so they can get in? Are you by yourself?

CALLER: Yes.

DISPATCHER: You're by yourself?

CALLER: Yes, and it's unlocked.

DISPATCHER: Okay. [To paramedics] Engine eighty-seven, be advised she is home alone by herself and the front door is unlocked.

CALLER: [Instantly stops crying; adamant] It's a *boy!*

DISPATCHER: It's a boy! I'm sorry, honey! [To paramedics] It's a boy!

CALLER: [Crying again] Oweeeee.

DISPATCHER: Don't move. Be real still.

CALLER: There's pressure on it either way.

DISPATCHER: Be real still. Real still. There's nobody with you at all?

CALLER: No one. My baby-sitter's next door.

DISPATCHER: Okay. Just be real still. And real quiet. Because if you move, that's when it hurts. So be real still. That way it won't bleed as much, either.

CALLER: Okay.

DISPATCHER: And they'll come right in the front door, so you don't have to worry. If you hear them, don't try to move and go help them because they'll come in. Do I hear somebody now?

CALLER: Yes. [Dejected] It's not the police.

DISPATCHER: Who is it, hon?

CALLER: It's the baby-sitter.

DISPATCHER: Okay. Okay.

CALLER: Don't! [Crying] Don't!

DISPATCHER: Tell her not to touch you! Not to touch you! Okay?

CALLER: Okay.

DISPATCHER: How old are you?

CALLER: I'm ten. [Elated] Hi!

DISPATCHER: Are they there now?

CALLER: They're here!

DISPATCHER: Okay, honey, bye-bye.

CALLER: Bye.

[The paramedics freed the boy's finger from the egg-beater. There was no permanent damage.]

PATTI WALTON, DISPATCH SUPERVISOR, OHIO

DISPATCHER: Fire and ambulance.

FEMALE CALLER: [Meekly] I, uh, I ate some cat shit. I ate kitty poop.

DISPATCHER: I'm sorry?

CALLER: I'm so ashamed of myself.

DISPATCHER: What's the problem?

CALLER: I need to throw up and I don't know how to induce vomiting.

DISPATCHER: [To another dispatcher] She stated she consumed cat feces.

SECOND DISPATCHER: Cat feces?

DISPATCHER: Yeah. She wants to know if it's going to hurt her or if she should try to throw it up.

SECOND DISPATCHER: Does she need an ambulance?

DISPATCHER: I don't know. That's why I thought I'd have her ask you.

SECOND DISPATCHER: Okay, ma'am, are you experiencing any problems?

CALLER: No, I just don't feel good, that's all.

SECOND DISPATCHER: How much of this did you consume?

CALLER: Quite a bit.

SECOND DISPATCHER: What's your name? How old are you?

CALLER: [Gives name] Twenty-eight.

SECOND DISPATCHER: Are you alone?

CALLER: I'm here at work. I work on a farm.

SECOND DISPATCHER: What's the address?

CALLER: I can't leave 'cause I gotta work.

SECOND DISPATCHER: Is there anyone else there with you?

CALLER: Yes.

SECOND DISPATCHER: Can we talk to one of them? Is there anyone nearby that can get on the phone?

CALLER: Uh, I'm so embarrassed. They're not here right now. [Starts crying]

SECOND DISPATCHER: What caused you to do this?

CALLER: [Crying]

SECOND DISPATCHER: Are you okay?

CALLER: Yes.

SECOND DISPATCHER: Are you getting sick to your stomach?

CALLER: No.

SECOND DISPATCHER: How long ago did you consume this?

CALLER: This morning.

SECOND DISPATCHER: When were you finished consuming this? How long ago?

CALLER: About ten A.M. this morning.

SECOND DISPATCHER: And you haven't gotten sick at all?

CALLER: Not yet, but a little bit.

SECOND DISPATCHER: When did you throw up?

CALLER: About ten o'clock.

DISPATCHER: [Returns from checking with doctor] Hello, ma'am?

CALLER: Yes.

DISPATCHER: There's not going to be any problem with your consuming it. It's not a toxic thing.

CALLER: Okay.

DISPATCHER: The only thing that could happen to you from consuming a large amount of it is you could get worms.

CALLER: Okay.

DISPATCHER: It would be a good idea not to do it again.

CALLER: What should I do?

DISPATCHER: For the time being, it's not going to cause you any harm. It's not toxic.

CALLER: Okay. Okay.

DISPATCHER: Do you have a family doctor?

CALLER: No, I don't.

DISPATCHER: Do you have transportation?

CALLER: Yes.

DISPATCHER: Okay. I spoke to the doctor at the hospital. It's not toxic. It's not going to hurt you. If you still feel sick, I advise you to drive to the hospital and be checked out.

CALLER: Okay. Thank you. You made me feel better.

DISPATCHER: All right. Just don't do it anymore.

CALLER: I won't. Bye-bye.

NAME WITHHELD, DISPATCHER, KENTUCKY

DISPATCHER: Fire and ambulance.

YOUNG BOY: Hey, motherfucker, eat shit!

DISPATCHER: I'm going to send the police to your house because I know where you are!

CALLER: [Quickly hangs up]

NAME WITHHELD, DISPATCHER, MINNESOTA

[A male caller is hiding in the closet from a possible home invader and is waiting for the police to arrive.]

DISPATCHER: The officers just came in? You see officers?

CALLER: No, but I see lights and I hear noises.

DISPATCHER: You hear anyone talking on the radio?

CALLER: No, they're saying, "Stand up over there. Don't move an inch, bud!"

DISPATCHER: Are they inside the home?

CALLER: "Down on your knees. Hands behind your head." Oh, my God, there *was* someone!

DISPATCHER: [To other dispatchers] They got somebody! He's hearing them talk. They're saying, "Down on your knees. Hands behind your head."

CALLER: Oh, my God . . .

DISPATCHER: Hang on. You just stay there.

CALLER: Okay.

DISPATCHER: Just relax.

CALLER: What?

DISPATCHER: Just relax.

CALLER: I am.

DISPATCHER: Take a couple of deep breaths. You hear the officers inside your room?

CALLER: Not my room. In the living room.

DISPATCHER: You just stay right there until we get a code four from them. That means everything is okay. You just stay right there on the phone.

CALLER: Shit, I'm not going nowhere. [Deep sigh] Thanks a lot, guys.

DISPATCHER: Hey, no problem. That's what we're here for.

CALLER: Oh, shit.

DISPATCHER: Tell me what else you hear.

CALLER: Nothing now. They're knocking on my door. Should I come out?

DISPATCHER: They're knocking on the bedroom door?

CALLER: Yep.

DISPATCHER: We got the code. You can go out and talk to them now.

CALLER: What do you want me to do?

DISPATCHER: Just get out of the closet. Go open the door and talk to the officers.

VOICE IN BACKGROUND AT CALLER'S HOUSE: You there?

CALLER: Yes, sir.

DISPATCHER: [To other dispatchers] I hear him. He didn't hang up the phone.

CALLER: [Long pause] You still there?

DISPATCHER: Yeah.

CALLER: Are you going to stay on the line?

DISPATCHER: No, I don't have to. Is everything all right?

CALLER: Yeah, I'm fine.

DISPATCHER: Okay, bye.

PATTI WALTON, DISPATCH SUPERVISOR, OHIO

DISPATCHER: Fire department.

EXTREMELY CALM YOUNG WOMAN: I want to report a fire.

DISPATCHER: Where?

CALLER: [Gives address]

DISPATCHER: What's on fire?

CALLER: Um, a person.

DISPATCHER: I beg your pardon?

CALLER: A person.

DISPATCHER: A person is on fire?

CALLER: Yeah.

DISPATCHER: Do you know how this happened?

CALLER: Um, I'm not real sure.

DISPATCHER: Is the person still on fire?

CALLER: Yeah.

DISPATCHER: Are they doing anything to try to put this person out?

CALLER: Pardon me?

DISPATCHER: Is anybody doing anything to put this person out?

CALLER: No.

DISPATCHER: He's just standing there burning?

CALLER: It's a female.

DISPATCHER: Do you know her?

CALLER: Yeah.

DISPATCHER: Okay. Is anybody doing anything for her?

CALLER: No.

DISPATCHER: Can you tell her to stop, drop, and roll?

CALLER: Yeah.

DISPATCHER: Why don't you do that?

CALLER: Okay.

DISPATCHER: Don't hang up.

CALLER: Okay.

DISPATCHER: Go tell her.

CALLER: Okay.

SECOND DISPATCHER: [To dispatcher] Fire, I'm still here. Still on the line.

DISPATCHER: [To second dispatcher] That sounded a little too calm to me.

SECOND DISPATCHER: [To dispatcher] Yeah, I know. It does, doesn't it?

CALLER: [Returns] Okay.

DISPATCHER: What's going on?

CALLER: [Deep sigh]

DISPATCHER: Tell me what's going on.

CALLER: I'll say it one more time. I know it's A shift. Right?

DISPATCHER: Who is this?

CALLER: [Gives her name and spells it]

DISPATCHER: [Recognizing caller's name from previous calls] Why are you asking if it's A shift?

CALLER: The person I need to respond is B.

DISPATCHER: Is who?

CALLER: B shift.

DISPATCHER: [To second dispatcher] Okay, you know what, cancel this. [To caller] Who is it that's supposed to be burning?

CALLER: Me.

DISPATCHER: Oh, you're burning? Okay. You said you're on fire?

CALLER: My feet and my hands. My feet primarily are all blistered, broken skin, bleeding, cracked, and some of my fingers are cracked and bleeding.

DISPATCHER: Okay. You told me a person was on fire. Do you understand the difference?

CALLER: Between what?

DISPATCHER: Between a person burning, on fire, and your feet hurting?

CALLER: No.

DISPATCHER: You don't know the difference?

CALLER: Have you ever seen anybody that's been burned by electricity?

DISPATCHER: Yes, I have.

CALLER: Where does the electricity exit the body?

DISPATCHER: Well, it depends. It could exit anywhere.

CALLER: It primarily comes out the hands, head, or feet.

DISPATCHER: So you're saying you were electrocuted today?

CALLER: No.

DISPATCHER: What are you saying?

CALLER: [Coughs] I'm sorry, what?

DISPATCHER: That's okay. Are you okay?

CALLER: Yeah.

DISPATCHER: So how long have you been feeling like this?

CALLER: Since the third.

DISPATCHER: Why did you specifically want B shift?

CALLER: That's the firefighter's shift.

DISPATCHER: What firefighter's shift?

CALLER: [Names a firefighter, "Don"]

DISPATCHER: Okay, and why do you specifically want him?

CALLER: Because he's the only one who can put it out.

DISPATCHER: Why is that?

CALLER: Because it was deemed so.

DISPATCHER: Deemed so by whom?

CALLER: A higher power.

DISPATCHER: By a higher power?

CALLER: Yeah.

DISPATCHER: Well, I guess you can't argue with that, can you?

CALLER: Nope.

DISPATCHER: Well, okay, I don't think he's working today.

CALLER: I know he's not.

DISPATCHER: So I don't think we can help you.

CALLER: What would you suggest?

DISPATCHER: Maybe put your feet in some water.

CALLER: I've been doing that.

DISPATCHER: And that hasn't helped?

CALLER: Not really. I've put in two and three trays of ice. And back and forth, and I've put special lotion from my friend who's a podiatrist . . .

DISPATCHER: Weren't you in the hospital the other day?

CALLER: I was in the hospital today. I took an overdose last night.

DISPATCHER: Oh, you did? How come you did that?

CALLER: Because he wouldn't come to me and I got to the point where I couldn't take it anymore.

DISPATCHER: Was he supposed to come to you or something?

CALLER: Yeah.

DISPATCHER: Oh, he was? Did you talk to him? Did he say he would or what?

CALLER: I haven't talked to him in three years.

DISPATCHER: Then why would you think he would come over yesterday?

CALLER: 'Cause I thought he would.

DISPATCHER: What made you come to that conclusion?

CALLER: A sign.

DISPATCHER: What kind of sign? Again, from a higher power, or what?

CALLER: No. I saw a pure white cat.

DISPATCHER: Is that kind of like the pure white buffalo thing?

CALLER: Yeah, it's all related. I'm surprised you know about that.

DISPATCHER: About the white buffalo? Oh, yeah, I'm part Indian.

CALLER: Oh, really? That's wonderful. When I saw that, I almost lost my breath.

DISPATCHER: That's something else, isn't it?

CALLER: It doesn't surprise me, but again it does.

DISPATCHER: So now this also applies to pure white cats?

CALLER: Well, see, Don is a cat in Western astrology. He's a rabbit in Chinese.

DISPATCHER: Oh, in the Chinese New Year you're talking about. The Chinese calendar.

CALLER: Yeah. I'm a dragon.

DISPATCHER: Maybe that's why you're burning!

CALLER: I didn't think of that.

DISPATCHER: Do you see the connection?

CALLER: My mouth is hot, too.

DISPATCHER: Well, see, if you're a dragon, a fire-breathing dragon . . . do you get the connection?

CALLER: Yeah. It makes sense now. I didn't think of that.

DISPATCHER: Interesting, huh?

CALLER: Yeah, it is. So why is he so stubborn?

DISPATCHER: Maybe you need to be more accepting. Maybe you are still in denial that this relationship is over.

CALLER: No, it's not over. It hasn't even begun.

DISPATCHER: Well, honey, you're barking up the wrong tree, then.

CALLER: I know, but we're having a baby. We have to make a baby.

DISPATCHER: Why is that?

CALLER: Because he has to be born on Christmas day.

DISPATCHER: Which Christmas? What year?

CALLER: This one.

DISPATCHER: And again, the higher power told you to do this?

CALLER: Yeah.

DISPATCHER: Why him?

CALLER: Who?

DISPATCHER: How did you meet him?

CALLER: Who? Don?

DISPATCHER: Don. Right.

CALLER: I was going to run for mayor. I said, "I know I can do it. I just don't have any money. I need to do a fund-raiser," so this firefighter gave me Don's name. [Mentions a popular firefighters' bar] I'd been in there before, but I didn't know who Don was.

DISPATCHER: Why would he give you Don's name? What association would Don have with your running for mayor?

CALLER: I have no idea. I don't know. So, it started a long time ago, but I got too outrageous, and so . . .

DISPATCHER: You got too outrageous? In your campaign?

CALLER: In my behavior. And he couldn't deal with it.

DISPATCHER: I don't think too many people would.

CALLER: What?

DISPATCHER: Do you blame him?

CALLER: No, not at all.

DISPATCHER: So why are you pursuing this? If it's been three years, and there's been no connection, why do you constantly call for him?

CALLER: Because I love him. He's my soul mate. We don't communicate with words. We communicate telepathically.

DISPATCHER: Oh, I see. So he has this power as well?

CALLER: He makes love to me without, uh . . .

DISPATCHER: Physical contact?

CALLER: Yeah.

DISPATCHER: So in essence, you could probably conceive without any physical contact as well?

CALLER: Yeah.

DISPATCHER: So why pursue him?

CALLER: Because I don't want to do it that way anymore.

DISPATCHER: So you're saying he's done this in the past?

CALLER: Oh, yeah, for three years.

DISPATCHER: I see. Well, honey, I don't know what to tell you. I think you're barking up the wrong tree, myself. I think you ought to come to grips with it that it's not going to happen and just let it go.

CALLER: No.

DISPATCHER: Maybe you ought to ask your higher power to send you a sign to make you realize that—

CALLER: No, the signs are there. All the signs are already here that it's the right thing.

DISPATCHER: And what signs are those?

CALLER: Everything around me.

DISPATCHER: For instance?

CALLER: [Sighs] Well, last summer, I flew into LAX to visit my daughter and my dad, and I landed twelve hours before Nicole [Brown Simpson] was murdered. Exactly twelve hours. The whole thing is heavy.

DISPATCHER: So did a lot of other people, I'm sure. Probably a lot sooner than you did.

CALLER: A lot sooner? What?

DISPATCHER: A lot of people landed at LAX the day she died. Why do you think it's a special sign for you? LAX is a busy airport. What significance does that have? What does that have to do with Don?

CALLER: Because O. J. and Nicole, that whole thing was a lesson for a lot of people. It wasn't so much a

black/white issue as it was about domestic abuse. I've
been beaten. Men have tried to kill me; they take my
children from me. Everything you can imagine that can
happen to a woman, I've been through. More than one
time. And the last two relationships I had before I met
Don, both of the men were abusive, and both said the
same thing to me, that I was not their equal, and I
replied to both of them that yes, I know, because I
would never hurt somebody like that. So I made up my
mind that when a man told me I was his equal, that
was the man. But I never told anybody. And one night
[at the bar] Don told me, "You know what I think?"
And I said, "What?" And he goes, "I think you've met
your match." When he said that, he opened my heart
chakra and I lost my balance. It was like an electric
bolt or something hit my solar plexus, and I kinda went
backward a few steps and I couldn't talk. I just totally
freaked out. . . . So, I know. And he knows.

DISPATCHER: Maybe you're making a little much out of
that. Maybe you misunderstood.

CALLER: You can think whatever you want. I know.

DISPATCHER: Uh-huh.

CALLER: So, I guess I'll just have to keep watching the
streets.

DISPATCHER: I really don't know what to tell you. These
calls are unfounded, and you're putting a lot of people's
lives in jeopardy with these false calls. Do you realize
that?

CALLER: Yeah, I do.

DISPATCHER: Okay, then that needs to stop.

CALLER: Well, I don't like doing it, but—

DISPATCHER: Then you need to stop doing it. Every time
these guys go out, Mach three down the street, you're
putting their lives in jeopardy. And all you're doing is
goofing off.

CALLER: Is what?

DISPATCHER: You're goofing off. You're playing around with the system.

CALLER: No, that's not true at all.

DISPATCHER: You're playing around with the system so that you can get together with him. It's not going to happen.

CALLER: [Hangs up]

CES HERRERAS, DISPATCHER, CALIFORNIA

4 Win Some . . .

It's a wonderful feeling to talk to someone who actually died or was clinically dead. Their stories are unbelievable. They remember everything that happened. They remember the drugs you administered. They remember the shocks. They remember the tubes being placed down their throats. The only thing they don't remember is what you just talked about a few minutes before. Almost all of them have short-term memory loss.

TOM HARRISON, PARAMEDIC, WISCONSIN

EMS is a young profession. You tell people you're a paramedic or emergency medical technician, and this glaze comes over their eyes. I don't think they really understand what it means. They think you drive around with red lights flashing and sirens wailing, running them off the road to get to who knows where. They don't understand where you're going in such a hurry—unless, of course, you're coming to their house. Then they wonder what took you so long.

Without exception, a medic's greatest satisfaction is a "save." That's when we find a person who is all but dead and who later, due to the treatment we gave them before arriving at the emergency room, is able to walk out of the hospital and lead a normal, productive life. What greater gift can you give to your fellow man? It makes all the other stuff tolerable.

THE STORIES

■ Probably the most savage incident I've experienced involved a man who was hiking west of the visitors' center, sixty miles out in Denali National Park, Alaska. He was exploring the terrain about two miles southwest of the center when he encountered a sow grizzly with a cub in the brush. Being unfamiliar with what to do in such an extremely volatile situation, he unfortunately made all the wrong moves.

The man had stumbled upon the sow at very close range, less than nine meters. He promptly did what most people would do—turned-and-ran. Alarmed by his fear and motion, the grizzly pounced, slashing him with her massive, clawed paw and biting him repeatedly.

The man's friends were hiking on a ridge above and witnessed the whole shocking attack. Screaming and throwing rocks, they eventually scared the bear away.

One of the man's friends, a strong, physically fit Norwegian, ran the whole two miles across a river and up a hill to the visitors' center. After catching his breath, he reported the incident.

I was fifty miles away when my radio relayed the emergency. The closest ranger was more than twenty miles in the opposite direction. Working the radio, I quickly discovered that a ranger at Walter Lake, twenty miles to the west, knew that a pair of emergency-room doctors from San Francisco was camping out near her station. She contacted them, and they agreed to come along.

After the fifty-mile drive to the visitors' center, we

hiked the two miles through the brush to the patient. The doctors were athletic types and covered the ground with little difficulty. When we arrived on the scene, I couldn't believe what I saw. The man's scalp was hanging by a single thread to the top of his head. He appeared as if he had been scalped by Indians.

The victim also had a deep laceration across the top of the orbital bone [near the eye], and a third gash where the bear's paw sliced across the maxilla [jawbone]. In addition, his body was covered with at least fifty puncture wounds from bites.

We took his pulse. Nothing. We slapped on the blood pressure cuff. Nothing. The needle didn't move. Incredibly, he was not only still alive, he was conscious. The man was even able to respond to our questions with nonverbal signals, mostly by moving his fingers.

Five minutes after we arrived, an Air Force helicopter touched down. We slipped a pair of military antishock trousers on the patient, inflated them, and were subsequently able to raise a pulse and get a blood pressure reading. [This medical device helps push blood from the body's extremities to the heart and helps stabilize broken limbs.] The hiker was evacuated to Fairbanks Memorial Hospital. There the ER doctors and follow-up surgeons performed some miracles. They not only saved the man's life, they seamlessly stitched his scalp back on.

The mauled hiker walked out of the hospital a few weeks later with a full head of hair and no permanent or disfiguring injuries.

NORM SIMONS, PARK RANGER AND
EMS COORDINATOR, ALASKA

■ It was my first day as a medic. I was working in Apache Junction, an Old West community east of Phoenix. My partner had hurt his back on an earlier call and took off to get treatment. The dispatcher said they were sending another medic to cover his shift. The next thing I knew, I was toned [called] out on a major medical emergency.

"I'm alone. I don't have a partner," I protested.

"Just go. Now!" the dispatcher ordered. "We'll send someone later."

I flicked on the siren and blasted down U.S. Route 60, balls to the wall. I approached some fire trucks and blew by them. The initial excitement masked my fear. This was my first call, and I was alone. I prayed it wouldn't be anything too difficult.

So much for my prayers. A bus full of orphans from Mexico had flipped and rolled when the two drivers tried to change positions without pulling over. The highway and half the desert looked like a scene from a natural disaster. Twenty-six injured children, a priest, and the two drivers were sprawled in the sand in every direction. Clothing, blankets, sleeping bags, toys, and food were spread out for a hundred yards.

A second priest remained standing. He was an older man, and was walking from person to person, giving comfort and praying.

The first priest, all the children, and the drivers were bleeding, screaming, and crying. Pedestrians and passersby started grabbing my arms and legs in an attempt to steer me to various patients. Just as one would pull me over to a little girl with a broken leg, another would yank me toward a boy with a gash in his head.

Although I frantically tried to do everything I could, I felt waves of panic. I was a lone, green medic trying to be in twenty-nine different places at once, and I was expected to perform a five-second miracle at each stop. I was ready to collapse from the stress and overwhelming pressure when I felt a hand on my shoulder.

"Just do the best you can, my child," the old priest said in Spanish. "Help will arrive soon."

I bandaged, braced, tubed, and bagged [oxygenated] children left and right. It seemed like I was alone out there for an hour before the first wave of firefighters and ambulances arrived to give me some relief. I'd actually been there only five minutes or so, but to me, it felt like an eternity.

We treated and loaded kids for the next hour. Miraculously, we saved them all! Every single child, plus the injured priest and two drivers, survived. The battered school bus had flipped and rolled, tossing the children around like rag dolls and spitting them out through the doors and windows, but not a single one suffered a broken neck or any other fatal injury.

When we loaded the last child, the old priest came by again.

"God was with us today," he said.

I looked up and noticed that his leg was bleeding. I inspected it more closely and realized that it was badly shattered. The bone had snapped and was piercing through the skin. I couldn't believe he was even walking, much less going from person to person, kneeling and praying like he had.

"Padre!" I exclaimed in Spanish. "You're hurt very badly. Why didn't you tell me? We should have taken you to the hospital long ago!"

He brushed me off. "The little ones needed my help," he said. "And so did you."

I waved over another medic and we gently placed the courageous old priest on a stretcher.

"A miracle happened here today, Padre," I said, tears welling up in my eyes. "A miracle from God."

He smiled and nodded.

"Just one of many," he said.

ROGER VIGIL, PARAMEDIC, ARIZONA

■ A man was playing in the surf with his seven-year-old daughter. She climbed on his back and began splashing around, having a great time. Suddenly a huge shark sprang from the water, grabbed the girl in its massive jaws, and attempted to rip her from her father's grasp.

The father went after the beast and tried to pry open its jaws. He battled the savage animal with total abandon, disregarding his own safety to save his daughter. The shark's teeth tore into the father's palms and pierced through the back of his hands. He ignored the agonizing pain, refusing to back off.

The courageous father finally snatched his daughter free and sprinted toward the beach. A team of paramedics rushed her to a hospital, where I was moonlighting in the ER.

The girl's leg was a ghastly sight. The shark had broken her right femur and shredded the flesh from her pelvis down. Despite her terrible injuries, the child was a trouper. She whimpered a bit but never cried. We didn't even have to give her pain medication. The only thing she seemed concerned about was that her favorite bathing suit had been torn apart.

A surgeon strolled into the ER, made a negative comment about her condition, and decided to amputate the leg from the hip down. I felt that was excessive. Even though the damage was severe, the child had a pulse in her foot and could wiggle her toes.

The doctor outranked me, ending the debate—or so we thought. After bringing the girl to surgery, I noticed a second doctor preparing to assist. He was a plastic surgeon I knew well.

"You've got to try to save her leg!" the ER nurse and I pleaded. "She can move her toes! She has a chance."

He promised to consider it.

The plastic surgeon did more than consider it. He diagnosed the situation the way we had and convinced his colleague to go for a total save. Together, they succeeded. The girl was in physical therapy for a long time, and still walks with a limp, but at least we saved both her life and her leg.

The ironic part is that the city council and police downplayed the situation just like in the movie *Jaws*. They announced that the child had been attacked by a nurse shark, a harmless, toothless creature that sleeps in the sand.

No way! The father described it as being at least eight feet long. The man has scars on his hands that prove it had teeth—big, sharp teeth! It was either a large bull shark or a tiger shark—both vicious man-eaters. But the city officials blamed it on a docile nurse shark and played it low-key so they wouldn't scare off the tourists.

JOHN OBJARTEL, PARAMEDIC, FLORIDA

■ We arrived at the drag strip and found a young motorcycle racer who lost control of his bike at 180 mph, hit a guardrail, and tore off his right arm at the elbow. His wife was part of his race team, so she was right there. The county EMS crew arrived first, and they already had the severed arm wrapped in a towel in a cooler.

The drag racer was awake and alert.

"I just want you to save my arm," he pleaded.

As we loaded him into the ambulance, his wife took me aside and said, "Please try to save his arm. He's a dentist."

During the ride to the hospital, he reiterated that it was critical that we save his arm, explaining, as his wife had, that he was a dentist, a right-handed dentist, and needed it to keep working.

At the hospital, the surgeons did all they could but were unable to reattach the limb. There was too much tissue and bone lost.

About four days later, we made another run to the

hospital and decided to visit the man. His wife was still by his side, and his sister had also come to be with him. I half expected him to be sullen and depressed, maybe even mad at us. Instead, he was the exact opposite. I couldn't believe how positive and happy this man was, how upbeat they all were. His entire career, his entire life in some sense, was tied up in his missing right arm. His wife was his medical assistant, so her job and income were also lost. And yet he was so positive, so happy just to be alive. He was thankful that we had done all we could to save him.

"I'm just going to have to learn to use my left arm," he told me.

Afterward, it was difficult for me to accept that he was being sincere. I couldn't believe someone could face a devastating tragedy with that positive a spirit. I wondered if he was merely putting on a show for us.

A few weeks later, we received a standard follow-up letter from the couple, responding to questions we routinely ask about their EMS care. The wife had written all the answers and remained supportive and thankful.

At the end of the letter, underneath her signature, was another name. It was a single first name scribbled in an awkward, childish fashion. I inspected it more closely.

It was her husband's name. He had signed it with his left hand.

NAME WITHHELD, PARAMEDIC, CALIFORNIA

■ I was in the first paramedic class in Arizona history, back in the early 1970s. I'd been an EMT prior to that, but the concept of giving medics extra training and allowing them to administer lifesaving IV solutions was in its infancy.

The ink was barely dry on my new certification papers when we were called on a dangerous mission. A hiker had taken a nasty fall while climbing the White Tank Mountains outside Phoenix. He'd scaled about 300 feet, lost his footing, and tumbled to a tiny, inaccessible ledge about 150 feet below.

I was a gung-ho kid then, nineteen, so I figured I could do anything. I volunteered to climb free-form up the mountain to determine if the man was still alive.

I made it up the rocks, scrub brush, and cactus and arrived at the ledge in one piece. The hiker was alive but in terrible shape. Blood was pouring from his nose, ears, and mouth, indicating extensive internal injuries. He also had multiple broken bones and a huge bruise covering his chest, and he was missing most of his teeth.

The ledge was so small there was no way I could move him around and maneuver myself in place to treat him. His situation was critical, so I had to think of something. I spotted a piñon tree growing out from under the ledge and got a wild idea. I climbed out on the four-inch trunk, straddled it with my legs, and began treating the patient from my precarious perch 150 feet above the ground!

I eased forward and hooked on a blood pressure cuff. His reading was sixty over zero, which meant he had virtually no blood pressure at all. I tried to place a stethoscope to his chest and nearly fell from the tree. Sitting on the small, spindly trunk was like walking a tightrope. I balanced my hand on some rickety branches and used my other hand to move the scope. There were no lung sounds. I started an IV, gave him oxygen, and cleared an airway—all while hanging on for dear life!

I cuffed him again. Bingo! The medication was working. I was able to get a weak blood pressure reading. We had a chance!

I didn't have a portable radio with me, so I was yelling my findings down to my partner at the base of the mountain. He, in turn, radioed the information to a doctor.

"I need CAMERA, quick!" I screamed, calling for the

Central Arizona Mountain Rescue Association. "That's the only chance this man has. We've got to get him down from here."

A fully equipped CAMERA helicopter and rescue crew just happened to be on a training exercise in the nearby Estrella Mountains. That cut their response time from an hour to just ten minutes.

Although we now had a chopper loaded with medical equipment, the problem was getting it near the patient. The ledge was too narrow to land on, and it cut in too deeply to drop a winch line from above. There wasn't anything close to a landing area in the vicinity. Once again, we had to improvise. The helicopter dropped a wire stoker basket to me so I could load the patient, then flew to a lower ledge. I watched with fascination as the pilot propped one wheel on a jutting bolder and hovered the helicopter at a cockeyed angle off the side of the mountain.

Marveling at the pilot's skill, I inched off my tree, strapped the man to the basket, lifted him down to the second ledge, and shoved him inside the oddly hovering craft. I then dove headfirst into the chopper just as the wheel slipped from the rock.

The helicopter plummeted sideways for a few frightening seconds before the pilot got it righted and regained control. My legs were still hanging from the door when the aircraft took off.

Pulling my feet inside, I was shocked to discover that my boots were smoking. The exhaust from the thrusters was so blisteringly hot it had melted my shoelaces into the tongue, practically welding my boots to my feet.

We landed at St. Joseph's Hospital and immediately carried the patient into surgery. Aside from his other injuries, he had a fractured spleen, four broken ribs, a collapsed lung, a torn liver, a fractured clavicle, and broken upper and lower jaws.

The doctors repaired it all. When I paid the man a visit

two weeks later, he was black-and-blue and bandaged like a mummy, but was well on the way to a total recovery.

In my thirty years as a medic, I've never had another rescue where everything fell into place like that. Had the guy taken his spill a few weeks earlier, there's no way we could have saved him. I wouldn't have been allowed to administer the IV solutions that kept him alive long enough for the helicopter to arrive. And if the helicopter had been at its base station instead of out on a training exercise, he would have died long before it got there.

The guy's number just wasn't up.

ROY RYALS, PARAMEDIC, ARIZONA

■ A man tossed a ladder down a fifteen-foot well and climbed in to clean it out. What he failed to consider was that over the decades, the sand and silt at the bottom had turned into a deadly form of quicksand. As he worked, he began sinking lower and lower. He didn't think much about it initially; he just went about his business. It was only when he sank to his thighs that he became concerned. He tried to pull himself up the ladder, but it also started sinking. At that point, he realized he was in big trouble.

A neighbor heard his screams and dialed 911. I responded with my crew. We backed the truck to the edge of the well and tied a rope to the truck, I proceeded to rappel down into the dark hole.

"I'm sorry to bother you guys," the man apologized when I reached him. "I can't believe I can't get out of this."

"Don't worry. We'll get you free."

By then he was waist deep in the thick, murky muck. I tested it with my boot. This wasn't the soft, watery jungle quicksand you see in the movies. This was a dense silt that was acting almost like cement. I feared that if we tied a rope around his chest and tried to pull him out with the truck, we'd rip his body in half.

That left me with limited options. The more I physically tried to pull him, the deeper he sank. I attempted to dig him out with my hands, but that just caused him to drop further. We started using buckets to bail out the muck and water, but that didn't work, either.

I'd been in the well for more than an hour, and the man was now trapped nearly to his chest. It was as if the earth was slowly eating him alive.

Despite his increasingly critical situation, the man remained calm and apologetic. He was more concerned about my safety than his own. That wasn't an issue—not in my mind, anyway. I was connected to a rope and harness that kept me from sinking in too deep, so I never really felt that I was going to get swallowed up with him. However, there were fleeting moments when I feared that he might not make it, that I'd have to hang there and watch him go under for the last time. I was determined not to let that moment arrive. There had to be another way.

Racking our collective brains, the rescue team hit upon a reverse-physics concept. If we couldn't get him out of the quicksand, we were going to try to get the quicksand out of him, so to speak. We had an industrial-strength electric pump brought to the scene and began pumping out the silt. That did the trick. After two harrowing hours in that deadly well, I was finally able to see the high-water line retreating on his chest. Fifteen minutes later, we freed him enough to pull him out.

We all knew enough to temper our celebration. Getting the man out of that literal hellhole was only half the battle. People in those situations—people who are trapped in some way—often suffer from what is known as "compartment syndrome," when the trapped part of their body instinctively shuts down to enable the blood to concentrate in the free areas and keep the person alive. When they're suddenly freed, the heart isn't prepared to send blood rushing into the empty areas and goes into cardiac arrest. This happens frequently with earthquake victims. You work all day to free them from the rubble, only to have them die from a massive coronary a few seconds after you pull them to safety.

I couldn't let that happen to this nice man, not after I'd worked so hard to get him out of that nightmarish well. Although he kept insisting he was fine and didn't need to be hospitalized, I knew better. I treated him almost like a cardiac patient in the ambulance to make sure his heart didn't suddenly explode. We rushed him to the ER for a thorough examination.

His heart held firm.

That was my first, and I hope my last, well rescue. And to this day, I don't know how or why people clean the inside of old wells. I just know it's not a good idea.

KEVIN WARD, PARAMEDIC, UTAH

■ The two-story home was fully engaged when we arrived. Smoke and fire poured from the windows. A woman was jumping up and down on the front lawn, screaming hysterically, "My daughter's inside! Oh, God, please help. My daughter's inside!"

My partner and I ran through the burning frame of the front door, determined to find the little girl. We climbed the stairs through the smoke and fire and split up in the hallway.

"You take those rooms and I'll take these," I said.

I dashed into a bedroom and dropped, crawling on the floor. A tiny child was unconscious under a bed. She was covered with soot. I grabbed her in my arms and ran out of the room—only to discover that the entire hallway was now a sheet of flame.

I ran back into the bedroom and broke open the window. Still carrying the girl, I climbed out and hoisted her to the roof. I then chinned myself up and started giving her mouth-to-mouth and CPR—right there on the hot roof of a burning house.

A ladder slapped against the drainpipe. A second medic scurried up and began assisting me. After getting a semblance of a breath and heartbeat, we quickly carried the girl down the ladder and into the ambulance. I worked her with a passion the whole way. Her breathing and pulse were sporadic. I knew it was touch and go.

Six weeks later, I was sitting at our picnic table outside the station when a woman approached. Holding her hand was a beautiful little girl. The woman stopped about five feet way. The little girl dropped her mother's hand and edged forward. I rose to greet her. Without saying a word, the little girl gave me a great big hug, then turned and walked away. They silently returned to their car and drove off.

It was the best thank-you I've ever had. I still get tears in my eyes thinking about it.

LOU CARLUCCI, EMT, OHIO

■ There was a massive forest fire up in the rim country that burned for nearly a month. It consumed twenty-eight thousand acres of Tonto National Forest, including the home of famous Western author Zane Grey. Firefighters and medics from all over the state banded together to battle what became known as "the Dude Fire."

I arrived home from my honeymoon and was immediately sent into the fray. My first assignment was a wild one. A crew of prisoners recruited to battle the blaze were overcome by what we call a "blowup." That's when the fire shifts direction and overtakes the firefighters. The prisoners had been trying to clear the underbrush from bulldozed fire lines, sections of land cleared in order to stop the inferno's spread.

Five prisoners and a female corrections officer were killed. Others were injured. I was ordered to respond to the highly dangerous area and try to rescue whoever remained standing.

"There could be more blowups," my captain cautioned. "Be careful."

I drove along a forest trail as far as I could until I reached a cabin near a partially burned out area. I left the vehicle and began searching for the victims on foot. Suddenly I heard a overpowering noise that sounded like a half-dozen freight trains barreling toward me. I turned and froze in shock. It was a blowup! A wall of fire fifty feet high was coming directly at me! It was consuming so much oxygen that a gust of wind nearly sucked me into the flames.

Medics and firefighters are given a heat-resistant aluminum foil-like tent that we're supposed to use in such situations. The theory is, you hit the ground, cover yourself with this fireproof material, and allow the zillion-degree fire to burn over the top of you. The questionable technique makes no concession for the fact that as the fire passes, there's no air to breathe. On top of everything else—intense heat, crashing trees, paralyzing fear—you're supposed to hold your breath.

Despite my misgivings, there was nothing I could do. I was trapped. I spread out the tent and hit the ground, fully aware that this was exactly what the perished prisoners had tried to do. I figured I was history. My new wife was going to be a widow one day after our honeymoon. Just as I was about to crawl under the foil, I heard someone yell. I looked back and saw six paramedic-firefighters emerge from behind the cabin. They were carrying a man on a backboard and appeared to be totally exhausted.

"Come over here!" they yelled. "We need your help!"

I jumped up and ran toward them, ignoring the mountain of fire that was about to overtake me. It didn't matter. I was there to save lives. I was going to do my job or die trying.

As I ran against the wind, I immediately started gulping for air. It felt like I'd run a mile instead of a few feet. I realized then why the six medics were having so much trouble with a single patient—there was so little oxygen left in the air that any exertion left them gasping. They'd already carried the victim for two hundred yards and had little energy left.

I made it to them and immediately lifted the board with my fresh strength. Glancing back, I saw the wall of fire make a sharp left, as if it were turning a corner. It was like God had blown it away with His breath. Alternately taking turns and collapsing from exhaustion, we lugged the injured prisoner up a hill where a helicopter was supposed to land. The ground was so hot beneath our feet, we couldn't even pause to rest. With barely any oxygen to breathe and the smoldering earth scorching our boots beneath us, it was a long, draining climb. Taking courage from each other, we powered onward and somehow made it to the top just as the chopper arrived. The prisoner was flown to a hospital and survived.

We, however, remained on the hill, very much in danger. When we climbed down the opposite side, I was shocked to see nearly two hundred paramedics and firefighters huddled together in a small bulldozed clearing. The theory is that the fire, finding no fuel in a cleared area, will leave it alone.

We danced the hotfoot in that clearing and watched the fire rage all around us. It shifted directions a half-dozen times or more, sometimes whipping toward us, while at other times mercifully retreating in the opposite direction. Its helter-skelter pattern was caused by the fact that the massive fire was creating its own wind currents, which blew around us in every direction.

Normally a forest fire burns the underbrush so fast that

it ignores the larger trees. This one was so hot that the trees started exploding like bombs. They'd smoke for a while, and then with a thunderous whoosh would burst into flames like giant matches.

We also began to hear a series of piercing whistles followed by ear-shattering booms.

"Propane tanks," a fireman beside me explained.

The tanks were mounted outside the numerous cabins in the fire's path. As they heated, they'd vent their pressure and then explode.

After three agonizing hours, the fire consumed the forest around us and headed off like a hungry monster to seek more food. When the ground cooled enough to let us escape, we discovered that the paint on our fire trucks had blistered, and all the plastic parts, including the headlights, sirens, and flashers on the roof, had melted.

I was awarded a Medal of Valor for my activities that day. The six other paramedic-firefighters were given similar awards from their departments, including being selected as Firefighters of the Year. Despite the honors, the psychological aftereffects ran deep. I'd been an avid camper all my life. In fact, I'd just spent my honeymoon camping in the forests of Utah and Nevada. After staring down that wall of fire, though, I wasn't able to set foot in the woods for more than a year.

HOWARD CLARK, PARAMEDIC, ARIZONA

■ I guess everybody's heard the saying that the greatest lies in the world are "I'll love you forever" and "The check's in the mail." Soldiers and park rangers have their own version: "The helicopter will be back in an hour." One of my most memorable rescues falls into this category, only in my case the helicopter was gone a lot longer than an hour.

We were called out on a technical rescue of an injured mountain climber on the face of Cathedral Wall at Rocky

Mountain National Park. The man had taken a long fall, landing in a heap on a ledge. He'd fractured his arm and leg and had unspecified internal injuries. I was part of the rescue team. My job was to station myself fourteen thousand feet high on a plateau above the ledge and keep the [climbing] ropes from kinking as the rangers descended the wall.

As I monitored the critical ropes, a pair of highly skilled rangers rappelled with a rescue sled five hundred feet down to the ledge. After they reached the patient, we had to lower him another five hundred feet to a clearing.

By the time we secured the patient and eased him down, night had fallen. Because of time, weight, and visibility concerns, it was decided that the helicopter would immediately rush the injured man to the hospital. That meant leaving us on the mountain. And we weren't going to be abandoned for only an hour or so—not even close. Because of the darkness, we were forced to spend the night on the cliff.

The pilot promised to rescue us at first light.

Even though it was late summer, it was still bitterly cold that high in the Colorado Rockies. To complicate matters, we didn't have any backpacks, blankets, sleeping bags, food, supplies, or anything of that nature with us. We had flown there empty-handed in order to get all the members of the rescue team and the rescue equipment into the helicopter.

We huddled together and did our best to try to keep from freezing during the long, cold night. Sleep eluded most of us.

Fortunately, the helicopter arrived at daybreak and got us out of there in time for a nice hot breakfast. And better yet, the guy we rescued survived.

NORM SIMONS, PARK RANGER AND EMT, COLORADO

■ We were dispatched to an unknown problem and found a thirty-year-old female in complete cardiac arrest. Usually when they're that young, narcotics are involved. We started CPR and did the other ALS [advanced life support] procedures, and she was all over the gamut. We kept trying—drugs, CPR, drugs, CPR, shock, shock, thump, the whole thing.

"Does she have a history of drug abuse?" I asked her husband.

"No. No way."

I kept asking him because all the signs pointed to that and we needed to know what she was on. He kept denying it emphatically. Her most significant past history, in fact, was that she was a marathon runner. It didn't add up.

We put that aside and worked her and worked her. Lidocaine, dopamine—we put everything we had into this woman. We got a pulse and a reasonable [breathing] rhythm, so we loaded her into the unit. As we did, her arm moved.

Hey, this is going to be okay, I thought.

On the way, we lost her pulse, got it back, lost it, got it back. We finally made it to the ER.

"How long have you been working her?" the doctor asked.

"About an hour."

"An hour?"

The ER crew kind of hemmed and hawed and were moving in slow motion. *What are you guys doing?* I thought. *She keeps going in and out. We need to get on it. Keep working her.* I wanted to hang around, but we received another call and had to run.

Afterward, I couldn't get her out of my mind, so I drove back to the hospital. I braced myself for the worst, figuring she was a code seven down in the cooler. Instead, they had gotten her pulse back, and she was up on the [recovery] floor.

It turned out that she had a rare cardiac-related problem, a one-in-ten-million illness, and had to have an external defibrillator put on. She also suffered some partial blindness. But what really got to me was that she worked as a counselor for the county drug rehabilitation program! Here I was, hounding her poor husband about a drug overdose, and the woman's a drug counselor!

A year later, I was breezing through the local newspaper when a story jumped out at me. The woman we saved had run another marathon.

SCOTT JOHNSON, PARAMEDIC, ILLINOIS

■ A church van ran over a lady on a moped. She was trapped under the van and had a severe head injury. We didn't have the big air bags back then [which elevate the vehicle], so the only way we could get the vehicle off her was to drive it off. Because I'm thin, I was chosen to crawl under the van and assist an equally thin police officer in holding the woman down. We spread our arms and legs on top of her and prayed for the best.

The woman regained a measure of consciousness and began fighting us. That's common with brain injuries. Not only did we have to keep our heads down and watch out for the tires, we had to do so while wrestling with a delirious patient.

The church van was driven off without further injury to the woman—or us. We rushed her into the ambulance and off to the hospital.

Although her recovery was slow, the lady not only survived, she wrote a critically acclaimed book about her experience!

VICKI IEZZY, PARAMEDIC, FLORIDA

■ A Sun City resident was out riding his bike when he collapsed. He was sprawled in the street when I arrived. I checked his pulse. Not a beat. He wasn't breathing, either.

In Sun City, when you find them dead like that, they usually stay dead. I did what I could and took him to the hospital.

Three weeks later, I was watching television at the station and heard a knock on the door.

"I'm looking for Roy," the elderly man said.

"That's me," I answered.

He stared for a moment. "You don't recognize me, do you?"

I looked him up and down. I couldn't place the guy.

"You remember a man lying in the middle of Balboa Street a few weeks ago?"

"Oh, yeah. I ran that call," I said, figuring he was one of the patient's friends.

"Well, that was me. I just wanted to thank you for saving my life!"

My jaw dropped. That guy was dead when we arrived at the scene and dead when we got to the hospital.

As I stood there slack-jawed, he proceeded to say something that I've never forgotten, something that has governed the way I've handled patients ever since.

"I also wanted to tell you that I'm not upset about that crack you made about me being fat."

My eyebrows shot through my forehead. At some point while I was trying to revive him, I'd expressed my frustration: "I'm having trouble getting the IV in because he's so damn fat!"

I couldn't believe the guy was lying there dead and he'd heard that. It made me realize that things are happening between life and death that we don't understand. A patient's body may not be functioning, but he could be conscious. Or they might be having an out-of-body experience or something and are watching everything I'm doing.

Either way, I've learned to comfort and speak soothingly to patients regardless of their condition.

ROY RYALS, PARAMEDIC, ARIZONA

■ We were sitting around the station one evening when I heard a screech outside. A woman came running.

"He's choking! He's choking! Can you help me?"

I ran out and threw open the passenger side of her pickup, expecting to find a baby or child. Lo and behold, there was a big springer spaniel–type dog lying on the floorboard, frothing at the mouth. There were no visible respirations, and his eyes were rolled back and glassed over. I thought he was dead.

"He's choking on a ball! Please! He's choking on a ball!" the woman shouted.

I wasn't sure what to do at first. I expected a human. I was trained to treat humans. *What the heck,* I thought. *A life's a life.*

I opened the dog's mouth and peered inside. Sure enough, there was a hard rubber ball lodged in there. I reached in but had a difficult time getting hold of it because it was stuck tight and was all slimy. I tried to squeeze it, but it wouldn't compress.

I dug in deeper, sticking my hand into the dog's mouth up to my wrists. I finally got my fingers around the ball, used a little carotid pressure, and pushed it up. It popped out. The dog's mouth immediately clamped down on my hand. I pried my hand out, then gave him a sternal rub to stimulate his heart. There was no response.

I lifted him from the truck, laid him on the ground, and knelt to give him mouth-to-snout resuscitation. I grabbed his nose to start and saw his eyes flicker. He was coming around. Not wanting to have my face buried in his mouth when he revived, I backed off and started rubbing his side. He lay there, real passive, and eventually started panting. We gave him some water.

"Harley! How are you?" the woman cried.

Harley perked up. His tail started to wag. He was going to be all right.

I've taken a lot of grief about that call. The guys ride me. I get dog biscuits delivered to the station. But to me, it was really satisfying. The owner was elated. The dog was happy. And I ended up getting on *Rescue 911*.

RICHARD WARK, PARAMEDIC, MAINE

■ We were returning from a call late one night when I spotted something lying in the road.

"Might as well check it out," I said, glancing at my partner, John Broderick. "We're here to save lives."

He smiled, flicked on the reds, and swung the ambulance around.

We pulled over to the shoulder and hopped out to treat our "patient," a gray striped cat. It had been clobbered by a car and was struggling to move. I backed off, knowing that I'm severely allergic to cats. One whiff can make my eyes water and my body swell.

The animal looked at me with big hazel eyes, pleading for help. I could tell it was in anguish. *So much for my allergy,* I thought, deciding to ignore the consequences of continuing.

"What should we do?" I asked.

"Let's handle it like we would any other patient," Broderick said with a shrug.

My partner masked the animal [administered oxygen] while I ran and grabbed a KED [back] board. I still wasn't sure what we were going to do with the injured feline at that point. I just knew we had to do something.

By this time, other motorists, attracted by the flashing

lights, began pulling over to observe. Surprisingly, no one seemed shocked or miffed that we were wasting our time and resources on a stray cat. They all seemed to think it was the most natural thing in the world.

"There's a veterinarian about a mile down the road," a woman informed us. "You should take it there."

Much to the delight of the crowd, we immobilized the animal on the board, lifted it into the van, and ran a "level one, kitty" to the vet.

Unlike the crowd, the vet met us with bewilderment. She couldn't believe a big ambulance had arrived with lights blazing and nothing inside but a tiny cat! However, when she shook the sleep from her eyes, her healing instincts took over. She accepted the patient.

We received another 911 call and sped off. For whatever reason, I hadn't so much as sneezed during the entire operation.

The next morning, my partner drove back to the vet's before going home. He discovered that the doctor and her crew had worked all night trying to save the cat's life.

"I think it's going to pull through," the exhausted vet said.

We visited the animal diligently for the next week, thrilled by its remarkable recovery. On day eight, Broderick took the cat home with him. That was five years ago, and the cat—which he named Trauma—remains with him today.

JIM HAYDEN, EMT, ARIZONA

■ "A woman's been attacked by a cat," the dispatcher announced. "Proceed with caution." We checked the location. It was the local zoo. Obviously, they don't raise house cats out there. We nervously hopped into our ambulance and took off, figuring it was a lion or tiger.

Close. It was a leopard!

The victim was a young zookeeper. She and her partner

had neglected to place the animal in lockup the night before. The next morning she went in to clean the area and forgot to count black spotted heads. She stepped through the fence—and came face to face with an angry leopard that had been out all night and was cold and hungry!

The big orange cat leaped on her. The woman managed to get off a single, blood-curdling scream before the animal grabbed her by the throat and shut her down. A number of fellow zookeepers heard her cry and rushed into the area. They distracted the cat enough to convince it to let the woman go.

The first thing we noticed was that her trachea and chest were bubbling, meaning her airways had been severely punctured. Her pupils were dilated and she was cyanotic [blue]. It looked like we were going to lose her.

We started an IV, ran oxygen at 100 percent, monitored her pulse, and hoped for the best. Although we made some progress, we were frustrated by the fact that she wasn't coming around. It was obvious that she had some other type of injury that we weren't picking up on.

Fortunately, the director of the zoo had jumped into the ambulance with us. He explained that when a leopard attacks, it doesn't merely bite the throat, it squeezes and holds on until the prey stops moving. That explained it. The big cat had not just punctured her neck, it had suffocated her!

We pumped in more oxygen and got her to the hospital alive.

It was touch and go in the ER, but the healthy young lady made it. She recovered quickly and was back at the zoo within two weeks.

To see her working again, to hear her thanks for saving her life—that was fantastic. It's what this job is all about.

**DOUG CARRELL AND DANIEL NATION,
PARAMEDICS, NEBRASKA**

■ A group of seven fishermen was trapped on an ice floe that had suddenly broken loose from the shore. They'd floated out to a point where the rough, frigid water was sixty feet deep. When a chunk breaks away like that, it usually disintegrates rapidly, plunging its victims into the bitterly cold water. Hypothermia and death quickly follow.

Another fisherman sprang into action. He paddled out in a rowboat and rescued three of the men. However, by the time he deposited them on the bank, the howling wind had pushed the runaway floe too far from shore for a successful return trip. The situation was critical.

Our department had just purchased a hovercraft to better handle emergencies of this nature. Lucky for these guys! We hopped in, sped to the floe, and quickly loaded the stranded fishermen before the ice crumbled beneath their boots. We got them aboard in the nick of time.

Once they were safe, they began to badger us about rescuing their elaborate equipment from the vanishing floe. Typical fishermen.

TOM HARRISON, PARAMEDIC, WISCONSIN

■ The two-year-old was lying on the couch in a fetal position, foaming at the mouth and frothing around her madly twitching eyes. It was absolutely horrifying. I'd never seen anything like it before. Her parents waved their hands in the air and shouted at us in Spanish. I couldn't understand a word they were saying. That was critical because we needed to know what happened.

The mother ran out the door and returned with a neighbor who could translate—barely.

From what we were able to comprehend, the girl had been playing on the back porch. The next thing they knew, she was unconscious and foaming. We'd pretty much already determined that. No one had a clue as to why.

Not knowing what else to do, we loaded her into the van and ran a code three to St. Luke's Hospital. The toddler continued to foam and froth the whole way. Her eyes kept spinning in that frightening manner. I was certain we were going to lose her. I'd never lost a child before and was already starting to sense the emotional devastation I'd heard so much about.

At the hospital, the doctor took one look and said, "Do we have any scorpion antivenin?"

"How do you know that?" I asked, shocked.

He pointed to her bubbling eyes and mouth.

"Classic scorpion sting," he asserted, administering the lifesaving drug. "We get a lot of that around here."

The child, thankfully, made a full recovery.

So did I.

JIM HAYDEN, EMT, ARIZONA

■ My partner, Brad Kooner, and I went on a possible drowning. This kid had been drinking and had fallen into a well. We fished him out, and he was in bad shape. In the ambulance, the guy started fighting us, trying to keep us from intubating him.

"Look, you've got to be still," Brad ordered.

The kid was having none of it and kept fighting. He had already aspirated a lot of water into his lungs, so it was critical that we tube him.

Brad cupped his hands.

Bam! He boxed the kid's ears and rang his bell. That quieted the boy down. We got the tube in, suctioned him, and it was unbelievable, the amount of grass and stuff we pulled out of his lungs.

Thanks to Brad's well-timed whomp, we saved him.

SCOTT JOHNSON, PARAMEDIC, ILLINOIS

■ It was my day off. I was driving by a creek with a steep incline. I noticed some tracks where it appeared as if someone had driven off the road and plunged into the woods. I slowed and spotted a car. It had spun off the road, crossed a ditch, plowed through a field, and had come to rest nose down on a bank. I didn't know how long the car had been there, but the marks looked fresh. I pulled over and climbed down to check it out. A man was slumped inside the car. His body was warm, but he didn't have a pulse. I could tell that he'd had a heart attack. I sprinted to my truck and radioed for an ambulance. I then ran back and started CPR. By this time, a crowd had gathered across the road, but no one would help me. The spectators probably figured that he'd been hurt in the accident and they shouldn't intervene or move him. I tried to holler at them and explain that whatever injuries he sustained in the crash didn't matter—he was dying from a heart attack, so if he had hurt his back or broken his leg, that was secondary. If we were going to save his life, we had to get him out of there and get his heart beating.

No one listened, so I had to lift the man out of the car myself and carry him up the embankment. I continued the CPR on the shoulder of the road until the medics and ambulance arrived. We loaded him in, started an IV, and managed to get his breathing and pulse back. Although he was in full cardiac arrest, he made it to the hospital alive.

The next day, his wife called me and said he was out of danger. He was going to live! "He's alive because you stopped to help," she said, tearfully thanking me. "If you hadn't been there . . ."

It's a tremendous feeling, knowing that you brought somebody back to life like that. And it's so gratifying to know you have the training and skills to stop, even on your day off, and rescue someone from the brink of death. If I hadn't stopped, if I hadn't been passing by, this man, this woman's husband, this father, would have died alone and helpless in a ditch while all the people on the road watched.

DARYL BURTON, FIREFIGHTER AND EMT, FLORIDA

■ Three teenagers packed themselves into a tiny, two-seat Alfa Romeo sports car and went for a ride. Somehow the car ended up wrapped around a tree. One of the passengers, a young man, suffered massive head and lung trauma. We worked him furiously at the scene, inserting chest tubes and decompressing both his collapsed lungs so he could breathe. At the hospital, skeptical doctors told us they didn't expect him to make it through the night.

The kid survived that touch-and-go evening and pulled through. After six weeks of intensive rehabilitation, he was discharged.

In May 1994 I received a call from the boy's parents. They said their son was graduating from Yale Law School and wanted me to attend the ceremony. The family paid my way and set me up for the entire weekend. It was an unforgettable experience.

GREG HESS, PARAMEDIC, INDIANA

■ It was fall. We responded to a possible heart attack at the home of an elderly lady. We started working this lady and worked her until the second wave of paramedics got there. The medics did their thing pushing the drugs and all that. We worked her together all the way to the hospital.

Around the middle of December, I got a Christmas card from someone I didn't know. The name on the return address didn't register. Curious, I opened it and started reading.

"This is a card thanking you for letting me spend another Christmas with my family. If it wasn't for people like you, I wouldn't have been there."

Boy, that really hit me. That's where the satisfaction comes in, knowing that somebody appreciates what you did. Knowing, at the very least, you gave someone another Christmas.

KEVIN HOLLEY, FIRST-RESPONDER AND EMT, FLORIDA

... Lose Some

> *My wife says I don't have a heart, I have*
> *a rock. It's like I've turned off my emo-*
> *tions for so long that it's hard for me to*
> *dig down there and find them. I know I*
> *have them. I've seen them on a few*
> *occasions.*

HOWARD LEVINSON, PARAMEDIC, MONTREAL

EMS training never prepares you for death. It teaches us how to save lives. Death is something we have to learn to deal with after we're out on the road. It is, by far, the most difficult part of the job.

"It's easy to harden yourself to what is actually happening to the patients," notes Missouri paramedic Bruce Groteweil. "This shouldn't be misunderstood as callousness. It's a defense mechanism. We're not immune to it."

There's a fine line between the patient's desire for compassion and the EMS professional's need to be dispassionate. It's a juggling act we face every day.

"I have to disassociate the patients as actually being human beings," adds Florida paramedic Diane Crawford. "You have to or it would just weigh you down. You see it so much, especially young teenagers who blow their brains out. What for? You look at these kids and think,

What a waste. Or the young kids who OD on drugs and you get there and there's nothing you can do for them. And you just go, *Why? Why can God let this happen?* And the children, the SIDS deaths, that's another story. But you have to think, *It's part of life,* and go on with it, or otherwise you couldn't handle it."

THE STORIES

■ Snowmobile accidents are the worst. The machines slip and slide all over the place while the driver is totally exposed. In a wreck, nasty things happen.

One evening both my husband and son were out playing Evel Knievel on their sleds. A call came in for a snowmobile accident in that area. My heart stopped. Was it my own husband and son? I rushed to the scene. There were two snowmobiles flipped over. A black-clad body was lying motionless between them. A trail of crimson blood extended from the body for sixty feet across the bright white snow.

In snowmobile suits, everyone looks alike. All snowmobiles look alike. Fear and dread gripped me as I approached.

Please, God, don't let this be someone I know, I prayed. *Please don't let this be my family.*

My partner slowly removed the helmet from the person sprawled on the ground. I closed my eyes, then opened them.

I breathed a huge sigh of relief. It was a woman.

"Thank you, God," I whispered.

I immediately shifted into my medic mode. It may not have been my husband or son, but it was definitely somebody's daughter, and maybe even somebody's wife or mother. We loaded the beautiful young woman into our unit and proceeded to cut off her suit, starting with an area on her left leg where there was a slight tear in the fabric. As I cut away the material, I became increasingly shocked at how the wound kept getting bigger and bigger. The more pant leg I sliced away, the longer the gash grew. I kept having to ask for bigger and bigger bandages, because none would fit.

Despite the relatively tiny opening in her suit, the woman had been sliced from her hip all the way to her ankle. She was cut so deeply that there was a tube of Chap Stick embedded into her leg, right near the bone. The only thing I could figure was that the ski of the other snowmobile had torn through her suit, cut up her leg, caught on her flesh and dragged her for sixty feet, and then come back out through the same small opening in her pants.

From her identification, we discovered that she was only twenty-three. She had a firm, very tan, athletic body. We worked her all we could but couldn't revive her. The ER doctors told us that she broke her neck on impact and died instantly.

I returned home with mixed feelings. I was sad for this girl but happy it wasn't my family.

When I walked through the door, I was met with another shock. While I was on the call, my son had plunged his sled into the lake. He'd managed to escape the frigid waters—no easy task there—and emerged covered with ice from head to toe. Not only that, but he had stubbornly compounded the problem by refusing to leave the scene until they dragged his precious snowmobile from the lake.

It took me three days to warm him up.

After that harrowing day, I never sat on a snowmobile again.

DONNA

■ "My friend's been shot!" the small voice cried. "We need an ambulance!"

It was a snow day, and all the schoolchildren were home. A young girl, twelve years old, was playing with some friends when they heard what sounded like a prowler outside. She grabbed her father's shotgun and took off toward the living room window. On the way, she dropped the weapon, which kicked back and went off, firing a single deer slug into her stomach. She was lying unconscious on the carpeted floor when I first saw her. There was a quarter-sized hole in her upper abdomen just below her breastbone.

We masked her, put on the antishock suit and inflated it, dressed and bandaged the wound, applied the cardiac monitor, and did an IV. Her pulse was weak and her breathing was shallow. We picked her up and placed her on the stretcher. She opened her eyes, yanked the oxygen mask from her face, sat up, and stared right at me.

"Oh, wow! What a dream!" she said.

She lay back down and died. We did everything we could, but we couldn't bring her back.

I walked outside and cried. I was ready to quit the job, give up my career, everything. That look just ripped through me.

I've been to her grave seven times in the past twelve years. I probably should let go, but something keeps drawing me there. I don't bring flowers or anything; I just visit her for a while. Why? For my own mental health.

I wish it had only been a dream.

BRUCE GROTEWEIL, PARAMEDIC, MISSOURI

■ It had been a quiet day. We had a couple of auto accidents, but they didn't amount to anything. Then we pulled up to this one scene. Everything was very calm, peaceful.

There were two vehicles, a car and a pickup truck. We figured we had a fender-bender, no injuries.

We got out of the unit with our flashlights blazing through the darkness. I'd expected to merely chat with these people, make sure they were okay, then cancel the call. I shined the light into the truck and gasped.

The young male in the small pickup had been forced off the road and crossed over to the other side. In the process, his truck hit a chain-link fence and ripped part of it down. He pulled up enough of the fence that he tore into the top rail. A section of the rail came through the windshield like a missile, plunged through the steering wheel, knifed through the kid's neck, missed the back of the seat, then blasted out the back window and soared completely over the bed of the truck.

I winced as I directed the light to the front of the truck. The rail remained in one piece and was still attached to the fence!

Tracing the rail's course with the light, I noticed that it snaked down the hood of the vehicle and reunited with an unbroken section of the fence as if nothing had happened. Shining the light back the other way, I shivered with revulsion. The opposite, severed end of the rail remained lodged in the youth's neck. A good seven feet or more had passed through his body and was sticking out behind him. It was as if the kid had become part of the fence, the way a tree will grow through barbed wire over the years.

We studied the patient. He looked exsanguinated [as if he had lost a lot of blood]. His face was totally white. I checked his wrist. Miraculously, he had a pulse! Despite the horror of what he had been through, and what he was still going through, we had a chance to save him. But how? How could we free him from the fence? His head was contorted around in such a position that we couldn't really get to him. I observed a few agonal respirations, but he was not breathing by any human standards.

There was no easy way to fit him with a demand valve for oxygen. Frustrated, we huddled outside the truck and tried to come up with a plan to lift this kid out of there.

"Let's get an IV on him," my partner said. "We'll take it from there."

That was a good suggestion. Since he had a pulse, he'd probably lost a lot of fluids. The least we could do was to keep him hydrated. We also had to breathe for this kid. If a patient doesn't have oxygenated blood, he or she isn't going to last long.

We decided to take out the back window so I could crawl through and gain access. I grabbed my equipment and climbed in.

I now had a closer view of the horrifying situation. The youth was sitting in the driver's seat, but his head was doing a 180-degree turn. When the pole hit him, it twisted his head completely around. Even if we tried to mask him, he couldn't receive oxygen in this position. There was no way air was going down his trachea. We had to get him out of there, and fast.

But how are we going to cut the pole? I wondered. *With a hacksaw, or what?* There was no real answer. A paramedic's training in vehicle extraction covers removing the patient from the vehicle. It doesn't cover anything like this.

I racked my brain for the proper solution—or any solution. A line from a training manual interrupted my thoughts: "*Impaled objects are to be immobilized where they are and transported with the patient to the hospital.*"

I had to repeat the line over and over in my head before I understood the meaning. The manual was telling me to take the rail with the patient to the hospital!

But that was impossible. The top rail was twenty feet long, maybe longer, and was attached to the fence. No way could I take the whole damn rail. The only way to free him was to cut the pole on both sides. But that would take too long. This kid only had a few minutes, if that.

"Guys, we have to get him out of here, *now!*" I shouted.

I had a brainstorm and called for a scalpel. The pole went through his neck and left a thin layer of skin and tissue on one side. I decided to shuck the manual and perform some on-the-spot surgery. Instead of freeing the pole from him, I'd free him from the pole. I knew it was a controversial decision. It went totally against everything that I'd been taught to do or was licensed to do. If something went wrong, I'd be hung out to dry.

The hell with it, I thought. *The books don't tell you about calls like this. I'm on my own out here.*

The books don't teach us about darkness, either. Trying to do intubations and delicate surgery in the dark is almost impossible. All I had to work with was a scalpel and three wavering flashlights shining on this huge hole in this kid's neck.

There wasn't time to bitch. I raised the surgical blade and moved it toward his neck. Looking closer, I could see fragments of cartilage from his trachea. The pole had completely taken out the larynx. I sighed and continued on. He was in such bad shape, there was little I could do to make it worse.

I called for an ET tube and used my hands to pull the trachea out of the way. When I maneuvered the tube down in the trachea, I started bagging him [pumping air into his lungs]. Next I began working the scalpel, cutting away the flesh. Halfway through, a piercing thought froze my hand: *What if his carotid artery went to the outside? If I come to the critical artery, what do I do? Severing that would kill him instantly.*

I asked my partner to redirect the light. As far as I could tell, the carotid had been squeezed to the inside of the pole. How the rail missed the carotid and jugular the way it did, I still don't know. It was a minor miracle that gave me hope.

My ad-libbed surgical technique worked. I pushed gently on his head and shoulders and freed him from the pole. Incredibly, he was still alive!

"He's got to have some spinal damage," I said. "We need to immobilize him. Get me a C-collar."

Someone handed me one through the window.

"What am I going to attach this to?" I mumbled to myself. "He's only got half a neck!" With the help of the others, we somehow got it on. We immobilized his head the best we could, enabling us to carry him out. Amazingly, we got him to the hospital alive. We'd done our job.

The youth was put on a respirator and survived six more days before he finally died. There was nothing they could do. The fence had done too much damage. They were, however, able to remove some of his healthy organs and pass them on to other people, including some needy children. You take whatever small victories you can.

BRUCE RYDER, PARAMEDIC, FLORIDA

■ The paramedics brought a man into the ER who was suffering from a superficial gunshot wound. Since his injury wasn't life-threatening, I put him in a holding area and started working on more critical patients.

His wife arrived a short time later.

"Do you have my husband here?" she asked the nurse out front.

"Yes."

"May I see him?"

"Sure."

The nurse, figuring the woman would be happy to see that her husband was okay, led her inside to the trauma unit.

The wife promptly pulled a pistol from her purse. *Bang! Bang! Bang! Bang! Bang!* She proceeded to shoot her husband five times at point-blank range. Five *more* times, to be precise—as we later learned, she was the one who shot him in the first place!

I came running over, but by then it was too late. The man's wounds were no longer superficial. He died on the spot, right there on a cot in ER!

As I stood in shock, the wife calmly placed her spent weapon back into her purse, walked to the lobby, and quietly waited for the police. We were all kind of numb. I never even determined what the poor guy had done to infuriate her so, just that they had been arguing.

DR. JAMES GRATE, EMERGENCY
MEDICINE SPECIALIST, OHIO

■ The call came in as an alligator attack on a child. Our hearts sank the moment we heard the dispatcher's words. Most paramedics become hardened and callous over the years; you have to in order to survive with your sanity. However, few of us have become so hard that children don't get to us.

It took seven minutes to get to the scene. A woman was standing on the shore of a lake in a residential area, screaming hysterically. She told us that her son said that he and his little sister had been walking by the lake when an alligator suddenly sprang out of the water, grabbed the girl, and dragged her below.

My partner and I began walking around the shore, searching for a clue—anything to help us gauge the location of the gator. I found a pink tennis shoe, painfully small, and drag marks leading to the water. After that, nothing. Even though so much time had passed since the attack, we frantically searched on, clinging to the hope that by some miracle the little girl could be saved.

After our futile search, we reluctantly radioed for a police dive team. They needed time to prepare their air tanks and equipment, so I knew they wouldn't arrive for another hour. Speed isn't an issue with them, anyway. Divers fish for bodies, not patients.

I was too upset and agitated to stand around doing nothing while we waited. I commandeered a dory and rode around the lake, scouring the grassy areas for the gator—or the remains.

A group of alligator hunters came next. At first I resented their presence as an intrusion on our turf. That opinion quickly changed. Instead of being trigger-happy yahoos, they were professionals who knew exactly what to do in this situation. They started "shining." That's the technique of flashing lights into the water to spot the shining, beady eyes of the gator. Sure enough, within minutes they found the alligator.

The hunters called me over. I looked down and saw the most horrifying sight I've ever seen in my life. This massive green monster, nearly twelve feet long, was swimming about two feet below the surface. It was pushing the little girl's body through the water just ahead of it.

"It's taking her to its den," one of the hunters said between spits of chewing tobacco. "That's what gators do. They like the meat to age a little before they eat it."

The hunters promptly shot the gator dead, disturbing the eerie silence of the lake with their violent eruptions. When the quiet returned, we fished the body from the water. My heart sank when I saw her. She was little more than an infant, about three or four years old. There was hardly a scratch on her—except that one of her legs was missing. She looked like a broken doll.

The hunters dragged the gator to shore and cut open its stomach. Inside was the little girl's leg, fully intact. I picked it up and placed it under her body, as if I could snap it back on.

Then I went home and cried.

When the police and game authorities later investigated the incident, they discovered that the girl, her eight-year-old brother, and their new puppy had been playing by the shore. Gator attacks on humans are rare, so the experts concluded that the beast was apparently attracted by the movements of the puppy. The puppy probably sensed the attack and darted away. The gator, in a feeding frenzy, made a split-second decision to settle for the larger, slower child. Whatever happened, it gave me nightmares for months.

STEVE LONG, PARAMEDIC, FLORIDA

■ A man was been tossed out of a discotheque in the South Bronx for fighting. He came back and firebombed the stairway. It was an old building, and the whole place just went up like a match. A few people escaped by jumping out the windows. Most didn't.

Seventeen people died huddled together in a tiny bathroom. They crowded in there to get away from the smoke.

We ended up having to cart twenty-four bodies out of the place, loading them into pine boxes. It was my duty to check each box. None of the people were burned. They'd all died from smoke inhalation and were laid out in their Saturday night party dresses and suits with their shoes shined and their hair fixed up and everything.

The images of those young people haunted me for months afterward.

MIKE SCHULZE, PARAMEDIC, NEW YORK

■ I remember one call where this young fellow ran into a train in Bonita Springs and was thrown out of his car. He was nineteen and didn't have a scratch on him—just dusted himself off and walked away. About a month later, in Fort Myers, I went on another call. Some guy ran a stop sign and was crushed by another car. He was thrown out of his vehicle and his head smashed against a telephone pole. I approached and eventually realized that it was the same guy who'd survived the train wreck. This time, his luck ran out. He was a code seven [deceased].

JOHN NIPPER, FIRST-RESPONDER, FLORIDA

■ Some calls have been so emotionally trying that I've just wanted to take the clipboard, throw it out the window, and tell them to come and get their ambulance. One of these was on an Easter Sunday. This man, forty-five, was dressed to go to early services with his family. He sat down for a moment, had a major heart attack, and fell to the floor. When we got there, he was in cardiac arrest and his wife and three children were standing around in their Sunday clothes, half in shock. We tried to save him, but it didn't work out.

The hard part was telling his family.

"Sorry, there's nothing we can do," I explained. "We've done everything we can. We did everything the emergency room would have done."

When I finished, the older son, a teenager, began pounding on the wall, crying, "Why, why, why? Why my father?"

I could tell there had been some kind of conflict between them, and the boy was blaming himself.

It was a real bad scene. It killed me not being able to help them. I'll never forget the image of those kids all dressed up for Easter Sunday, and how they had to watch their father die in front of them.

Not long afterward, it happened again. A guy had been mowing his grass and had a heart attack. He was sitting by his pool when we arrived, and he promptly went into full cardiac arrest. We put him on the floor and tried everything we could, to no avail.

Suddenly the front door opened and his teenage daughter walked in. She saw her father covered with a sheet and just screamed. I'll never forget her scream.

SCOTT JOHNSON, PARAMEDIC, ILLINOIS

■ One of my first calls was an elderly man having difficulty breathing. He was on the bathroom floor. He wasn't having difficulty breathing—he wasn't breathing at all! We tried to clear an airway and couldn't. My partner reached into his throat and began pulling out blood clots. He was splattering them on the floor, wall, everywhere. But no matter how many he pulled out, we still couldn't get a tube in. The guy had an artery rupture in his stomach and simply bled to death. We placed him on a gurney, pulled a sheet over him, and brought him to the coroner.

I was sitting alone in the ambulance when I heard this grunting sound. My body tensed. I heard it again. I was terrified. I sat dead silent and started hearing these gurgling, bubbling sounds.

I rushed up front.

"The patient's alive! He's making sounds!"

The two veteran medics just looked at each other.

"Grunts and gurgling sounds?"

"Yes!"

"Those are the sounds of silence," the medic informed me. "The sounds of death. Gas. Ignore it."

DONNA

■ I had a patient, twenty-seven, who had a cast on his leg and was complaining of pain. We immediately thought he might have an embolism. He did, and he died right there in my arms. That really affected me. It was very frustrating being in a BLS [basic life support] system in Montreal. We had fifty ambulances and only two doctors, and the doctors were forty minutes away. If you're working a cardiac arrest, that's just too much time. The frustration led to stress, and the stress came to a point where I couldn't do it anymore. I couldn't keep watching these people dying needlessly. The way I dealt with it was to move to the United States, where there are more medical facilities.

HOWARD LEVINSON, PARAMEDIC, MONTREAL

■ This guy was in the late stages of AIDS, and they don't even look human. I hadn't seen anything like that before. In San Francisco there's a lot of AIDS patients. Sometimes it amazes me what happens to someone in that amount of time. They just shrivel up to nothing. They're like death itself lying there.

NAME WITHHELD, PARAMEDIC, CALIFORNIA

■ The sugar beet farmers in our area store their sugar in bins approximately 110 feet high. Workmen frequently labor in and around these bins, scouring the tanks and reclaiming the sweet powder. They're supposed to wear safety harnesses. Sometimes, tragically, they choose to be brave.

A worker going the brave route tumbled into the tank, hit an air pocket [a soft spot], and disappeared beneath a mountain of the sugar. My partner and I joined some firefighters in responding. We strapped on our harnesses and dived in, squeezing down through sixteen-inch chutes. Within seconds we were surrounded by walls of powdery sugar ten to fifteen feet high.

We located the man's arms and tied his hands to a safety rope, but we couldn't risk trying to drag him out. The sugar was so fine and viselike that even when we dug down to his knees, we still couldn't pull him out. It was too late, anyway. The man suffocated and had been dead far too long to revive. We struggled for nearly two hours to free his body from the sticky, quicksandlike sugar and claustrophobic confines.

When we returned to the station, a secretary, thinking she was being nice, brought us a chocolate meringue pie. We couldn't even touch it, not after having been nearly swallowed inside a sugar tank.

RANDY MEININGER, PARAMEDIC, NEBRASKA

6 Coping

*It helps to be able to come home after a
bad day and give the wife a kiss and the
kids a hug. That eases the stress.*

DANIEL NATION, PARAMEDIC, NEBRASKA

I remember my first death. I transported this gunshot
patient to the emergency room. He was DOA. I went outside, sat on the curb, and cried. My partner, a veteran
paramedic, came out, listened to my sobs for a while,
then gave me a hug.

"You can't take it personally," he said.

After that, I just hardened. People became little more
than biological units, human machines. Nothing bothered
me. But that wasn't the answer, either. Losing my humanity didn't make me a better paramedic. I gradually
reached the point where I could work EMS, do my job,
keep my emotions under control, and still show compassion for my patients.

It wasn't easy. I experienced one ghastly call after
another, covering every imaginable form of human misery. Afterward I'd have to hold myself together on my
own. In the early days, we didn't have group therapy or
critical incident stress debriefing seminars. There was no
such thing. They just threw us out there and told us to
save lives.

The medics I've run with, interviewed, and studied

have all worked hard at developing their own personal emotional survival techniques. They talk it out among themselves. They party at the local tavern—sometimes far too often. They exercise at health clubs to relieve the tension and frustration. They pursue elaborate hobbies to try to erase distressing mental images from their minds.

Most of all, we cry.

A lot.

THE STORIES

■ I guess it was one of the craziest things I ever did. In our state, a dead body legally belongs to the coroner. That means a body can't be moved from the scene until the coroner arrives and gives the okay.

This was a really weird call. We were told that it was a possible pediatric death seven or eight miles away. The police officers were already there when we arrived. I walked into the door and spotted two uniforms talking to a young man. I could hear the anguished wails of a young woman coming from the living room.

"Do something! Do something!" she cried.

I walked over and spotted an infant lying on the couch. It was obvious the child was dead and had been dead for quite a while. There was a great deal of lividity in the front of the body.

I asked a police officer if he had started CPR.

"No, I couldn't get the baby's mouth open. My fingers were too big to get an airway," he said.

The first thought that went through my head was that this poor woman was going to have to go through "the procedure." That means that before a body can be removed, we have to call the coroner and wait for him to arrive. The coroner then tries to ascertain the cause of death. It's a long, drawn-out process that can be torturous for the grieving family, but especially so for a young mother.

I was overcome with the desire to spare the mother this terribly insensitive process. There was a legal loophole that allowed me to do just that: If a patient is still alive, we can take them out of there.

I snatched the baby's body and herded my partner toward the van.

"Come on. We're going to the hospital," I announced.

"Are you nuts?" the medic exclaimed. "It's too late."

"We're running a code," I insisted. "We're getting out of here."

I cradled the stiff body and ran to the unit. Inside, I was able to get my little finger into its mouth. I freed its tongue and started mouth-to-mouth. We radioed the hospital that we were in code with a five-month-old male.

At the emergency room, they were prepared to attempt a resuscitation on what they thought was a viable patient. They put the monitor on, but it was stone flat. The doctor noticed the lividity and stiffness.

"Why did you run a code on this child?" she demanded.

I saw my career flash before my eyes. There was nothing to say but the truth.

"I didn't want to leave it in the house with the mother. She was hysterical," I explained with a shrug.

The doctor shook her head and waved for an orderly to wheel the baby away.

"This isn't the job for the softhearted," she said, moving on to her next patient.

"I know," I answered meekly.

While we were en route to the station, we received a call from the dispatcher. She said the coroner was on the phone and wanted to know what we had done with the deceased baby. I struggled for something to say.

"Tell him I kidnapped it. Over and out."

Nothing more came of it. I survived to go on a thousand more runs. The kicker is that some weeks later, we heard that the parents blamed us for the baby's death. They went around town telling everybody that we hadn't done our best to save the child. That hurt. My partner was utterly devastated by these accusations. He had been especially heartbroken about losing a baby. It was a totally unfair assessment. We chalked it up to the family's going through the grieving process. We found out later that the baby died of crib death, and it had been dead probably five to six hours before the parents discovered it and called us. They couldn't live with the guilt, so they blamed us.

That was the thanks I received for putting my career on the line.

DONNA

■ It was the evening of the Fourth of July. A drunk driver ran a stop sign and T-boned a small station wagon carrying a family of six. The impact was so powerful it knocked everyone from the vehicle. The bodies of the mother and father landed in a muddy cotton field sixty feet away. A third adult was lying on the shoulder. A girl, about eight, was a shorter distance away in the cotton field. Two smaller children, a three-year-old girl and a four-year-old boy, were lying face up in seven inches of water in a canal. The little girl was wearing white shorts with red polka dots and a white T-shirt. The boy had on a pair of jeans.

The accident happened at a rural intersection where cars rarely travel at that time of night. Because of the seclusion, the crash wasn't reported for ten minutes. It was so far out, it took us another ten minutes to arrive. By then, the fates of all those involved had already been decided.

I've worked many auto accidents in my career and have

witnessed every form of human suffering imaginable. Most of what I saw that night didn't affect me—the adults in the field, the grandparent on the shoulder, the scattered belongings of the family, the toys . . . it was all sadly familiar.

The children in the canal weren't. The instant I approached them, my brain tried to shut off. I couldn't bear the sight of these two little kids floating in that muddy water. The little girl was the same age as my own daughter, a factor that heightened my increasing anxiety. It just tore me up inside to see her like that.

We treated the older child, the only one in the family who survived, and sent her off in an ambulance. As fate would have it, the drunken driver also survived. He was hardly injured at all.

"What happened?" he slurred. "Was there some kind of accident?" He had no idea what he had done. He was so out of it there was no sense in even being mad at him. I treated the guy and motioned for a unit to take him away.

Then came the hard part—studying the bodies. I expected that the initial shock of seeing the two kids in the canal would wear off and enable me to dispassionately complete my task. It didn't. Every time I tried to look down, my senses screamed in renewed horror, forcing me to turn away. It was like I was living a nightmare I couldn't escape.

I steeled myself and lifted the little girl out of the mud. I could feel her shattered bones moving around in her limp body. Touching the child and bringing her close made it even worse. I put her back down and walked like a zombie over to our scene commander.

"I think we're going to need some debriefing on this."

"You think so?"

"I think so."

"I'll set it up," he promised.

When I went home that morning, I couldn't shake the

images from my mind. A snapshot of horror had seared itself into my brain. I couldn't focus on any activity. I couldn't do anything to divert my attention or erase the haunting memory.

I suddenly had an overwhelming desire to go out into the sunshine and cut the grass. I needed some mundane diversion just to keep my sanity. I mowed and mowed, but the image remained.

My wife knew something was wrong but pretty much left me alone.

"Are you all right?" she asked.

"Yeah. I just had a bad call, that's all," I explained. "I'll be okay."

The debriefing was set for the following day. Remarkably, all thirteen firefighters and paramedics on the scene that night attended. That was comforting. I thought my reaction was unique to me, that everyone else had toughed it out and forgotten it, like we always do. But those kids in the canal affected everybody. The same terrible snapshot was tormenting everyone.

We each stood up, one by one, and started talking about how we felt. Some of the guys cried. Others leaned on their religion to try to rationalize it. Almost everyone expressed a bitter frustration that there was nothing we could do. We're trained to save people, or at least to have a fighting chance at saving them. In this case, we never had that chance. We all felt so helpless.

It was amazing how similar everyone's feelings were. The tears of my fellow medics, their heartaches and nightmares, all combined to help me understand that I wasn't alone.

It took a long time, but the images finally did fade. I was able to go back out there and do my job.

KURT MICKELSON, PARAMEDIC, ARIZONA

■ One fall afternoon, my partner, Greg, and I were called to an apartment on an accidental pediatric drowning. Halfway to the scene, we were given an update.

"Caution is advised," the dispatcher warned. "Incident is possibly violent in nature. A second unit has been dispatched. The police have been notified and are on the way. Be careful, guys."

Four minutes after receiving the call, we arrived on the scene. We were met at the curb by two agitated men.

"Someone's inside killing a baby," one of the men insisted.

We grabbed our equipment and ran to the apartment, ignoring the caution. I knocked on the door. No answer. I knocked again.

"Ambulance. Open the door!"

Still no answer. I heard what sounded like the cries of a small child, along with water running in a bathtub. We suspected the worst.

After a few minutes, the second unit arrived. Carl and Jimmy jumped out of their vehicle and ran toward us. We searched the building for another way to get inside the apartment, but all the windows were barred. There was no way in or out, except through the front door.

"Where are the police?" I muttered out loud, frustrated by our helplessness. "Didn't this call come in through them?"

I radioed our dispatcher for a police ETA. Shortly afterward a few patrol cars arrived. They approached with their hands on their weapons and knocked on the door.

"Open up. Police!"

The door swung open. We were greeted by a stark naked man well over six feet tall.

"I've been stabbed," he said with a hollow-eyed look that cut through me.

The naked man turned, walked into the living room, and sat down on a recliner. There was a frightening calmness about him.

The stench of burning flesh and hair hit us like a sledgehammer the moment we walked into the apartment. Puddles of blood were on the floor. A small girl, moaning in pain from numerous stab wounds, knelt in the kitchen. Her older brother was lying in a fetal position in front of a gas stove. He had also been severely mutilated.

That wasn't the half of it. The stove, that's where the real horror was. The severed head of their baby sister had been placed on the back burner. The pilot light remained on, gently cooking the infant.

We all turned away in revulsion. None of us could believe what we were seeing.

The police officers pulled their weapons and edged toward the bathroom, hunting for a maniacal madman capable of such atrocities. Bursting inside, the cops were visually assaulted by more unspeakable horror. The quartered body of the baby girl was floating in a bathtub full of bloodred water.

We were numb. For several seconds we just stood looking on in disbelief. We had been caught completely off guard. The baby's head was sitting in one place and the body in another. I tried to erase both images from my mind but couldn't. It was like they had been seared into my brain with a branding iron.

After regaining our senses, we rushed to the aid of the two live children writhing on the floor. Carl and Jimmy went over to Tasha, a four-year-old whose face and tiny body had been burned so badly she was certain to be disfigured for life. She had also been stabbed in the abdomen.

Greg and I stumbled in a daze over to Tony, a six-year-old. Tony had suffered through the same brutal, ritualistic torture, including stab wounds to his chest and abdomen. The wound to his chest was so deep that his right lung was visible. When I reached down to check for a carotid pulse, he took his last breath.

I felt like dying myself.

Greg brushed me aside, picked the boy up, and carried him to the vehicle. We intubated him and initiated CPR, both to no avail. He was transported to one of three level-one trauma centers in Cleveland. Carl and Jimmy took Tasha to another level-one trauma center and burn center.

The father's wounds, apparently self-inflicted, were minor. The police cuffed and arrested him.

After entering the emergency room and giving my report, I felt really strange. I was numb all over and was shaking visibly. An X-ray technician approached. Her eyes were wide with shock.

"What the hell happened?"

I couldn't bring myself to tell her. I couldn't even talk.

I staggered to a telephone, tears rolling from my eyes. I advised our supervisor that I'd never seen anything like this before and that we would not be going back into service—at least not for a while.

"Roger, Bonnie. We'll cover. I'll be right over," he said.

I went back into the nurses' lounge and sat down, just staring at the walls. I had a run sheet in my hand but couldn't put anything on it. I just couldn't bring myself to describe what I'd just seen. I couldn't understand why a father would torture and murder his children in such a way. I sat there and cried. Greg joined me in the room, and he too had tears in his eyes. His shirt was covered with the blood of our young patients. I couldn't even look at it anymore.

I thought about Carl and Jimmy. I wondered what they were going through at that moment. I later learned that they were consumed with the safety of their own children. Jimmy sped home to make sure his young daughter was okay. He hugged her and told her over and over how much he loved her.

It took almost three hours for the four of us to pull ourselves back together. We dug down deep and mustered enough strength and courage to go back to work. We kept telling ourselves that other people needed us and we couldn't let them down. The public just wouldn't understand why two ambulances weren't available. Fortunately, the remainder of the shift was uneventful.

Tasha died shortly after arriving at the hospital. Her brother had died earlier on the kitchen floor. The father was sent to prison. He never really explained why he'd done what he did. He mumbled something about his wife leaving him, about losing his job and being unhappy. But nothing could excuse it.

Dr. Gayle Galen, the emergency-room physician on duty that day, was given the unenviable task of officially pronouncing the children dead, including the headless baby. It emotionally devastated her. After struggling to come to terms with her own feelings, she organized a debriefing session led by a psychiatrist specializing in emergency medicine. Everyone involved in the incident was invited to attend. The session served as an effective outlet for the rage and pain we had locked inside us. One by one we opened up.

Dr. Galen spoke of how her faith in God was shaken. She even contemplated giving up medicine. She told us how she delved into the Bible to find something to help her through. She also turned to close friends for support.

Dr. Galen described how one friend, a psychologist, had her come to the office and bring the gown she wore that day, the clothes she worn beneath it, and anything else that reminded her of the children. It was all placed in a brown box. A prayer was said and the box ceremoniously buried. For Dr. Galen, the horrible memory of the massacre was buried with it.

Carl spoke next. He explained how he experienced a loss of reality and direction. He repeatedly had to ask a dispatcher for directions to a hospital he'd been to hundreds of times before. He said that he didn't feel angry until after the care of his dying young patient had been turned over to someone else. Then became outraged and wanted to somehow avenge the children's deaths. After telling his story, Carl expressed appreciation for being able to share his feelings and vent his anger. He also voiced the need to attend counseling sessions like this more often.

Greg spoke of the nightmares he had and the frustration he felt on the scene. He remembered hearing the cries when we were outside and not being able to do anything about them. He vented his anger very strongly and he felt a sense of relief afterward.

My turn came. I relived the entire run and felt frustrated and inadequate all over again. I remembered the cold shiver that ran through me when the father looked at me. My anger blazed against the police department because of their slow response time. I also expressed my anger with the TV news people. Throughout the week that followed the incident, they televised special reports on the effect the murders had on the family, their friends and neighbors, and the police officers. They failed to consider us, the ones charged with caring for and transporting the young victims. Never once were we mentioned. That hurt.

During the debriefing, I found a great deal of comfort in knowing that I was not alone. I appreciated being able to share my feelings. I told Dr. Galen how much it helped when she told Greg and me that we had done a good job that day. I was able to get through the rest of the shift knowing that we had done our best. That generous compliment carries me through even today.

Jimmy didn't attend the session for his own reasons, but he later told me how he felt. He recalled how upset he was when he first entered the apartment. He recalled seeing his own little girl's face in Tasha's.

"It hit home," he said.

He also remembered the ride to the hospital. Little

Tasha clung to his fingers and would not let go. Whenever he moved away, she cried. The sound of her cries was more painful for Jimmy than the knowledge of what had caused them.

Jimmy also said something that is true for most of us: We handle trauma in an adult a lot better than we do in a child. Perhaps this is because we think of children as being innocent and helpless. We know that much of what happens to them of a traumatic nature is the result of careless or uncaring adults. In this case, it was a disturbed father who caused their deaths. This is what we came together to discuss, to come to terms with, and to get past.

We're still trying.

BONNIE ALLEN, PARAMEDIC, OHIO

■ We arrived at this local canal area that children use for swimming. A man waved us over and frantically explained that two small girls were missing. I was the rescue diver for the fire department, so that meant I had to slap on my equipment and jump in.

The water was very murky around the surface, but down about seven or eight feet, it cleared. I immediately found the first girl. She appeared to be about seven, and was lying on her side in a fetal position on the bottom. My heart raced as I grabbed her, pulled her to the surface, and swam as fast as I could toward the shore. I practically threw her on the dock to the waiting medics, trying to save every second I could. I turned around and went back down.

A minute or so later, I saw this other little girl, about thirty feet from where I'd discovered the first one. She was about five. Like her sister, she was in a fetal position on the bottom. Unlike her sister, her long hair was flowing beautifully in the agonizingly clear water, and she had this eerie, happy expression on her face.

The image haunts me to this day.

I picked her up and rushed her to the dock. We all began doing CPR, trying for nearly an hour to breathe some life into the little girls.

No luck.

Normally I know how to handle my emotions, but this was too much. I have two girls of my own, practically the same age. I'm sure that's part of why it hit me so hard. Not only did I have to struggle with the memory, but I also had to face all the things that went with it—the news stories and the interviews with the various representatives of all the social and governmental agencies that become involved in such tragedies.

As a rescue diver, I was used to picking up bodies. That's part of the job. You do it and go on. But this time I just couldn't shake it. I couldn't go on.

I never really had the time, or took the time, to deal with it, deal with my emotions. I just tried to suppress them. That only made it worse. After a while it was too late to try to do anything about it. The mental scars had become permanent.

I was never able to perform my duty as a rescue diver again. Even when I try to pleasure-dive in the ocean, I'm tormented by the images of those two little girls, especially the happy-looking one.

I wish that back at that time they had the critical incident stress classes and psychological debriefings that they have today. That might have helped.

**TERRY PYE, ASSISTANT FIRE CHIEF
AND PARAMEDIC DIVER, ONTARIO**

■ We'd been running all day and were called to respond to an accident. That's all I remember, so the rest of this was told to me by others. The accident was in the center of a four-lane road. The car we were dealing with had come to rest across the center line. We pulled the ambulance in front of the car.

As we were working the scene, a guy in a truck shot over a nearby bridge and for some reason didn't realize that we were in his lane. A firefighter tried to push me out of the way, but the truck caught my left side, hip, leg, and shoulder. My head hit the truck's mirror, ripping the mirror off. I was thrown about ten feet or so and knocked out cold. I felt no pain, nothing.

When I came to, I was still at the scene. I saw my captain leaning over me.

"Don't bullshit me, man, are my brains hanging out?" I demanded.

I'd recently been on a call where a guy was talking to me and his brains were in my hands, so I thought that had happened to me. I wasn't that critical, but I apparently knew I was in bad shape.

My associates plugged my head wound, took care of me, and got me to the ER. From what I've been told, six ambulances responded without even being officially toned out.

The next thing I knew, I was looking up at my wife. I'd been out for more than an hour.

I ended up with a plate and five pins in my left leg. My tibial plateau had to be rebuilt with a bone supplement—an implant of coral. My fibula was fractured, my fascia was ripped, and to this day the muscle on my thigh is still hanging out—I have a pouch on the side of my leg. My knees are in bad shape. I can't lie on my back. My legs burn. When I bend over, my legs feel numb. I have post-concussive syndrome and say words that are not appropriate in a sentence—I flip them. I'm still basically banged up from it.

The guy who hit me was given a ticket for exceeding a safe speed limit in an emergency zone, a small infraction. The guy with him in the truck was drunk, but he apparently passed the field sobriety test. I haven't forgiven the guy yet. I probably won't for a long time. He took something away from me. Because of all my injuries, my days in EMS are numbered. I can see the handwriting on the wall. I'm having trouble getting down to intubate people, and my shoulders aren't that strong. Mentally, I have problems taking in a lot of data at once and coming up with the right answer.

I hope workmen's comp will take care of me, but that's been a battle. It's hard to believe, with the injuries I've sustained, that they still treat me like I'm one of the people trying to take advantage of the system. They treat everybody like they're a bunch of crooks.

On the up side, I'm living proof that EMS works. My buddies and the others who responded saved me. I know that.

SCOTT JOHNSON, PARAMEDIC, ILLINOIS

■ I ran with this group of guys that were real cutups. There was nothing too gross or tragic that they wouldn't make light of. Since I was the only female on the team, I was usually the butt of their jokes. One afternoon we responded to a possible DOA in a mobile home. I followed my partner to the door. He opened it slightly, took a whiff, then quickly swung around, pushed me inside, and slammed the door behind me.

The air was so thick and putrid that I thought I was going to die. The staggering smell of rotting human flesh nearly suffocated me. I started seeing spots and grew dizzy.

"Let me out!" I screamed, pounding on the door. "Please let me out! Please!"

For a few agonizing minutes, all I heard was laughter. I vowed to strangle those clowns the instant I got my hands on them. They finally opened the door and allowed me to escape. I coughed, gagged, sucked in the fresh air, and fumed. However, the moment I looked at their stupid faces, I couldn't help breaking down and laughing with them.

"You guys are assholes!"

We regrouped and went back inside to do our job.

The body was lying on the couch. The lead medic looked at me, nodded toward the man's right leg, nodded toward a new EMT we were training, and winked. I instantly knew what he meant. They were about to play another horrendous joke, but this time it would be on one of the guys. I would be part of it.

I have to admit that I felt a wonderful sense of acceptance. I was being included, for once, as the joker instead of the jokee. They were telling me that I'd made the grade. I belonged under the spinning red lights.

I positioned the trainee to the rear of the body and took my place with the other guys at his head. We lifted. The trainee grabbed his legs—and one hand clutched nothing but empty trouser. The corpse had only one leg!

The young medic freaked. He screamed, dropped the good leg, and ran out of the trailer. We howled with laughter.

Outside, the guy refused to come back and help us. Mind you, this was the same man who had been laughing at me a few minutes earlier. We finally had to recruit a cop to help us lug the body.

Needless to say, I stayed on the team. The young medic didn't.

DONNA

■ I was in an aerobics class and received a call from one of my supervisors. She told me that Ray Barnett, a paramedic coworker, had died in a crash. A dump truck ran a stop sign and hit him broadside, killing him instantly. The medics who responded didn't even recognize him because his facial features were completely destroyed. Ray was a real loving, caring person. I just couldn't believe it when it happened. It was like somebody punched me in the stomach. I just wanted something mentioned in your book to remember him.

LISA COLLINS, PARAMEDIC, FLORIDA

■ I'll never forget the day Ray Barnett died because it was the first anniversary of my marriage. Everybody was shaken about it. At Ray's funeral, they covered his ambulance, Medic Two, with black ribbons and parked it in front of the church where they held the services. Toward the end of the service, Lee County EMS dropped all the different [emergency radio] tones for each of the seventeen stations. The dispatcher came on and said, "This is for you, Ray Barnett. This is your last call." It was a very, very emotional moment for everybody there.

This is for you, Ray Barnett. All of us love you and miss you.

VICKI JONES, PARAMEDIC, FLORIDA

7 Fear

Every time we roll down the road, we all have a little cringe of fear. We never know what we're going to roll into.

RICHARD WARK, PARAMEDIC, MAINE

Fear hitches a ride on virtually every 911 call. The moment you flick the switch to turn on the red flashing lights, your heart starts pounding, and one question invariably stabs at your brain: What life-threatening hell am I about to face this time?

We confront all forms of danger every day. We deal with patients who have smoked, inhaled, or injected the happy stuff and who think we're the Wicked Witch of the West riding on a pink dragon. Or the drunk who beat up his wife, locked the kids in the attic, and drowned the family dog; brandishing his shotgun, he thinks we're there to repossess his pickup truck.

"Yeah, I've been scared," admits New York paramedic Mike Schulze. "I've been attacked. I've been chased. I've been beat on. Sometimes you pull up to a call and you kind of get a weird feeling that something's not right. You're a little leery, so you approach the scene with caution. I don't think that we get enough respect from the people in the streets. A lot of them don't know what we're all about. Recently we've gotten some publicity, but basically the public doesn't know what our job is. They think of us as a bunch of meat-wagon attendants or body snatchers."

Norm Simons, a park ranger and EMS coordinator in Alaska, says that fear is a routine part of the job in the rough country he patrols.

"Anybody who says they've never been scared is a liar. I've certainly been scared a number of times, especially when you're talking about high elevations, high-angle technical rock rescues when you have nothing but a couple thousand feet of air between you and the ground."

As with death and stress, we've all learned to handle fear in our own way.

THE STORIES

■ I was working for a volunteer rescue squad one afternoon when my pager beeped. I called the dispatcher and was told that there was a possible heart attack a half-block from my home. I responded in my personal vehicle, knowing that an ambulance was on its way and would be there in about five minutes.

I went to the front door, knocked, then pushed it open. A young boy was sitting in a darkened room watching TV.

"What's the problem?" I asked.

"He's in there," the boy answered, pointing to a back room.

I walked a few steps into the kitchen, looked around, and didn't see anyone. I glanced down the hallway. It was dark, but I could make out the shadowy image of this massive figure lumbering toward me, stumbling into the walls.

"What the fuck do you want?" the man bellowed.

He came into the light. Three observations struck me at once: He was disheveled, drunk, and had a gun. That's always a bad combination.

"Get the hell out of here!" he screamed, waving the pistol.

"I need to talk to you," I answered calmly.

The man peered at me, his anger momentarily draining. He winced in pain and clutched the side of his chest.

"Sit down, please. You may be sick," I ordered.

He did as told. Once seated, his demeanor changed.

"I want to die," he said, breaking into tears. "I beat up my wife and she left me. I'm going to kill myself."

Despite his self-pitying tone, I knew enough to remain on alert. Guys like him usually don't keep the rage to themselves. Any nearby target will do.

I was Ms. Nearby.

Sure enough, a darkening in his eyes signaled a sudden mood swing. I tensed. The ambulance would be there any second, red lights flashing and sirens blaring. That was the last thing this dangerously demented drunk needed. I had to alert my colleagues, who were about to arrive. I couldn't allow them to come busting through the door, only to get shot in the face. But how could I warn them?

I thought of sprinting toward the door. No good. Even a drunk with a trembling hand could shoot me from that distance.

The phone rang. The man made no effort to answer it.

"Can I get that for you?" I asked.

"Go ahead," he said dejectedly.

I picked up the receiver. It was a woman, his wife.

"Is he okay?" she asked.

"No, not really," I said, stalling. This was my chance. I wanted to give her a message without setting off her husband. I searched my mind for what to say, how to walk this life-and-death verbal tightrope. Fortunately, his wife was thinking the same thing.

"Does he have his gun?" she asked.

"Affirmative."

"What should I do?"

"Please inform the authorities. Have them come in silence."

"Come again?"

"Just tell them what I said."

"Okay."

As I hung up, I heard the sirens in the distance. *Please let them get the message,* I prayed.

The man lifted the gun and put it to his head. He sobbed louder. Then, as if some demonic thought hit him, he did exactly what I feared—he pulled the gun from his temple and pointed it at me.

"Why am I shooting myself? I should shoot you!"

I swallowed hard and fought to remain calm. I was caught in that horrible dilemma paramedics so often face: Do you save yourself and risk losing the subject, or do you hang in there at all costs and risk dying in someone else's drunken nightmare?

"You don't want to do that," I whispered calmly.

"Why not?"

It was a good question. I fumbled for an answer that wasn't self-serving.

"That won't accomplish anything. Your wife called. She's concerned about you."

That cooled his temper for a moment, but only a moment. The man spent the next two or three minutes—an eternity in that situation—alternating between threatening to shoot himself and threatening to shoot me.

In the midst of this dangerous mental tug-of-war, I noticed that the sirens had been muted. Time was passing. Where were the paramedics? Where were the police? How much longer could I play this unnerving game with this man?

The front door opened very softly. I noticed it. The man, fortunately, didn't. A medic quietly stepped in.

"How are you two doing?"

"This man is my friend and neighbor, and he's okay," I

responded. I turned to the man. "Joe here is a medic. He's here to help. He just wants to talk to you."

The man nodded his acceptance. He started crying again and waving the gun around. The medic, true to form, suppressed his own fear and sat down with us. As we talked, he whispered to me that the sheriff was outside with a force of men. They were waiting for some signal from us—either that or the sound of a gun going off.

"Thanks," I whispered back. "Mighty nice of them."

More time passed. Working together, the medic and I tried to convince the man to go with plan C—give himself up rather than shoot himself or one of us. Our argument was simple and to the point, the kind of straightforward logic that works best in these situations. He could either kill himself very painfully and never see his wife or children again, murder us and spend the rest of his life in a wretched prison playing housemaid for a brute, or walk out of there with no harm done.

He hesitated for a moment, then laid the gun on the table. The medic went to the door and motioned for the police to come in. They grabbed the gun and restrained the patient.

We began treating him and determined that he was suffering from a mild heart attack. We rushed him to the emergency room.

As I was walking out of the hospital, a policeman waved me over.

"Did you have the wife send the message to kill our sirens?"

I nodded.

"Good thinking. Probably saved your life. The guy could have shot you."

"I know."

DONNA

■ We used to have a contract with the county to pick up mental patients. Many of these were people who were being committed by a guardian or relative, so they weren't too happy about the process. Similarly, we weren't too happy about doing it. These calls were time bombs.

I was dispatched to a fleabag Phoenix slum hotel. The place was a rathole, complete with filthy floors, dingy walls, and the ever-present smell of urine. When I arrived at the door, I did my standard police knock, meaning I stood in the hallway and stretched my arm out to the door. That's done to shield my body in case the man or woman inside welcomes me with a shotgun, bazooka, .357 Magnum, hacksaw, switchblade, or similar fun thing.

"Who is it?"

The voice sounded pleasant. My tension eased.

"This is Roy. I need to talk to you."

"Are you the ambulance service?" he asked.

"Yeah."

"I've been expecting you. I'll be right there."

The man seemed nice enough. I stepped from behind the wall and stood in front of the door.

Bad move.

The door swung open. In a flash, the guy stuck a knife into my gut and plunged it all the way to the handle. It happened so fast I didn't even have time to react. I just stood there and ate the four-inch blade.

I instinctively stepped back, a move that probably saved my life. The knife popped out, preventing the man from doing more damage by trying to slice up my chest. As I stood there bleeding, my first thought was, *I don't want my guts to spill out on this rotten floor.* I was certain that if that happened, I'd get some wretched disease. Terrified by the prospect, I reached down and tried to squeeze everything back inside.

"I've been stabbed," I whispered into my radio.

"What?"

"I've been stabbed. Cut up. We're going to need another ambulance."

"Are you still in danger?"

"I don't think so."

"Where's the patient?"

"He went back inside."

My partner contacted the police, then helped me out of the building and drove me to the hospital. It was strange being on that end all of a sudden. I was also kind of embarrassed, coming into the ER bleeding like that in front of all the cute nurses I was always hitting on.

My ER friends wheeled me into surgery and repaired two loops of my bowel. The doctors and nurses treated me great. They never even sent a bill. I recovered to ride again, but that was a scary one.

ROY RYALS, PARAMEDIC, ARIZONA

■ There was thunder and lightning and it was raining like crazy when I pulled the fire truck out to respond to an infant code. An ambulance also responded. We stabilized the baby and sent it to the hospital, where it recovered. On the way back, I lost control of the big red truck in the storm, slid off the road, and plunged into a ditch. When I got out, I noticed that I'd stopped right next to a pet cemetery.

For some reason, that really gave me the creeps. I think it would have been better had it been a regular people cemetery. The whole thought of being surrounded by the ghosts of dogs, cats, parrots, and goldfish was starting to freak me out.

I radioed for help. I could hear the dispatcher, but they couldn't hear me! I tried and tried, but no one could read me. What was going on? There was no earthly reason why my radio wasn't working. My mind played tricks on me. Were the animal ghosts conspiring to keep me there for some sinister reason? Was I caught in some *Twilight Zone* time loop? I looked out across the cemetery. The whole place had this eerie glow about it. Goose bumps exploded on my body.

"Please, can anybody hear me?" I pleaded on the radio as flashes of lightning illuminated the tombstones of Fido, Paws, Tweety, and Goldie. "This is unit seventeen. I've gone down in a ditch! I need assistance. Please, can anybody hear me?"

The minutes passed. The storm grew worse. Nobody responded.

Finally, after a torturous hour, I was able to get through.

"Please, I've gone down in a ditch. Send a tow truck! Fast."

"Is this an emergency? Are you injured?"

"Uh, no, but I'm, uh, I'm next to, uh, a pet cemetery!"

"Repeat, please."

"I'm stuck near a pet graveyard, dammit! Please get me the hell out of here!"

"Okay," the dispatcher said, laughing. "I understand. We'll get someone right on it."

It was another hour before the tow truck arrived—the longest hour of my life. To this day, I've never set foot near another pet cemetery.

GEORGE RUIZ, EMT, ARIZONA

■ There was this twenty-year-old student who went on an overnight backpacking trip in a pretty easy area of the park. We'd never had any problems in that section before. Apparently the girl panicked when the weather deteriorated, and she ended up on a high ridge that was actually fairly close to a road. For some reason, possibly disorientation, she descended down the north side, lost her pack, and then somehow crossed the river. That was the last anybody saw of her.

I was in charge of the three-day search. One of my duties was to interview her family and friends and go through her diary to try to find out what I could about her state of mind, her background, or anything else that might help us locate her. I talked to people she had gone to school with, people she'd attended a backcountry leadership management program with, and others who knew her. I delved into many intimate aspects of her life. I knew her goals, ambitions, and personal desires. I learned an awful lot about this young woman. In a way, you could say I got to know her.

We scoured the area with helicopters, fixed-wing aircraft, and ground searches, but we couldn't find a trace of her. For a while we figured that this might be a life insurance setup or a planned disappearing act, although from what I'd learned, it didn't seem in character. On the third day we found her. She had drowned trying to come back across the river. Her body had been swept downstream and lodged against some rocks.

Another district ranger and I had to identify the body and perform the basic physical examination for broken bones and other gross injuries.

The investigation, interviews, reading her diary, then touching and studying her body all combined to have a strange effect upon me. I began having eerie dreams about her.

"I don't want to be dead. I want to live. I want you to help me. Find me. Please!" she pleaded night after night. It really shook me.

I never said anything to anybody about the haunting nightmares until a former district ranger went to a critical incident stress debriefing program in Tucson, Arizona. After he came back, we had a four-hour class on these types of incidents, and it was only then that I was able to open up about my dreams. That made me feel a lot better. More important, the dreams never recurred.

NORM SIMONS, PARK RANGER AND
EMS COORDINATOR, ALASKA

■ There was a big shoot-out at the armored-car company down on South Boulevard. We pulled up directly into it. The shooting was still going on. Bullets were flying everywhere. We had to duck for cover. A police detective I knew, Bob, was the first casualty. He had taken a slug in the knee and was trying to duck behind a row of cars. I saw him and jumped out of the unit.

I ran behind the cars, creeping lower with each shot, and reached the injured detective. I lifted him over my shoulders and carried him back to the ambulance. Fortunately, neither of us was shot on the way. The firefight continued as I treated Bob's shattered knee. It turned out to be a bad day all the way around. A deputy and one of the perpetrators were killed. Bob and a hostage were wounded. A second perpetrator was arrested.

Bob recovered and was back on the beat within months; he wasn't a desk-job kind of guy. That was extremely fortunate—for me.

One night we went down into what's called a "hill area"—a low-income part of town where violence and mayhem are common and paramedics, despite our angel of mercy mission, are often viewed as an extension of the police—meaning we're the enemy. The patient was cut all over his chest, arms, and face. They were mostly just nicks and scratches, nothing fatal. He told us that a man by the name of Clarence had knocked him down with a club and he had fallen into a crown-of-thorns bush. The bush had inflicted most of his wounds.

The police arrived. One of the uniformed officers

asked me if it was all right if he interviewed the man while we treated him.

"Yeah, no problem," I replied.

The cop hopped in the ambulance and began asking the man questions while I stood outside behind the van's open double doors, half listening to the victim's story. He was describing what Clarence looked like. In the middle of his description, he stopped and said, "There's Clarence!"

No one paid much attention, including me. Then he said it again: "There's Clarence!" I looked at him, and he was looking right through me. That gave me a chill. I turned around, and sure enough, there was Clarence—a huge, enraged man wielding a baseball bat. He peered down at me with the red, angry eyes of a wild animal. I saw him raise the bat.

My body instinctively went into a defensive posture. I was planning to duck, block the blow with my arms, or run, whatever was most expedient. Before I could do any of those, I heard a strong, authoritative voice behind me.

"Drop it, Clarence!"

Clarence turned his blood-red eyes toward the voice.

"Drop it, Clarence!"

Clarence dropped the bat. Easing up, I looked around. There was my old pal Bob the detective, standing with his 9 mm gun pointed at Clarence's head.

When the tension subsided and Clarence was cuffed and under control, I asked Bob what he would have done if Clarence hadn't dropped the bat. Bob looked at me and grinned.

"I would have blown his fucking brains all over the ground. You forget, I owe you."

ERNIE EBERHARD, PARAMEDIC, FLORIDA

■ We were called to an unknown distress. I was riding with a rookie EMT. Usually you wait for a deputy before you enter a place, but this time it didn't seem like it was any drastic, hairy problem, so I went up to the house. I told my partner to bring the first-aid kit. When I hit the front door, I found myself looking at the end of a rifle barrel. The man holding the gun ordered me to kneel on the floor inside. I was as scared as I've ever been in my life, certain that I was going to die.

I looked to my right and spotted a woman sprawled on the living room floor.

"Hey, can I just go check her out?" I offered.

"No. Shut up and stay right there," he shot back.

My partner, thank God, realized something was wrong and called for help. He didn't even know the codes that well, so he stumbled over them. When we heard the tape later, it was kind of funny, but not then.

The deputies and SWAT team arrived within minutes and set up their perimeter. Meanwhile, I kept talking. When I get nervous, I just talk and talk and talk. I can't help myself.

"You don't want to kill me. What's the point? I'm pregnant. I'm going to have a baby," I argued—truthfully. I was six months along at the time. "You don't want to kill a pregnant woman."

"Just shut up, lady. You open your mouth one more time, I'm going to shoot you."

That was asking too much.

"Come on, why don't you just let me go?" I continued.

The man walked over and put the barrel right to my neck. *This is it,* I was thinking. *I'm going to die because I can't shut up!*

The anxiety started eating at me. I couldn't keep quiet, and I couldn't handle the stress.

"If you're going to kill me, kill me, because I can't stand the suspense anymore!"

"Shut up!" he repeated, pulling the gun away.

Outside, the police started working the bullhorn.

"Come out with your hands up!"

The next thing I knew, the house was filled with tear gas. I started coughing and crying. The gunman stumbled toward the back of the house.

Bang!

The police heard the shot and figured that he'd killed me. They charged in, exploding tear gas left and right. I ran for the door, tears streaming down my face. I was totally freaked.

Outside, I fell into the nearest officer's arms.

"Are you okay?" he asked.

"Yeah, I think so, but I don't know about the people inside."

Ever the EMS trouper, I composed myself and promptly marched back into the house to do my job. The woman on the floor was dead. I walked into a back bedroom and discovered the body of a five-year-old boy. He had been shot to death like his mother. In the next bedroom, a three-year-old girl had suffered the same terrible fate.

They were the man's wife and children.

I walked out and caught my breath. Knowing what he had done made me realize how close I had come to being killed myself. I'm not even sure why I wasn't.

DIANE CRAWFORD, PARAMEDIC, OHIO

■ We loaded a motor vehicle accident patient with a broken ankle. There was some alcohol involved, but generally this kind of patient doesn't give us much trouble.

Generally.

I walked around back for a last-minute check and discovered that the man was sitting up and clutching a knife. My partner had his back turned, and the man was about to ram the blade between his shoulders. Was I scared? I was petrified! I couldn't even talk, much less shout.

Thinking fast, I grabbed the patient's broken ankle and

gave it a twist. The excruciating pain caused him to reconsider killing my partner. He dropped the weapon.

Hearing the guy scream, my partner turned and looked at me like I'd gone nuts. He figured I'd gone mad and attacked a patient.

"Look on the floor!" I yelled. "Look on the floor!"

He glanced down and spotted the knife. His eyes bulged.

We subdued the patient and transported him without further incident. We never determined why he wanted to kill the person who rescued him. We just dropped him off and went back to work.

DOUG CARRELL, PARAMEDIC, NEBRASKA

■ A small boy was swimming at a local gravel pit. A woman and her three children had also been swimming there, and they reported that the boy had run down a hill, plunged into the water, and immediately had begun thrashing around. He disappeared a few seconds later.

In Florida, that usually means one thing—a bad bull alligator. That presented us with a paralyzing dilemma. The only chance the child had was if we immediately dived in and tried to save him. That, however, could have resulted in one or more of us being attacked and dragged to the bottom by the giant gator. As I stood at the edge of the water, fear coursing through my body, I thought that if that had been my child, I'd want somebody to take the chance at all costs.

"The hell with it," I said, startling my equally frightened cohorts. "Let's go for it." I jumped in. My action loosened the legs of my associates, and soon we were all in the water. We were terrified but determined.

It was a small pit, and it wasn't long before we found the body. I thought that maybe we'd have a chance, but it was too late. As I laid his young body on the gravel, I noticed that his limbs were intact and there wasn't a mark on him. It definitely wasn't a gator.

So what happened?

The coroner later discovered that the kid had been chewing a wad of grape bubblegum practically the size of a boulder. When he hit the cold water, the shock took his breath away and sucked the gum right into his windpipe, cutting off the air. That's what killed him.

In this tragedy is a major lesson: Children should never be allowed to chew gum when they swim.

ERNIE EBERHARD, PARAMEDIC, FLORIDA

■ A car was speeding off just as we arrived at the scene of a shooting. The police went after it. We figured it was the assailant making his escape, so we busted through the apartment door. Bad guess. The gunman was sitting inside clutching his rifle!

My heart pounded. That's not a good situation to be in, by any means.

"Uh, where's the guy you shot?" I clumsily asked.

"He's in the bedroom over there," the man answered, pointing with the rifle.

"Do you, uh, mind if we work on him?" That was probably not the question to ask. Obviously he hadn't shot the guy because he wanted him to be saved. He shot him because he wanted him dead!

"No, go ahead," he said.

We ran to the bedroom and discovered a man with a nonfatal chest wound. We started treating him, all the while wondering when the gunman was going to appear with his rifle and finish him, and us, off.

"The assailant is inside the house!" I whispered into my radio. "He's sitting on the east wall with a rifle. Please assist."

The police arrived shortly thereafter. The gunman

quietly handed over his weapon. It worked out okay, but that was a tense one.

ANDREW ARNOLD, PARAMEDIC, TEXAS

■ I was transporting a man on crack cocaine. He kept staring at me funny.

"I'm going to kill you, rape you, cut you into little pieces, and dump you out all over the road," he threatened.

For some reason, fear or just stupidity, I started laughing.

"You're in no position to be talking to me like that."

"I'm going to kill you, rape you, and cut you up, and nobody's ever going to find your body," he repeated.

"You see those two back doors?" I countered, motioning toward the back of the ambulance. "I'm going to open those doors and shove you out on the road and watch you roll."

After that, he didn't say another word.

VICKI IEZZY, PARAMEDIC, FLORIDA

■ We had a weird SIDS [sudden infant death syndrome] situation. We asked the mother to show us how she'd found the baby. She led us to the crib and said the infant had been lying facedown on a small pillow. It had apparently suffocated.

After the medical examiner arrived, we looked around the house. There was an older sibling, probably four or five. She had a doll the same size as the baby, wearing the exact same sleeper. The doll was lying facedown on the girl's bed, with its nose and mouth buried in a pillow. I felt a chill when I saw it. I wondered whether the sister was jealous and somehow suffocated the child.

The medical examiner, however, ruled it a natural death.

PATRICK WALSH, PARAMEDIC, ILLINOIS

■ We arrived at a trailer and found a groggy 260-pound woman in a waterbed with her husband.

"She's taken an overdose of pills," the husband stated.

"No, I didn't," the wife countered.

I took her vital signs. She appeared lethargic but otherwise okay.

A little girl came running into the room.

"Leave my mommy alone!" she screamed.

The child's piercing voice acted like a switch that instantly altered her mother's mood. The big woman sat up and angrily ripped off the blood pressure cuff.

"See what you've done!" she huffed, scrambling for a nearby purse.

Fear gripped me. *She's got a weapon in there,* I thought, heading her off.

"You can't have it!" I insisted, reaching it first.

The woman lunged for the purse and managed to get her hands on a corner. This set off a violent tug-of-war. As I was yanking and pulling, the little girl started beating on me.

At this point, all I thought about was protecting myself. With strength fueled by anger, I snatched the purse and pinned the woman to the bed.

"You're not going anywhere," I yelled, fighting to control a woman who outweighed me by 120 pounds.

"You #@$%!@#%$," she spat back, calling me every name in the book.

My partner, Tammy Maurer, rushed in and leaped on the waterbed to help me hold this big woman down. During the ensuing struggle, Tammy tried to radio for help. As she did, the woman punted the radio out of her hands, knocking it between the frame of the bed and the liner.

A fireman on call with us heard the commotion and joined the fray. The woman's husband joined in on her side. The three of us good guys were now bouncing on the waterbed trying to subdue this woman while her husband and little daughter flailed away at us.

Meanwhile, her other children proceeded to lock all the doors to the trailer, shutting out the police and remaining firefighters. The children just stared blankly at them through the windows as they attempted to come to our rescue.

The little girl who started it all disappeared for a moment, then returned brandishing a butcher knife! We had to call a time-out from the wrestling match and take it away from her before someone ended up being killed.

The police finally broke in. In quick succession, the husband was Maced and arrested, the children were subdued, and the woman was taken first to the hospital and then later to the health department for a complete psychiatric evaluation.

We dusted ourselves off and went back to work.

VICKI IEZZY, PARAMEDIC, FLORIDA

■ A lumberjack was hit by a falling tree deep inside a swamp forest. The only way to get to him was by traveling for three miles through waist-high mud. My partner, Lynn, and I parked the ambulance and hopped aboard a skidder, a tractor made to haul trees out of the muck. After loading our equipment, there was room for only two people in the cab—the driver and Lynn. That meant I had to stand outside on the blade! One slip, and I'd fall under the tractor and be buried forever in the sludge.

It was a rough ride. Mud, slippery mud, was flying left and right. Sometimes we'd dip down like a boat and just plow the mud everywhere. I was scared to death the whole way, but I tried to focus on the job I had to do.

After all that, the guy was dead. He died the instant he got hit by the tree. Yet, scared as I was, and knowing the patient's outcome, I'd do it again. As far as we knew, we had a viable patient, and it was my duty to help him.

RICHARD WARK, PARAMEDIC, MAINE

■ There were more than a hundred people milling around the scene of a late-night shooting. It was a low-income area, and the situation was critical. People were yelling, carrying on, and fighting. The shooting victim was sprawled on the pavement of a parking lot. A handful of police officers with dogs were trying to control the area.

We quickly loaded the patient and prepared to take off so we could get away from the explosive situation.

The man had a gunshot wound to his hip. He was conscious and extremely violent, really hyped. We speculated that he was on crack. I tried to calm him, talk him down, but I wasn't getting through.

I reached over to get the blood pressure cuff. As I did, the man reared up, grabbed me around the neck, and started choking me and slamming me against the sides of the ambulance. I couldn't breathe.

"I'm gonna kill you, lady!" he screamed.

I was more frightened than I'd ever been in my life.

It seemed like forever, but my partner finally realized what was going on and waved over the police. They jumped in back and pulled the man off me. We regrouped, then handcuffed the patient to the stretcher.

Afterward I was shaking all over. I couldn't talk. I was just so stunned. My partner got in the back, and I took the wheel. My body shook uncontrollably all the way to the hospital.

When we arrived, my fear turned to anger. It was all I could do to keep from barging into the ER room where the patient was and giving him a piece of my mind.

It was a busy night. We were called out on another violent incident in a bad part of town, a stabbing. I had yet to recover from the previous incident, and there I was, back in the fray.

My husband, a police officer, heard about what happened and made an unscheduled visit to the hospital. He located the patient and informed him that he wasn't happy about what happened. The guy responded by jumping up and trying to attack my husband! The patient was treated and arrested.

My husband then found out where the second call was and went to the scene. When I saw him, I broke down and started crying. I wasn't emotionally prepared to go into another hostile area so soon after what had happened to me. Seeing my husband was a huge relief. He got me through the night.

TAMMY MAURER, PARAMEDIC, FLORIDA

■ I was pacing back and forth at the station, certain that something terrible was about to go down.

"What's up with you?" a coworker asked.

"I don't know. I just have a bad feeling about today."

An hour later, we received a call about a possible shooting. As we approached the back of the house, I heard two explosions: *boom, boom.*

"Hit the floor, Marcia!" I ordered, instructing my partner to get down.

The shooter wasn't after us. He'd blown the windows out of a police patrol car, injuring the deputy.

We pulled back and drove to a nearby convenience store to take cover. A man approached us.

"My mom's been shot!" he exclaimed. "You guys have to go in and get her!"

"We can't go in until the scene's secure," I explained. "Your father's still shooting."

"You've gotta go now!" he insisted.

"We can't."

The son reached through the window and started taking swings at me. A fireman had to chase him away with a halagon tool [a ten-pound clawed crowbar used for breaking into buildings].

Meanwhile, there was some confusion among the police as to which house the shots were coming from. The rattled deputy who'd had his windows blown out thought it was the second or third house on the block.

A second deputy arrived, a friend of mine named Ronnie. He pulled up near the first house, opened his door, and got out. Tragically, the deranged gunman was in the first house! He put a bead on Ronnie and squeezed the trigger, blasting a volley of deadly 16-gauge buckshot through Ronnie's driver's-side window and into his gut. Ronnie dropped on the spot.

Other deputies arrived and tried to rescue their fallen comrade. The first one who tried was met with a blast that blew his radio off his hip.

Patrol cars swarmed the scene, fourteen in all. The house was surrounded. Yet with all that firepower, the gunman still had Ronnie pinned down beside his unit. Every time somebody tried to get close, the gunman would blast them.

I radioed headquarters for instructions. Our duty officer ordered us to hang tight and wait until he arrived with another team of paramedics.

"Don't try to be heroes," he said.

That didn't sit well with me. My friend Ronnie was dying, and every second counted. Plus, Ronnie and his wife had just had a baby girl. I couldn't let him bleed to death alone on the ground in front of some crazy man's house.

"We have to try to get Ronnie out of there!" I pleaded when my captain arrived. "He's hurt bad!"

As I argued my case, the gawkers began to arrive. In the confusion, the police failed to block off the street or set up a perimeter. People began parking their cars in plain view, as close to the house as they could. There were parents standing out front with little kids running around, all within easy range of the gunman. It was insane.

I shook my head and turned my attention back to Ronnie. "We've got to try," I said.

I finally convinced my captain to let us go. I knew I was risking my life, but I had to do it. I pulled the ambulance as close as I could to Ronnie's patrol car and dashed out with a stretcher. Staying as low to the ground as possible, Marcia and I loaded him. We lifted him slightly and managed to slide him onto the floor of the ambulance.

The gunman, for whatever reason, held his fire.

Ronnie was breathing and his eyes were open, but he was dazed and didn't have a pulse. We drove a block away and stopped to intubate him and start a couple of lines. Then we hauled butt to the hospital. A block from the ER, Ronnie went into cardiac arrest.

In ER, they cracked his chest and shocked him with the cardiac paddles, all to no avail. The doctors discovered, after opening him up, that one of the deer slugs had severed his descending aorta. That meant that even if he'd made it to surgery, it wouldn't have mattered. He was gone.

As I was grieving for my friend, we received a call to go back to the scene. I couldn't believe it. We were being ordered to pick up the shooter! That's just what I wanted to do, rescue the SOB who just killed my buddy!

The shooter was already being treated by another medic team when we arrived. He had placed the shotgun under his chin and blown off his face from his nose down to his Adam's apple. He had two lines and a MAST suit [military antishock trousers] on and was ready to be transported. Unfortunately, he was still alive.

We rushed him to the hospital—to the same ER doctors who tried to save Ronnie. They stabilized him and got him to surgery. As luck would have it, the guy survived. He recovered well enough to stand trial. The jury convicted him of first-degree murder.

I ended up transporting three other injured deputies that afternoon, along with the gunman and his wife. Everyone survived except my friend Ronnie.

The incident affected me deeply, and affects me to this day. As a result of it, I joined our county's critical incident stress debriefing team. We now have a psychologist and peer debriefers to help medics, firefighters, and police officers cope with bad calls.

PATRICK WALSH, PARAMEDIC, ILLINOIS

■ A young boy broke his leg jumping for fruit in an orange grove. We took the chopper and landed in a big open pasture as close as we could to him.

Grabbing my kit, I walked across the field, crawled under a barbed wire fence, crashed through some underbrush, and came out at another open area. I could see the grove just beyond the opposite fence.

Halfway across the field, a bull appeared and decided I didn't belong there. He came stampeding after me. I took off toward the distant fence. The bull kept gaining on me until his murderous horns were only a few feet from my heels.

I reached the fence and did my best martial arts jump-and-roll over three strands of barbed wire. Any second I expected to hear a twang as the beast blasted through the spindly fence and pounced upon me.

The animal stopped short.

We eventually got to the kid, but that's as scared as I've ever been in my life.

MIKE EDWARDS, PARAMEDIC, FLORIDA

8 Laugh Till You Cry

Waiting for the next call can sometimes be the hardest part of the job. To break the boredom, we do the same thing that paramedics and EMTs do worldwide: We tell war stories and complain about how lazy the crews on the other shifts are.

RALPH HENDRICKS, PARAMEDIC, TEXAS

Paramedic humor is of a different breed. We find laughs in the strangest places. Sometimes people are bleeding to death, dying, and something happens that breaks us up. We don't laugh on the scene, of course, but we do back at the unit, when the day is done. We laugh because it keeps us from crying.

"We go back to the station and find something funny about a call, no matter how tragic it was," admits Ohio paramedic Diane Crawford. "If you don't, you just fall apart. Some people think it's pretty sick humor, but the people in the field, they know exactly what I mean. You see everything. You hear everything. You touch everything. There's got to be something funny about it somewhere, and that's the aspect of EMS that you have to find. . . . You can't really connect with these people or it would bother you to the point where you couldn't handle yourself."

Outsiders may feel that we're a twisted bunch, and maybe we are. But people just don't understand. We deal with death and tragedy every day. If we can't relieve the stress with laughter, the relentless onslaught of misery will destroy our souls.

THE STORIES

■ It was a hot, miserably humid summer day. We were dispatched to the residence of an elderly lady who had not been seen by her neighbors for days. When we arrived, we found the small house completely closed. The windows and doors were locked and the shades were drawn. This is common among elderly women who fear crime and realize how helpless they would be against an intruder.

As per policy, we waited for the police to arrive and break into the place. Inside, we found the woman lying facedown on the living room floor. She was wearing a pair of polyester stretch pants and nothing on the top.

The temperature inside the suffocating home had to be nearly a hundred degrees, and the smell was awful. We all became drenched in sweat immediately upon entering. I ignored the heat and studied the victim. She had fallen forward and her arms were pinned inside her toppled walker. Her legs were bent and useless beneath her. She was semiconscious and disoriented, and she was mumbling incoherently.

We immediately removed her from the walker. Her legs still wouldn't straighten. When we tried to take her vitals, she became combative and verbally abusive, cursing us. We ignored her furious wails and treated her for heat exhaustion and dehydration, hooking up an IV.

When we placed her on a gurney, we were finally able to straighten out her legs.

I carried the front of the gurney as we proceeded out of the house. Just as we exited, the woman reached up, clutched the front of my blouse in a death grip, and ripped it and my bra completely off. There I stood, topless, in front of my fellow paramedics, the police, and the dozens of neighbors who had gathered around, attracted by the commotion.

I had two choices—let go of the gurney to cover myself and drop the woman on her head, or give everyone a peep show as we made our way through the crowd to the distant ambulance.

The crowd cheered as I chose option number two.

DONNA

■ My partner and I arrived at the scene of a shooting in a bad part of town. A guy had been shot in the stomach, and a big crowd gathered. My partner addressed the injured man.

"Where's the son of a bitch who shot you?"

The patient lifted up his hand and pointed to a big man standing right next to me!

My partner, always fast on his feet, didn't miss a beat.

"Well, you probably deserved it, then!"

PATRICK WALSH, PARAMEDIC, ILLINOIS

■ We had a guy in our unit, Bob, who was a straitlaced Mormon. Never cussed or peeked at *Playboy* or anything like that. He was squeaky clean.

One night a man came to the station house complaining of some unidentified physical ailment.

"I'll handle this," Bob said. "You guys go on to bed."

It was pretty late, so we took him up on it.

About a half-hour later, we were toned on a call. We jumped from bed, hopped into our boots and pants, and ran to the truck. When we reached the garage, we all stopped as one. Our eyes bulged and our jaws dropped. There was a man standing bare-assed in the middle of the garage with his pants and underpants down around his ankles. Bob was on his knees in front of him with his face and hands buried in the man's groin area.

Bob's face peered out from behind the man's hairy ass.

"You guys go on," he said matter-of-factly. "I'll follow later."

We looked at each other in shock, then jumped on the truck. Someone was injured and needed help, so there was no time to deal with Bob. We ran the call, but we were all numb. We couldn't shake the image of good ol' Bob down on his knees.

Back at the station, Bob and his patient explained what happened. The man had gotten a cock ring, a device used to prolong erections, caught on his penis. He couldn't get it off and was panicking. Good Samaritan Bob retrieved a ring cutter from our unit and was performing the intricate surgery when we were awakened.

We laughed about that for months.

DAN COUCH AND MANNY DEVALLE, PARAMEDICS, ARIZONA

■ An Hispanic guy called and said his wife had been hit by a Jeep. We dispatched it as a code four, a motor vehicle accident. The crew was ready for the worst. Pedestrian-auto accidents can be gruesome.

The medics picked up the wife and checked her out. She didn't seem to be the worse for wear. They called it back as a personal injury. I radioed for clarification because I needed to log it correctly.

"Is it a personal injury or a motor vehicle accident?"

Laughter rang out on the radio.

"It's a minor personal injury," the paramedic announced.

Back at the unit, the guys explained that the caller and his wife had been visiting a small farm, where they were petting a goat. The wife bent over, and the goat rammed her in the rear end. The husband mistook the goat for a sheep. When he called, his heavy accent did the rest, translating *sheep* into *Jeep*.

MELANIE CARR, DISPATCH SUPERVISOR, FLORIDA

■ We were dispatched to a Hyatt Regency on a minor "general weakness" call. I was in my first week of training and was running with my field instructor, who was very exacting about how to take vitals. The patient was this absolutely gorgeous twenty-five-year-old woman wearing a bright red knit dress. Not only was she a knockout, but she was very well rounded. In the ambulance, I reached the point of my general assessment where I needed to record lung sounds. My field instructor refused to allow me to take them through clothing. I hesitated. Back then I was a naive, backward sort of person, very shy and introverted. I didn't know how I was going to get lung sounds on this beautiful woman and I didn't want to try. I nervously stuck my head into the front of the ambulance.

"Do I have to take lung sounds on this lady?" I asked my instructor.

"Are they equal on both side, no wheezing, no rales?" he answered.

"I don't know."

He gave me that "Well, find out, stupid!" look. I went back to the patient and explained that I needed to go under her clothes.

She didn't protest.

I slid the stethoscope down the left side of her dress and told her to breathe. I heard nothing, not a sound. My heart raced.

What's going on? I thought.

I moved the stethoscope over to the right side. She took a deep breath. I still heard nothing.

Those were the upper lobes. Next I had to listen to the bases, which entailed weaving my hand further inside her bra in and around her mountainous breasts. With trembling fingers, I eased the scope in—and heard absolute silence. As far as I could tell, this woman wasn't even alive! There I was, with my hand deep into her bosom, and I suddenly realized that I didn't have the earpieces of the stethoscope in my ears—they were hanging around my neck!

I looked at her sheepishly. She nodded her head and gave me the sweetest, most knowing smile. I scrambled to put the earpieces in my ears and instantly began hearing wonderfully healthy lung sounds.

JEFF COLE, PARAMEDIC, FLORIDA

■ We received a call to go to a local bar for a possible fractured leg. When we got there, we found a lady moaning and crying in pain. Somehow, in the push of the crowd, her ankle had been crushed.

The bar wasn't the kind of place where someone's misfortune was going to spoil the fun for everybody else. The loud rock music and lively activity onstage proceeded as normal, despite our presence.

This particular activity happened to be a wet T-shirt contest. There were three of us EMTs on the call, all men. As we tried to work on this lady, our eyes kept being drawn to the wet, seminaked women bouncing around just a few feet away.

The injured woman wasn't happy about that. She kept screaming at us to pay attention to her ankle. She was right. We were there to treat her, not to enjoy a show. We went back to work.

The crowd suddenly whooped, drawing our gaze back to the stage. A particularly well endowed contestant ended an extremely seductive striptease by ripping apart her wet T-shirt and allowing the shreds to fall to the floor. As she ripped, she came close to us and blew us kisses.

"Can you rescue *these,* guys?" she teased, squeezing her supple breasts.

We were mesmerized into complete inactivity. Suddenly the lady with the broken ankle let out a blood-curdling scream that could be heard halfway around the state.

"My ankle, dammit!"

The temptress on the stage laughed, jiggled her contest-winning boobs at us, and continued her dance.

It was by far the slowest rescue we've ever performed.

KEVIN HOLLEY, EMT, FLORIDA

■ An attractive young woman baby-sitting her sister's children had had a private party after the kids fell asleep. She drank and smoked and titillated herself with her brother-in-law's vast collection of porno magazines and homemade X-rated videos. She subsequently passed out with a cigarette burning and set the house on fire. The kids, eight and ten, rescued her from the deadly slumber just as the king-size waterbed burst.

We treated the lady and the children for minor smoke inhalation and then went about dealing with the fire. After drowning the blaze, we searched the house for any further complications.

"Hear that?" my partner asked.

I stopped and listened. There was an audible buzz coming from somewhere.

We combed through the smoldering home to locate the cause of the disquieting noise. Was an electrical outlet or cord exposed? Was some appliance ready to explode?

Our ears led us to the master bedroom, the place where the fire originated. It was quite a room. The waterbed sat under a mirrored canopy and rested upon an elevated pedestal with a dozen drawers.

We cocked our heads and determined that the buzzing was coming from one of the drenched drawers. As we searched, we began unearthing a plethora of strange sex toys and weird gadgets that obviously went along with the porno magazines and videos. The kinky couple must have owned at least two dozen different dildos, in every shape, size, and color.

Searching the drawers further, my partner finally uncovered the cause of the persistent buzz. He smiled as he waved a huge vibrating egg with the switch still very much in the on position.

"No wonder she fell asleep," he cracked, nodding at the wildly throbbing device. "She was exhausted!"

HOWARD CLARK, PARAMEDIC, ILLINOIS

■ The eight-year-old was in the bathroom on his hands and knees when we arrived. The dispatcher had said he'd been poisoned, but he didn't appear to be very ill.

"What's the matter?" I asked.

"I, uh, I, uh, I accidentally swallowed a bee and it stung me in the throat."

There was something fishy about his story. I glanced over at his little brother. The tot looked like he was about to explode with a secret.

"He threw up outside!" the younger boy blurted.

"Can you show us where?" I asked, needing to inspect the discharge.

"Sure!" The little boy beamed, obviously thrilled with the assignment. "Follow me!"

The eager tyke led us to a spot outside. I bent down to study the puke. There was no sign of a bee. There were, however, at least two dozen black caterpillars with gray stripes.

"Those things are toxic," my partner intoned in his best entomologist voice. "No wonder he's sick."

I ran back upstairs to grill the kid. He sheepishly confessed that another boy had promised to give him a snake if he'd eat fifty caterpillars. He made it to twenty-seven before he barfed.

We placed the kid on a gurney and took him to the hospital as a precaution. The media got wind of the story and played it big. The television stations, newspapers, and radio all wanted a piece of the caterpillar boy. For a while he was on television more than the governor. And even though he never made it to fifty, he got his snake—compliments of the morning DJs at a local radio station.

RICH FITSHEN, EMT, ARIZONA

■ We arrived on the scene of a bad motorcycle accident. A young EMT fresh out of training led the way. The driver's leg was scraped, broken, and just plain mangled. He was screaming in agony. The young medic knelt down beside him and asked, "Have you ever had this problem before?"

Despite the condition of the poor victim, I had to turn away to keep from bursting out laughing. When I looked at the young medic, he just shrugged.

"That's what the book says to ask every patient."

RON BURTON, PARAMEDIC, OHIO

■ I was crawling on the floor in a burning house, dragging in a hose, when an unnerving warning came over the radio.

"Be advised that the owner said there are a large number of reptiles in the house."

I stopped dead in my tracks and stared wide-eyed at my partner through the smoke. He motioned for me to get on the radio.

"Did you say 'reptiles'? Can you repeat that?" I asked.

"That's affirmative," the dispatcher replied. "The owner says there are a large number of reptiles in the house."

"Is that 'a large number of reptiles' or 'a number of large reptiles'?"

"Large number."

My partner and I shuddered with fear. Crawling around in a burning building is dangerous enough without having to worry about coming face to face with a king cobra! And since the house was on fire, any reptiles we encountered weren't going to be in the best of moods.

"What kind of reptiles? Snakes? Iguanas? What are we talking about here?" I demanded, the hairs on the back of my neck starting to stand up.

"Unknown at this time."

That answer didn't cut it. This was Arizona. Reptiles and arachnids in Arizona usually mean three things— rattlesnakes, scorpions, and poisonous Gila monsters!

"Can you please clarify? We're in here on our hands and knees in the middle of a fire in a house that might be full of giant killer lizards."

The radio went silent. We waited a few harrowing minutes, certain we were about to be attacked by an angry crocodile.

"The owner says they're nonpoisonous reptiles."

"Yeah, right," I barked. "An Arizona reptile dealer? Are you kidding? The guy wants us to save his house! What the hell do you expect him to say?"

"That's all the information we have."

Scared as we were—and we were terrified—we proceeded to bring in the hose and douse the fire. Sure enough, when the smoke cleared, we discovered that the place was packed wall to wall with cages and aquariums full of exotic reptiles—including scores of nasty-looking lizards, snakes, and whatnot. There was also a tank full of tarantulas, whose existence the owner had conveniently failed to mention.

We put on our paramedic hats and saved most of the slimy critters—although I'm not sure we were doing anybody a favor.

KURT MICKELSON, PARAMEDIC, ARIZONA

■ Looking good on the job can be nearly as important as a save. Plus the crowds of nosy neighbors that invariably gather at the scene of accidents and emergencies are expecting a show. Over the years, I've learned some important tips that can turn a bad day into a tolerable one.

- Hold the intravenous fluid bag, catheter sheath, penlight, or anything else between one's teeth while moving a patient to the unit. Crowds especially love this.
- Pop the little yellow caps off the D-50 bolus and syringe so that they come off at the same time and make a graceful arc through the air at least two feet above your head.
- Clear the air out of a syringe by squirting the medication so that it catches the light in a sparkling glitter as it tinkles to the floor.
- Talk in EMS lingo whenever a crowd is listening in. Toss in such terms as *bicarb, D/W, KED, micros, MAI, tubing,* etc.
- Yell "Everybody clear!" with authority even when no one is in the way.
- Always look serious, thoughtful, and knowledgeable even if you don't know what the heck the

reading on the EKG you just ran means.

- Snap the tourniquet off just after the hitting the vein so that it makes a neat popping sound.
- Fashion tip: Antishock trousers always look cool even when they're not inflated.
- Fashion tip II: Drape around your neck a stethoscope that is color-coordinated with your clothing.

On the other hand, looking good can also be accomplished by not looking bad. Here are favorite paramedic and EMT no-nos.

- Don't forget to unhook the oxygen tubing before removing the patient from the ambulance.
- Don't forget to remove a tourniquet after you hit that hard-to-find vein with the IV. Patients usually require a clear blood flow to all parts of their body, and ER nurses aren't happy when a patient's arm turns black.
- Never yell "Everybody clear" and then proceed to shock yourself with the defibrillator.
- Try to avoid having the cot wheels roll over the IV tubes, yanking them out. Patients, neighbors, and family members hate when that happens.
- Try not to vomit after doing mouth-to-mouth resuscitation. This grosses out everyone but small boys.
- Don't dramatically scoop up the trauma kit on the scene without having secured the latches.
- Avoid running out ten miles of EKG paper because you forgot to turn off the monitor.
- Always avoid getting your nifty, color-coordinated stethoscope tangled up in the ambulance shoulder harness as you exit the rig in front of a big crowd.

RALPH HENDRICKS, PARAMEDIC, TEXAS

■ I was running with a woman, Dawn, who had an aversion to blood. She would get nauseated if she got real close to it. But she was very good at patient relations—talking to people and getting information from them. So we had an agreement that if it was anything she couldn't cope with, I would deal with the blood and she'd do the interviewing and paperwork. If there was no blood, we'd take turns.

We were called to a trailer park one afternoon. It was freezing outside, and it had snowed heavily the night before. I was the first one to the door. I knocked. An elderly gentleman answered.

"What's the problem?" I asked.

"My testicles are swollen," he whispered.

Not quite sure I heard him right, I asked him to repeat it.

"My testicles are swollen," he said, a bit louder.

I immediately turned to Dawn, took the clipboard away from her, and motioned for her to go ahead and examine him. She walked over. As I suspected, she hadn't heard him say what his problem was.

"Sir, what's the problem?"

"*My balls are swollen!*" he said in a loud, irritated voice.

I looked at Dawn. She appeared shocked and completely dumbfounded. I turned around and stifled a laugh.

We eventually stuck the driver, a male EMT trainee, with the task of examining the patient. He applied an ice pack to the subject's testicles and transported him to the hospital.

Back at the unit, as news spread of my prank, Dawn shot me an icy stare and swore to get even.

DONNA

■ I was on a mountain rescue treating a patient who had fallen to a ledge. I didn't have a portable radio with me, so I was yelling my findings down to my partner, an inexperienced EMT, at the foot of the mountain. He relayed the information to a doctor.

The old-fashioned method of communication produced some strange moments. I screamed that the patient had an "acute abdomen," meaning her stomach had swollen and was rock hard from internal injuries. My partner scratched his head and told the doctor that I'd said she had a "cute abdomen."

Fortunately, the doctor knew what I meant.

Similarly, the doctor wanted me to give the woman "a lactated ringer," which is an IV solution. It was relayed to me as a "laxative ringer."

"That should take care of her cute abdomen," my baffled partner cracked.

ROY RYALS, PARAMEDIC, ARIZONA

■ One of my dispatchers went off shift and decided to ride with the paramedics for a while to get out of the control room and get a feel for what the street units go through. She hopped into one of the station wagon ambulances that have emergency lights on them. She was hungry and asked the medic if they could stop first and grab something to eat at a nearby convenience store. He said sure.

As she was gathering her things to go into the store, she looked over and spotted a man coming out of the door wearing a towel over his head and waving a gun.

"They're being robbed!" she exclaimed.

"Who?" the medic asked.

"The store. Look!"

The medic glanced up. The robber, at that precise instance, noticed him. Their eyes met.

Inside the unit, the EMS crew had a bad feeling about what was going to happen next. Sure enough, the dimwitted robber saw the emergency lights, thought they were the police, and let them have it. The medics and dispatcher hit the floor. Glass shattered all around them, raining down like a hailstorm. A few seconds later, everything quieted down. The dispatcher poked her head above the crumbled windshield. The robber was gone. She glanced around the inside of the unit. There were bullet holes everywhere. She looked at the medic in disbelief. "You wanted to know what it's like on the streets?" the exasperated paramedic said. "*This* is what it's like on the streets!"

MELANIE CARR, DISPATCH SUPERVISOR, FLORIDA

■ Not only was an auto accident victim decapitated, but parts of her body were scattered around everywhere. I had to gather them up. The hardest part to deal with was an eye that was just lying there on the street. As I bent down to pick it up, a state trooper walked over and said, "Here's looking at you, kid."

DIANE CRAWFORD, PARAMEDIC, OHIO

■ We were at the station watching the movie *The Exorcist* when we were dispatched on a call about someone who was mentally ill. My partner, Pat Crawford, and I arrived and knocked on the door. A woman answered and asked us a strange question.

"Are you guys also drunk?"

"Excuse me?"

She led us inside. A mom-and-pop team of volunteer EMTs was already there. They were both in their sixties and were definitely on the sauce. We brushed them aside and took over.

The scene got stranger by the moment. Two young girls, about eight and six, were standing wide-eyed in the living room. They looked like they'd seen a ghost. Back in the bedroom, there was a skinny, naked man, about 120 pounds, lying on the bed. Another man, about 300 pounds, was on top of him, holding him down.

"What's going on?" I asked.

The woman explained that the little man was a preacher. He had been speaking at a revival or something for five days straight without eating. Apparently the devil took advantage of his weakened condition and grabbed him.

Remember, we had just been watching *The Exorcist*, a film about demonic possession that's one of the scariest movies ever made. It's so scary one of the paramedics at the station had refused to watch it. And now we had to deal with a man who was saying that the devil had him. Fortunately, my partner knew just what to do. With a dramatic flourish, he launched into his best Ernest Ainsley/Jimmy Swaggart impression.

"What's wrong with you, my child?"

"The devil's in me and he won't let go!" the little man cried.

"The devil's in you? Lord have mercy! We'll have to pray." My partner took his hand. "Do you believe in Jesus Christ as your personal savior?"

"Yes, I do! Oh, yes, I do. But the devil's in me and he's got a hold of me and he won't turn me loose!"

"Well, grab my hand. Feel the power of Jesus in my hand," my partner preached.

"I feel it! I feel it!" the man responded.

"Do you believe in Jesus Christ as your savior?"

"Oh, yes, I do! I do, Lord. Please help me!"

"I'm helping you, my son. I'm helping you. Feel the power of Jesus that's in my arm going into your body."

"I feel it! I feel it," the man repeated.

"Okay, get up from that bed and get on that stretcher!"

Sure enough, the little man hopped off the bed and lay down on the stretcher. We were able to get him to the hospital, get some fluids in him, and bring him around.

I don't know if his blood sugar was out of whack or what, but his wife's story was pretty much what happened. He returned home from the revival, took off all his clothes, and started showing his two little daughters the devil.

PATRICK WALSH, PARAMEDIC, ILLINOIS

■ I was working on Thanksgiving morning when we received a call about a possible drowning. We got there as fast as we could and pulled up to the lake. Two Mexicans had been duck hunting for Thanksgiving. One guy swam out to retrieve a duck and never come back. His friend kept diving in but never found him. When we arrived, the friend was sprawled out on the bank in near shock from the ordeal.

The fire department divers had been called, so we concentrated on the guy on the shore. He was exhausted but okay. We put him in the unit and took off for the hospital.

A mile or two down the road, things started flying off the ambulance engine. I pulled over and called for another unit. While I was waiting outside, I suddenly felt a stinging sensation all over my body. I was covered with fire ants! I was standing on a huge mound, and they had crawled all the way to my neck!

My partner started taking off my blouse, pants, socks, everything, right there in the middle of the road!

After we knocked off the ants, I got dressed and sat down inside the unit. My partner was really concerned because I'm allergic to bees and I had hundreds of bites.

"Are you sure you're okay?" he asked.

"I'm fine," I insisted. "I'll go to the hospital with the patient and let them check me out."

Well, the longer I sat there, the worse I felt. My throat was closing up. Then I went into anaphylactic shock! The second unit arrived and rushed me to the hospital. The

ER doctors hooked up an IV and were able to stabilize me. With their help, I made it home for Thanksgiving dinner.

Back at the squad, the big joke was that my partner was always trying to get into my pants and now he finally had—in the middle of the street!

DIANE CRAWFORD, PARAMEDIC, OHIO

■ "Now *this* might be fun," I said with a wink when the call came in to respond to a local strip joint.

"It's probably just an old drunk," my partner cautioned.

"Let's keep our fingers crossed."

An inordinate number of fire trucks were already on the scene when we arrived. I figured there must have been a hellacious bar fight. Inside, a group of county paramedic-firefighters and EMTs were kneeling in a circle near the stage. It was obvious that the entire shift had responded. I edged closer. A beautiful redhead with huge breasts and a body that could make a man's heart stop was lying on the floor. The exotic dancer had fallen coming down the stairs of the stage and had twisted her ankle.

Despite the extraspecial attention she was getting from all the paramedics and EMTs, I couldn't help but notice that no one had bothered to cover her up. She was lying there stark naked, and had been for quite some time.

The eager-beaver county medics slowly placed her on a backboard and reluctantly handed her over to us—still unadorned. When we reached the door, I stopped.

"Don't you think we should, uh, cover her before we bring her outside?" I asked my partner.

"Uh, no. Why?" he answered in his best Beavis and Butt-head voice.

I laughed, shook my head, set the backboard down,

and laid a towel across the patient's gorgeous body. Another dancer appeared with the redhead's dress, which she put on in the ambulance.

Suffice it to say, she lived to dance again.

GEORGE RUIZ, EMT, ARIZONA

◼ A commercial airliner arrived at the airport. After the passengers were unloaded, the stewardess went to awaken a sleeping woman. There was no response. When we arrived, we determined that not only had the woman passed away, she'd been dead for hours. They had a layover in Atlanta, and apparently she was already dead at that point. Since she didn't have to change planes, the flight attendants left her alone.

The woman had been in a sitting position for an extended period of time, and rigor mortis set in. She was stiff as a board. We had to somehow get her off the plane. What we did reminded me of the Chevy Chase movie in which Aunt Edna [played in the film by Imogene Coca] died in the car in the middle of nowhere. The kids were too afraid to sit by her, so they had to strap her to the roof of the vehicle. She was stiff and was propped up there in a sitting position with a blanket over her.

That's what we did. We couldn't straighten the woman and lay her down, so we had to put her in a chair stretcher and cover her with a blanket, just like in the movie. Then we had to wheel her through the crowded main terminal to reach the clinic area. I'll never forget the looks on the passengers' faces. So many people are afraid of flying to begin with, and there we were, wheeling this corpse through the terminal in a sitting position.

TAMMY MAURER, PARAMEDIC, FLORIDA

■ We were called out to this country club. A man had fallen on some steep stairs. He was a big man—he barely fit on the stretcher. I'm not the strongest person in the world, and I was running with a medic who had a bad back. We tried to get the patient down the stairs but lost control. The guy started bouncing down the steps by himself! There was an incline at the bottom, so he continued sliding down the incline. My partner and I frantically chased the runaway gurney. We finally caught up, apologized, and maneuvered the patient into the unit.

At the hospital, my knee gave just as we were bringing him out of the ambulance. I collapsed underneath the stretcher. The guy fell over and bounced on the pavement. He came to a stop right next to me.

"Honey, are you okay?" he asked, peering at me under the stretcher.

"Yeah, how about you?"

"I could be better."

I laughed so hard over that. I guess you had to be there.

DIANE CRAWFORD, PARAMEDIC, OHIO

■ A car ran off the road and hit a telephone pole. We couldn't get the door open, so I peered inside. The driver was sitting there, calm as could be, bleeding profusely from the head while smoking a big fat marijuana joint. The guy was definitely one toke over the line.

"Put that down!" I yelled. "The police'll be here any second. You're in enough trouble already!"

He just flashed a smile and kept puffing away.

A corner of his windshield had popped out, so I crawled through and plopped down beside him.

"Hi," he said. "What's happening, pretty lady? Want a hit?"

"You're happening," I said, swabbing the blood off the gash in his head. "Now put that thing down."

He took another big drag, then flicked the roach away.

The firefighters arrived and cut the door open. We lifted the guy from his seat and put him on a backboard. He passed out the moment he lay down.

Inside the unit, as we motored to the hospital, I did what we call a "ninety-second survey." That's where you start from the top of the head and literally feel the body all the way down for injuries or trauma. When I reached his pelvic area, it was as if I'd flicked a switch. He jerked to life and sat straight up.

"Get your hands off my dick!" he yelled, then launched a right cross that popped me right between the eyes, breaking my eyeglasses. I did a back flip, bounced against the jump seat, then rolled to my feet.

My anger cut through the pain and penetrated the stars spinning around my head. I was ready to lash the guy down and give him a piece of my mind. However, when I hovered over him, he was out again—stone cold out of it. Apparently he'd had some kind of knee-jerk reaction, only it was more of a dick-jerk reaction that connected right into his consciousness. Damnedest thing I've ever seen.

We got him to the hospital without further incident. He recovered to toke again.

DONNA

■ An elderly woman tried to wake her husband in the middle of the night and couldn't get him to move. She covered him with a sheet and called 911 to pick up his body.

I waited for a police officer, then we entered the house together. The officer approached the bed and pulled down the sheet.

"Whoa, whoa! What's happening?" the man said, springing up to a sitting position.

The officer and I nearly jumped through the ceiling. Our hearts raced.

"Y-Your w-wife said you were dead! Said she c-couldn't w-wake you!" I stammered, trying to catch my breath.

"I'm not dead! I was just sleeping. What's the matter with you, Erma?"

We looked at Erma. She just shrugged.

"I've got to get a better job," the police officer sighed outside, placing his hand to his still-pounding heart. "You're going be carrying me in that ambulance one of these days."

"That's if I don't end up there first," I said.

MARK SECRIST, EMT, ARIZONA

■ After treating a pedestrian hit by a car, we sped off to the hospital. Some firefighters who had helped us at the scene left all the doors and compartments open in the ambulance. As we drove away, stretchers and backboards fell out of the vehicle and started bouncing down the road.

I pulled the ambulance to a halt. My partner lept out.

"I'll take care of this," she exclaimed. "You get the patient to the hospital."

I continued on, wheeling the injured man into the ER. When I came back outside, I discovered my partner unloading our stuff from the car of a bewildered-looking family. Included in the group was a small boy who was standing there wide-eyed, gawking at the ambulances and lively emergency room.

Apparently my partner had jumped out into the street, waved her EMT badge, and commandeered the first passing car! She stuffed our wayward medical equipment into it and ordered the father to the hospital on the double. He'd dutifully obeyed.

PATRICK WALSH, PARAMEDIC, FLORIDA

■ A mother accidentally locked her toddler inside her sport utility vehicle. In Arizona, such an accident can be deadly. The intense desert sun can heat an auto interior to nearly two hundred degrees in a matter of minutes.

We used our jimmies and slim jims and all our available tools to try to open the door. No luck. It was a new Trooper, Blazer, or the like and had been specifically designed to resist break-ins.

Desperate, I started making goofy faces to try to befriend the little tot. He smiled and laughed. I motioned toward the lock and made a pulling motion.

"We tried that. It won't work," my partner said. "He's too young."

Undeterred, I tried again. I made a big face, pointed to the lock, and went into my wildly exaggerated pantomime act. The boy reached out his tiny paw and pulled up the lock.

HOWARD CLARK, PARAMEDIC, ARIZONA

■ My old supervisor used to fingerprint bodies for the police department. He was always complaining how tough it was because of rigor mortis. It was like trying to get a print from a store mannequin. This one body arrived at the morgue in a condition that solved the problem. It came in three parts—both arms had been severed.

Great, the supervisor thought. *This'll be an easy one.*

He wrapped one of the limbs in a plastic bag, then stuck it under his arm to place the hand on the print sheet.

As he did this, he got the feeling that someone was watching. He turned and spotted a janitor standing behind him. She looked at him, mentally counted arms, then dropped her mop and took off screaming down the hallway.

MIKE SCHULZE, PARAMEDIC, NEW YORK

I was a new, gung ho medic. We received a call to respond to a migrant camp. Instead of waiting for the police, I just barged in—to the wrong address! Worse, it was a bad choice of wrong addresses. I was right smack in the middle of a drug deal!

The heavily armed men pointed their weapons at me. I'm certain that if I'd been wearing the uniform I wear today, which looks like a SWAT cop's coveralls, I'd be dead. But back then we wore medical smocks.

"Get the hell out of here!" one of the dealers ordered, waving his weapon. "Nobody needs a stinkin' doctor!"

I did as I was told.

NAME WITHHELD, PARAMEDIC, CALIFORNIA

■ An intoxicated patient was having difficulty breathing. He owned a monster Rottweiler, and we kept yelling at him to put the dog in a bathroom so we could treat him. He was too drunk to comply. The tension increased rapidly. The drunk was agitated, the dog was agitated, we were agitated, and the police were agitated. Unable to calm the situation, the police gave up. The two officers withdrew and stood next to our ambulance.

"A friend of his is inside," the first officer explained. "He's trying to get him to leash the dog."

Suddenly the friend came flying out of the door. "The dog's loose and he's pissed!"

The friend disappeared into the next house. A second later, this furious monster dog came rocketing out. Apparently the owner passed out. But before he did, he barfed all over the dog! The dog was madder than hell and was going to make somebody pay.

The moment they saw the dog, the rest of the crew scattered like quail. One cop ducked into his unit while the other jumped on the hood. My partners bolted for the ambulance and shut the back doors.

Me? I just froze. Everything happened so fast, I couldn't even move. So there I was, standing between the patrol car and the ambulance, and this raging Rottweiler was five feet in front of me. He was snarling. He was barking. He had puke rolling off him. He was definitely one pissed-off pup!

I sensed that he either wanted to pass between the vehicles or eat me alive. He was debating which move to make. I was debating my own moves. I'd always heard that you can't show a dog fear or else they'll attack, so I struck a martial arts pose.

"You don't want to bite me," I said.

He charged. I stuck out my forearm. I was going to sacrifice it to keep the dog from getting my throat. At the last second, the dog hooked right and blew past me, disappearing behind the cars.

I heaved a sigh of relief and fetched my partners. We entered the house. The man inside was simply drunk and didn't want to be taken to the hospital. All that excitement for a "no transport."

ANDREW ARNOLD, PARAMEDIC, TEXAS

■ A doctor couldn't sleep and decided to go for a late-night drive. He got into a wreck, and his car caught fire. The accident scene was like a Fourth of July celebration gone bad. Thunderous mortars and colorful roman candles were whistling, spinning, and slicing through the air left and right. Cherry bombs exploded like grenades all around us.

The guy had a trunk full of illegal fireworks! We had to hunker down and dodge every manner of holiday explosive to put out the blaze and keep the rest of the potent load from igniting.

The doctor made it out of the vehicle okay, at least physically. Aside from the illegal fireworks, he also had an unregistered .44 Magnum under the front seat. The highly agitated police ended up tossing him in jail for a few days.

BILL ROSE, PARAMEDIC, OHIO

■ An airplane crashed into a building and exploded in a ball of fire, consuming a man who was inside talking on the telephone. The body was burned beyond recognition.

During the accident, a tiny sixteen-penny nail had fallen from somewhere and stuck into the man's chest.

"We obviously know what killed this man," the medical examiner said, plucking the nail from the guy's horribly charred body. "It was this nail!"

JOHN OBJARTEL, PARAMEDIC, IOWA

■ We were sitting in a pizza restaurant waiting for our order. We had just returned from a traumatic auto accident and started talking shop, describing the event rather graphically.

A woman in the booth behind us started to retch. Her husband had to escort her out of the joint.

"Can't you guys talk about anything else in a restaurant?" he growled as they left.

PAT CRAWFORD, PARAMEDIC, FLORIDA

■ The young couple was lying stark naked in their bed. They appeared to be in perfect health.

"What seems to be the problem?" I inquired.

They kind of looked at each other. The man finally spoke.

"I, uh, I, uh . . . I couldn't do it!"

I glanced at my partner in disbelief. The guy had called 911 because he couldn't get it up!

As we talked further, I could see that this was apparently the first time it ever happened to him, and they were both very distressed about it. To him, it was a true medical emergency.

RANDY MEININGER, PARAMEDIC, NEBRASKA

9 The Weird and Bizarre

> My problem is recurring nightmares. It's always this baby in a car wreck. He's alive and alert and looking up at me. People are standing around. "Help him! Help him!" they shout. All the baby's organs are outside his body. I have to put them back in the right place. The dream is tremendously stressful. I keep having it and having it, and it just eats me up.
>
> **ANDREW ARNOLD, PARAMEDIC, TEXAS**

Aside from everything else we have to deal with, paramedics and EMTs encounter a good dose of spine-tingling, blood-chilling strangeness. And sometimes, just when things appear to be proceeding as normal, fate throws us a whopper of a surprise ending.

At times, I've felt that *Twilight Zone* host Rod Serling was riding in the ambulance with me, right next to his pal Alfred Hitchcock. Upon arriving at a scene—imagine a dark, creaky house hidden among the trees—the two famous purveyors of all things creepy would hop out and provide a narrative introduction to what I was about to encounter inside.

Whether it's a full-fledged terror or a quirky slice of life-or-death, things can sure get freaky out there.

THE STORIES

■ A hospital bed had been set up in the living room of the house. It was obvious that the elderly man on the bed had been ill for a long time. He was on his last legs. The grim reaper was all but carrying him away when I arrived. Aside from myriad other problems, the patient had gone into cardiac arrest.

I lifted him off the bed, laid him on the floor, and began CPR. An old woman suddenly appeared and went nuts. "Leave him alone!" she screamed, pounding my back with her gnarled fists. "He's been sick too long! Let him go."

That, of course, was a moral and legal decision outside my authority. To the contrary, the law stated that I had to keep performing CPR until I was either told to stop by a doctor, was relieved by another medic, or was too exhausted to continue. I ignored the woman and did my job.

"Leave him alone," she ranted, punching and kicking me with renewed fervor. "Let him go!"

I refused.

The woman then jumped on my back like a demented witch and tried to drag me off. Luckily for me, she was nearly as weak and frail as her husband, and for the most part I was able to brush her away. She eventually retreated to try a new tactic—she grabbed a telephone and dialed her physician.

"I want you to tell her to stop what she's doing," she demanded. "Stop the CPR!"

The doctor chose not to order me to cease and desist.

Stymied on that front, the old woman nevertheless remained fiercely determined to let her husband die. She proceeded to lock all the doors in the house so the second wave of medics couldn't come inside with their specialized equipment.

A police officer knocked next, and she let him in. That, however, was only because she figured she could force him to order me to stop. Her logic backfired. Instead of yanking me off, the cop prevented her from beating on me any further.

By that time, I was physically and emotionally drained—and pretty peeved to boot. I'd responded to the beeper in my personal car and didn't have any equipment. With constant distractions, no help, and no medical tools, I wasn't able to get an airway on the guy. Totally exasperated, I gave the crazy old bag her wish.

"The hell with this," I muttered. "This is done. I'm done. I quit."

Convinced that her beloved husband was indeed history, the lady finally opened the door and let everybody in. But, just in case, she refused to allow us to move the body. No doubt she was terrified by the prospect of us reviving him in the ambulance.

The next day, the woman filed an official complaint against me with the state. That was a good one—I was cited for trying to save someone's life.

"We tossed it into the circular file," a licensing official assured me.

The final irony was that this woman had been very active in fund-raising for our unit and had always made a solid personal contribution as well. Because of me, she ended both activities. That's the thanks you get.

DONNA

■ A man and his wife were speeding down I-74 on a motorcycle when a thunderstorm hit. The rain came down so hard they were forced to pull over, and the wife hopped off the powerful machine. Just as the man was about to join her, a bolt of lightning crashed through the clouds and struck him square on the shoulder. It speared him at the precise moment when he had one foot on the grass and the other on the motorcycle. That grounded the man and sent the million-volt charge coursing through his body.

My father, Richard Neibert, was on duty as a fire-fighter–first-responder. He received the call, jumped into a basic life support ambulance, and, together with a pair of EMTs, was the first to arrive at the scene. The crew found the man sprawled in a nearby ditch. His wife was pacing in front of him, screaming hysterically,

"Take the wife to the unit and calm her down," one of the EMTs directed. "Get her away from here."

Dad put his arms around the woman's shoulders, comforted her the best he could, and sat her down on the back step of the unit. The second medic grabbed the radio and requested a Lifeline helicopter. The pilot radioed back that the storm was too intense.

"You'll have to go with a land ALS unit," he said, explaining that they'd have better luck with an advanced life support ambulance.

Although I was off duty, I heard about the incident over my scanner and raced to the scene in my own car. A paramedic named Kim Cobb also picked up the broadcast and came in her vehicle. Shortly after I arrived, my dad's ambulance went completely dead. Both the engine and the electrical power shut down simultaneously—an unusual occurrence, because they're separate systems. Even the backup power in the bed of the ambulance mysteriously went out.

The darkness caused the man's wife to panic. She began screaming again. "Leave him alone! Let him die in peace! Please leave him alone," she cried. Dad again tried to calm her.

As Kim held a tarp overhead to shield us from the rain,

I inspected the patient. The lightning struck his right shoulder and came out through his groin and leg. The zipper on his pants had been welded shut, the stem on his watch melted into the timepiece, and his shoes had blown completely off. The burns caused by the massive electrical jolt were still giving off a bluish smoke. The patient had no pulse and wasn't breathing. Hard as we tried, we couldn't revive him.

Suddenly a strange woman appeared among us. I looked up and felt a chill sweep over my body. The woman was wearing a long black wool dress with a high collar, like something out of the nineteenth century. She had on black boots and was holding a Bible in her hands. She had flowing black hair, big brown eyes, and dark skin. An antique hand-crafted silver cross hung from her neck. A matching ring decorated her long, slim fingers. She looked like a Native American and was by far the most beautiful woman I've ever seen in my life.

"I can save him," she said in a soft, silky voice that cut through my soul. "I need to talk to him."

Normally we don't let civilians anywhere near a patient on the scene, especially someone who was so oddly dressed. For some reason, though, I moved aside.

"Let her do what she needs to do," I heard myself say. "She can't hurt him."

The woman dropped to her knees, placed the Bible over the man's heart, and began to chant in a language none of us understood. As she chanted, she repeatedly raised the Bible and pounded it on his chest. She followed that by reciting the Twenty-third Psalm, the one that begins "The Lord is my shepherd, I shall not want. . . ."

We all stood stunned, mesmerized by the eerie scene that was playing out before us. It was only then that I realized that the woman was completely dry. We were all soaked head to toe from the pouring rain, yet this person didn't have a drop of water on her anywhere.

After a few minutes, the woman stopped, smiled at me with the most loving smile I've ever seen, then rose. I looked down and saw the patient's color return to his body—not from the face down, as it normally does, but from his ankles up, a process that was contrary to the laws of science. The patient began to breathe, and his heart started beating. I turned to thank the stranger, but she was gone.

"Where'd she go?" I asked. Everyone just shrugged and shook their heads. I ran out in the rain to find her, and was startled by the lights of my father's ambulance flashing back on. On top of that, the engine restarted without anyone turning the key!

A few seconds later, the ALS unit arrived and the Lifeline helicopter appeared overhead. "We decided to give it a shot," the pilot said after landing. The medics loaded the patient and flew him to the hospital.

The patient, who turned out to be a firefighter himself, fell into a deep coma. The doctors said he would probably never come out of it, and if he did, he wouldn't be able to walk or talk. Nine weeks later the patient opened his eyes. Not only could he walk and talk, he made a complete recovery.

In keeping with the events of that day, the injured firefighter told us that after he was hit, he found himself walking through a wondrous pasture and spotted his deceased father sitting under a big tree. They talked for a while, but he had no conscious recollection of what they said.

"If that's heaven, then I want to go there," he told me.

I know it sounds crazy, but all of us who were on the scene that day are convinced that the woman who helped us was an angel, a belief supported by the area's history. The place where the accident occurred is near a lot where a large Methodist retreat had once stood almost a century before. Behind the retreat is a Native American burial ground. A spark from a train had caused a flash fire that burned the retreat to the ground years earlier. Even since then, area children, myself included, were told never to go back there.

Two years after that fateful rescue, I was cycling in Acton with my fiancée when another thunderstorm erupted. We ducked for cover inside an old nineteenth-century church that had been turned into a historical museum. I walked inside and froze in shock. There, draped over a mannequin, was the exact dress the angel had worn. Sitting on a table next to the mannequin was a Bible.

The incident with the angel and everything surrounding it changed my life. It ignited a spiritual awakening inside me, a steadfast belief in God and Jesus Christ that remains my guiding force. I know there is life after death, because I've seen it.

RANDY NEIBERT, FIRST-RESPONDER, INDIANA, WITH RICHARD NEIBERT, FIRST-RESPONDER, AND KIM COBB, PARAMEDIC

■ We were called to the site of an eighty-gallon chlorine gas tank in Charlotte County that was leaking. The wind was blowing the poisonous gas toward a trailer park. We had a special repair kit to cap off the spot where the tank was cracked, but the airpack I was wearing went bad, and I inhaled quite a bit of chlorine; I collapsed shortly afterward. They called a helicopter and flew me to the hospital.

When chlorine gas gets into your lungs, it turns to an acid that cuts off your breathing. I struggled to breathe the whole way to the hospital, which seemed like forever.

As I passed the emergency-room desk, I heard a doctor say that they needed to look up how to treat chlorine inhalation because they'd never had a case like that before. That didn't fill me with confidence.

They laid me on the ER table, hooked on some breathing apparatus, and started to take my blood. I'm not a big fan of needles, so not being able to breathe and my fear of needles combined to stop my heart.

Suddenly I was engulfed by a bright white light and had a warm, peaceful feeling all over. I was breathing easily and felt no pain. I discovered, to my shock, that I was floating above the room, looking down on myself lying on the table! I saw the doctors and nurses working on me and could hear them talking among themselves, asking for specific drugs.

Despite the euphoric sensation, I was convinced that it wasn't my time to go. I fought my way back into my body. How, I'm not really sure. I was just determined to survive. Whatever I did, whatever the reason, I made it back. I woke up on the table, in a whole lot of pain but thankful I was still in this world.

I remained in the hospital on oxygen for two and a half weeks. After that, I was okay. But it sure put a scare in me.

I used to smoke two, three packs of cigarettes a day. Needless to say, from that day on, I haven't smoked anything. Not a pipe, cigar, cigarette, anything. I already know what it's like not being able to breathe. If people went through what I did, I don't think anybody would smoke.

DARYL BURTON, EMT, FLORIDA

■ The call came in as a DOA in the trunk of a car. There were several police cars there, and the officers were standing around, chatting and smoking cigarettes. I walked to the trunk, opened it—and the guy moved! Scared me half to death.

The man had been changing a flat tire when another car hit him and slammed him into his trunk. His right leg was broken in half. The ball of his right foot was up against his chin. His left leg was wrapped around the bumper of the car. It was broken in so many places it had molded itself to the shape of the car. His upper body was in good shape and both his arms were okay, so he was desperately trying to push himself out of the trunk, bleeding to death, while the cops stood around nonchalantly shooting the breeze. From the outside, with his legs mangled and all, I could see how the police thought he was dead.

This was before we had paramedics [at that time there were only EMTs], so we called some ER staff out to the scene. They started an internal subclavicle line on him and removed him from the trunk. He died on the operating room table three hours later. He'd just lost too much blood out there before anyone noticed that he was alive.

MIKE SCHULZE, PARAMEDIC, NEW YORK

■ A TR–4 sports car missed a turn and crashed headlong into a fake waterfall at the entrance of an apartment complex. The waterfall effect was created by two huge plates of glass fifteen feet high and ten feet wide. Although the nose of the car penetrated the glass at the base, the structure was still standing.

The driver's legs were trapped in the small well underneath the steering column of the tiny convertible. I laid my body across the passenger seat and tried to crawl under to free them. While I was down, I heard the siren of an arriving fire truck pierce the night. Then I felt a strange vibration and instinctively pulled myself up to check it out.

I'll never forget what happened next. One of the plates of glass dropped down in front of my face like the blade of a giant guillotine. I screamed as it chopped the driver's legs off at the thigh.

I sat there, completely stunned. If I'd stayed down a second longer, the glass would have cut me in half at the waist.

The driver cried out in pain and shock, rocking me back to my senses. Since he was now free, we were able to lift his torso from the seat and get him out of there. The firefighters subsequently cut apart the car and retrieved his legs. We managed to limit the bleeding and save his life, but the surgeons weren't able to reattach his mangled legs.

Usually a paramedic arrives long after the damage has been done. That time, I was right there to watch it happen. I was almost right there to watch it happen to *me*.

ROY RYALS, PARAMEDIC, ARIZONA

■ It was a rainy Valentine's Day. When we arrived at the well-kept house, the first thing I noticed was that the dinner table was beautifully set. There were black glass plates, thin-stemmed wine goblets, and red napkins. It was like something out of a magazine.

I wandered into the bedroom, where it looked as if a massacre had taken place. There was blood all over the walls, floor, everywhere. Standing in the middle of the blood was a man wearing heavy makeup, black high heels, a hot-pink-and-black teddy, a black feather boa around his neck, false breasts, a wig, and dangling earrings. In his hand was a blood-covered pair of rusty hedge clippers.

I stared at his groin area in shock. The guy had tried to make himself into a woman! He had used the nasty clippers to take three whacks at his penis and testicles—once, twice, three times a lady!

His makeshift surgery was anything but precise. The poor man had severed and mashed his penis, leaving it hanging by a thread of skin. He'd completely chopped off one testicle and smashed it. Only a single testicle remained intact.

My partners, all men, were pale and sweating, which I thought was pretty funny. Anyway, we got him onto the backboard and into the ambulance and started a couple of lines.

"Oh, please, let me die. Let me die!" he wailed. "Don't sew it back on. If you sew it back on, I'll just want to die."

Not knowing what to say to calm him, I proceeded to give him a firsthand account of how wonderful it is to be a woman. That seemed to comfort him. Fortunately—or unfortunately, depending upon one's perspective—the ER doctors managed not only to save his life but also to save the remaining testicle.

I later learned that the man's medical insurance wouldn't cover a sex change operation. In addition, he didn't want to go through the yearlong course of psychotherapy required before a physician will perform such a radical procedure. Frustrated, he'd decided to celebrate St. Valentine's Day with his lover by going at it with the hedge clippers.

VICKI IEZZY, PARAMEDIC, FLORIDA

■ A pair of idiot armed robbers tried to hold up a bar in the midst of a bustling Saturday night. One guy stationed himself at the entrance, while his partner sneaked through the back door in case there was any trouble. They were both armed with shotguns.

The owner, no rocket scientist himself, grabbed a pistol and decided to shoot it out with them. The guy at the front door fired away. Not only did he kill the owner, he sprayed half the people in the bar, including his own partner! The injured robber was so angry that he blasted his companion in crime, dropping him in a pool of blood in the doorway. The police then came in and finished off the injured back-door man, adding three .38 slugs to his collection of shotgun pellets.

The scene was absolutely chaotic when we arrived. People were yelling and screaming and crying and bleeding all over the place. Aside from the three dead bodies, eight patrons, both men and women, were in various states of shotgun agony. Most had wounds in their arms and the tops of the heads, indicating that they'd had time to duck and cover up during the deadly firefight.

We began calming and stabilizing the customers, then sending them off, two by two, in the ambulances. Although the robbers and the owner died on the spot, we managed to save all the customers.

The night was a perfect example of the standard police advice that if someone tries to rob you or your business, let them have the money! It's not worth your life.

LOU CARLUCCI, EMT, OHIO

■ We were called on a "devil possession." This guy led us to a creepy back room where the walls were covered with pictures of naked men. A woman was lying totally nude on a bed. The man who greeted us said that something attacked her while she was taking a shower and that she had started screaming for help.

I examined her. She had these odd scratch and bite marks all over her torso, back, and legs. I looked at the guy.

"I didn't do it, I swear," he pleaded.

The woman was okay, nothing serious, but it was the eeriest call I've ever been on.

VICKI JONES, PARAMEDIC, FLORIDA

■ A life flight air-evac medic crew was transporting an elderly woman from Las Vegas to her home in Canada. She and her husband had been vacationing in the gambling mecca when she'd suffered a stroke. The plane refueled in Rapid City, then encountered problems on takeoff, when a wing dropped, hooked the ground, and sent the aircraft cartwheeling down the runway.

We found the male nurse three hundred feet away. He was sitting upright and was conscious and alert. He had a collapsed lung and some fractured ribs but made it.

The elderly woman was hanging upside down, still strapped to her cot. She was fine. Her husband was similarly strapped to his seat.

The pilot was the only one who didn't make it. He was killed on impact.

The couple decided that they didn't want to fly home anymore. We had to drive them to Canada. That was understandable. It hadn't been the best vacation.

DANIEL NATION, PARAMEDIC, SOUTH DAKOTA

■ The patient was sitting in the middle of the living room floor in a straight chair. There were four dogs running around the house, with smelly droppings all over the place. We had to step around the piles to get to the man.

"What's the problem?"

"I don't feel very well," he said.

I took his vitals. His pulse was slow and barely audible. I opened his shirt and noticed something strange around his neck. I inspected it more closely. It was a flea collar!

I checked further. He had additional flea collars around his wrists and ankles.

My partner and I began to slap at something biting our ankles.

"Why are you wearing dog flea collars?" I asked.

"To keep the fleas off me, of course!"

"You can't do that. Those collars are poisonous to people!" I exclaimed. "They'll eventually stop your heart."

We cut the collars off, gave him some oxygen, and shooed him to the hospital. The guy recovered.

DONNA

■ The dispatcher said a woman had a cue ball stuck in her vagina. We all figured it had to be a crank call. Sure enough, the woman had indeed gotten a cue ball stuck up there. We removed it without too much difficulty.

Curiosity, of course, got the best of us.

"By the way, how'd it get there?" I asked.

The woman explained that she and her man had been playing pool and gotten a bit frisky. They decided to see if the heavy ivory ball would fit. It did going in; it just didn't coming out. That necessitated the trip to the emergency room.

I guess the guy didn't put enough English on the ball.

ANDREA GEARY, EMT AND ER TECHNICIAN, FLORIDA

■ We were doing a routine transfer one night, taking a patient from the hospital to his residence. I was sitting in the back with the man, conversing, when all of a sudden my partner yells, "Hang on! We're going to hit a moose!"

Bang! Thud! We were rocked hard.

I looked out the back window. The battered moose was flipping down the road.

"We hit a moose!" the driver screamed on the radio. "We hit a moose!"

The patient was strapped in, and everybody was wearing seat belts, so nobody got hurt. We easily could have been. A moose can weigh over a thousand pounds and can do a lot of damage to a vehicle. Luckily, we'd caught this one with our side bumper.

Looking back, it was kind of funny. But when it happened, it was scary.

RICHARD WARK, PARAMEDIC, MAINE

■ A low rider collided with a Harley chopper being ridden by a biker and his lady. The low rider's bumper caught the woman's leg and ripped it off, carrying it three hundred feet down the road.

We responded within minutes. The woman, about twenty, was close to death. We treated her, tried to stop the bleeding, retrieved her leg, and radioed for a helicopter to air-evac her to the hospital.

Meanwhile, word of the accident spread through town like wildfire. The low rider's Mexican gang pals flooded into the area and lined one side of the street. The biker's burly brothers materialized out of thin air and lined up their noisy bikes defiantly on the other side. Furious about the gruesome injury to their buddy's lady, they began shouting threats and insults across the street. The macho Mexicans, not ones to back down for anything, screamed their own insults back.

As I was treating the woman, desperately trying to keep her breathing, I sensed the crowd edging forward. It was a tinderbox. Any second there was going to be a vicious rumble between fifty mammoth bikers and about a hundred sociopathic gang members. Worse yet, my partner and I were caught right in the crossfire!

"We need more police here immediately!" I radioed. "As many as you can spare. We're about to have World War Three!"

As the crowds moved closer, the helicopter touched down, temporarily diverting everyone's attention. By the time we loaded the patient, dozens of patrol cars had arrived, defusing the situation.

A month or so later, the lady and her biker pals came strolling into the station. She had been fitted with a prosthesis and seemed to be handling it well. Biker ladies, of course, aren't usually the shrinking-violet type to begin with. She and her bearded and tattooed companions thanked us profusely for our quick response in saving her life.

"You won't ever have any trouble with us," their leader promised.

After that, whenever we had a call at their lively colony—a drug overdose, stabbing, beating, stomping, ass-kicking, etc.—we were treated with the utmost respect no matter how explosive the circumstances. If anybody tried to hassle us or mouth off, they'd be slapped down on the spot.

It made life easy for a while.

KURT MICKELSON, AIR-EVAC PARAMEDIC, ARIZONA

■ One day we got a call from a woman who said, "I just woke up. I've got to go to work! My husband, he's dead!"

It was like it was such an inconvenience that her husband had died on her. It was interfering with her going to work. But the more I spoke with her, the more I realized that she was shaken up. I could hear it. She was panicking and couldn't even give her address. She gave me a street number but no street name. I had to go easy with her to try to get the information we needed. Still, she couldn't pull herself together enough to give me anything. When this happens, we can look at the 911 computer screen and get an address, and that gets us back on track.

I'll always remember this woman's first comment about being late for her job. It was like, "You guys deal with this and get my husband's body out of the way so I can go to work."

MELANIE CARR, DISPATCH SUPERVISOR, FLORIDA

■ A guy lost control of his Corvette at 150 mph and rocketed through a field, shattering the vehicle into four separate pieces. The driver and the passenger came down more than a hundred feet apart.

Incredibly, both were alive! They were in their individual

chunks, still strapped to their seats by their seat belts. The pair were busted up a bit, but easily survived.

I've never witnessed a better testament to seat belt use than that.

BILL ROSE, PARAMEDIC, OHIO

■ My captain and I responded to a shooting in progress on Christmas Eve. When we arrived, sure enough, gunshots were sounding. This old guy was chasing his brother-in-law around the yard with a .38. The guy with the gun was seventy-one. The brother-in-law was sixty-nine. The gunman had already shot his brother-in-law five or six times; when the gun was empty, he went into the house, reloaded, and came out firing again. After he emptied the chambers a second time, he proceeded to pistol-whip the guy and was kicking him as he lay bleeding on the ground. We couldn't do anything about it until the sheriff's department got there, not with a man waving a live gun around.

Remarkably, the brother-in-law was still alive when the police finally arrived. He survived all the way to the hospital but eventually died from the multiple wounds. At the trial, the shooter said that his brother-in-law had been aggravating him for twenty years and he'd finally gotten tired of it.

JOHN NIPPER, FIRST-RESPONDER, FLORIDA

■ A woman with a history of aneurysms decided to have a baby, against her doctor's advice. She made it to full term and delivered. Afterward, the doctors discovered that she had an enlargement of the right and left carotids [neck arteries] with aneurysms afflicting both. That was extremely dangerous. They decided to immediately airevac her to Denver for emergency surgery.

I was in her room in intensive care, preparing her to

leave, when they brought in the baby. It was pretty emotional to see the mother say good-bye to the child, knowing that she'd probably never see it again. It was doubtful that she'd even survive the flight.

The stress of parting with her newborn got her pretty worked up. Her blood pressure rocketed, causing one of the aneurysms to rupture. She died right before my eyes.

It was the worst moment I've experienced in my career. I came home at 2:00 A.M. in a trance and had to wake my wife for support. I also woke up my six-month-old son just to give him a hug.

DANIEL NATION, PARAMEDIC, NEBRASKA

■ We arrived at a house and discovered a frail, elderly man who appeared to be ill. However, after examining him, I couldn't find anything wrong. I decided to take his blood pressure. I put on the cuff and pumped it up, but it wouldn't register because his arm was so skinny and frail. I turned to my captain and calmly explained that I couldn't get a reading.

Just then, this ex-nurse riding with us looked at the instrument and screamed, "Oh, my God, he's got no BP!"

The poor guy glanced up at us, eyes full of fear, and promptly went into a fatal cardiac arrest.

That proved to me that people can die from fright.

TERRY PYE, PARAMEDIC, ONTARIO

■ There was this really pretty little girl, seven or eight, hanging from a tree by a rope around her neck. An old metal dinette chair was on the ground next to her. Her little sister, about four, was crying and clutching at her dangling ankles trying to pull her out of the tree. It was a horrible sight. I braced myself for the worst.

"She's alive!" I screamed to my partner after checking her out. "Let's get her down."

Fortunately, the little girl was so light that the rope failed to tighten—even with her sister tugging at her legs. It just braced her under her chin and the back of her neck. We untied the noose, slipped her head out, and transported her to the hospital. She recovered without any brain damage or side effects of any kind.

Apparently some neighbor kids had been taunting her, telling her she was ugly—which she wasn't—and it depressed her so much that she tried to kill herself. It turned out well, but it was still one of the saddest calls I've ever been on. Kids can be mean.

PATRICK WALSH, PARAMEDIC, ILLINOIS

■ Sometimes it's not the call the amazes me, it's the strange way people live. This case qualifies.

We were called on a "blind date," an unknown problem. When we got there, we had to break in. Searching the house, we found nothing unusual until we reached the kitchen. A woman was lying on the floor having a seizure. That wasn't the weird part. The problem was, she wasn't technically lying on the floor. She was lying in a sea of cat litter.

The lady had four cats and apparently had decided to turn her entire kitchen into a giant litter box. She'd covered the floor from wall to wall with three inches of cat litter. She must have figured it would cut down on the need to empty the box, because the grainy, absorbent stuff was dotted with lumps of cat shit.

It got worse. Not only had she turned the kitchen into a litter box, but it was still functioning as a kitchen! That's where she prepared her meals, right in the middle of the cat litter. In fact, she'd been making breakfast when she collapsed.

I tiptoed through the tulips, knelt beside her, and, without thinking, put my hand down to brace myself. *Squish!* My hand bull's-eyed a big, stinky blob of cat shit. I became queasy and nearly threw up. Focusing on my duty, I wiped my fingers off and gave the woman oxygen. We eventually got her out of there and off to the hospital. She recovered and went back to her cats—and her bizarre kitchen.

DONNA

■ We were taking this woman's sister to the hospital for some minor complications and the sister demanded that we drop her off at a specified parking lot.

"That's against our insurance regulations," I informed her. "Besides, we're not a taxi. You're here with your sister and you're going to stay with her until we reach the hospital."

The sister didn't take kindly to that. She proceeded to open the door while I was speeding down the road. My first thought was that she was going to jump out and get crushed by the wheels and that I was going to be sued. I don't have a lot of possessions, but what I have I wanted to keep. I grabbed her arm.

"You're not going anywhere!"

The sister went ballistic, hitting me, scratching me, and beating on me while I was navigating the ambulance through traffic. I managed to radio for help and pull the cumbersome vehicle to a stop without killing us all. Two city police cars and a state trooper arrived within seconds. They yanked the wildcat out of the van and arrested her.

The battling sister turned out to be a drug-addicted prostitute who had every disease known to man. I was lucky I didn't catch any.

VICKI IEZZY, PARAMEDIC, FLORIDA

■ I used to live on a big lake in Ohio. One day I spotted a patrol boat speeding across the water with the blues flashing.

"There's a problem out there," I said to my husband, Ben. I focused my binoculars and saw them toss out the dragline. "Uh-oh, someone's drowned. Get me over there!"

We ran to our dock, hopped into our boat, and zipped to the scene. The park ranger immediately recognized me.

"You have to help us," he pleaded. "Get that woman out of here!"

The ranger pointed to a small group of people in a nearby vessel that had run aground. We edged closer. Two of the boaters were hysterical over their missing friend. A third person, the victim's wife, was beyond hysterical. She was in neurogenic shock, violently screaming and crying.

"Oh, my husband! My husband!"

I asked Ben to take the wheel of their boat so we could get them out of there and let the rangers do their job. I also wanted to bring them to a dock near a road where an ambulance could arrive. After freeing the vessel, we took off. That only infuriated the wife further.

"Let me die! Let me die with my husband," she begged, trying to leap overboard.

I grabbed her and prevented her from jumping. She fought me like a bear, clawing my face and arms with her long red fingernails. Although she was twice my weight, I managed to knock her down and sit on her—all while radioing for the ambulance.

Hell-bent on killing herself, the woman struggled to get up, ranting and raving and repeatedly slashing my legs with her nails. If that wasn't bad enough, the people on the shore started cursing at us and waving their fists because we were raising a massive wake in a no-wake zone, splashing huge waves against their precious homes, boats, and docks.

I had bigger problems than angry neighbors. I quickly turned my attention back to the suicidal bronco I was riding. I hung on long enough to get her safely to the dock. The medics took over from there. They carried her into the ambulance and transported her to the hospital to be sedated.

The investigation revealed that it was an all too typical boating accident. The two couples had been drinking heavily and decided to go for a swim. The victim, normally a good swimmer, became disoriented by the alcohol and vanished into a deep trench.

It wasn't exactly Miller time.

DONNA

■ It was a bad pediatric drowning, one of those days that makes you want to quit. There was a mix-up over life jackets among siblings, and a little boy, about three, had gone under in a backyard lake. He had curly brown hair and big brown eyes that were open and fixed, eyes that haunted my partner and me for months afterward.

The mother freaked out at the scene, begging us to perform a miracle. We couldn't. It was the same terrible ordeal we'd so often experienced. Only this one, for us, wouldn't end.

"I wake up in the middle of the night, and I keep seeing those eyes," my partner confessed a few days later. "This is eating me up."

For me, it was even worse. The woman's husband, in a typically male reaction, decided that they would never talk about the boy again. They couldn't even mention his name in the house. The man wasn't being mean; that was just his way of dealing with his own horrible grief. He had to blot it out.

The mother, in a typically female reaction, needed to do the exact opposite. She had to talk. She began calling me—and calling me and calling me, day and night, talking about the boy's life and going over and over his death. I knew she just needed to get it out of her system, but the constant reminder was wearing me down. I hated having to relive that tragic call again and again, but I suffered through it, knowing that her pain was far worse than mine.

Three weeks later, my partner and I were invited to their house. The father, an executive with a big firm, told us they wanted to donate some pediatric lifesaving equipment to our squad in their son's name. He gave us a healthy check, and we put it all to good use. When the materials arrived, I had an IN MEMORY OF . . . tag placed on each item.

DONNA

■ I was working as a EMS training officer and sometimes responded to scenes at my own discretion. I heard about a multivehicle auto accident on a four-lane highway and drove out to help. It was pretty chaotic. There were four cars involved, including an unoccupied parked vehicle. Several rescue units from different agencies were already there. I did a general survey of the scene, checking in with the different crews. Things seemed to be under control; there were injuries, but none appeared to be life-threatening. While I was walking around, a paramedic grabbed me.

"I want you to look at this patient. She's breathing awfully fast."

He led me to an eight-year-old girl.

"I told my boss about her, but he said she was just excited and scared," the medic continued.

"What about her lung sounds?" I asked.

"They're diminished on the right side."

I examined the girl. She indeed had decreased lung

sounds, and her belly appeared to be overly firm. Her other vitals were okay.

I checked and found that they had her scheduled for a basic life support ambulance. I relayed my findings to the paramedic in charge, and he repeated that he felt she was just upset and didn't need to be upgraded to emergency status.

I remained concerned and went to inspect the car. There was a two-foot invasion into the compartment where she had been sitting. In addition, her car had struck the third vehicle and then smashed head-on into the car that was pulled off the road near a ditch. The way I saw it, there was significant reason to believe that her injuries were worse than they appeared.

I immediately ordered a waiting unit to load the girl. I ran to my unit, grabbed a trauma box and EKG, and jumped into the girl's ambulance before it left. I instructed the driver to run it as an emergency. En route to the hospital, I started an IV and monitored her. Her blood pressure dropped a bit, and her pulse and respiration rates increased.

At the hospital, I took her directly into the pediatric trauma room. They did an abdominal tap to see if there was any free blood in the abdominal cavity. As they inserted the catheter, a stream of bright red blood squirted up. It turned out that her liver had been cut.

As I walked out of the emergency room, a shirtless and very agitated young man came at me.

"You son of a bitch, I'm going to kill you!"

"Who are you?" I wondered.

"I'm the girl's father!"

"Why are you going to kill me?"

He reached out his hand and showed me his daughter's jewelry.

"They just put her necklace in my hand and told me that she was in critical condition and may die. It's all because of you!"

I had absolutely no clue what he was talking about. If anything, I had saved the girl's life by overruling the paramedic in charge and rushing her to the hospital in time to have her liver repaired.

I tried to explain this to the father, but he wouldn't hear it. He kept insisting that it was my fault and remained dead set on killing me. I left before things got worse.

It took me a while to sort out what had happened. Apparently there was a man lying underneath the fourth car when the accident occurred—he had pulled over to work on his engine. When the car that the little girl was riding in struck his vehicle, he was killed instantly. His car was knocked to the edge of a nearby ditch, and his body ended up pinned under her vehicle.

I had no idea there was a body under the car when I went to inspect it. The father knew, and concluded that I'd deserted his dying daughter in the ambulance while I went over to gawk at a dead man under the car.

That was the thanks I got.

JEFF COLE, PARAMEDIC, FLORIDA

■ The elderly woman went into cardiac arrest inside the ambulance. I reached down to rip open her cotton robe and was nearly blinded by the light reflecting off a huge diamond necklace around her neck. I shielded my eyes and gave her CPR, bringing her back around. We got her to the ER and were later informed that she would recover.

A week later, I received a call from someone at the hospital.

"That old lady you rescued is telling everybody that you saved her life and she's putting you in her will! She's rich. You're set! You're gonna be on easy street!"

It was a paramedic's dream come true, the exact scenario

we often fantasize about: An elderly patient is so thankful for our help that they leave us their fortune. For a while, my head was in the clouds. I figured that if all she did was will me that diamond necklace, I could sell it and retire to a life of leisure. No more patients throwing up on me, baby!

Ten days later, the woman caught pneumonia in the hospital and died. She never made it home in time to call her lawyer and change her will. So much for easy street. It was back on the mean streets for me.

DONNA

10 The Horror, the Horror

For years, the way I handled the horror of what goes on out there was, first, through denial, and second, I'm an alcoholic. That's how I handled it.

NAME WITHHELD, PARAMEDIC, LOUISIANA

Blood. It's a wonderful, life-giving liquid that courses through our arteries and veins, neatly tucked inside our bodies. Few people actually see much of it, but not us—we see it everywhere. Lots and lots of blood. We can't put it back, so we have to know what to do with it.

Mostly mop it up.

THE STORIES

■ We received a code four call, designating an auto accident. At the scene, I saw that a new Buick had been broadsided by a large construction truck. That's usually not good. We immediately sent for the fire department to bring the jaws of life. It was obvious that extrication was going to be necessary.

Upon approaching the car, I saw a body in the passenger's seat. I was shocked when I looked closer. It appeared that the body had two heads! Examining further, I determined that there were actually two bodies. One of the men had been thrown on top of the other and was sitting on his lap. The man on top had extensive head injuries. Blood was everywhere. Both victims were unconscious.

The firemen arrived and gained access to the back door behind the passenger. They proceeded to pry apart the twisted metal to extricate the bodies. When they made some room, I crawled into the backseat to treat the victims. I could see that the man on top was not a viable patient. Despite having a pulse, brain matter was seeping out of the top of his head. He was beyond hope.

The guy underneath had a stronger pulse and fewer visible injuries. If we acted quickly, he had a chance. The trouble was, I had to get the other man off him. I reached under the arms of the guy on top and lifted him up so that the firemen and medics could get to the man on the bottom and get a backboard under him. I lifted with all my might.

"Higher," one of the firemen said.

I lifted again.

"Higher."

A third time.

"Higher."

I heaved with everything I had. Suddenly his head sort of flopped over on my right arm, dangling by some shreds of tissue. I was looking right down into his neck stub!

"Higher," the fireman ordered.

I suppressed my shock and lifted again. This time the head detached from the neck, rolled down the man's body, smacked the edge of the car, and bounced into the street. It rolled to a stop.

"Pick it up! Pick it up," I ordered a stunned EMT trainee standing nearby.

The woman didn't move. She just stood there, mouth agape, staring down at the head.

"Pick it up!" I screamed.

Startled, she jerked, then bent over and did her job, carrying the head with her arms outstretched like it was a bomb.

After that, we were able to free the other man. We rushed him to the hospital, to no avail. He never regained consciousness.

Back at the scene, the police officers found $18,000 in a paper bag in the Buick's trunk. Apparently the headless man, an older gentleman, didn't trust banks and carried all his money in his car.

The story didn't end there. A few days later I had to drop off another body at the local funeral home. The funeral director, a funny, upbeat sort of man, waved me over.

"I want to show you something," he said.

When an overly excited funeral director makes that statement, it's usually time to hightail it in the opposite direction. For some reason, though, I pressed forward.

He led me into a dark, horror-movie-type room. Bodies were lying on tables everywhere. He stopped at a particular corpse, switched on a spotlight, and pulled back the sheet.

I immediately recognized the headless man from the Buick. The proud funeral director had sewn everything back together with black thread.

"Don't you think I do good work?" he said, beaming.

DONNA

■ A woman put her four-year-old son in the backyard with a pair of young German shepherds so she could spend some time with her boyfriend. The dogs began to playfully use the boy as a sort of rope to tug between them the way dogs like to do. They played this horrifying game for hours, oblivious to the devastation they were causing the child. The game reached a point where the child was being tossed into the air like a rag doll. The dogs, barely more than puppies themselves, hadn't acted in malice or anger. They hadn't even growled. They were just playing.

The result of their play was the most shocking and haunting image I've ever seen. The boy was bitten in more than a hundred places. Both of his ears had been ripped off. His testicles were shredded and hanging by threads. His arms and legs were gnawed nearly to the bone.

Through it all, he remained alive. He was conscious on some level, although I couldn't say exactly how. His eyes were wide open. He was staring blankly, an inhuman stare. I looked at him and a chill washed over me. It was as if his soul had left his body to escape the horror. As I helped prepare him for transport, I noticed an eerie smell. The boy smelled like a dog.

At the emergency room, there was a woman whose sole duty was to hold his hand and talk to him while the doctors worked. I thought that was a nice touch.

I returned a week later. To my surprise, the boy was doing well. His ears and testicles had been reattached, and his bites were stitched and healing. He was playing games as if nothing had happened.

Despite the happy ending, it was the previous images of horror that remained locked in my memory. I'll never forget the lifeless look in the boy's eyes, the dog smell, and the massive injuries. To this day, I hate dog bites. Although I have two dogs of my own, and two children, I cringe when I have to respond to a bite.

ROD MORTENSEN, PARAMEDIC, ARIZONA

■ A man committed suicide by jumping off an elevated subway platform. The train ran over him, and his mangled body was caught up there in the trusses. The police had to take him down piece by piece, tossing the parts to us. The ribs fell in one clump. Half his head fell in another. An arm plopped down after that. People flocked into the area by the hundreds to watch the ghoulish show. Some even had binoculars.

Halfway through, this ratty little stray dog ran up, grabbed a piece of the guy, and took off down the street, running kind of sideways. A big, fat cop went lumbering after him. It would have been funny if it wasn't so sick. The dog easily outdistanced the cop and disappeared. I guess the mutt had a good meal that night.

At the morgue, a police officer arrived with the guy's leg. It was found three stops down the line. The cop heaved it into the pile of other body parts like it was a basketball.

MIKE SCHULZE, PARAMEDIC, NEW YORK

■ A huge, snarling bull with long, bloodstained horns was standing over a terribly wounded man. The brutal sight came as a shock. All we'd been told was that there was a man down in a field. Nobody said anything about a 1,400-pound beast hovering over him.

The man been gored in the abdomen, chest, groin, and head. The bull had hooked its deadly horns into the guy's clothing and tossed him around, ripping his clothes, and his flesh, to shreds.

We suspected the man was dead, but we're not paid to make a long-distance diagnosis. We had to get to him, but how? The bull appeared hungry for more victims. We stood behind an electric fence and considered our options. The bull postured in front of us, snorting, kicking the ground, generally letting us know that he meant business. A man lay dead or dying, and we were in a standoff with a furious monster.

I radioed the station and requested a firefighter who I knew lived on a farm. He came and bravely fought off the powerful animal with a pole. When he pushed the bull back fifty feet, he waved us in.

We ran to treat the patient. I glanced up, nervously checking the whereabouts of the bull. Instead of retreating, he was now pawing the ground, ducking his head, and creeping forward.

"Get the guy out of there!" the firefighter screamed. "The bull's not going to hold off much longer."

Normally we don't move a patient until we've checked for broken bones and spinal injuries, but there was no time for that. We had to get him, and ourselves, the hell out of there. We grabbed the guy and ran in the opposite direction. The firefighter managed to hold off the animal long enough to enable us to retreat behind the electric fence.

After all that, there was nothing we could do for the man. He was gored beyond belief. The bull intended to kill him and made sure there wouldn't be any doubt. If he'd have gotten his horns into us, we'd have been in the same shape.

TOM HARRISON, PARAMEDIC, WISCONSIN

■ A pickup truck was doing over a hundred when it flipped into a ditch, trapped the driver underneath, and caught fire. We could see the flames from a quarter-mile away. After we arrived, my partner went running toward the truck with a fire extinguisher. I yelled at her to come back before the vehicle exploded, but she didn't listen. I'd known her for thirteen years. She was my best friend.

"If she's going to die, I'm gonna die with her," I vowed, charging after her.

I caught up and was assaulted by a ghastly sight. The driver's body, from his chest down, was pinned inside the burning truck and was fully engulfed in flames. Only his head and shoulders were free. Although parts of his lower body had already burned away, he was still conscious!

"Get me out! Please!" he screamed in agony. "Please get me out!"

We sprayed our extinguishers to try to keep the fire away from him, but had limited success. Flaming fuel was dripping on what remained of his back, feeding the inferno.

I knew it was hopeless, even though he was conscious and screaming. What remained of his legs and back was covered with third-, fourth-, and fifth-degree burns, meaning the skin and bone were gone. The only reason he hadn't died immediately was that he was facedown in the dirt. That position shielded the front of his ravaged body.

The fire department arrived and doused the truck for a good fifteen minutes before the fire subsided. There was so much water that we had to dig holes in the mud with our hands and lift the guy's head up to keep him from drowning.

The firemen used the cutters to slice open the car. When they got to the man, his body had melted into the interior of the truck. They had to use air bags to pry him loose and slide him onto the board.

Incredibly, he survived the whole way to the hospital.

"When are they going to let me go home? I'm fine," he kept insisting. "I just want to go home."

The man, of course, never made it home.

VICKI IEZZY, PARAMEDIC, FLORIDA

■ After we pulled the guy from the truck and got him to the hospital, I found an empty room and sat down and cried. I had to let it all out. I mean, the man had talked to us the whole time. . . .

My lieutenant came to the hospital, and I just fell into

his arms, crying like a little baby. The stress was so bad from seeing another human being suffer like that. They immediately set up a debriefing for myself, my partner, Vicki, the ER physician, and the firefighters on the scene. That really helped.

TAMMY MAURER, PARAMEDIC, FLORIDA

■ I hate suicides. Why people do the things they do to themselves, the moral implications, and how life gets so bad that they have to end it—these are just terrible calls all the way around.

I was dispatched on one of these downers one afternoon. A young man, nineteen, had propped a shotgun under his chin and pulled the trigger, blowing off his face and the top of his head. I noticed something weird lying beside him and bent to take a closer look. It was his brain! The pinkish organ was perfectly intact, just lying there on the floor. The impact of the blast had popped it out of his head in one clean piece.

I hate suicides.

DAN COUCH, PARAMEDIC, ARIZONA

■ A young man tried to kill himself with a 9 mm gun. He had placed the powerful weapon under his chin but flinched at the last second.

He was standing in his doorway with a bloody towel to his chin when we arrived. He dropped the towel to show us the damage. I recoiled in shock. He only had half a face! Instead of sending the bullet into his brain, he'd blown off his entire lower jaw.

The poor guy was trying to communicate with us but couldn't talk—there was no jaw to move to form words. I'll never forget the look of horror in his eyes. It was like he was pleading with us, "What do I do now?"

We treated him as best we could and got him to the ER. They stopped the bleeding and saved his life—whatever life a man with half a face could have.

KEVIN WARD, PARAMEDIC, UTAH

■ I was rocked from a dead sleep at 4:50 A.M. to respond to a fire. That's all we expected, a simple house fire. Four minutes later, a frantic woman ran up to the truck and handed me a badly burned eighteen-month-old baby boy. Her husband gave my partner the boy's severely burned twin sister. The babies screamed in agony and squirmed in our arms. Their blistered skin peeled off in our hands.

I tried to shake the sleep from my brain and deal with the anguish that suddenly confronted me. One minute, I was fast asleep; the next, I was trapped in an absolute nightmare.

A third medic, Crystal Sorenson, helped me mask the boy and wrap the terrible wounds. My partner, Richard Frankland, treated the baby girl. There was little more we could do. We held the babies, listened to their tortured cries, and waited for the rescue helicopter. I felt so helpless.

After we turned the twins over to the helicopter paramedics, Richard fell to his knees and cried. I had to do all I could to keep from breaking down myself. We both have small children of our own, and seeing what happened to these two just devastated us. I couldn't go back to sleep after that. The department quickly arranged a CISD session, which helped.

I learned later that the power company had withdrawn the electric service to the family's house because of a billing problem, and the family turned to lanterns and candles to light their home. One of the candles apparently fell off a table in the twins' room and ignited a playpen. The fire quickly spread.

At the time, I was also working as a pitcher for the Seattle Mariners replacement team during the Major League baseball strike. I had a game that same afternoon. As I put my uniform on and warmed up, I couldn't shake the terrible images of those two burned babies. The only time I was able to put it out of my mind was when I took the mound. I concentrated on throwing strikes and pitched two innings of scoreless relief—relief in a fantasy game, and relief from the awful reality of what I'd experienced.

There was a lot of animosity during that bitter strike. For me, however, the resurrection of my baseball career was tremendously therapeutic. It was the only time I wasn't haunted by the memory of those twins.

DAVE GRAYBILL, EMT, ARIZONA
[GRAYBILL WAS A MEMBER OF THE 1984 U.S. OLYMPIC BASE-
BALL TEAM AND WAS DRAFTED OUT OF ARIZONA STATE
UNIVERSITY BY THE MONTREAL EXPOS]

■ A troubled young man decided to kill himself using a powerful elephant rifle. He put the barrel under his chin, braced the stock between his knees, reached down, and pulled the trigger. The tremendous impact exploded his head all over the room.

What the man failed to consider was where the slug might end up. After blasting through his brain, it cut through the ceiling and lodged in his son's shoe. The child was sleeping on the floor upstairs, next to his siblings' beds.

That was too close.

BRIAN BURKELAND, PARAMEDIC, WISCONSIN

■ When I was a kid, I used to put coins on a railroad track so the train could flatten them. We were always half scared that the pennies would derail the train, but fortunately all we ever got was a neat-looking piece of squashed copper.

After I became an EMT, I responded to a call that was a gruesome variation of the old penny-on-the-rail trick. A drunk had chosen a terrible place to pass out—right across a railroad track. The Amtrak train didn't see him in time and hit the guy full force. His body just exploded.

I found what was left of his head thirty feet away. A leg had traveled sixty feet beyond that. An arm was hanging across a nearby bush. Various other parts of his body were all over the place. What remained of his torso was split down the center, exposing his upper and lower intestines.

I had been shown a film of an autopsy in EMT school, but seeing everything scattered around like that was a whole different experience—and not one I'd like to repeat.

MARK SECRIST, EMT, ARIZONA

◼ We responded to the call of a patient with difficulty breathing. When I walked into the house, it smelled like a butcher shop. There was a distinct smell of fresh blood. We started down the hallway and discovered a man lying on a bed of blood. I mean, blood was everywhere. It was like a sea of red in the room. We didn't know what was going on until we edged closer and examined him.

Turned out the man had throat and lung cancer and had a stoma [an opening in the trachea]. Blood was oozing out of it. Whenever his heart would pump especially strongly, a real gusher would shoot out.

I glanced around the room. There were trails of clotted blood about six inches wide and a foot long on the sides of the bed. Some of the pools of clotted blood were a quarter-inch deep on the floor.

The guy was still conscious! I tried to hook up the

suction to try to control the blood, but it was useless. The paramedics arrived and started a couple of lines on him, and we got him out of there.

Incredibly, the guy survived. I don't know how, but he lived.

KEVIN HOLLEY, FIRST-RESPONDER EMT, FLORIDA

■ An intoxicated teenager, on a dare, decided to run naked from one farmhouse to another on the coldest night of the year. It was forty degrees below zero, with a wind chill factor of sixty below. Not smart.

When we found him, he looked like he'd been thrown into a pot of boiling water. He was as red as a lobster and was suffering from second-and third-degree frost burns.

As we warmed him, his skin started peeling off like a snake's. It was phenomenal—and incredibly gory. Surprisingly, the teen not only survived, but he didn't lose any arms, legs, fingers, or toes to frostbite.

He just lost a whole lot of skin.

RANDY MEININGER, PARAMEDIC, NEBRASKA

■ One afternoon we responded to a call at an air park in our district. An aircraft went down with two PIs [pin-ins]. The rescue unit I run with had the [jaws of life] extraction tool, so we took over.

The guy up front was in bad shape, but his injuries didn't initially appear to be fatal. His feet were broken and were turned upright at a ninety-degree angle. The balls of his bones were sticking out of his heels. That was caused by the impact with the runway. The other guy's feet were identical.

The first guy was still breathing. Looking closer, I could see that he had no teeth and that the back of his head was crushed in. I figured he didn't have much of a chance. His last breath could come any second.

The guy in the back turned out to be even worse. He was the owner of the plane and was teaching this young man how to fly. For whatever reason, they slammed nose first into the runway. The owner had been thrown forward and his face rammed the young man in the back of the head. The tremendous impact just flattened his face. In addition, the top of his forehead had an inch gap all the way across. There was really nothing I could do. The owner was dead and the student was dying. But we still had to get the bodies out, so we began the process of dislodging them.

When we got to the guy in the back, we had to lean his head forward to get him out. Suddenly this brown substance began pouring out of the crack in his head. It looked like extra thick coffee and just oozed all over me. I stared in disbelief until I realized what it was. It was his brain! The crash had just scrambled his head and liquefied his brain. That was nasty.

The incident has kept me from flying—in anything, anywhere.

KEVIN HOLLEY, FIRST-RESPONDER EMT, FLORIDA

■ The patient had been dead in his home for quite some time. The gases in his decaying corpse got trapped under his skin and had actually separated the skin from his body. It looked like he was encased inside a balloon.

I've never seen anything like that in sixteen years.

DOUG CARRELL, PARAMEDIC, NEBRASKA

■ A gentleman pulled into a gas station for a fill-up, and the attendant noticed that there was a body underneath his car! Apparently the guy didn't even know he'd hit someone.

We responded, and it was a mess. The victim was facedown, right in the center of the car, near the rear axle. His belt was caught on the axle. The highway patrol estimated that he had been dragged like that for two miles or more.

The fire department lifted the vehicle so we could get the man's body out from under the car. Half his face, chest, abdomen, and legs had been eaten away by the pavement. His chest was wide open and his intestines were exposed. That was the strangest call I've ever run.

TAMMY MAURER, PARAMEDIC, FLORIDA

■ The call came in as an unstated illness. We arrived at a filthy, dilapidated trailer—never a good sign. I was running with another female medic, and we had a woman driver, so it was just us three ladies. When we arrived at the scene, I noticed that the driver was hesitant about getting out of the unit—another bad sign. The other medic and I looked at each other and sighed, then we entered the trailer.

We were led to a back bedroom where an emaciated woman was lying on a bare mattress that had been tossed on the floor. She was weak and disoriented. Her skin was encrusted with dirt.

I knew we wouldn't be able to get a gurney into the trailer, so I picked her up in my arms and carried her outside. Inside the unit, we took the woman's vitals, gave her oxygen, and transported her to the hospital.

On the way back to the station, I was sitting in the front seat, next to the driver, when I started scratching. I looked over at my fellow medic, and she was also scratching. A message came over the radio: "Unit five-fifty-five, return to the hospital immediately."

The driver made a U-turn and back we went. A nurse greeted us in the emergency room. She was holding a small jar, which she held before our eyes. Inside, I could see these tiny bugs jumping around.

"The lady you just brought in was covered with body lice," the nurse explained.

"Argh!" we screamed in unison, horrified by the thought.

We rushed back to the station, itching, scratching, and totally repulsed. After scrubbing the unit, I dashed home, tossed my uniform and underwear into a washing machine, and jumped into the shower, scouring myself with Kwell, a lice-killing ointment. That was the first time I got lice on a call. Unfortunately, it wasn't the last.

DONNA

■ Early in my career, I was called out to a fiery car crash. A twenty-one-year-old woman was trapped in a car, burning to death. I could hear her screams, but we couldn't get to her. The two men with her had been thrown out. One was lying in the center of the street, moaning in agony. The second was running through the nearby woods, totally ablaze. It was the most shocking sight I've ever seen.

We went after the guy who was running. He finally dropped, and we managed to carry him into the ambulance. It was awful. He had third-degree burns on his entire body. His skin was so hard it was like trying to start an IV on the bottom of a shoe.

All three patients died.

When I got home that evening, I kept seeing the image of that horribly charred man in my apartment. And the smell—I couldn't get rid of the smell. I wasn't able to eat chicken for a long time, especially barbecued chicken. The aroma turned my stomach.

I called my supervisor. "I can't handle this job," I said, ready to quit. "I don't deal with this kind of thing well."

"No one does," he said, reassuring me. "Give it some time. It'll pass."

It did. I look back on it now, and it's just another call.

SHERRY OBJARTEL, PARAMEDIC, MICHIGAN

■ A semi crashed into a car, crushing it. I'd never seen a vehicle so destroyed. I walked from one side to the other looking for the remains of the driver.

"Where is he?" I asked an officer.

"He's right there!" he answered, pointing to the wreck.

"Where?"

"Right there."

My partner walked over and said, "He's right there. Can't you see him?"

"What are you guys talking about? Where's the driver?"

They leaned in and pointed him out. I was stunned. The guy *was* right there, only he was so entangled with the twisted and broken metal that he looked like part of the wreck. He was totally camouflaged. I'd been staring right at him all along.

TOM HARRISON, PARAMEDIC, WISCONSIN

■ The schoolkids in our area started playing a dangerous game—bouncing their knapsacks off the tires of passing trucks. The sacks, held by their long straps, would kick back, spin the thrower, and wrap around the them, giving the kids a thrill.

You can see where this is heading.

A blond, blue-eyed girl, about ten, decided to play. She flung her knapsack toward the dual rear tires of a gasoline truck. The strap got caught, jerked her through the air, and sucked her in between the huge tires. Her body flapped around until there was nothing left but splats of blood and flesh. It took us more than an hour to peel what was left of her from between the wheels and place the material in a small bag.

"Let's get out of here before her mom comes and sees this!" I kept imploring the Department of Transportation investigators, trying to speed them along. "Do what you need to do, but hurry!"

They ignored me and took their sweet time. The mother arrived. A single shoe was all that survived the carnage intact. It was the only thing we could use to make an official identification. I showed the mother the shoe. It was one of the most horrible moments of my life.

"That's it! I don't need this anymore," I snapped at the station afterward. "I quit!"

Someone convinced me to take a two-week sabbatical instead. I did, and decided to stay. But that one nearly did me in.

PAT CRAWFORD, PARAMEDIC, FLORIDA

[Kansas paramedic Ted Stramel wrote the following letter to his friend, paramedic Joe Williamson, after Stramel held a gun in his mouth for more than an hour, contemplating suicide.]

■ The only time that death bothered me was about two weeks ago, when a young girl aborted two babies. One was at her house and the other at the hospital.

When we got the call they said she was bleeding from the vagina. We got there, and it was altogether a different story. We found a young girl lying on the hallway floor who had aborted a fetus about five months old. She was crying out loud that this was never going to happen again. I felt sorry for her, but then I looked down and here was a little creature lying there with no chance of survival. Not one little chance at all. It looked like E.T. from the movies. It was so tiny and fragile that it took me what seemed like an hour to pick it up with a bloody towel and put it into a bedpan. I guess this child just deserved more respect from me than throwing a life away in a bedpan.

I wonder what the fuck those people thought of me when I did that. What are they going to think of me the next time they see me? How does the mother feel about me?

Nobody seemed to care about it except for myself and Brent [another paramedic]. How do you gracefully pick up a dead fetus from a dirty carpet and dispense with it in front of people you don't even know?

Something is missing. I don't understand why I even do this job anymore. On the one hand, I felt that I did what was right, but on the other, I'm not sure.

My own mother's death didn't bother me as much as this incident. And I didn't cry as much, either. I just can't seem to get this out of my mind.

I work with about twenty-two people. We kind of resemble a chain. Somewhere, within this chain, is [me] Ted. Sometimes he thinks he is the whole chain. Other times the chain gets so tight that the link which is Ted wants to snap. Sometimes the temper in the link loses some of its strength. What does one do when a link gets weak? Buy a new chain, or do you replace the weak link?

Don't worry, Joe, I won't kill myself. I could never hurt my mother even if she is no longer with me. Well, she *is* with me. Her spirit, anyway.

I guess a person who does this kind of work should get used to it. But a person, or at least me, can't turn my emotions on and off like a lightbulb.

I hope this doesn't upset anyone. I didn't mean for it to. And I'll work it out sooner or later. If I have to, we'll take a walk together. God, I hate the way you walk.

TED STRAMEL, PARAMEDIC, KANSAS
[STRAMEL, WHO BATTLED A DRINKING PROBLEM,
HAS SINCE DIED OF CANCER]

11 The Weird and Bizarre, Part II— Pathos, Bathos, and Poignancy

One of our supervisors was arrested in the Son of Sam murders. He had a car that matched Son of Sam's car, and he used to drive around with a scanner and back us up on calls. The police saw him hanging around and they arrested him. Paramedics get no respect in New York.

MIKE SCHULZE, PARAMEDIC, NEW YORK

Everybody loves happy endings. Unfortunately, life ain't always peaches and cream. Ask a hundred medics about their most memorable calls, and ninety-five will reel off the ones that either broke their hearts, tormented their souls, or haunted their dreams—in essence, the stories that fall far short of the standard *Rescue 911* happy-face hero stuff.

To top it off, a good percentage of these gripping tales include an element of the absurd. Maybe I've been in the rescue business too long, but these bizarre, hard-to-categorize anecdotes—the ones that sift through the darker side of the human condition—are my personal favorites.

THE STORIES

■ A family docked their camper in a state park beside a large lake. There were five people in all—Mom, Pop, two daughters, and a grandmother. It was a hot summer day, so as soon as they stopped, the two girls jumped out and dived into the cold water.

Only one, the smallest, came back up. It was as if something had swallowed the older girl and dragged her to the bottom.

When we arrived, not only was the teenage daughter missing, but the grandmother was having chest pains and was in shock. As I treated her, I saw the drag boats appear. To shelter the family from that gruesome scene, I ushered them all back into the mobile home.

After finishing with the grandmother, I went to check on the search. The little girl insisted on coming with me. Just as we reached the shore, I saw the hook on one of the boats catch. That meant they netted the body. A few seconds later, I could see the teen rolling over the edge of the boat.

I did an immediate turn and shooed the sister back to the camper. The park rangers brought the teenager's body to a boat house and laid her out. She was very peaceful-looking, so young and beautiful with long, thick blond hair. It was heartbreaking to see her like that, a life aborted for no apparent reason.

The investigators were never able to determine what made her drop to the bottom like a bag of bricks. The only clue was like something out of a horror novel: I later learned that a couple of years before, that same family lost another child in that same part of the lake.

DONNA

■ A guy overturned a Subaru Samurai on I–17, killing the young coed riding with him. Her body was lying by the side of the road when we arrived.

I walked over to check her out. Sometimes the police tell us someone's dead when they're not, so we have to make our own determination.

The girl was dead, all right. She'd suffered a severe head injury. However, what I remember is she had the prettiest little hands. Her nails were pink and perfectly manicured. I also noticed a tiny ring made of twisted gold on her finger.

As I turned to leave, I saw her long blond hair blowing in the wind. I kept thinking, *She can't be dead. She's going to get up any minute. She's alive.*

I'd walk a few more steps, turn around, and feel the same strange sensation. I was certain she was going to get up.

For whatever reason, that girl haunted my dreams for months. It seemed like every time my head hit the pillow, I'd see her hair, her hands, her fingernails, and that ring. I'd never see her face, just her hair and hands. No matter how many times the dream repeated, it never varied. Not once did she get up, talk, or do anything weird. It was just her hands, fingernails, ring, and hair, night after night.

Of all the vividly gruesome and horribly tragic calls I've been on, that simple accident is the only one that's ever penetrated my subconscious. And I can't even begin to explain why. If the girl's trying to send me a message, what is it? And why won't it stop?

MANNY DEVALLE, PARAMEDIC, ARIZONA

■ I guess every town has their village idiot. Today that term is woefully politically incorrect, but that's what we called him. He was young, in his thirties, a nice-looking man who was "mentally challenged," as they say now. He spent his time wandering around town. Everybody knew him. He never talked, though. Not a sound. Whenever he needed something, like at the grocery store, he'd write a note and hand it to the clerk.

The man spent a great deal of his time standing across the street in front of the station house. He was just mesmerized by the ambulances. Whenever we pulled out with the reds flashing and sirens blaring, he'd jump up and down and clap his hands and go wild with excitement. Inside, he was just a little boy.

I used to be kind of leery of him, as people tend to be when confronting the unusual. However, as time passed, we all got used to his being out there. We'd wave whenever we passed on a call.

One day, we were toned out on a possible hemorrhage. We pulled up in front of a house, and there sat our buddy on the front porch. He was waving at us and smiling brightly.

"What's wrong?" I asked.

He showed me his thumb. There was a small cut on it, the kind you get from a broken teacup or a paring knife. He was absolutely elated about it because the injury meant that the great flashing ambulance had come for him! He was finally going to get a chance to ride inside it and go to the emergency room!

My partner was having none of it, though.

"I'm not taking him anywhere," the paramedic growled. "I'm not bandaging his damn hand. This is ridiculous."

"Can't we do it this once?" I pleaded. "Come on. What'll it hurt?"

"What if we get a real call and someone dies because

we're playing Paramedic Friendly with this idiot?" he argued.

It was a good point. Although it would have been nice to give the guy a ride, we couldn't risk it. Instead, I got out my bandage kit and tied this bodacious bandage on his thumb. That seemed to please him just fine.

After we left, I was curious about something. I called the dispatcher and had her play the 911 tape. A man's voice came on, speaking perfect English. He was using the first person singular. It was the guy! He'd made the call himself. He could talk just fine.

I guess he never really had anything important to say before.

DONNA

■ The call was a 918, a crazy person. I responded with a female medic. The patient was a woman in her forties. She seemed okay and didn't protest when we led her to the ambulance.

The woman began staring at me.

"I know you're trying to sniff my cunt," she said. "Don't sniff my cunt!"

"Believe me, lady, I'm not sniffing your cunt," I replied.

"Don't lie to me. You're sniffing my cunt. You're just like my dentist. He puts me under, then he sniffs my cunt and fucks me."

"You're not going to be put under, and no one is going to touch you," I assured.

I could hear laughter emanating from the driver's compartment. My partner was greatly amused, but I was getting the creeps.

The woman was quiet for a moment, then started up again.

"Stop sniffing my cunt, I said!"

"Listen, lady, you've got your clothes on. I couldn't sniff you if I wanted to."

"You're sniffing my cunt. I know it!" she insisted. "You're just like my dentist."

It went like that the whole way to the hospital. With each breath I took, she fired another vulgar accusation. That was one patient I was glad to see go out those double doors.

MICHAEL QUEN, PARAMEDIC, ARIZONA

■ A man was shot in the chest as he stood in front of his apartment in the projects. He stumbled into the living room and collapsed.

When we arrived, his five-year-old son was sitting on the couch watching cartoons. As we treated his father, the boy walked closer and started craning his neck so he could look around us and see the television. He was totally oblivious to the fact that we were battling for his father's life right on the floor in front of him.

We saved the guy, but I'll never forget the emotionless reaction of the son. It's a searing indication of what life is like in the ghettos of our inner cities. The violence is so prevalent that by the time kids are out of diapers, they don't even notice it anymore—even when it happens to their own parents. Sad.

LOU CARLUCCI, EMT, OHIO

■ A child was playing near an elevator shaft and fell in. He was hanging upside down at the bottom of the shaft, leaning against a power line. A cop saw him move.

"I think he might be alive. You want to check it out?"

One of the medics with us volunteered to climb in. He reached the kid and felt for a carotid pulse. The next thing I knew, the medic went flying backward and landed on his butt. A powerful electric jolt had nearly knocked him senseless. We rushed over to treat him.

"Are you all right?" I asked.

The medic responded by opening his paramedic shirt. Underneath, he was wearing a blue T-shirt with a big *S* on it.

"Of course I'm okay," he said. "I'm Superman!"

MIKE SCHULZE, PARAMEDIC, NEW YORK

■ The local flasher was brought in suffering from a heart attack. He was dead as a doornail when we got to him. I noticed a large lump in his pants. We cut them off and discovered a big dildo strapped to his groin. It had a metal tie device that enabled him to lift it up and down.

Apparently the guy had been displaying his new toy around the local Wal-Mart and the excitement got to him.

ANDREA GEARY, EMT AND ER TECHNICIAN, FLORIDA

■ It was another "blind date," a problem-unknown call.

"He won't leave," a small elderly woman announced as she greeted us at the door. She appeared to be in perfect health.

"Who won't leave?" I asked.

"Him! He came in here and demanded that I fix his breakfast, but I just want him to leave."

We searched the house and found nobody anywhere.

"He keeps coming here and he won't go," the lady continued.

"Who?"

"Him! He's sitting right there," she said, pointing to an empty chair across the table from her.

"Oh, that guy!" I said, nodding, now fully understanding the problem.

"He's been coming to my house at all hours of the day and night. He came last night in his pickup truck and had a machine gun. He pointed it at me!"

"No!"

"This morning he came back and started looking at me through the windows. Then he boldly marched in and asked me to fix his breakfast. I don't want to fix his breakfast. I don't even like him!"

While she talked, I went through her things to find the number of a family member I could call. I finally located a number, and her relatives arrived and took it from there.

It was the first time I'd seen a delusion that vivid. It gave me the chills. It also emphasized that families shouldn't allow their elderly relatives to live alone. Loneliness, among other things, can play tricks on the mind.

DONNA

■ A young man was suffering from a toothache. He lived in a trailer with a large family, and it seemed every member had an illness of some kind. They had a row of medications lined up on a shelf.

To seek relief from this throbbing tooth, the man began sampling all the medications. He took his mother's painkillers. Didn't work. He tried his father's cardiac drugs. No relief. He swallowed his grandmother's diabetes pills. The tooth still hurt. He took his grandfather's blood thinners. The pain remained. He continued down the line, taking half a pharmacy's worth of pills, all to no avail.

He was woozy but still hurting when we arrived. I told my partner to relay to the doctor the entire list of drugs he had taken so we'd know what to do.

"Is that it?" I asked when he reached the end.

"That's it," he said, lifting his eyes to the shelf. "No, wait. There was something else." He reached up and grabbed a tube of Ben-Gay ointment and handed it to me.

"What'd you do with this?" I asked.

"I rubbed it on my tooth."

"Okay," I said, walking over to my partner. "He said he took one more, Ben-Gay."

My partner got on the radio and tried to relay the last bit of information, but she couldn't. She suddenly got a bad case of the giggles. Every time she tried to say "Ben-Gay," she just broke down, laughing until she cried. The doctor was not amused. I took the radio.

"He rubbed Ben-Gay on his gums," I said.

"Okay, that shouldn't be a . . ." the doctor began, then stopped. I heard muffled laughter. "That, uh, that shouldn't be a problem," the doctor finally managed, breaking down himself.

ROGER VIGIL, PARAMEDIC, ARIZONA

■ A man had taken a nasty spill and kept trying to tell us something. We told him to shut up because he'd sliced his external carotid [artery] and was bleeding like crazy. Every time he tried to talk, he'd bleed even worse. Turned out that he had a partial plate [false teeth] and it was stuck in his throat. He was trying to tell us that he was choking to death! We saved him, but after that, I learned to listen to my patients.

DIANE CRAWFORD, PARAMEDIC, OHIO

■ A man and a woman were getting out of their car to unload some groceries when the transmission slipped out of park and locked into reverse. They were both knocked from the vehicle. The car ran over the man's foot, then dragged the woman halfway down the driveway before she rolled free.

We responded and treated the pair. The man had a broken leg, and the woman suffered broken ribs. They were both taken to the hospital.

With the couple out of the way, we turned our attention to a bigger problem—the car. It had backed out of the driveway and was now moseying down the snow-covered road in a pattern of overlapping circles, bouncing from curb to curb, chewing up bushes, mailboxes, landscape lights, small trees, and trash cans along the way.

I surveyed the situation. The street came to an abrupt end a couple hundred yards away. Twenty feet below was a very busy thoroughfare. If the runaway car plunged down the incline, all hell would break loose.

I huddled with the cops.

"Let's shoot the tires out. That'll slow it down," an officer suggested.

"No, that'll just alter its course," I cautioned. "It may end up going straight down the street even faster, or it could crash into one of the homes. At least right now we know what it's doing."

Someone suggested trying to dive Hollywood-style through the flapping driver's-side door as it swung open, but that was deemed too risky. The person trying it could end up with a pair of broken legs if the door whipped shut at the wrong time. Hopping onto the hood like Indiana Jones and trying to get control that way was also ruled to be too dangerous.

We tossed out a half-dozen more ideas over the next thirty minutes as the circling vehicle crept closer to the ravine. We finally decided to call in a bulldozer with a shovel full of sand. The bulldozer would anchor itself behind the car and allow it to crash into the shovel.

The couple's son arrived while we were waiting for the bulldozer. "What are you doing?" he screamed, unhappy with our inactivity. "Stop the car before it gets to the highway!"

"We've got a plan," I explained. "Let us handle it."

The son didn't like our plan. He ran to his car, cranked it up, then zigzagged his way through the row of fire trucks and police cars on the scene. Once clear, he crashed his vehicle into the back of his parents' runaway car. That did the trick.

"Why didn't we think of that?" the cop standing next to me cracked.

HOWARD CLARK, PARAMEDIC, ILLINOIS

■ A young girl, no more than ninety-nine pounds soaking wet, was zonked out on angel dust. She was on her knees in the middle of the street, furiously banging her head on the pavement, bleeding like a stuck pig. I grabbed her and tried to lay her down flat so she couldn't do any more damage, but she fought me with the strength of three men—which is a common side effect of angel dust. I lay on her and hooked my feet behind her knees. She countered by spinning me like a top. We rolled all over the street, back and forth from curb to curb, until I was so dizzy I couldn't even think.

My partner slapped some plastic restraints on her. The tiny woman snapped them like they were strands of spaghetti. He had to run back and get some metal handcuffs, leaving me to rock and roll some more. We finally got her cuffed and strapped on a gurney in the ambulance.

I spent the next couple of hours picking tar, rocks, dirt, and grit out of my chest, legs, and knees—which led me to wonder why the hell they call that demonic drug *angel* dust.

DONNA

■ We call them "chicken breathing" calls. That's when one of my fellow Mexicans phones 911 and is so hysterical she runs her words together: "She can't breathe. Chee cint breathe! Chee cintbreathe! Cheecintbreathe. Chicken breathe!"

We get these all the time.

We ran a "chicken breathing" call and arrived to find a boisterous fiesta in progress. Someone led me to a back bedroom, where a young woman was writhing on the sheets and screaming at the top of her lungs. She was either drunk or drugged, or her boyfriend broke up with her, or one of the usual things, and she didn't appear to be physically ill. When I tried to take her vitals, she started fighting.

"Let me go! Let me go!" she wailed.

My partner and I fought to hold her down while our captain, a man who never wanted to get his hands dirty, just stood by and observed. A pair of frantic women sprinted into the room. They were the girl's two equally hot-blooded sisters.

"You're hurting her," they yelled. "Stop it!"

The older one proceeded to jump on my head and started yanking my hair. "Get off her!"

"We're trying to help. You called us!"

"I don't care. Get off her!"

The second sister took the cue and leaped on my partner like a deranged gargoyle and started beating the hell out of him.

I glanced over toward my captain. *Surely he'll intervene now,* I thought. Nope. He just stood there watching.

"The police are on the way," he said, refusing to budge from his spot in the corner. "They'll be here any minute."

That was a relief. I held on, waiting for a tag team of burly, weight lifter–type cops to lumber into the room and take care of the sisters from hell.

The terrible trio was still pounding on us when a lone officer strolled into the room. I looked over and winced. Instead of the two hoped-for gorillas, it was a tiny policewoman!

"What do you want me to do?" she asked.

"Get these two lunatics off us!" I cried, figuring I was asking too much of this glorified meter maid.

The next thing I knew, the tiny cop grabbed the older sister by the hair, yanked her off my back like a dishrag, and dragged her out of the room. The officer marched back inside and did the same thing to the second sister. She returned, stood in the doorway, and screamed, "Clear this room, *now!*"

The music stopped. Everything went dead quiet. Then, as if on cue, the men, women, and teenagers bolted as one from the apartment, terrified by the minicop.

I turned to my partner and said, "Man, that little lady kicked some ass!"

Outside, the supercop singlehandedly arrested all three of the sisters, including the one on the bed, whose alleged illness was never determined. After that, my partner and I never doubted the abilities of a female officer.

ROGER VIGIL, PARAMEDIC, ARIZONA

■ A regular patient of ours was walking along the train tracks, oblivious to the approaching train. Although the engineer blasted his horn, the guy just kept walking. At the last minute he turned, smiled at the conductor, waved, and then was slammed by the huge iron beast and knocked for a loop.

I expected to find bits and pieces of a horribly mangled body. Instead, we discovered a viable patient.

"Don't do that," he protested, waving his arm as I tried to tube him.

The guy took a point-blank hit from a megaton locomotive and came away with nothing more than a fractured arm and a few broken ribs. Pretty doggone amazing.

DOUG CARRELL, PARAMEDIC, NEBRASKA

■ A young dentist was severely depressed over the deterioration of his relationship with his girlfriend. Although the guy seemed to have it all—money, a successful practice, a beautiful condo, and a hot sports car parked out front—he couldn't deal with what was happening with this woman.

The pain of lost love became so unbearable that he couldn't go on. He took a hundred Valiums and went to sleep, certain that he would never see the sun again. During the night, however, his body rejected the medication, forcing him to throw up. He was too groggy to notice it at the time, but when the sun came up, he was still alive.

"You really didn't want to kill yourself," I heard a callous cop say to him on the scene. "If you really wanted to kill yourself, you'd have used a gun."

A week later, we were dispatched to the same address. The dentist had taken a .357 Magnum in one hand and a .38 in the other, placed them to both temples, and fired. This time there was no margin for error. I'll never forget the look of utter despair frozen on what was left of his face. I'll also never forget the insensitive cop who all but challenged the dentist to do it right the next time.

DAN COUCH, PARAMEDIC, ARIZONA

■ A man was hit by a train and his body was mangled. A woman came to the station and asked if anyone had seen her husband.

"Did he have on brown shoes?" a medic asked.

"*Sí! Sí!* Brown shoes."

The medic showed her the shoes taken from the body. The woman identified the shoes as belonging to her husband and freaked out.

Only it wasn't her husband! He came home in one piece a short time later. They must have been a popular brand of brown shoes.

MIKE SCHULZE, PARAMEDIC, NEW YORK

■ A Jeep had overturned in five feet of water in a canal. When my partner and I jumped on top, we heard a knocking sound from inside. I looked across the undercarriage and saw what appeared to be a trail of blood running from the engine to the gas tank.

Before it hit the canal, the Jeep had bounced off a utility pole, breaking one of the power lines. That made the whole situation extremely dangerous. If we took a hit of electricity while wading in the water, we'd be instantly killed.

We heard the knock again.

"Someone's trapped inside," I exclaimed. "We've got to go in."

For the next half-hour we splashed around in the mud, frantically trying to save the person in the car. We fished inside with our arms. We held our breath and swam around. We dug underneath with shovels. We did everything humanly possible, but we couldn't find the driver!

A crane arrived and lifted the vehicle. I immediately dived under the dangling Jeep—a risky procedure—and searched anew. There was nobody anywhere. Not in the car, in the canal, buried in the mud, or on the bank.

We slogged to shore, covered with mud and totally exhausted.

A pair of police dogs arrived and picked up a trail. With their help, the police eventually ran down the driver, who was hightailing it across a cornfield. Apparently he was intoxicated and didn't want to get a DUI.

The guys at the station razzed us pretty good for that one. The blood was nothing but transmission fluid. The knock was who knows what. But even so, there's a lesson to be learned. Please, if you ever have an accident, don't leave the scene for any reason. You may be endangering the life of an EMT or paramedic.

LOU CARLUCCI, EMT, OHIO

■ We were dispatched on a cardiac arrest at the community center of a trailer park. When we arrived, the lights were low, music was playing, and a party was going on full force. I figured it was a false alarm, but someone finally noticed our presence and led us to a corner where a man was sprawled out on the floor, dying. I couldn't believe it. This guy was having a heart attack, but these people didn't let it interfere with their good time. They just kept right on eating and drinking, slow-dancing in the soft light.

We brought the man to the hospital DOA.

"Should we go back and tell the people at the party?" my partner wondered.

"Nah," I said. "I don't think anybody cares."

MICHAEL QUEN, PARAMEDIC, ARIZONA

■ A lady called 911 and said something was burning in her house. We arrived, and sure enough, there was a noticeable odor. We searched and searched, but we couldn't find the source. We guessed that it was a wire or something inside a wall.

Making one last pass at her bedroom, I spotted a quarter-sized burn hole in her drapes. That was curious. Tracing back, I discovered the culprit. The woman had a two-panel makeup mirror on her dresser. The two mirrors were set in such a way that the sun coming through the window bounced from one mirror to the other and reflected a concentrated beam back toward the drapes—a beam intense enough to burn through the curtain.

She was extremely lucky that the curtains, and the house, hadn't burst into flames. We advised the lady to keep her mirror closed when she wasn't using it.

HOWARD CLARK, PARAMEDIC, ILLINOIS

■ My father worked a subway accident where a man was

decapitated. The victim's head was shaved and he had no facial hair, so there was no easy way to pick the head up. Dad didn't want to put his fingers in the corpse's mouth, so he lifted it with the palm of his hand like a waiter holding a food tray. He started walking down the tracks, doing a little jig and singing "I Ain't Got Nobody."

A freelance photographer shot a picture and sent it to the *National Enquirer*. The tabloid splashed it across a centerfold.

Dad got chewed out, but the photo has lived on in infamy. The picture remains on the wall of a police department in Brooklyn—thirty years later.

MIKE SCHULZE, PARAMEDIC, NEW YORK

■ I blinked in disbelief and asked the dispatcher to repeat herself.

"Man stuck in washing machine."

I looked at my partner, shrugged, and flicked on the reds.

Sure enough, a man was jammed inside a washing machine. He was a big guy, about 220 pounds, and his body was wrapped around the agitator. He'd been trying to fix it, slipped, and tumbled in.

His legs, pants, belt loops, everything had become entangled with the machine. He was in agony, and we couldn't get him out! We finally had to call the fire department. They tore the machine apart and eventually got him free. He had some pretty nasty bruises and muscle pulls, but he was generally okay.

NAME WITHHELD, PARAMEDIC, KENTUCKY

■ We were toned out to assist a rural emergency team thirty miles away near a lake.

"Don't spare the horses," the dispatcher said.

We linked with the other unit on the highway. When I opened the ambulance doors, blood came pouring out from the floorboard. A teen had been hit by the propeller of a boat, and his leg was severely lacerated. There were four EMS personnel in there with him, and they had yet to tie on a tourniquet to stop the bleeding, because the teen was semiconscious and extremely combative.

I ordered them to put on a pair of tourniquets as high as they could, then I inspected the damage. The leg was cut in a spiral pattern from the buttocks all the way to his knee. Some of the cuts were so severe they went to the bone.

We moved the boy to our ambulance and tilted the cot so that blood would flow to his upper jugulars. We then put two bags of IV ringers into him. The boy had suffered a vascular shutdown, so I had to tie blood pressure cuffs around the IV bags so we could squeeze the solution in.

At the hospital, I asked the doctor to clamp his femoral artery, but the doctor refused. Sometimes that can be a tough decision. We're taught to be very careful with tourniquets and clamps, because once you put them on, you generally lose the limb. I'm sure this doctor was thinking that he could save the leg.

Well, in saving the leg, you sometimes lose the patient. I was convinced that this was the situation we were in. To complicate matters, there were no surgeons at the hospital. We had to emergency-transport the boy to another city. I went with a doctor and nurse, and the whole time we squeezed volume expanders [fluids] into him. He was still bleeding pretty badly, and the doctor continued to avoid clamping the artery.

At the second hospital, I noticed a pencil-thin line of blood streaming to the floor as the boy was being prepped for surgery. Nobody was doing a thing about it! I barged in there, put on a pair of gloves, walked to the patient, and tightened the tourniquets. I then put my hand on the femoral artery and pressed down as hard as I could.

"You've got to hold this all the way into the operating room," I instructed a nurse. "You've got to stop this bleeding. You've got to slow it down!"

They were all shocked that I would be so forward and say that. I guess I was pretty emotional at the time. Whatever, the nurse did what I asked.

Despite all our efforts, the teen died on the operating table. The nurses cried. The doctor was shocked. It was tragic for everyone involved.

I tell this story to all my paramedic classes. It's a classic call. There comes a time when you have to make a decision to lose the limb. It's a hard call to make, but you've got to save the life first. We teach that you never put on a tourniquet except as a last resort. Well, you have to know a last resort when it's looking you in the face. What we had on this run was a last resort.

It's been six years since that happened, and I still think of that boy all the time. I wonder if he'd be alive today if they'd gotten the tourniquets on sooner and if the doctor had clamped the artery. After all, it was just a leg. No one should die from a leg injury.

NAME WITHHELD, PARAMEDIC, MONTANA

■ A man overdosed on the roof of a building and was being helped by his wife and brother. The guy's girlfriend showed up and proceeded to get into a vicious fight with the wife. During the clawing and fisticuffs, the stoned boyfriend/husband was accidentally knocked from the roof and plunged to his death!

That only enraged the women more. They battled their way down the stairs and out to the street. Neighbors started pouring from the nearby buildings and began taking sides. Pretty soon a full-blown riot had broken out. As we barricaded ourselves on the roof, we watched as our ambulance was turned over and burned to a crisp—along with half the block!

An army of cops responded in school buses. It took fourteen hours to get things under control—all because of a catfight over a dead drug addict.

MIKE SHULZE, PARAMEDIC, NEW YORK

■ Two high-school girls'-bathroom calls have had an indelible effect upon my life and career.

The first was when four young ladies stuffed a commode with toilet paper and set it on fire, setting the toxic vinyl seats ablaze as well. I went inside with an MSA oxygen mask and promptly collapsed with what appeared to be a heart attack. Additional medics had to come in and rescue me. At the hospital, they determined that the MSA tanks were contaminated with carbon dioxide. I was in intensive care for nearly four days before I pulled through.

Some time later, it was back to a bathroom again. A 400-pound teenager passed out on the commode. I couldn't believe it when I saw her. She was wedged between the toilet and the stall wall and was absolutely huge! There was no way I was going to be able to lift her. All I tried to do was center her a bit so we could get more people in there to help me. I had her part of the way up when she suddenly lurched forward. I heard my back pop. It didn't hurt so much right away, so I continued working. We were carrying her on the stretcher when my back popped again, this time even louder.

The girl turned out to be okay, but that was it for me. My career was over. I had three back surgeries and retired on a disability.

BILL ROSE, PARAMEDIC, OHIO

■ I walked up to an auto accident scene and couldn't believe what I found. A Camaro hit a bridge, and the guardrail smashed through the windshield, sliced off the top of the driver's seat, and blasted out the back window. I edged closer, fully expecting to find a beheaded corpse lying on the floorboard. There was nobody inside.

I searched the area, figuring the mangled body had been ejected. There was no sign of anyone.

A few minutes later, a man approached with a teenager at his side.

"That's my son's car," the man said.

I looked at the boy. There was hardly a scratch on him. In any case, he was feeling no pain.

"You were driving?"

"Uh-huh," he slurred, obviously intoxicated.

"How'd you survive?" I asked.

The teen smiled sheepishly.

"I ducked."

PATRICK WALSH, PARAMEDIC, ILLINOIS

■ There was a shooting at a bar. We wanted to wait for the police, but a mob of about 150 people rushed the ambulance and began pounding on the doors, screaming at us to get inside. We made the mistake of complying.

A gentleman was lying on the floor. As we bent down to treat him, the taunting started.

"If he doesn't make it, you're going to die," a voice threatened.

"If you lose him, we've coming after you," another seconded.

Then the opposite side spoke up.

"Let him die!"

"Don't you dare help him!"

"Let the SOB die!"

There were definitely two different sets of opinions at work in the bar, as well as a large number of mean and intoxicated patrons. The crowd grew increasingly ugly and unruly. They began to push and shove and started threatening each other as well as us.

"This is a scoop-and-run," I whispered to my partner. He agreed. We rolled the victim onto a stretcher and carted him out of there before the place blew.

The guy made it, and so did we.

DOUG CARRELL, PARAMEDIC, NEBRASKA

■ A deputy who died in a shooting had been drinking coffee a half-hour before the shoot-out. After he was hit, he constantly vomited the coffee. That's the kind of stuff they don't show on television. When human beings are gravely injured, it's usually not pretty. At that time, we didn't have EOAs [a balloon-tipped tube inserted into the stomach to prevent vomiting]. I ended up dodging this vile coffee vomit the entire trip to the emergency room. Later, back at the unit, I discovered that it was all over me. I nearly threw up myself. For years after that, the smell of coffee made me sick.

Unfortunately, I wasn't in a profession that allowed me to shy away from much of anything, least of all coffee. A few months later, on another call, I found myself treating a man who suffered a heart attack in a department store. His family was standing around, screaming and crying, while dozens of customers watched. It was one of those moments when a paramedic is on display for all the world to see.

I'm trying to tube this guy, and he starts vomiting coffee. That was it. I lost it. I started vomiting myself, right in front of his family and all the shoppers. Still, I didn't lose sight of my job. I kept trying to tube him; he kept pitching his coffee, and I kept pitching my lunch. I'd recover, drag him to a clean spot on the floor, and we'd start the process again. It would have been funny if it wasn't so disgusting.

ERNIE EBERHARD, PARAMEDIC, MICHIGAN

■ A pair of college kids on spring break slammed their van into a huge boulder outside a beachfront restaurant. A teenage girl they'd picked up along the way was thrown through the windshield. The van tumbled in the soft, sugarlike sand and came to rest on top of her.

After determining that the guys were okay—they were wearing their seat belts—I grabbed a flashlight and crawled under the vehicle. The first thing I noticed was the light shimmering on the girl's long auburn hair. The rest of the picture wasn't so pretty. She was lying on her side with an axle pressed against her head. The sand around her had turned to red clay from the blood.

"Can you hear me?" I asked.

A small hand, caked in bloody sand, reached toward me. I wrapped my fingers around it. She squeezed.

"Please don't leave me. I'm so scared," she pleaded.

"I won't. I'm right here. Don't worry."

A large group of college kids gathered around the van. I could hear them arguing with my partner.

"We're going to roll it off!" someone announced.

"We'd better wait for the fire department," I suggested. "She has a head injury."

A young man bent his head down to talk to me.

"The firemen are nowhere in sight, man!" he said. "I don't even hear any sirens coming. You'd better get out, because we're going to get it off her—now!"

There was no sense arguing with the determined mob.

"You can roll it away, but I'm not leaving her," I said. "Just roll it off us both."

I turned to the girl and explained what was going to happen.

"Please don't let me die," she cried.

"I won't," I assured her. "We're going to get this off you and take you to the hospital."

I watched as a dozen pair of feet began scurrying around the van, getting into position.

"On three!" someone commanded.

The boys lifted. The girl squeezed my hand—then stopped breathing as the vehicle came off.

I did mouth-to-mouth and revived her. She took a few breaths, then stopped breathing again. I spit the sand and blood from my teeth and revived her a second time. We rushed her into the ambulance.

When we arrived at the ER, the door was locked! We couldn't get in! The girl was dying, and we couldn't get into the damn place!

I frantically banged on the windows and doors until somebody finally appeared. By then, the girl had stopped breathing—for the last time.

"Why'd you bring her here?" a gruff doctor challenged, implying that we should have taken her directly to the morgue.

"Because this is a hospital, isn't it?" I shouted back, furious about the locked door and his callous attitude.

It took me a long time to shake that one. I can still feel that girl's dainty hand squeezing mine as her life escaped. I pray for her soul every day.

PAT CRAWFORD, PARAMEDIC, FLORIDA

■ A woman was mowing her lawn with a John Deere ride-on mower when it accidentally flipped over and killed her. There wasn't much we could do after we arrived but try to comfort her husband.

"You know, she's been telling me for months that

something was going to happen," he said. "She kept saying that an angel visited her on the patio. The angel always told her that he was preparing to take her home.

"Here," the man said, thrusting a little book into my hands. "She wrote it all down in her diary."

I thumbed through the pages. Sure enough, there were numerous references to an angel sitting with her on the patio. When I got to the last page, an entry she had written just a few hours earlier, goose bumps rose on my body.

"Two angels came and visited me this morning," she wrote. "They told me, 'Today is the day we are taking you home.'"

RANDY NEIBERT, FIRST-RESPONDER, INDIANA

Win Some More

> *If you stay after it, if you keep training and you work on your systems, EMS can make a difference and save lives. It doesn't always have to be such a horrifying occupation.*

JOE WILLIAMSON, PARAMEDIC, KANSAS

Saves—oh, those glorious saves. Although they're a lot rarer than the television rescue shows would have you believe, there's no mistaking the fact that this is what we're all about. Can't beat a happy ending.

THE STORIES

■ In the desert, we have all these dry beds and washes that can turn into roaring rivers with the slightest rain. Many of these "instant rivers" course right across main thoroughfares, forcing us to shut down roadways until nature can literally run its course. Most desert dwellers are used to this and learn to adjust. However, there's always somebody who tries to push it. When that happens, it's my job to come to the rescue—or clean up the mess.

A period of heavy rains in the mid-1980s made the wash situation the worst I'd ever seen it. The Phoenix metropolitan area became crisscrossed with roaring rivers where there had been nothing but parched desert. One of the largest was downstream from the Lake Pleasant dam near Sun City, the famous retirement community. Aside from the natural rain runoff, this particular wash was being fed by controlled water releases from the dam.

We received a call at 5:30 A.M. that a body was in an overturned car. When we arrived, all we could see were four tires sticking up through the muddy water. Although the intersection had been barricaded, the driver had stopped his car, removed the barricades, backed up, and floored it in a woefully misguided attempt to blast through the water. He didn't make it. The river stopped his car dead and overturned it.

The vehicle came to rest under an overpass. That enabled my partner and me to rappel down the side of the bridge and swing out to the undercarriage. Our intention was to hook on a tow cable and drag the car to shore. If there was a body inside, we could fish it out later.

As we were standing there in the morning light, we heard a loud *knock knock knock* under our feet.

"Shit!" I exclaimed. "There's somebody alive in there!"

My partner lay across the gas tank and tried to reach through the window. I held on to his legs to keep the water from washing him away.

"I feel a foot!" he said. "Must be the one that's been kicking the floor. But I can't pull him out."

We yelled to the firefighters on dry land that we needed more help and additional equipment.

"Negative," the reply came via bullhorn. "They've opened the gates of the dam. You've got seven minutes to get the hell out of there."

A chill ran through my body. A tidal wave of water, probably another ten feet high, was rapidly heading our way. If we were still standing there when it hit, the vehicle, the man inside, and my partner and I would be swept halfway to Nevada before they found us.

"We've got to go in the car, *now!*" I barked.

"You're kidding!"

"No time to argue. We've got six minutes!"

We tied our ropes to the axle and jumped into the cold, raging water. Hanging on for all we were worth, we managed to pull the man feet first through a window and hoist him to the undercarriage.

I glanced at my watch. We had about three minutes left. The man was suffering from hypothermia and was going in and out of consciousness. We slipped a life jacket on him, tied a rope around his waist, and signaled for the firefighters to reel him in like a fish.

As they pulled him through the rushing water, I could hear a distant rumble. The wave was coming!

"Let's get out of here!" I ordered.

My partner and I swung back to the bridge and began frantically climbing up the ropes. Id scaled a good ten feet into the air when all of a sudden the water was licking at my boots again. I climbed with renewed vigor and made it to the top. My partner followed a few seconds later.

"Damn, that was close!" I said, catching my breath.

"Yeah, too close," my partner shot back. "All for some idiot! We should have let him drown!"

I looked below. The river was now twice the size it had been seconds before. It was halfway to the top of the bridge, a good thirty feet deep. And if it was raging before, it was absolutely furious now.

I pointed to the spot where the vehicle had been, where we'd just been standing. There was nothing but acres of cold, dark water.

My partner and I shivered from the cold and the fear, then snapped back to attention. There was no time to sightsee. We were the only paramedics on the scene, and we still had a patient to save. We ran across the bridge to the ambulance.

The man had regained consciousness and was angry and combative, a typical reaction with hypothermia. I checked him over. Incredibly, he had only minor injuries. We plunged in an IV to speed up his heart rate and took off for the hospital. There they put him in warm water to get his body temperature back to 98.6 degrees. Despite all he'd been through, he was released that same afternoon.

A few days later, I was called into my administrator's office.

"That man you pulled from the wash filed a complaint against you," my boss announced.

"What? What kind of complaint? I nearly died saving that SOB!"

"He said you stole his watch. He wants ninety dollars deducted from his ambulance bill."

"What a jerk!" I exclaimed. "I can't believe this."

My boss laughed and tossed the complaint into the garbage.

"Like I said," my partner said with a shrug, "we should have let the river have him. Sometimes it's best to remove his kind from the gene pool."

I filed that one under the heading NO GOOD DEED GOES UNPUNISHED.

ROY RYALS, PARAMEDIC, ARIZONA

■ A crowd had already gathered below the 150-foot water tower when we arrived. The people were craning their necks and pointing skyward. I looked up and could just make out the outline of this little figure dangling off the edge of the huge tower.

"He's the painter!" someone explained. "He must have slipped. He's hanging by his lifeline!"

I huddled with my partners.

"How are we going to get this guy down?" I wondered.

One of the medics, a guy who had a sick sense of humor, went to his unit and brought back a body bag.

"However we get him down, we're going to need this," he cracked.

A firefighter who'd also responded, a young, healthy stud, volunteered to play hero. "I'll climb the ladder and check it out," he said, and up he went, scaling the small ladder that went through the center of the tower.

When he reached the work station at the top, he had a shock. A woman was sitting there calmly reading a magazine! She had a rope tied around her waist that extended above her head and snaked over an elevated railing. The other end of the rope was tied to her husband, who was hanging over the edge. The poor lady had no idea what he was going through. She couldn't hear his screams from where she sat, and the railing was bracing his weight, allowing her to read her magazine undisturbed.

The woman spotted the fireman and started to stand.

"No! No! No! Don't get up!" he ordered. "Stay there! Stay there!"

The firefighter explained what was happening and took control before the newly enlightened wife could panic. Together, they managed to pull the rope and haul the guy back to safety. We took him to the hospital, but he was more scared than anything.

Before we left, however, he did have a few choice words for his beloved.

DONNA

■ A man was walking through a private arboretum when he was nailed by a giant rattlesnake that bit completely through his tennis shoe. It was most vicious snake attack I'd ever seen.

People fear a rattler's poison, and rightly so, but in

many cases it's the blunt trauma that does the most damage. A coiled rattler that suddenly springs can shatter a car windshield from six feet away.

In this case, the man had gotten the worst of both evils. The king rattler not only blasted his foot with the force of a cannonball, it dug in its fangs and sprayed a staggering amount of paralyzing poison into the guy's bloodstream.

"I'm going to die! I know I'm going to die!" the man screamed.

"Nobody's going to die," I calmly assured him as I applied a constriction band around his calf. "We haven't lost a snakebite victim in decades."

That was true. A rattler bite of that force and severity would have indeed been deadly in another era. However, thanks to the age of rapidly responding paramedics, death from snakebite has been virtually eliminated.

Which was lucky for this guy, because he'd taken a whopper of a hit. The man's entire foot was swollen and purple, and the frightening discoloration was visibly creeping up his leg. Despite the constriction bands and IVs I'd administered, the poison had reached his knee by the time we made it to the hospital. "I'm going to die. I know it," he repeated as his leg continued to swell.

"No, you're not. The poison has a ways to go before it reaches your heart. You'll be fine. Just relax."

I returned to the hospital a week later to check the progress of the patient. I have to admit I was shocked by what I saw. The man was black and blue from his foot all the way up to his back. He was also really sick from the ravaging effects of the antivenin. The poor guy was in misery, but the good news was that he was out of danger. That issue had been settled the moment a paramedic arrived at the arboretum.

ROGER VIGIL, PARAMEDIC, ARIZONA

■ A hiker deep in the Utah forests lost his step trying to cross a steam and plummeted sixty-five feet down a waterfall, shattering his ankle and leg. It took his companion more than an hour to reach civilization and call 911.

There was no way to get to the victim by air or car. Despite the time involved, the only option we had was to hike in. I was part of a six-member rescue crew that made the trek. We carried a stokes basket with us and headed out into the forest.

It took us about ninety minutes to find the man. He was, suffice it to say, in a whole lot of pain. We checked him out, stabilized him, then strapped him inside the basket to keep him steady. The fear was that he'd fallen so far that he'd probably suffered unknown internal injuries. We needed to get him to a hospital, fast.

Although there were six of us, it was a nightmare trying to carry the basket through the dense forest and rocky terrain. We had to hoist him over, under, and around branches, bushes, thorns, and weeds. It took so long to maneuver him through the woods that an inky darkness washed over us two-thirds of the way out. Working blind slowed us down even further.

Tough as it was on us, you can imagine how it was on him.

We finally got the patient out of there—two and a half hours after we started. We slid him into the ambulance and rushed to the hospital. There, the ER doctors were able to determine what we already suspected—that despite his long, hard fall, he'd somehow managed to avoid fatal trauma to his head or body. If he had, he probably wouldn't have made it out of the forest.

They set his ankle and leg and sent him home a few days later. That was one lucky hiker.

KEVIN WARD, PARAMEDIC, UTAH

■ It's incredible how much the human body can endure. I worked a car accident where a bunch of kids flipped their vehicle on a bridge. One was ejected and skidded over the windshield glass that peppered the pavement. Shards of glass were impaled all over his body. When I approached him, he was leaning against the post of the bridge talking to one of his buddies. I couldn't believe it. He was a solid sheet of red. I couldn't see any clothes on him. I couldn't see any hair. And he's, like, having this casual conversation with his friend.

"Dude! How are you doing?" the friend asked.

"I'm okay. I'm just hurt a little here and there."

I stared at him and said, "Have you looked at yourself recently?"

"No. Why?" he asked.

The guy was drunk out of his mind. When I work teenagers, they're usually intoxicated. It's terrible. They have no idea what they're doing to themselves. I convinced the guy to gaze down at himself. He got the message.

"Oh, jeez, I must really be hurt!"

"No shit!"

As gruesome as he looked, this turned out to be one of the happy ones. The ER doctors were able to pluck out the glass and send him on his way, terribly sore but none the worse for wear.

VICKI IEZZY, PARAMEDIC, FLORIDA

■ There was a thunderous, head-on collision between two long-haul tractor-trailer trucks. One was loaded with beer and the other with mattresses. The driver of the mattress truck was pushing it to get home and had fallen asleep at the wheel. He bounced across the divider and smashed full force into his fellow trucker.

It was one of the most destructive accidents I've ever seen. The cab of the mattress truck had been crumpled to the size of a refrigerator. The fiberglass cab of the beer truck just shattered. The engine and transmission were ripped out of the chassis and were lying on the road.

Beer cans and mattresses were scattered everywhere. The beer cans were in a mound along the side of the road for more than half a mile. That's a lot of beer. Cans were popping and foaming left and right. I peered inside the jackknifed trailer. There was a single can sitting in there, all alone.

We figured both drivers were dead.

Something caught my eye in a nearby ditch. I couldn't believe it. There, lying in the middle of a huge puddle of beer and diesel fuel, was the driver of the beer truck!

My partner and I waded through the slippery sea to reach him. His legs, pelvis, arms, and shoulders were all fractured, but he was conscious! With an assist from the fire department, we managed to get him out of there and into the ambulance. We got three lines on him and kept him alive until we got to the hospital.

He was one tough trucker. Despite his massive injuries, he not only survived, but walked out of the hospital on his own power a month or so later. A few weeks after that, he was back in another truck, hauling the good brew.

PATRICK WALSH, PARAMEDIC, ILLINOIS

■ We had five inches of rain in thirty minutes. Cars started spinning down a rampaging river that materialized like magic through the city. They were swept into a drainage ditch and began smashing into each other, stacking up door to door.

A call came in that there were four people stuck in a van that was squashed against a large drain. The only way to get to it was by crossing a picket fence and hopscotching from one submerged vehicle to the next. I grabbed an ax, jumped the fence, danced my way across, then chopped out the van's windows—only to discover that it was a false alarm. There was nobody inside! The van had been parked in front of a house when it was caught by the floodwater.

As I turned to leave, I spotted a car trying to cross a flooded section of the road. The water stopped the vehicle dead, then spun it around. It started floating backward down the street at a high rate of speed.

I'd observed earlier that as each new vehicle smashed into the deck of cars, it rolled and stacked on top of the others. That meant I was standing in an extremely precarious position! I hopped across the roofs and made it to shore just as the car slammed into the end of the line, crunching the vehicles even more tightly together.

I mopped my brow and took a breath. Glancing toward the new addition, I saw something move. A woman and two small children were trapped inside the car! The vehicle had flipped onto its side and was being buffeted by the rushing water. Any second, another car could come barreling down the river of rain, caving in the first car's roof and crushing the family.

Back I went, playing my deadly game of hopscotch—only this time, I had to slide part of the way across a drainage pipe. The water below my feet was being sucked into a hidden drain, creating a massive whirlpool. I felt as if I was walking on the edge of a giant toilet that had just been flushed. There was no margin for error—one slip and I'd be swallowed by the water.

I concentrated on what I had to do and managed to reach the overturned vehicle. The mother pushed her two children up through the passenger-side window. One was a three-year-old girl and the other an eleven-month-old baby boy. I clutched one in each arm and tread carefully across the pipe and car roofs, painfully aware that I now was responsible for two lives besides my own. If I stumbled and lost a child, I'd never forgive myself.

I navigated over four teetering cars, then handed the girl to a friend, Tony Stegman, who met me halfway out. The baby was clinging to my neck so tightly I had to pry him off. Tony carried the boy and girl to some waiting firefighters who had formed a human chain to the bank.

I made a third trip over the slippery pipe and car roofs to help the mother escape the car and get to shore.

We were as wet as drowned rats, but everyone survived—including me.

The ironic part is that twenty minutes later, the rain stopped and the water practically disappeared. What had been a deadly river was now nothing more than a soft trickle.

JOE WILLIAMSON, PARAMEDIC, KANSAS

■ A Native American woman was in labor and wanted to be taken to the Phoenix Indian hospital. I was sitting in back with her, trying to keep her calm, when a gush of water erupted from between her legs like a fire hydrant, shooting across the ambulance and splashing against the back doors.

"We need to divert to the nearest hospital, *now!*" I told the driver.

"Why? Has her water broken?"

"Affirmative. It nearly broke the back door!"

We rushed her directly to OB, but the kid was having none of it. His head popped out in the hall. When the OB staff arrived, I shrugged and pointed to the healthy baby boy.

"I guess the little fellow was anxious to get out," I said.

DAN COUCH, PARAMEDIC, ARIZONA

■ The elderly woman was sitting calmly in her living room dressed in a pink nightgown. She was pale, sweaty, and clammy, and spoke of having chest pains. We escorted her to the ambulance and put her on oxygen.

Two blocks down the road, she went into full cardiac arrest. I started CPR while my partner cleared an airway. We worked on her the whole trip and finally got the monitor lines moving just as we were pulling up at the hospital.

As with so many cases, we were immediately toned out again, and the day's activities quickly blurred together. We never determined what happened to the cardiac patient.

Two months later, I was attending a meeting at the station when someone walked in and asked for me.

"Yes, may I help you?" I inquired.

"I want to thank you for saving my life," she said.

My mind started working. I'd been on hundreds of calls since that afternoon. Who was this? Something finally clicked. The woman in the pink nightgown!

She certainly looked different. She was wearing makeup and had her hair done up all fancy. Most of all, she appeared healthy and alive. I couldn't believe it was the same person who lay near death in the ambulance for so long.

I struggled for something to say.

"I-It's our pleasure," I stuttered.

She touched my hand, then turned and walked away. I kind of stood there, stunned but happy. I'd saved another life!

DONNA

■ One time we went on a "breathing difficulty" call. This elderly, obese gentleman had just finished eating a nice Italian meal and drinking about half a bottle of wine. After we arrived, he went into cardiac arrest, and we started to perform CPR. As we did, he began to vomit—a lot. All that wine and Italian food was coming back up in torrents.

We loaded him into the ambulance and started toward the hospital. On the way, the guy started projectile vomiting, which is as bad as it sounds. He was putting out streams at least a foot high. At that point, I couldn't go on. I couldn't continue the CPR. I had to run to a window and stick my head out to get some fresh air.

When we arrived at the hospital, I just bailed out and let the ER workers handle it from there.

Afterward I worried that my inability to stomach the situation had resulted in the man's death. No matter how horrible and personally intolerable the circumstances, I was wrong to abandon my efforts to save him.

About three months later, I was on a routine call for another breathing difficulty. I walked inside and froze in shock. The same guy was sitting there on the side of his bed like a ghost!

"You're supposed to be dead!" I blurted without thinking.

He smiled and proceeded to explain that he had survived the previous run. Then he lifted up his shirt and showed me hand prints on his chest.

"Those are yours," he said. "You saved my life!"

Incredibly, the outline of my hands was still visible on his body from the vigorous CPR that I had apparently managed to perform.

I was happy that he was still alive, but seeing him sure gave me a start.

TERRY PYE, PARAMEDIC, ONTARIO

■ A little girl was playing on the lawn of an apartment complex when her left leg suddenly vanished into the ground. She'd stepped into a small sewage treatment pipe and had been swallowed up to her groin.

The poor child was whimpering and had the saddest look in her eyes that I've ever seen.

"Please help me," she pleaded.

We tried to lift her gently, but her leg wouldn't budge. By then, a large crowd had gathered. Her mother, suffice it to say, was frantic.

"We're going to have to cut the pipe," I announced.

We dug a hole next to her about two feet down. I crawled inside with a hacksaw and sawed through the pipe.

We now had her free, but the pipe was still glued to her leg. We laid her on the grass and huddled to determine what to do next. I tried to maneuver her shoe so that I could slip her leg out, but it wouldn't budge.

Back to work I went with the hacksaw, this time far more delicately. I sliced the pipe sideways at the bottom and pulled that section apart. I then untied the girl's shoe and slipped it off. After that, we were able to slide her leg out of the pipe.

The crowd cheered as we carried the girl into the ambulance for a precautionary ride to the hospital.

HOWARD CLARK, PARAMEDIC, ILLINOIS

■ A cat, running from a dog, smashed headfirst into a chain-link fence. The impact not only knocked its head through one of the links, it twisted it around and threaded it through a second link. The animal came to rest looking backward across its body.

I would have sworn the dang thing broke its neck, but it was still breathing! I guess it was using lives one through eight on this one.

I asked the lady who lived at the residence if we could cut a link in order to free the feline. She went inside the house, consulted her husband, and reappeared with the bad news.

"He said no."

"We can't get the cat out without cutting the fence!" I argued. "His head's wedged in there tight."

"My husband said you can't do it," she repeated.

Rebuffed, we called central, ordered some cooking oil, and greased the cat. Hard as we tried, we couldn't dislodge it without strangling the poor creature or breaking its neck.

Unwilling to give up, we worked on it another twenty minutes before pleading our case again.

"I don't think we're gonna be able to get this cat out of here," I lectured the lady. "It looks like you're going to have a cat skeleton sitting in your fence!"

She went back inside and talked it over with her husband, who never bothered to come out.

"Nope, he still won't let you cut the fence."

"Well, okay, we'll try the oil one more time," I sighed.

Somehow we managed to pop the cat's head through the second link. That enabled him to get a little more oxygen to his brain, and he revived a bit. It also meant the fight was on. The feisty stray tried to slash and climb anything and everything, me and my partner in particular.

It took us another five minutes, and a lot of cat scratches, but we eventually busted him loose.

Once free, the animal skittered off sideways and crawled under the couple's portable storage shed.

"I don't suppose you can get him out from beneath our building?" the woman asked.

"No, lady, I don't suppose we can. I reckon he'll come out when he's ready."

ANDREW ARNOLD, PARAMEDIC, TEXAS

■ A preteen boy needed to move one of his family's cars from the driveway in order to play basketball. The car was parked behind a second vehicle, which was in the garage. It had a standard transmission and was left in first gear as people often do. The instant the youth turned the key, the car lurched forward and crushed his four-year-old brother between the two bumpers.

The little boy's body was lying on the living room floor. He had no pulse and wasn't breathing. He was essentially dead. I'll never forget the look of horror on the parents' faces. They had no idea what to do for him.

We prepared our air bags and oxygen masks to attempt to resuscitate him. To our shock, all the glue holding the masks together had cracked in the hundred-degree Arizona heat. The facepieces had fallen off, rendering the masks useless.

I had to physically perform mouth-to-mouth. The boy had vomited, so I was blowing in and spitting out vomit, blowing in and spitting out vomit. I ignored the bitter taste and continued.

From the first breath, I had a powerful sensation that his life had returned, that all he needed was that initial air. There was no explanation for it, but I knew, despite his massive injuries, that this kid was a fighter. He wasn't ready to die.

I checked his pulse. There was a faint beat! We tubed him, put in an IV, and air-evaced him to the hospital.

In those days, we didn't follow up on calls. We did the best we could and moved on to the next one. Even though I'd experienced that strong feeling that he was going to make it, I didn't check to confirm it.

Six months later, I was home reading the newspaper when a story popped out at me. The boy had survived a series of operations and was recovering from a long hospital stay. Six months after that, a second story announced that he was returning home fully recovered.

My time with him had been short, only a matter of minutes, but they were important minutes. I was there when his life, and his will to live, returned.

ROD MORTENSEN, PARAMEDIC, ARIZONA

■ I was strolling through a local mall when I heard the

sound of an airplane sputtering overhead. I ran outside and saw a small prop engine heading right for a restaurant. My parents were eating inside!

I grabbed my gear and rushed over. On the way, I saw the aircraft skip over the restaurant and crash onto the flat roof of an automotive center.

Some people in the crowd helped lift me to the top of the two-story building. The minute I got up there, I smelled gasoline and saw steam rising. I didn't know if the plane was about to blow like a bomb—which usually happens—or if the steam was coming from puddles of rainwater being heated by the plane's scalding engines.

There was no time to determine which was which. As I moved in to assist the passengers, I prayed it was theory number two.

I shouted down for a tire iron and used it to pop open the plane's door. There were two people in the front seat and a third person under a bunch of clothing in the back. The woman up front had originally been in the back. The impact ripped the moorings of her seat from the floor and threw her forward. She was badly injured but alive. The pilot had multiple fractures and contusions, but he too was alive. A frightened young girl lay under the clothing in the back. Incredibly, she appeared to have nothing but a few cuts and bruises.

By then, additional medics and firefighters had arrived. We got the family out of the plane, eased them down from the roof, and sped the lucky trio to the hospital. All three made it. Although the woman ended up being paralyzed from the waist down, in an airline crash you take that outcome any day over the other alternative.

The plane, suffice it to say, didn't explode.

I was awarded a Medal of Valor and retired from the service a short time later. I figured a triple rescue was a good way to cap my career.

BILL ROSE, PARAMEDIC, OHIO

■ A man had fallen into the pool at a motel. Someone pulled him out, but he still wasn't breathing. We thought it was a heart attack. I had this feeling that there was something else going on, something different about this call. I don't know what made me do it, but I took my finger and went way in the back of his throat. I felt something and grabbed hold of it. It was part of a sandwich.

He had been walking beside the pool when he choked, fell in, and hit his head, knocking himself out. As soon as I got that chunk of sandwich free, he started breathing. Otherwise, he might have died right there.

DIANE CRAWFORD, PARAMEDIC, OHIO

■ We responded to a shooting and found the victim standing in a phone booth. He had taken a shotgun blast to the chest at close range. He was a big, tough guy and was alert and talking despite the gaping hole in his torso.

"You wait here and we'll get the stretcher," I explained.

As I was lifting it out, I felt this huge weight on my back. The man had walked over to the ambulance, then collapsed on top of me. We got him on the stretcher, strapped him down, put on a C-collar to protect his spine, and started two lines.

Back at the station, I was amazed how much of the man's blood was on me. It had soaked through my jumpsuit and T-shirt and was all over my skin. Considering the size of the wound and the amount of blood he'd lost, I figured he wouldn't make it.

The guy walked out of the hospital a few days later.

PATRICK WALSH, PARAMEDIC, ILLINOIS

■ A man was in full cardiac arrest when we arrived at the

golf course. We tried everything we could on the scene but couldn't raise a pulse. I was certain this was going to be one of the bad ones.

I kept working him in the ambulance. His pulse came back. I worked him some more and got a faint blood pressure reading.

We went on a few more calls, then returned to the hospital to see if he made it. I was shocked to find him sitting in a chair in his room.

"Hi," he said. "You must be the man who saved my life."

I couldn't believe it. Not only was he alive, he was almost fully recovered.

"What's that lump in your pocket?" I asked, noticing a bulge near his hip.

He fished around and pulled out a golf ball.

"I'd hang on to that," I said. "That's your good-luck charm."

"I will!" he promised.

MICHAEL QUEN, PARAMEDIC, ARIZONA

■ I was sent on an OB-GYN call in the projects. We walked in and found several wailing women and children running around all over the place. They led me into the bedroom. A woman was on the bed screaming in pain while two televisions blared in the background.

"Get me to the hospital!" she pleaded.

"What's wrong?"

"I'm in labor."

She was lying on her back, knees up. I lifted her dress to examine her and received the shock of my life. The head of the child had completely delivered—and the mother was still wearing her panties!

I jerked back to gather my wits. The whole scene was bizarre. The children—there must have been at least a half-dozen of them—were all gathered around the bed. The two televisions were still on, and this woman's poor newborn was struggling to push its head through her panties and get out.

We quickly yanked off her underpants and freed the eager child. Despite the unexpected obstacle, he was perfectly healthy.

I've done thousands of calls since then, all kinds of situations, but none that have had that kind of emotional impact on me. It was a powerful moment.

NAME WITHHELD, PARAMEDIC, CALIFORNIA

■ It was Christmas Eve. We were toned to a large house where a big party was in progress. The owners had a newborn, about two weeks old. They put it to bed in an area that was also doubling as the coatroom. One of their friends came by with a dress she had just gotten from the cleaners. She changed and then, not knowing a baby was there, tossed the thin plastic bag right on top of the infant.

The child's breathing sucked the plastic to its face. It quickly became covered like a doll wrapped in deadly cellophane. The baby started bleeding from the mouth and stopped breathing. The parents and guests were nearly hysterical.

A nurse at the party started CPR. When I took over, the infant still wasn't breathing. I tubed the baby, bagged it, and gave it an adrenaline IV. We got a pulse and a breathing rate.

A helicopter arrived and flew the baby to Good Samaritan Hospital, where the doctors took over. The child made a full recovery without any permanent damage.

A month later, the entire family came to the station with the baby. The child was happy and alert, and both the mother and father were crying with joy. It had truly been a merry Christmas.

ROGER VIGIL, PARAMEDIC, ARIZONA

■ My partner and I ran a cardiac arrest on a fourteen-year-old girl. Heart attacks are bad enough on older people, but when they happen to kids, it's really distressing.

We worked this girl, defibrillated her, and brought her to the hospital, where they determined that she had a congenital heart defect. The surgeons equipped her with an internal defibrillator.

Ten years later, we responded to a local business where someone was having difficulty breathing. This same girl worked there and assisted us on the call. It was strange, in a neat sort of way, to see this person again and have her help us. She was basically dead back then, and now she'd blossomed into a grown woman.

It makes the job worthwhile.

RANDY MEININGER, PARAMEDIC, NEBRASKA

■ A woman was lying across the threshold of her home, giving birth to a premature baby. It was twenty degrees outside, and steam was rising from her body. She was twenty-seven weeks into her pregnancy and was unable to make it through the door, much less get to a hospital, when the child decided to emerge.

I assisted her as best I could with the emergency delivery. The child was so tiny—one pound nine ounces—that it fit in the palm of my hand. For an instant I thought about just letting it go. It wasn't breathing, and even if it had been, it was so small that its chances weren't good. Plus, babies that small are usually saddled with crippling birth defects. On top of that, the mother was poor and unwed. From every angle, the odds didn't look favorable.

I dashed the dark thoughts, scooped the baby into my hands, and rushed it to the unit. It was too tiny to tube or bag, so I had to do old-fashioned mouth-to-mouth. A couple of times I got it to take a few breaths on its own, then it would immediately stop. I again thought about just letting it pass, letting nature take it course. No, I decided. If it was my child, I'd want someone to try. I continued breathing for it, mouth-to-mouth, all the way to the ER.

"I need help! Right now!" I shouted as I rushed inside. A doctor ran over, took the child from me, and worked on it for nearly an hour, finally locking in a breathing rhythm. It was then transported to another hospital, one that had a premie ward.

Although the doctors were skeptical, the tiny little girl made it through that night—and the next four months. When her weight increased, I was called to take her home. Despite the weight gain, the baby was still so diminutive that her mother had to buy Premie Cabbage Patch Doll clothes so she would have something to wear.

Happily, while the courageous little girl was clinging to life at the hospital, things were looking up at home. The child's father, an army recruit, accepted responsibility and married the mom, giving the baby a stable family to come home to.

It's just a small story, one that's not untypical in a paramedic's life, but it affected me deeply. I truly believe that part of my soul is in that baby.

GREG HESS, PARAMEDIC, INDIANA

■ It was the worst twelve-wheeler truck wreck I'd ever seen, and I've seen a lot of them. The cab was a shapeless mass of broken and twisted fiberglass. I grabbed a flashlight and searched through the rubble on my hands and knees. From what I could surmise, the driver was lying on his stomach with the shattered cab on top of him. The only things visible were his legs from the knees down—just like the witch under Dorothy's house in *The Wizard of Oz*.

I inspected his legs. The blinker switch was embedded in his right calf muscle. It was sticking out like another appendage.

Finding his legs was a start, but I really needed to get to the other end. I had to find his head to see if he was breathing.

That proved to be impossible. There was too much weight bearing down on him. I couldn't even reach my hand in any farther than his waist.

"Hey, can you hear me?" I yelled, trying to determine if he was alive.

He responded with a grunt and a groan.

"He's alive!" I screamed to my comrades. "Let's get him out!"

I ducked back under and started an IV on his leg so we'd have medical access to him while we waited for our next move.

The first thing we tried was the jaws of life. We attempted to cut a pathway through the wreckage, but the fiberglass kept crumbling and falling back into place. It was like trying to empty a sand pile with a fork.

When that failed, my chief radioed for a wrecker. The wrecker operator backed his truck up and tied a series of chains to anything he could. After using five separate chains to spread out the weight, he began lifting the cab an inch at a time. That enabled me to reach in and locate the driver's hand.

I checked his pulse. It was strong.

"Squeeze my hand," I instructed him. "Can you squeeze my hand?"

He squeezed it weakly.

"He has a good pulse and can respond to commands," I explained to my associates. "We've got to get him out!"

On the way back in, I noticed that his leg was bleeding

profusely from the hole where the blinker switch had been.

"What happened to the blinker?" I demanded.

A bystander inched forward. "I pulled it out for you."

That was the wrong thing to do. When something's sticking out of a person, you bandage the area and leave the object in until you get to the hospital, because the foreign object might be the only thing keeping the blood from gushing out. I grabbed a pressure bandage and managed to control the bleeding.

Meanwhile, the wrecker had slowly lifted the cab about a foot off the ground—enough room for me to crawl completely under.

"Do you want to go in?" my chief asked. "You don't have to. We can try to get it higher and then slip a backboard under him."

"I can do more good inside," I responded. "If something happens, I can protect him with my bunker coat and helmet." The unmentioned "something" was the strong possibility that at any second the entire cab could come crashing down.

Ignoring the danger, I eased myself underneath, breaking away remnants of fiberglass along the way. When I reached the driver, he was alert and oriented times three, meaning he knew his name, where he was, and the day and date.

"There's something pushing on my right hip and shoulder. Otherwise I'd have crawled out of here myself," he said.

"Okay, here's what we're going to do," I explained. "I don't know if you have any spine or cervical injuries, so I'm going to have them pass a backboard between us. I'll lay it flat, and then we'll roll you on your right side a little bit and get it underneath you. Then we'll slide you out."

"Okay," he said.

Our first attempt didn't work because parts of the cab continued to press on him. I instructed the wrecker to lift the pile another inch. It creaked and cracked and rained fiberglass on us from every direction. The whole cab seemed ready to collapse.

The extra inch enabled me to get the board under him. Now all I had to do was get him out. He was a hearty soul, a good 280 pounds. There was no way I could slip him through a narrow opening. We had to go for broke and raise the cab another five inches.

Chunks of fiberglass slammed down around us as we rushed to get him—and me—out of there in time.

We made it.

Once free, I helped carry him to the ambulance. As we were loading him in, I heard a thunderous crack and turned my head. The chains had broken through the cab, and the entire mangled heap crashed down in an explosion of splintering fiberglass.

I stood and stared in shock. I'd been on the scene more than an hour at that point. Much of that time was spent under the cab with the driver. Had we been there a minute longer, we would both have been crushed like eggs. It was as if something, some unseen force, was holding it up for us until the moment we got out.

"Attaboy!" my chief said, slapping me on the back, knocking me out of my stunned state. "Just in time."

The trucker had a fractured hip, the punctured calf, and some minor cuts and bruises—small potatoes, considering what he'd been through. He was back driving the big rigs in a matter of weeks.

ANDREW ARNOLD, PARAMEDIC, TEXAS

13 Oklahoma City

I don't think of myself as a hero. I was just doing my job. There were a lot of people out there who went above and beyond the call of duty. Nobody had to go barging into that building when the dust was so thick you couldn't breathe, when there seemed to be a new bomb scare every ten minutes or so, and the walls and spearlike cables were still crashing down around us.

TIFFANY SMITH, PARAMEDIC, OKLAHOMA

Sometimes a single devastating incident offers a lifetime of experiences for the paramedics and EMTs who respond. On April 19, 1995, such a disaster occurred in Oklahoma City. Here's the story from the EMS perspective—the good, the bad, and the painfully ugly.

THE GOOD

■ I was on the scene six minutes after the terrorist bomb destroyed the Alfred P. Murrah Federal Building. While we were still en route, I spotted a man on the street with blood shooting out of his arm. I signaled for the driver to stop and ran over. The injured man was in his forties and was wearing a juror's tag.

"What happened?" I asked.

"I don't know. Something blew up!"

"How'd you hurt your arm?"

"I don't know. It just started bleeding."

I bandaged the juror's arm, put in an IV, and escorted him to a transport unit. An EMT riding with me rounded up two more cut and bleeding jurors who had escaped the smoking building. They appeared dazed and confused.

"Something blew up," they kept repeating. "There was an explosion."

After treating the pair, we parked near the south entrance. From that angle, the building appeared relatively normal. Windows were blown out, and broken glass sparkled like diamonds on the pavement, but the structure looked intact.

I figured a gas line had burst in some isolated section, injuring a dozen people or so. I couldn't even imagine the massive destruction on the opposite side or the heartbreaking human tragedy that was about to unfold.

Suddenly a scream rang out from across the street.

"There's a man inside with two broken legs! He can't get out!"

I grabbed a spine board, tossed my medical equipment into a garbage bag, and headed for the building. There were two flights of cement stairs that I had to climb before reaching the doors. At the top of the stairs, in the patio area, a man wearing a red windbreaker was stumbling around in a trance. He was covered with blood from head to toe.

"I'm bleeding bad. Help me! Please," he pleaded.

He was an awful sight. His hair was burned off. Shards of glass jutted out of his arms, legs, and chest. His face was both burned and cut to ribbons, obscuring his features. He could have been my husband and I wouldn't have recognized him. It looked like the bomb exploded in his face.

"Don't worry," I assured. "I'll take care of you. You're going to be all right." I gently laid him on the board. A sheriff's deputy helped me carry him down the stairs to medic Scott Scammahorn's ambulance.

I grabbed a second backboard and jogged up the stairs, still determined to rescue the man with the two broken legs. By the time I reached the top, another victim had staggered out of the building and was braced against a light post. This man was wearing what remained of a business suit and was in the same condition as the previous patient—burned, bleeding, and cut to pieces.

"I need some help," he said calmly.

I inspected him more closely. Underneath his once crisp white shirt, he had a massive abrasion that covered his entire chest. "How did you get that?" I asked, my eyebrows arched with shock and surprise.

"I don't know. I was sitting in my chair, and something blew up. I hit something, or something hit me. I can't really recall."

I transferred the patient to paramedic Nelda Smith and headed back toward the building. A deputy was now standing near an employees' entrance.

"There's supposed to be a man inside with two broken legs. Do you know anything about it?" I asked.

"Somebody already got that guy," he explained. "We're bringing someone else down from the fourth floor who's critical."

"Let me go get some more help. I'll be right back."

I ran down the stairs and recruited EMT David Dunafin. We climbed back up just as they were carrying the latest victim out. As I approached, I heard a scream that I'll never forget. The voice came from deep inside the shattered hallway.

"We've got kids!"

The next thing I knew, the police officer at the door handed me a tiny African-American baby girl. She was unconscious and completely covered with dust and soot. I didn't see any noticeable injuries, so we put her in a vacuum splint to immobilize her spine. David carried her to the truck. I never saw her again and don't know whether she survived.

After treating and transporting that child, I was promptly handed another. This was a white boy about three who was burned really badly. His hair was gone and his body was singed so severely that his skin just peeled away in my hands. His mouth and nose were packed with plasterboard dust. He wasn't breathing.

There was nothing in my training that taught me how to deal with this, so I had to improvise. I dug my fingernail into each nostril and pulled out a thimbleful of dust. I repeated the procedure with his mouth, and he started to breathe! Tears welled in my eyes as I handed him to another medic. This boy made it.

A few seconds later, I found myself holding the latest tiny victim, an African-American toddler, about two years old. He was passed to me by a quickly developing human bucket brigade. This child was in worse shape than the others. His hair was gone, more than half his body was covered with deep burns, and his arm was broken. I could hear him wheezing and guessed that on top of everything else, he had asthma. I again relied upon my long fingernails to dig the dust and debris out of his nose and mouth. That cleared an airway, and he started breathing—and wheezing—louder. Despite that positive sign, I figured this poor little boy didn't have a prayer.

Because of his severe condition, I carried him all the way down the steps myself. For some reason, I felt a strange attachment to this child. I knew he didn't have a chance, but I couldn't let go.

Well, I was wrong! He survived! Not only that, but little

P. J. (later identified as Phillip Allen) was dubbed the "miracle toddler" and featured in newspapers around the world.

For me, P. J. made everything I'd experienced that day worthwhile.

After tearfully letting go of P. J., I climbed the stairs for the umpteenth time and was immediately handed a limp little girl with beautiful blond hair. She was about three. She was bleeding from her head, arms, and body, but was breathing strongly. I treated her wounds and handed her to David. As with P. J. and the others, I talked to her in a comforting manner the whole time. Even though they were unconscious, I felt that maybe these children could still hear me, and if they could, I wanted them to know they were going to be okay.

Although my day was far from over, the blond girl was the last survivor I handled that morning. Over the ensuing weeks, I've leaned on this, on the children I helped save, to get me through the horrors of what later happened [see "The Ugly"]. I've had to tell myself that hundreds of paramedics, EMTs, and firefighters from around the nation worked the disaster that morning—and for weeks afterward—and only a handful were able to actually rescue anyone. I have to keep telling myself how lucky I am to have gotten there as early as I did, to have freed airways and saved lives, especially the little lives, like P. J.'s. I thank God for the special children He spared.

I'm just glad I was there so early, because I didn't want these kids to die.

TIFFANY SMITH, PARAMEDIC, OKLAHOMA

■ "What the hell was that?" I exclaimed as the station rocked with what sounded like the sonic boom from an F–18 fighter jet. We ran outside and saw smoke coming from downtown. I picked up a telephone. It was dead. All the phones were dead.

"Let's roll!" I ordered.

The smoke column loomed larger as we approached the city. At least thirty children from a nearby day care center were sitting on a corner, wailing and sobbing from fear. People were running in every direction. *What's going on?* I wondered.

The answer came with the first shocking look at the Alfred P. Murrah Federal Building. The whole north side had been blown away, and I knew we were in for a long, agonizing day.

It was my job to create a triage [medical command] center, try to organize the chaos, and make sure my paramedics—especially my headstrong wife, Tiffany—didn't get themselves killed trying to be heroes.

We quickly rounded up our crews and ambulances and established the traditional tag system to designate the type of treatment to give each patient. In some cases we actually use colored tape to literally tag people, but in this instance there were too many patients and too little time, so we organized them by area.

Red-tag patients were critical. They required immediate attention and transport. Yellow tags indicated those who needed urgent care and were next in line. Greens meant patients who were less critical and could be treated on the scene until secondary transport was available.

The black tags just needed body bags.

After getting the system working, I took the time to make a foray into the building. My main concern was to monitor my crews to make sure they weren't overextending themselves and putting their lives in danger. However, I was dramatically detoured when I came across a small boy passed out in the rubble. His foot was caught under a piece of cement. He was breathing but bleeding profusely from the head. I cleared the cement and carried him out in my arms. He was red-tagged and whisked away. I don't know if he made it or not.

Things were going smoothly until the ATF [Bureau of Alcohol, Tobacco, and Firearms] agents suddenly ordered everyone out of the building. Word spread that they had a five-hundred-pound practice bomb stored in the basement and needed to defuse it. I rushed back in to clear out my crews. Many protested, but I had to firmly overrule them. It wouldn't serve any purpose to have my entire squad obliterated in a second blast.

The wait proved to be insufferably long. We weren't given the go-ahead to continue our rescue efforts until ninety minutes later. And even then, additional bomb scares constantly interrupted our efforts throughout the day.

Despite the chaos, delays, and sheer number of victims, I'm proud of the way our unit operated that day. We transported 110 patients in the first forty-five minutes alone. I've since learned that the government is rewriting their official disaster plans based upon how our company, EMSA, responded to the bombing.

The paramedics and EMTs who worked the Oklahoma City disaster stand out as models of EMS at its best. We risked our lives, not for the company, but for the profession.

DON SMITH, PARAMEDIC, OKLAHOMA

THE BAD

■ We were sitting around the station house when the place was rocked by what sounded like a thunderous sonic boom. *No way,* I thought. *That was too powerful.*

I ran outside and saw a big cloud of smoke coming from downtown. "Something bad's happened," I announced, not even bothering to be officially dispatched. "Let's go."

Two minutes later, we were dodging chunks of debris, wire, and broken glass in the street. Parked cars were burning and exploding all around us, their tires bursting like bombs. *This is just too weird,* I thought. It was like we had entered some futuristic, post–nuclear holocaust scene.

As we approached the source of the smoke, the Alfred P. Murrah Federal Building, the debris on the street became so thick we couldn't differentiate between the road and the shoulder.

The instant we stopped, twenty-five people rushed toward us. Most were splotched with blood. Virtually all were screaming, crying, and pleading for help. We tried to organize the mob, and ourselves, as best we could, determining which ones were hurt the worst and treating them first. The others were told to be patient.

Some of the people who continued to pour out of the building were frantic; others were dazed. Those who could talk weren't making much sense. Everyone made reference to some kind of explosion, but no one had a clue what specifically had happened.

At some point I managed to glance up. Suddenly all the screaming and clamoring for help faded into the background, and my mind and body grew numb. Half the building was gone! "There's going to be a lot of dead people," I mumbled.

Turning away to shield my eyes from the harrowing sight, I spotted a soldier in uniform sprawled on the sidewalk. Another soldier was standing over him, trying to help. I walked over to see what was wrong.

"My arm's broken," the soldier said. "My back hurts."

I bent down to assess his injuries. Aside from his arm and back, he had a big, bloody gash on his head. I then noticed that he was black. His face, arms, and hair were covered with so much plasterboard dust that he initially appeared to be white.

"You're going to be all right," I said. "Just wait here and we'll get you some help."

By that time, additional emergency units began to arrive. The situation outside appeared to be stabilizing. The survivors who made it that far generally had nonfatal cuts and burns. It was obvious that the people who were trapped inside needed our help the most.

We returned to our truck to prepare for the next phase of the rescue operation. That's when we made a critical discovery. The driveshaft of the Ryder van that we later learned held the terrorist bomb was on the ground next to us. "It was a car bomb," my partner, Don Carter, correctly surmised, waving over some federal agents.

The criminal investigation wasn't my concern. I grabbed my kit and headed toward the building's garage. The sprinkler system had ignited and was operating with a vengeance. I peered through the eerie mist and spotted a woman thrashing about in the puddles and wet debris. She was frantically trying to free herself from the chunks of concrete crushing her legs.

As I eased through the indoor rainstorm, I discovered three other bodies, all squashed beyond recognition. I shuddered, then moved deeper into the abyss. I was scared to death. There was stuff—big, heavy stuff— falling all around me in every direction, splashing violently into the pooled water. The whole structure creaked and cracked like the building was about to crumble any second.

I ignored my fear and pressed forward, finally reaching the woman. She had a severe head injury and was delirious and combative. I quickly realized that there was no way I could lift the heavy concrete slabs off her legs. I ran back outside to get help. The firefighters hadn't arrived yet, so I recruited the first person I saw, a man in his mid-thirties who was just standing around gawking.

"There's a lady trapped in there!" I choked, nearly out

of breath. "I can't get her out. I need help! But it's dangerous—the debris is still falling. You'd be risking your life
to help me."

"Let's do it," he said.

We charged back in and managed to get the woman
free. That only made her scream and thrash around even
more. I wrestled her to a backboard and, together with
the good Samaritan, carried her to an ambulance. They
transported her to the hospital alive, but she died in
surgery.

Outside, I reunited with Don just as a firefighter
handed him a baby. The firefighter, Chris Fields, and the
baby, Baylee Almon, would later be pictured in newspapers around the world. Don took the child, and we both
grimaced in horror. Her skull was cracked like an egg.
There was nothing we could do.

Don had twins of his own, and holding this infant devastated him. I knew I had to get her away from him, get it
away from everybody. Anyone who saw her would be horrified. I took the child in my arms and walked a block to
the triage center.

"Mike, I have a dead baby here," I explained to my
supervisor, Mike Murphy. "I don't want to leave her just
anywhere."

"That truck's not leaving," he said, pointing to an
ambulance being used as a supply center. "Put her there."

I gently wrapped the baby in a sheet and placed her in
the back of the vehicle.

"God loves you," I whispered as the tears fell from my
eyes. "God will look after you now."

As I walked back toward the ruins, I overheard someone say that there was a day care center in the building.

Oh, God, more children, I thought.

A police officer frantically waved me over.

"There's a guy alive up there on the third floor!"

I focused my eyes on where he was pointing. Sure

enough, there was a man calmly sitting on the shattered edge of what had once been a floor. He could have been fishing, for all the emotion he showed.

The police constructed a makeshift ladder out of a broken fence and slapped it against the building's jagged edges. Don and I climbed up. When we reached the man, we discovered why he was so calm. He was dead! His right leg had been torn off, his left leg was pinned under him, and the back of his head was sheared away. I have no idea what was holding him up like that. We covered him with a sheet, so that nobody else would think he was alive, and left him there to be dealt with later.

We proceeded to search through the rest of the floor for survivors but couldn't find any.

By then, the firefighters had tunneled their way to the day care center. That's when the real horror began. The firefighters dug the children out, one by one, and handed their broken bodies to us. Some of the kids had their clothes ripped right off them. Others were perfectly intact. The massive concussion from the bomb had simply blown out their lungs. It was pretty horrific. Each time I held another dead baby, it just tore my heart out.

Our misery was interrupted by more misery—a bomb scare. We were told that we were standing on a huge practice bomb owned by the Bureau of Alcohol, Tobacco, and Firearms and that we had to evacuate the building. Some of us thought that was bullshit and refused to leave. The rumor spread that the FBI just wanted time to investigate the crime scene and was using the alleged bomb as a ruse to clear everyone out.

Whatever the truth, we were forced to abandon our rescue efforts for nearly two hours at the most critical juncture. I sneaked back in a couple of times, desperate to search for any child that might need help, but was shooed away each time.

"If you go in one more time, Jana, I'm going to pull you from the scene," a supervisor scolded.

"But there are people dying who need us!" I protested.

"I know, but I don't want you to be one of them."

The long wait combined with the ghastly images to drain Don and me of what little energy we had left. I was soaking wet from the sprinklers, filthy, covered with blood, and totally exhausted, both physically and mentally. As it turned out, neither of us ever entered the building again.

I've since undergone extensive CISD. And I've cried. Boy, have I cried. To this day, when I drive to work, I start crying. I keep asking myself, *Why? Why did this happen? Why the babies? Why here in Oklahoma City?* It just doesn't make sense. I can understand a natural disaster, but a mass murder like this?

I've had constant nightmares since that morning. In my dreams, I keep seeing those dead babies covered with white plasterboard dust. They look like ghosts. Hard as I try, though, I can't get to them.

It's been tough, but I don't think I'll quit being a paramedic. I plan to keep working. We've all received a lot of support from each other. I think if we stick together, if we keep talking about it and don't clam up and let it eat at us, we'll be all right.

We'll never forget it, though. Never.

JANA KNOX, PARAMEDIC, OKLAHOMA

THE UGLY

■ After helping rescue more than a dozen people in and around the south entrance of the Alfred P. Murrah Federal Building, things suddenly took a dramatic turn for the worse.

I'd been on the scene about fifteen minutes, frantically treating, bandaging, and comforting survivors of the bombing, and I still had no concept of the damage that awaited me inside. Except for broken windows and a sea of shattered glass, everything appeared to be normal from my limited vantage point. I continued to labor under the belief that a gas line had exploded in some isolated area and that the casualties were all a result of that.

I about to enter the nine-story structure for the first time when I spotted an FBI medic carrying a forty-pound Thomas pack [first-aid kit]. He looked like he knew where he was going, so I tagged along.

I couldn't believe it when I stepped inside. There were mounds of plasterboard, overturned office furniture, snarled wires, and twisted metal everywhere. The entire place was a mass of rubble.

A distant voice echoed out of the darkness: "We have people here who are hurt!"

I took a few steps in the direction of the voice. Suddenly there was nothing in front of me! I was standing on the edge of a huge crater that had eaten through the center of the building up to a point four or five floors above me.

"What happened here?" I exclaimed. "How could a gas line do this much damage?"

"It wasn't a gas line," the FBI agent said, acknowledging my presence for the first time. "It was a car bomb."

I looked around, soaking in the disturbing images. A woman's bright blue purse was jutting out from under a chunk of cement. An overturned file cabinet was visible in the center of the crater. A high-heeled shoe was next to it. I listened. I could hear muffled sobs, cries, and screams for help from distant parts of the building.

"Oh, my God," I whispered to myself in horror. "There are people all over the place under these rocks!"

A team of firefighters was already down in the crater,

trying to claw their way to something, or someone. A weak cry sounded from in front of them. I strained my eyes. *Oh, God,* I thought. I could see the outline of a woman underneath the debris! She was covered with heavy chunks of sheet rock. I watched as the firemen dug her out and placed her facedown on a spine board. Her head was dangling over the edge. I knew the firefighters were doing the best they could, but they should have known better than to place a critically injured patient on her stomach and allow her head to flop around like that.

When the board came my way, I reached over to take it. In Oklahoma, firefighters have only EMT training, and by law, private paramedics like myself have authority on the scene. The firefighters often resent this and give us a hard time, especially if the paramedic is a woman. In this instance, I figured everyone would suspend such animosity and pull together.

I figured wrong. The firefighters passed the victim right by me, as if I wasn't there. The woman, who was three months pregnant, went into full cardiac arrest and died outside on the street.

I was pissed! I couldn't believe these guys were playing their macho game in a tragic situation like this. Fortunately, that kind of attitude wasn't prevalent among the firefighters and rescue workers. The task was so difficult, the job so horrible, that like it or not, we all began to work together.

Our next attempt to dig out a victim met with frustration and failure. The chunks of plasterboard and cement were so massive that, even working together, we couldn't free this man. The extraction would have to wait until the rock cutters and other heavy equipment arrived. The guy was DOA, so the delay wasn't critical.

I stood to catch my breath. Someone walked over, handed me something, and walked away. I looked down. It was a baby—a dead baby with a crushed head! I recoiled in horror, unable to mentally handle what was in my arms, but unwilling to drop it or get away from it. I burst out in tears and became sick to my stomach. I just wanted to scream.

"My God, there are little kids down there!"

As the whole world now knows, the building had come crashing down upon, among other things, a jam-packed day care center. Amid all the twisted steel, severed cables, and hunks of cement, there were bodies. Lots of little bodies.

I wrapped the child in a sheet and passed it down the line. We all stood there, frozen in shock, thinking the same thing: *I hope this is the only one we find that's dead. Please, God, let the others be alive!*

A few minutes later, I was holding another toddler. Another dead toddler. I couldn't tell if it was a girl or a boy. It was wearing red shorts, and its face was caved in.

A third baby was handed to me. The infant's brains dripped like wax onto the cement. The baby was still breathing, but that was only an added horror. There was nothing salvageable about the child.

"I'll take this one," paramedic Jule Spicer whispered, bravely relieving me of the nightmarish infant. "I'll take it outside myself and stay with it until it dies. No baby should die alone." As promised, Jule held the baby until it took its last breath.

We were now out of sheets. I knew there were more victims to come, so I used the shortage as an excuse to get out of the hellish catacomb, walk into the morning sunlight, and collect myself. Momentarily distracted, I nearly collided with someone. It was my husband, Don, our company's supervising paramedic. Don was busy establishing a triage center, organizing the rescue squads, and directing the ambulances. I looked at him, tears falling from my eyes. "There are dead babies in there," I said, collapsing in his arms.

"I know, honey," he whispered, stroking my hair and taking the time to comfort me. "I know."

I pulled away. There were too many people who desperately needed help for me to start feeling sorry for myself.

"I've got to get back," I said, brushing the tears from my eyes. "If they find someone alive, I want to be there."

Once again, I headed up the stairway to hell, entered the door, and took my position. My friends and fellow paramedics, Jana Knox and Don Carter, stood beside me as we braced ourselves for what was to come.

With each passing minute, more workers began to file into the building. The firefighters were spread out everywhere. I watched with growing admiration, and my previous anger melted away as I saw them lift massive chunks of cement with superhuman strength, boulders that under any other circumstance they wouldn't have been able to budge.

A pile was cleared, unleashing a wail of blood-chilling despair from the rescue workers who cut through the building. The firefighters had uncovered another pocket of dead babies.

In quick succession, three more bundles of horror passed through my arms. They were broken, bloody, and mangled, each covered with soot and dust. I felt my body, my entire soul, begin to crumble. *Dear God, how much more of this can I take?* I thought.

There was another break in the action, so I excused myself and went in search of more sheets. There weren't any more anywhere. I ran down the street to another command post and bumped into Nelda Smith, a paramedic from our company.

"Tammy's here," Nelda said, referring to my best friend, who worked as a paramedic in an outlying city.

"Where?"

"She's right over—"

"*Run!*" someone yelled in the distance. "Everybody get out of there!"

I turned and saw hordes of firefighters and rescue workers sprint out of the building in a mad panic. I grabbed someone and asked, "What's happening now?"

"There's another bomb in the building!" he said.

"I don't care," I answered, heading back toward the rubble. "There are babies in there. We have to get them."

A firefighter stopped me from going any farther.

"You don't understand," he said. "ATF [Bureau of Alcohol, Tobacco, and Firearms] has a five-hundred-pound training bomb in the basement, right underneath where we were standing. We can't go back in until they defuse it."

The ATF delay took more than ninety minutes—ninety long, frustrating minutes. I couldn't help thinking of the babies we might have been able to save if we hadn't been called off the scene—both then and the six subsequent times we were flushed from the building because of various bomb discoveries and threats.

I used the time to track down Tammy Chaffin. She was visibly upset.

"Have you seen the other side of the building yet?" she asked.

"No."

"It's gone! I mean, it's totally gone! There are so many dead."

An Hispanic woman wandered over. She appeared to be okay physically but seemed stunned. "I was in a storage room when the building collapsed," she said, her eyes dead and glassy. "All of a sudden, everything just came down on me. I don't understand what happened. My back hurts," she moaned.

"You've got to let us take you in," I insisted. "You're numb. You might be hurt worse than you know."

The woman sighed and leaned on me for support. Paramedics Artie Coffman and Daryl McKnight saw what happened and converged on us. Daryl flagged down a small pickup truck.

"We need to take someone to the hospital!"

"Hop in," the driver said. "That's where I'm going."

We eased the patient into the truck and piled aboard. The driver turned out to be a nursing student called in to help with the disaster.

When we arrived at the hospital, there were people outside waiting to process the victims. They quickly took control of our patient and ushered her into the facility.

I hitched a ride back to the scene. On the way, I finally got to see the front of the building. I froze in shock and awe. The entire north face had been blown away, just as Tammy had described. I couldn't believe the devastation. It was a wonder anyone survived.

We still couldn't go back inside, so I began pacing again. My pager went off. It was a message to immediately report to the triage center in front of the nearby county courthouse. When I arrived, it turned out that my husband had simply been worried about me. He wasn't aware that I'd taken a breather before the bomb scare and thought I was still inside or, worse, that I'd been crushed underneath some falling debris.

He gave me a big hug of relief.

"You know, you really shouldn't be out here in your condition—"

"I don't want to hear it," I said, cutting him off. I'd recently been in an ambulance accident and was on limited duty while I recovered from my injuries—muscle spasms in my shoulder and neck and pounding headaches. That, however, was the furthest thing from my mind that morning.

Our risk management and workmen's compensation representative came over, probably at my husband's urging, and tried to pull me from the detail.

"There are babies in there!" I countered. "When we

get the go-ahead, I'm going back in. Don't try to stop me!"

"Okay. Okay," he said. "Just be careful."

My husband spoke up next. "All right, everybody. We've moving the triage center, now!" he barked.

"What going on?" I asked.

"Another bomb threat. This one at the courthouse," he explained, nodding toward the building right behind us.

I just shook my head. When would this nightmare end?

After moving our ambulances and equipment down the street, we were finally cleared to reenter the building. Things slowed down considerably at that point. There were only three or four more survivors pulled from the rubble the rest of the day, including a woman who had to be abandoned in midrescue because of the ATF bomb, and a teenager pinned in the basement who had to have her leg amputated. A thick air of gloom swept over us as we realized that from this point on, it would be little more than a body salvage operation.

Physically exhausted and emotionally drained, I was ordered to go home at three-thirty that afternoon. This time I relented, but when I got to my apartment, I couldn't rest. The images of those mangled babies flashed in my brain. The phone rang. A relative told me that my cousin, Lisa Goins, had been in the building on the seventh floor and had survived. She was knocked unconscious but was one of the lucky ones that were found early.

The phone rang again. The caller, another relative, told me that another cousin, Lanny Scroggins, had also been in the building and was among the missing. That hit me hard. I'd known Lanny since I was a small child. He dated my mom's best friend and was always coming over to the house. He was a great guy—and now he was somewhere trapped inside that hell. Was he alive? Was he hurt and bleeding, just waiting for someone to get to him?

Those questions began to torment me. Lanny won a Bronze Star in Vietnam for heroism. After that, how could he end up being blown apart while working at some mundane, nine-to-five accounting job at the Department of Housing and Urban Development? It didn't seem fair.

I was so nervous and agitated, I couldn't stay in the apartment. I'd experienced the nightmare of the bombing up close, but until then it hadn't been personal. I jumped into my car and joined the desperate flocks making the rounds at the churches, hospitals, and Red Cross stations that were keeping track of the victims. After spending the entire day in and around the bombed-out building, I was now spending the night walking like a zombie among the tragedy's second set of victims—the numb and shattered relatives. We were all scouring the death lists to determine if the broken bodies of our mothers, fathers, brothers, sisters, aunts, uncles, cousins, friends, and lovers had been dragged from the ruins.

Mixed emotions tore at us. On the one hand, we wanted the name to appear so we could be assured that our loved one wasn't alive in there, dying slowly and alone in horrible agony. On the other hand, not finding the name held out hope that our loved one had escaped earlier in the day and had gotten lost in the shuffle.

I found no mention of my cousin Lanny.

My search brought me back to the building. It looked different now. As horrible as it had been in the light of day, it appeared even more menacing in the darkness. It was like a giant tomb that was doing everything it could to hang on to the hundreds of bodies it was holding hostage.

I walked inside and wandered through the broken corridors and gutted hallways, asking anyone and everyone if they'd seen my cousin Lanny. They hadn't, of course, and even if they had, no one would have known it was Lanny. Still, I wandered and searched long into the hellish night.

Someone told me that four bodies had been brought out at 6:30 P.M. and that Lanny's was among them. I called my relatives and we dashed to the hospital. False alarm.

Thursday passed. More bodies, dozens and dozens of bodies, were taken from the building, but still no word of Lanny.

By then I knew he was gone. I just wanted his body found. I needed closure. After all I'd been through, I needed to put this one last thing behind me.

On Friday the Red Cross reported that Lanny had been "accounted for." They wouldn't confirm if he was dead or alive, just that he had been "accounted for." It was infuriating terminology, but, being a paramedic, I understood what the Red Cross was going through. They didn't want to make a mistake. They didn't want to declare anyone dead who was alive, or vice versa. Emotions were running high enough already.

It wasn't until late Friday that I found out what happened to Lanny. His had been one of the first bodies taken from the scene. The medical examiner was using a refrigerator truck as a makeshift morgue, and Lanny had been put on ice; it had taken a while to untangle the paperwork.

With Lanny "accounted for," I no longer had something to focus on to occupy my mind. The images from that initial morning began coming back in waves.

When I was handed that first dead child, I'd have traded my life on the spot if God would have allowed the infant to live. I'd have given my life to save just one of those kids. It's horrible enough to see an adult in that condition, but to see a little kid like that . . . it just breaks your heart.

I've since been tormented by the thought that some of those babies and toddlers might have taken hours, or even days, to die. How many lay there under the debris, frightened and afraid, crying out for their mothers, waiting for a rescuer who never came? Can you imagine the physical and mental agony?

Although I've seen a psychologist and sought CISD counseling, I can't get the images of those babies out of my mind. And I can't stop crying.

They tell me it's a slow process but that eventually the images will fade. I hope so.

TIFFANY SMITH, PARAMEDIC, OKLAHOMA

14 Gripes and Suggestions

We always get these cat-up-a-tree calls. They're a pain. A lot of paramedics and firemen have been seriously hurt or killed climbing trees trying to get cats down. When a stranger goes up there to get the cat, the stressed animal usually starts hissing and clawing like a tiger! Whenever I get called on a cat rescue, I tell everybody to get away and just have the owners put out a bowl of food. The cat usually comes down on its own when it gets hungry. It's not as dramatic or heroic, but I highly recommend that technique.

BILL ROSE, PARAMEDIC, OHIO

People don't realize how precious life is. We always believe that bad things happen to somebody else. Those of us in EMS view life differently. We see people die who are ready to die; we see people die who aren't ready to die; we see people die who shouldn't have died. And then, when it feels like the doom and gloom are about to crush us, we see someone live who shouldn't have lived.

That puts everything back into perspective.

I had a heart attack myself not too long ago. It was so different being on that end of the EMS process. I was lying in the emergency room watching the doctor shoot nitro into me and observing the nurse start a drip. I instinctively glanced at the monitor and saw that my pulse was bottoming out. I'd seen that so many times before that it was hard to fathom that this time it was *my* pong line going flat.

If I can only live a little longer, I prayed. *I have so many things I want to do. I have so many people I care about that I don't want to leave behind. Please, God, let me have some more time.*

An experience like that makes you stop and think about how precious life is. It doesn't matter if you're angry with someone, or if you don't have enough money to pay the rent this month, or if the car breaks down and the roof leaks. Those things suddenly become trivial. What's important is getting up every morning, feeling good, breathing fresh air, seeing the sky, smelling the grass, and looking out over the glittering ocean. What's important is visiting people you care about, hearing the sounds of kids laughing on a distant playground, and sharing memories with an aged relative.

In EMS I've had the opportunity to help some people realize this. I not only saved their life, but I also gave them a better life, one in which everything was in the proper order.

My gripe is, I guess, that it shouldn't take a near-death experience for people to realize this.

THE COMMENTS

■ This is the honest truth: In my ten years as a paramedic, I've never had to unlatch a seat belt to pull a dead body out of a car. I've seen some nasty collisions, and I've handled hundreds of dead people, but not a single one of them was wearing a seat belt.

Second, we have an alarming number of teenagers and young people involved in drunk driving accidents. It's not a pretty sight. It ruins a lot of people's lives whenever we make a call like that.

So I always try to get in these two pitches—always wear a seat belt, and promote education to teenagers about drinking and driving.

ANDREW ARNOLD, PARAMEDIC, TEXAS

■ What I do in the field doesn't stress me. It's the other things that stress me. The low pay, the union negotiations—those kinds of things make me angry. There's really no way to deal with it except by talking to my wife and talking to my friends.

Disappointments? Lack of respect from the outside world. The people who don't understand what's going on. In New York we're very much disrespected. We get no respect at all.

Here's another thing. When I was working in the complaint department, I used to get two or three calls a day in which somebody would complain about an ambulance running them off the road, blowing right by them with lights and sirens and then shutting down somewhere up ahead [without responding to an emergency]. I'd check it out, and nine out of ten times the call had been canceled en route. When that happens, we have to pull off to the side of the road and then proceed at a normal rate of speed. What do people want us to do, make believe we're still on a call just to appease everyone? People think we're using the lights and sirens to get through traffic or go to dinner. What's the famous line? "Oh, they're probably going for coffee." Believe me, we're not going for coffee.

MIKE SCHULZE, PARAMEDIC, NEW YORK

■ I'd like to see a national training program where everybody could decide uniformly what the goals of EMS are and what the protocols are, and provide some sort of annual funding. That may be a bit idealistic, but I think that's what's really needed if we're all to work effectively. Right now there's so much competition from one state to another to say who's the best in EMS. Everybody sets higher standards or different standards than the state next to them. Consequently it makes it extremely difficult for people to properly practice EMS. And that's a real shame, because a lot of people put a lot of time and energy, and sometimes their own money, into EMS training. Then when you move from one state to another, you're not allowed to practice because of competition or professional jealousy. That's one of my disappointments, but I think it could be remedied with a national registry or certification system.

**NORM SIMONS, PARK RANGER AND
EMS COORDINATOR, ALASKA**

■ The only personal problem I have is that my wife thinks I'd treat a stranger before I'd treat her. That's because sometimes when you're at home, you want to let it all stay at work. She'll get nauseated from being pregnant and she'll want me to sit with her in the bathroom. To me, that's something minor. That's something where you don't need a paramedic, you need a husband. We've only been married a short time, so I'm not accustomed to being a husband. But I don't think this will cause any long-term problems at home. We'll adjust.

The hardest part is taking off the uniform. You're an authority when you wear the uniform. When you go home, you expect your wife and children to live up to your standards, and it's partially your uniform speaking. It's not actually the way you really want things to be at home. It's just a matter of shutting it off. You need to take charge as a paramedic; you can't lose your cool on the scene. Then, when you get home, you say something wrong to your wife or son and the whole thing gets blown out of proportion. Luckily, I haven't had too many of these experiences.

As for the job, I don't like it when a patient's family yells at us to rush to the hospital before we've had a chance to stabilize the person. When we go into a house, it's like bringing the emergency room. But the families scream at us to get going and leave. We're professionals. We know what we're doing. We're there, and there's not much more that can be done than what we are already doing right in the house.

HOWARD LEVINSON, PARAMEDIC, MONTREAL

■ Being a paramedic isn't as rewarding as it used to be, and the chief reason is lawyers. As with so many other professions preyed upon by attorneys, excessive and frivolous lawsuits have altered the way we operate. And it's not for the better.

We used to be able to advise patients with minor injuries that they didn't need to go to the hospital. Not anymore. No matter how insignificant the injury, we have to say, "The safest thing to do would be to go to the hospital," and then leave the decision up to them. This has led to thousands and thousands of unnecessary transports.

Our paperwork load has also increased. We used to write reports to assist the doctors in their treatment. Now we write them to assist the doctors *and* to provide documentation for lawyers.

Similarly, lawyers have changed the way paramedics are being trained and recertified. The emphasis used to be on what to do to help people in need. Now it's what to do to protect yourself from being sued.

I became a paramedic to help people. It's an important job, and I love doing it. But I resent the fact that some lawyer is going to scrutinize and second-guess every move I made in a critical, life-and-death situation out on the street. Lawyers can make anybody look bad. Look what they did to the police detectives in the O. J. Simpson trial.

Admittedly, doctors have it even worse, but we're getting there.

ROD MORTENSEN, PARAMEDIC, ARIZONA

■ I'd like to see us have a closer relationship with the hospitals—especially in the rural areas, where there tends to be a kind of barrier. A lot of people at the hospital don't understand our job, don't understand our skills and what we're capable of. They see us as untrained. There's a lot of friction, and I'd like to see that eliminated. There shouldn't be a turf battle. If we can help them in the emergency room, that's great. We don't want to take their jobs; we just want to help.

RICHARD WARK, PARAMEDIC, MAINE

■ I think the public needs to be more aware of what we do. I also think there need to be more of us, more units throughout every EMS system. Another problem is dealing with nonemergency calls. I'd say 50 to 60 percent of our calls are people with sore throats or something minor who want to be transported to the hospital. These people are abusing us and the system. I don't think it's fair for us to be called out at 3:00 A.M. to pick up someone with a sore throat because he or she knows we have to take them. If we had more units, we could get to the scene and then call a nonemergency transport service. That would relieve us of these calls, along with all the paperwork that we have to do. We have to write up everything, take vitals—I mean, the whole works—for everybody we take in.

When you're on shift for five days—I'm talking twenty-four hours a day—and you're just running call after call, the dirtbag crowd, the drunks, start to get to you. Then all these bullshit calls really start getting to you. Night after night, you're getting up, you're not getting any sleep, and you're getting called out for bullshit. I'm tired of people who don't need an advanced life support ambulance calling and demanding that you take them to the hospital.

NAME WITHHELD, PARAMEDIC, CALIFORNIA

■ We ran a call where a woman was sleeping with her little girls and died during the night from complications of cancer. When we arrived, we took her through the whole process. We put her on the floor, tore off her nightgown, gave her CPR, shocked her with the paddles—all while her daughters watched.

A few days later, the older girl, about four, approached her father, a dispatch supervisor.

"Daddy, why did those firemen rip off Mama's clothes and beat her up?"

When we heard that, we all kind of went, "Wow, that's what we do. It must look horrible to a child."

It led us to reevaluate our way of handling calls, to make sure that if children are around, someone explains to them what we're doing so they aren't left with a confusing and frightening memory.

I guess you can file that under the need to show compassion not only to the patients but to their relatives as well.

MANNY DEVALLE, PARAMEDIC, ARIZONA

■ My biggest disappointment was how our ambulances were maintained. We'd be going to a call and part of the engine would fly off. I'd call headquarters and say, "Hey, our unit broke down."

They'd come back and say, "What's wrong with it?"

"How the hell do I know? I'm not a mechanic!"

And they'd say, "Get out and try to decide what's wrong with it."

Our units were constantly breaking down. That isn't the way it should be with emergency vehicles.

Regarding my being a woman, yeah, a lot of guys may have resented it. One of my supervisors never wanted women on his shift, and I happened to be the first woman ever on his shift. He resented me, resented women in general. He didn't think they belonged in this profession.

About a year later, I ended up working directly with him. We worked together for eight months. He now has a different opinion about women. He told me later that he knew I would always back him up, and that meant more to me than anything.

But it's always been hard for me, from the fire department on up—I've always had to prove myself because I'm a woman. I had to prove that I'd be strong enough and that I would do anything for my partner.

Something ironic happened when I was a firefighter. We went into this burning house, and there were supposedly children inside, so it was a critical situation. I was leading with the hose, with my buddy behind me. I forgot exactly what happened, but I remember feeling behind me and there was no buddy anymore. He'd gotten scared and left me there, stuck. I'm the woman and he left me. *I've* never done that.

DIANE CRAWFORD, PARAMEDIC, OHIO

■ I've had wonderful female partners in the past and I have absolutely no problem working with them. I do have problems working with female or male partners who cannot pull their own weight. I mean that figuratively and literally. I don't know that I've ever worked with a male who couldn't do that, but I have worked with females who were unable to pull their own weight physically. When it came time to lift or maneuver patients—whether it's bringing them out of a third-floor apartment on a stair chair or taking them through the roof of a car on a backboard—I've had female partners who were unable to pull their weight. I've never seriously injured myself working with someone in that sort of situation, but I've come close. It's not a problem with their sex; it's a problem with their abilities.

As for EMS in general, I'd make it more difficult for paramedics. I would require that every paramedic have a two-year degree, at least a two-year degree, in emergency medical technology, probably in cooperation with a college of medicine. This would include taking some courses in interpersonal relations and taking more anatomy and physiology. I would require EMS professionals to know more about medications. I would require EMS to be more of a profession. Nurses are considered professionals. Paramedics are considered technicians, and I think that's sad.

JEFF COLE, PARAMEDIC, FLORIDA

■ In our area, we have a pretty good rapport with our citizens. We work hard, and they see us all the time, see us everywhere. We're involved politically with our city council. We talk to the council members and attend meetings. They're used to seeing us, but they don't feel threatened. We don't feel threatened by them. That's the way it should be. If they want to come to the station and ride along with us, that's okay. We invite them, and they've responded.

TOM HARRISON, PARAMEDIC, WISCONSIN

■ I think the general public is naive about what we do. I really get upset when somebody calls me for a roach in their ear, a bloody nose, a split lip, or a toe they stubbed three days before. I think it's pretty lame. However, in this job, you've got to do what you've got to do, so we take care of the people and that's the way it is. I know a large number of my calls could probably be taken by private car, but that's okay. I do the job.

SCOTT JOHNSON, PARAMEDIC, ILLINOIS

■ Our county is pushing right now to sell subscriptions to the ambulance service for $60 a year. For that price, you get all the ambulance service you want. They're going to be surprised at the number of people calling to get their blood pressure taken. We don't have enough people to man the rigs now, and it's going to be a lot worse when they start this.

STEVE LONG, PARAMEDIC, FLORIDA

■ We need to have it so the whole nation has the same training and certification exam. Every county, everybody everywhere, paramedics and EMTs, should be the same. We should also have a uniform pay scale and more money. I think if we started with a national base pay—you know, like RNs—that would help.

Regarding sexism, sure, some of the men are chauvinist pigs, but I can deal with it. If someone's going to act like that, you just deal with them on their level. You encounter ignorant people in life like that all the time, so you have to get along. You use tact.

NAME WITHHELD, PARAMEDIC, CALIFORNIA

■ For some reason, men don't like to be around when babies are born. I've delivered fourteen in the field, and

I'm the one who delivers them because the man is usually like, "I'll be right back. I have to do something."

One of my pet peeves, however, is delivering crack babies. The mothers usually don't even know they're delivering because they're so high. The babies are sometimes as small as your hand, and they're practically transparent—you can see the lungs, heart, everything. Doing CPR on something that tiny, intubating something that tiny, it's sad. And they often end up living. One I delivered survived nine months, going through painful withdrawal before it finally died.

VICKI IEZZY, PARAMEDIC, FLORIDA

■ I don't think it's any more difficult for females to work in this field, other than maybe having to prove to the men that you can hold your own, that you can do the same job at their level. Sometimes it's hard convincing some male chauvinists that females do belong in EMS, that females are more sensitive to patients' needs. I definitely believe that this can be a career for both males and females. It doesn't have to be one or the other, and we can work side by side successfully.

TAMMY MAURER, PARAMEDIC, FLORIDA

■ Too frequently we focus only on the physical part of illness or injury, forgetting or feeling uncomfortable about the other components—the psychological aspects. We neglect to consider how the patient, the family, the bystanders, and even our fellow prehospital care providers feel about a problem and its outcome.

For example, the patient may experience fear, anxiety, depression, and anger. A teenage girl with a lacerated face may be more concerned with being disfigured than anything else. A working man could be consumed with worry about the financial problems his injury or illness will cause his family. A heart attack patient might be overwhelmed by impending doom.

The family and bystanders may endure guilt, anxiety, anger, or distress with the prehospital care providers. The medics, in turn, may become irritated, anxious, defensive, and sad.

At times, we medics do need to separate ourselves from the surrounding emotional and physical pain, not only to function as emergency personnel but also to function as loving and caring human beings when our work shift ends and we become part of the everyday world.

In the end, however, I feel it's our ability to provide simple human compassion toward our patients that enables us to treat their injuries and illnesses and to keep doing it day after day.

BRUCE GROTEWEIL, PARAMEDIC, MISSOURI

■ The greatest satisfaction is being able to do your job and make a difference. I think most of my disappointment stems from what goes on at the hospital. After we've worked our butt off on a patient, the ER staff works on them for five minutes or so and then calls a code [pronounces them dead]. It's kind of frustrating, but they're busy and you just have to go with it and trust their judgment.

PATRICK WALSH, PARAMEDIC, ILLINOIS

■ Yeah, there's a lot of things that need to be addressed that are being ignored. EMS is being treated as a stepchild in the public safety arena compared to fire and police. They have history. We don't.

Plus, police and firefighters are part of a universal system in which police officers and firefighters in New York are the same as their counterparts in Texas. But a medic in New York is nothing like a medic in Florida, who is nothing like a medic in Minnesota. The medical training and requirements are different state by state.

Even the EMS organizations are different. There are the independent EMS systems, like us. There are the fire-rescue systems, where you work for the fire department but you're also a paramedic. And there's private industry, the for-profit ambulance and rescue services. It can be confusing.

There also need to be changes from the patient or delivery side, the operations side, and the administrative side. When I first started working, the more training you had, the less patient contact you had. That doesn't make sense to me. I was two days on the job and had to have the ambulance driver tell me how to do CPR. That was crazy. I knew how to drive, and he knew how to do CPR, but our roles were reversed.

Training is extremely important. I'm real big into training. It's only through training that a person can learn their weaknesses. We put a lot of emphasis on training today, whereas sixteen years ago we didn't have any. It was really kind of funny back then. If you needed a first-aid card, somebody [at the fire department] would just type one up to make you legal or keep you current.

EMS in general needs to identify itself. There has to be, somewhere down the road, a separation from the fire departments. We need to develop our own stations and be more involved in the community. When you're in a combined fire-rescue system, are you a paramedic or a firefighter? Is it feasible to be cross-trained in both? Is it possible to be a great paramedic and a great firefighter? I don't think so. It's like trying to be a lawyer and a doctor. I mean, they're two separate and different careers.

At schools during Fire Prevention Week, you see the firemen show up with their fire trucks. We need to have something like Injury Prevention Week or Safety

Awareness Week, when we can get paramedics into schools to teach the students what to do in the event of a medical emergency. This would include teaching them how to access the 911 system and what information to have at hand to quickly help the dispatcher.

In addition, this private ambulance service business needs to be dealt with. Think of it: If I started a company to provide a community with police protection, I'd be laughed out of town. Yet people do this type of work for profit, and that doesn't sit well with me. You shouldn't make a profit off people's pain and suffering, charging them for a lifesaving service like that.

MARTY WILKERSON, EMS ADMINISTRATOR, FLORIDA

■We're moving toward a national licensing test for paramedics, and that's beneficial. However, we must remember that there are differences geographically. We can't expect paramedics and EMTs in Colorado to have much interest in learning how to treat stingray stings, a problem we see a lot here in Florida. Similarly, a Florida paramedic doesn't encounter cold-water immersion hypothermia cases, except for prolonged incidents in the Gulf or ocean.

As EMS systems grow, so does the bureaucracy. As with most governmental things, EMS is a bit too top-heavy. There are too many people with too little to do except draw a salary and have a title.

DR. JAMES GRATE, EMERGENCY
MEDICINE SPECIALIST, FLORIDA

■ Wives look upon EMS as a whore. Wives want to be loved. They want to be number one in our lives, but we can't give them that. We're chained to that beeper and radio. When someone calls and needs help, they need it immediately. No matter what you're doing, you have to drop it and run.

Spouses of medics begin to view EMS as another woman or man. EMS is someone their husbands or wives spend time with, someone they care for, someone who receives top priority. That takes a toll on marriages.

On top of this, we come home after dealing with sick, hurt, and dying people, and we don't want to hear about household problems. That's a mistake I've made, and it's a mistake other medics have made. We put too much emphasis on our EMS family. We don't spend enough time with our real families. I think we talk to our EMS family and share our feelings and emotions with them, when we should be doing that with our spouses and children.

RANDY MEININGER, PARAMEDIC, NEBRASKA

Epilogue

I'd like to finish with some words about my longtime partner, Frank Richards. Frank worked as an EMT with the Indian Lake Emergency Squad in Ohio. I met him during my first day of EMT school. He was older, like me, and had recently retired from the railroad after twenty years. He wanted to stay active in his retirement and contribute to his community, so he responded to the same enticing want ad that I had. We were both at a crossroads in our lives and were lured by the prospect of joining this newfangled emergency medical profession.

Frank and I hit it off right from the start. He was a nice-looking man who stood five feet ten inches tall, weighed 175 pounds, and sported a big mustache that matched his dark hair. Personality-wise, Frank was a dream. He was outgoing, funny, and friendly. To Frank, there was no such thing as a stranger.

The former railroad man asked a lot of questions in class. Although he hungered for knowledge, I could tell he wasn't book smart. He wrestled with the medical terminology and all the dry reading. Later, when we prepared to take the state exam, he was afraid that he wasn't going to make it. He wanted to be an EMT so badly, and he knew it would be a struggle to get over that final hurdle. Through sheer determination, he passed—just barely.

I never doubted him for a moment. I knew God wanted Frank Richards on the streets. He was the ultimate angel of emergency.

As I expected, once we rolled for real, there was no better medic in the world than Frank. He really cared about the patients. I could see the concern literally etched in his face when he went out on a call. He couldn't stand to see anyone in agony. If there was something, anything, he could do to make someone feel better, he did it. He felt their pain—long before that phrase became a political cliché.

Frank's empathy was tied in with his upbeat personality. He knew everybody in town, and everybody knew and liked him. He never had a bad word for anyone. Frank gave the whole town a sense of security. If anything awful ever happened, we all knew Frank would be there.

Frank was especially fond of children. He'd put in an extra effort for them, refusing to give up until all hope was gone. Whenever we lost one, he'd be devastated for days.

Because we were older and came up together, our careers were intertwined. We ran hundreds of calls as a team. We saved some lives, gave some comfort, and said good-bye to a lot of good people. Too many good people.

Through it all, Frank made me laugh and smile, and on occasion he even made me angry. That was okay. Sometimes I needed to be angry.

We'd been medics for only eleven months when Frank suffered his first heart attack. He took his medication and got right back on the ambulance. Despite the high stress and extreme tension involved in the rescue profession, Frank refused to quit.

As the years passed, Frank's spirit grew stronger, but his fifty-seven-year-old body couldn't keep pace. Once, when we were handling a cardiac arrest, I didn't know who was going to drop first, Frank or the patient. He was working the man's chest while I was handling the airway. I looked up and saw that Frank was chalk white. I could tell he was in severe discomfort. Although it was winter, sweat was dripping off his forehead and splashing down on the patient. Concerned, I pulled him off the vigorous CPR detail and told him to do the less strenuous airway.

Afterward, he was furious.

"If I can't do my job, then I have no business being here. Don't you ever pull me off a patient again!" he huffed.

EMS is not a job for someone with a faint heart. Frank had a second attack—and still kept running under the red lights. His ticker was fading fast, but he wouldn't concede defeat. It reached the point where we had to shadow him on his calls. Whenever he went out, we'd make sure there were extra medics on the scene, just in case we'd have to lay Frank beside the patient.

"If anything ever happens to me, I want you to take care of the patient," he announced one day. "Don't worry about me. The patient always comes first."

Frank's condition worsened to the point where the only thing that could save him was a risky heart transplant. We talked about it before he made the decision.

"I'm going to go for it," he decided. "If it works, fine. If it doesn't, that's okay, too. I've had a good life."

Frank was put on medical alert and given a beeper that was to advise him when a heart was ready. At any moment, he'd have to dash to the hospital and immediately undergo the radical procedure. Which meant, of course, that when the beeper went off, it could be his last day on earth.

We were sitting in a café having coffee one afternoon when the dreaded beeper came to life. The blood just drained from Frank's face . . . and from mine, too.

"This is it," he said. "They've found a heart. This is the moment of truth."

He ran to a pay phone, only to discover it was a false alarm. There was some problem with the beeper company. What a foul-up! That alone was enough to give Frank, and me, a fatal heart attack.

Frank finally did get his heart, but it didn't work out. He caught Legionnaire's disease at the hospital and was knocked down for the count.

"I just want to tell you that I love you," I said, hugging his frail body as he lay in his bed.

"I love you too, Puss," he whispered, calling me by my nickname.

Frank died two days later, on August 16, 1990. His funeral was the biggest in Indian Lake history. The whole town came to pay their respects to the man who had been everyone's guardian angel.

Frank Richards literally gave his heart for EMS. He embodied what EMS is all about—service, concern, and personal sacrifice.

I've had a chance, more than most, to see the evil and crime that permeate our violent society. I've witnessed firsthand the horrible things people do to each other. What keeps me from tossing it in is knowing people like Frank. As long as there are people like Frank among us, things are going to be okay.

If there's an emergency squad in heaven, Frank Richards is up there right now running under the reds.

Donna